FACETS OF THE BENCH

MYSTERIOUS ARTS
BOOK FOUR

CELIA LAKE

FACETS OF THE BENCH

The War changed everything.

Annice grew up wanting to carve jet. Born and raised in Whitby, on the Yorkshire coast, she learned from her father and grandfather, drawing beauty out of ancient stones. But now she's on her own, there are customs against women carving jet, and the stone's fallen out of fashion. It's 1927. People want to forget their grief, not wear it for all to see. For all those reasons and more, Annice is at a crossroads in her life.

Griffin has lived in Trellech, Albion's magical city, all his life except for his service during the Great War. He's loved the city nearly as long, years before he made a place for himself tending the magic of the courts as a solicitor and specialist. After the War, he came home willing to use whatever tools he needed - wheelchair, crutches, canes - to keep doing what he loved. But other people don't think he's still capable. Griffin's been stuck in a professional limbo that hasn't budged for years.

When the magic and the jet of one of the courtrooms starts failing, Griffin is the one who has to figure out how to fix it. On a trip to Whitby, it becomes obvious that he needs Annice's help to keep the inheritance court working as it should. If he can convince her to be confident in her skills - and give Trellech a try - there's a chance for the two of them to do much more together than they could on their own.

Facets of the Bench is about loving a place and sharing it with others, competence, and making the most of an opportunity. It features an ambulatory wheelchair user, a woman whose skills just need a little encouragement to blossom, and a city full of magic. Set in 1927, it's a romance with a happily ever after ending.

CHAPTER I

G riffin wheeled himself into his office. "Mind getting the door?"

"Never." Antimony followed him in. She was in full formal Guard uniform, down to the cravat and perfectly shined shoes. With the skirt, because the Honourable Magister Rollings had been presiding, and he had decidedly outdated opinions about women wearing trousers. Griffin was in a suit, a formal charcoal grey, perfectly fitted, because he couldn't afford to be sloppy about any of those details. Both of them picked their fights and put the effort in where it mattered. It was one reason he and Antimony had become allies over the past seven years.

Griffin flicked the kettle on and checked there were leaves waiting in the pot. He'd set it up this morning, and he'd expected to get a cup long since. The morning court had run long, though, and there'd been a need for two different consults before the afternoon sessions. His lunch had been half a sandwich and a cup of tea from the court offices. Tending the kettle done, Griffin turned his wheelchair neatly, parking it out of the way against the wall. He touched the brake charm on the side of the chair.

It left him close enough to the desk to use it for balance, taking suitably cautious steps until he was in his desk chair. The way the rest of the day had gone, he had half-wondered if his feet were going to dump him on the floor. Antimony turned away from the door to take the chair across the desk from him, and Griffin brought up the warding with a quick gesture. His wards sprang up like eager hounds, ready to do their work.

"It's not your imagination," Griffin said.

"I wanted it to be." Antimony grimaced, then shrugged out of her jacket and loosened the top button of her blouse. After a moment's consideration, she entirely removed the cravat, tucking it into the pocket of the jacket. "His Honour will be gone by the time we're done. He wants to get up north." Rollings was an avid outdoorsman, it was Friday, quod erat demonstrandum.

"We both have our devotion to the truth of the thing." Griffin said it as gently as he could, in large part because he was still grappling with the implications of what Antimony had pointed out on Wednesday as they were finishing in the inheritance court. She'd brought it up hesitantly, as if she weren't sure if her senses were playing tricks on her.

She hadn't given him anything to go on, just one quiet question. Would he pay attention on Friday to how the charms were responding?

One of the other things he appreciated about Antimony is that she didn't avoid asking him questions. She'd put the thing to him and let him decide how to deal with it. That was more rare in his life than he wanted, especially his professional life.

Now, he made his same bow to unbiased information.

"How about we both write it down, make a copy, and pass it over?" Griffin had been making notes in his own particular shorthand all day, in between his other duties. He nudged the drawer beside him open, pulled out a couple of spare sheets of paper, and handed them over. Antimony took out a fountain pen and began translating her own notes out of her shorthand into something he could read.

It made him chuckle, and she glanced up, grinned briefly, and went back to it. Just at about the point the kettle sang, they'd finished their notes, dotting their Is and crossing their Ts. She got up to pour the tea, to spare him fussing with it, and brought the pot back to sit on the edge of his desk. Silently, Griffin handed one sheet of paper over to her, keeping the duplicate for his own records. They'd both be starting a proper project file from this. He knew that much already.

She passed her page over, covered both sides in tight but readable letters. Griffin scanned it, then looked up to meet her eyes. "Same things. The magic's sluggish, but unevenly so, which is almost worse. And we had just done the reconditioning, what, last November? I'd have to check the dates." To be fair to him, it had been just before things had got truly hectic in the first half of December. Antimony had been well into that too, so after a moment he said, "It was right before that mess with Nico Lind. I remember thinking it was good we'd done the reconditioning early. Only now I'm wondering."

That had been an entire bit of chaos, and not the usual run of the demands of the courts. Though in the end, the actual judicial magics had been straightforward. Lind and his co-conspirators hadn't had the strength of magic on their own to fight the truth charms, and their attempts at evasion had only gone so far.

"I was wondering the same thing. That it had felt good to be ahead of it, only that's not long at all. Four months. Not even four. I think the jet's fading. Or whatever one calls a very black gemstone when it's no longer as much of a muchness as it used to be."

It made Griffin snort, despite the seriousness of the problem. "Do we think it's just the inheritance hall?"

"It's a tad hard to tell without an inheritance case elsewhere. Could you fit up the main hall for one?" Antimony reached for the small notebook she carried. "We don't have another inheritance case for a fortnight, do we?"

"No, but they'll want the main hall set for the investitures next month. That's not enough time to reset between." Griffin had a number of gifts. Thankfully keeping track of that kind of thing came easily to him. "Blast. Have you been in the other courtrooms at all, or should I ask around delicately?"

Antimony pursed her lips. She then shifted to pour the tea, dropping a single sugar lump in his and giving it a stir before handing it over. "I think we both should. Different people will talk to us. Though we should coordinate, we don't both want to be asking the same set."

"Quite." Griffin sorted through the web of contacts in his head. "You do the Guard, obviously. In confidence, avoid anyone who might gossip for right now."

She snorted, agreeably. "Come on, I've been doing this longer than you have." That was true. She'd earned her Captain's rank a couple of years before he finished his apprenticeship, so he couldn't even argue it was a technicality due to the War.

"Do you remember when the last time we reconditioned before November was?" There were major reconditioning rites about every twenty-six years, and more minor ones.

"1924," Antimony said. Right, he'd missed the previous minor. Two of the senior administrators had thrown a fit about him doing the work. They had sent him on a wild goose chase for unnecessary duplicates of records in Somerset House in London, which had occupied him for three solid weeks. He'd done what they'd asked, but he'd filed it as one more mark in the tally of people being unreasonably obstructive for their own reasons.

Somerset House had been the usual tedious need for the forearm crutches, though at least the staff there did all the tracking down of records and making copies. But London wasn't made for easy wheelchair use, despite the number of veterans - and others - needing them. Not that Trellech was a lot better, but at least Trellech sometimes made the effort, and he knew which places were easy to manage. Magic did help at least a bit of the infrastructure.

Silently, Antimony pulled out a list of dates from her notebook and handed it over. It went back to 1880. Roughly every seven and a quarter years, or rather at least that. It was sometimes less if there was a particularly useful transit or alignment to work with. He noted, particularly, that they'd had to do a short-term fix in 1919.

Griffin chewed on his lips, thinking about it. "I wasn't back here yet in 1919, but I read the notes. The theory was that reconditioning when Saturn was in Libra, in exaltation, was supposed to fix that, right?"

"It did. For a while." Antimony leaned forward. "I haven't cracked out the ephemeris and all the documentation. Besides, that's your job. But in 1919, Lockland argued that we just needed something that would hold until 1921. Only, we reconditioned again in 1924 - to take advantage of that Libra alignment one more time." Saturn moved back and forth in the sky, and sometimes comparatively slowly.

"And so we've got the next major in 1929, two years from now, but we need something to hold until then. Or rather, to make sure we can handle cases until then and that the major working will actually hold. After that, there's a long stretch where we won't have good alignments for any of that." Griffin was as skilled at the particular chronological and locational magics relevant to the Halls of Justice as anyone on the planet. Also, he was exceptionally modest and generally avoided pointing that out to people unnecessarily. People kept making it relevant, however, by arguing when they didn't know their precedent.

"And it's only February of 1927. 1924's certainly should have lasted much longer. Into the new decade. Even if we'd do it again in Capricorn, because we're not idiots." Griffin laid it out, mostly so they both knew it had been said. They had to make the best of the chronological moments that they could, for that sort of magic. The planets did not stand on human convenience.

"You'd think." Antimony leaned back, rubbing the bridge of her nose. "All right. How do we go about this?"

"We are still at you asking the Guard. Any of the ones who are thoughtful about the inheritance implications, in particular. Edgarton. Donovan. I don't need to make you the list." Griffin was making his own in his head, of course. "I'll make some inquiries here, and see about the other courts. I have reason to sit in at least three of them in the next week. I'll see what I gather from that. And who knows, it might give me another line of inquiry."

"I do love that you're a solicitor first, sometimes. Figuring out how to get at the fundamental question and what's needed to move forward. Very restful to give you your head and let you work rather than have to orchestrate it myself." She cupped her hands around her mug. "How's the rest of it? It's been, what, a month since we caught up?"

"You've been busy," Griffin pointed out. There'd been her daughter's wedding and a handful of other events. The wedding had been a larger affair, near two hundred guests, many of whom Griffin knew. He'd barely talked to Antimony all day. It might have made him a touch wistful - that wasn't a life he knew - but he'd enjoyed himself. "Mum and Dad are enjoying retirement. If things settle down here, I was thinking of taking a week or two and visiting. Perhaps over the equinox hiatus."

"Is that enjoying, or enjoying complaining about not having enough to do?" Antimony said, grinning. "Not that either of us know anything about that."

"Oh, Dad's still rotating through the same six arguments about why he shouldn't have handed the department store over to anyone else. Mum keeps managing him into other projects. He's been taking up woodwork." Griffin gestured at the chair. "I begged a favour, asked Seth to get him started, and it's actually turned out well. He's finished three side tables and a set of shelves so far, so if you need any smaller furniture, let me know. I'm trying to talk him into a better drinks cabinet, with doors that aren't annoying to manage. Something that slides."

"Huh. That would be handy, actually. And possibly take some of the locking charms a bit better. There's an interesting puzzle for someone." Then she heard a noise, and rummaged in her shoulder bag, pulling out her journal, which was chiming insistently. She flipped through a few pages of it for the current message. "Pardon. They're shorthanded tonight, and I need to go maintain some order in the chaos."

"Good luck." Griffin meant it, sincerely. "And we'll talk in, what, a week, about what information we have."

"A week. Send me a note, or I'll forget to schedule it." With that, Antimony was up, though she remembered to shift her cup to the tray for the cleaners to get later that evening.

Griffin opened the warding for her, leaving it that way. There was no reason he couldn't head home, and several reasons he should. Mrs Ellis, the housekeeper he shared with the main house on the lot, would have left him something easy to stick in the oven and heat. He had several books he'd been meaning to read, and an evening on the couch sounded comfortable.

CHAPTER 2
FEBRUARY 24TH IN TRELLECH

Three weeks later, they definitely had a problem. To be precise, they had several problems, starting with half a dozen people being needlessly difficult about this meeting. It had taken the last fortnight to get everyone involved to agree it was needed, and three attempts at scheduling and rescheduling. Now they were all here, seated round one of the long tables in the most posh of the conference rooms, and Griffin was at the head.

He'd selected the attendees carefully. It was a decidedly mixed group. Some of that was out of necessity, but some of it was a deliberate decision. They had two judges, including the Honourable Magister Rollings, both of whom heard cases regularly relating to inheritance. Both would hold their own counsel until they felt it was time to comment, but Griffin hoped they were both sensible and sensitive enough to have felt the impact on their own work by this point. Both Rollings and the Honourable Magistra Follett had decades of experience in the courts. And while both maintained a studious neutrality with Griffin himself, neither had gone out of their way to be unduly difficult.

After a little consideration, Griffin had also made a relatively simple and also challenging decision. He'd invited his two most senior direct colleagues with the overall responsibility for the magics of justice. Christopher Gregory was the easy one to deal with. He'd come up through Dunwich, from a long line of people who had done the same. Christopher knew how to weigh information as easily as trade goods. Griffin understood how the man thought.

Gloriana Hector, though, had been dubious about Griffin ever since he'd returned after the War. She was one of the ones who absolutely felt that no one with his sort of disability should advance further in the Courts than he had already come. He suspected she'd argue Griffin should not have his current position, either, except that he gave her no room for that.

She'd been like that since Griffin had resumed work after his recovery and sorting out how best to use his chair and canes and crutches and magic. For the last seven years, they'd been in a civil but chilly detente about it. On the other hand, it wasn't as if she'd be easier to deal with if she were left out of the conversation now. And she was good at her work, that was the thing, and she might well have useful insight.

Antimony was there, of course, along with Captain Donovan. They'd hoped for Edgarton, since he wore three hats to Captain Donovan's two. Edgarton was a magistrate, besides being a Captain in the guard and Lord of the land - or Lady, in Donovan's case. But he'd been on a complicated case for three days that didn't show signs of letting up. And Genevieve Donovan was definitely on Griffin's and Antimony's side in this.

They had two of the more senior clerks, Willis and Henning. Mistress Henning was certainly the most formidable of them. Her reputation for precision and the proper form were known well beyond the Halls of Justice. Willis was nearly as thorough about details, but he also had a tremendous memory for precedent and timing, which seemed useful here.

And, of necessity, they had both Nestor Aplin and Harriet Wilson, the other two potential Heirs to Trellech's land magic. There was no avoiding that, either. Harriet was fine. They had an amiable agreement with each other. But Griffin had never got along with Aplin before the War, and that definitely hadn't improved. Aplin was the sort - well, Rollings was too - to be all hearty outdoorsman whenever Griffin was in hearing distance. They were both skilled enough at rhetorical construction to make it clear that Griffin's need for a chair made him less in their eyes without ever coming out and saying so.

More fool them, but that was easier to say with conviction some days than others. Now, though, Griffin knew what he was about. More to the point, he knew how to apply his own mastery in Incantation, addressing the room with a clear "Order, please," that cut across the murmuring. Obligingly, everyone fell silent. Griffin nodded. "Thank you all for coming and your time. I believe everyone here knows all the other parties, save perhaps for my apprentice, Charlus Edwards, who will take our notes."

Charlus stood briefly beside Griffin. "Copies by end of day tomorrow, as usual." Charlus came from a notably more posh family than Griffin himself did - the forename was a certain amount of a hint there. But he'd also begun his apprenticeship by earnestly wanting to learn all he could. He was a third son, and going into the courts in some form was an entirely respectable vocation.

He was young enough he'd not seen the War up close.

But his older brothers had, and that turned out to make it easier for Griffin to get on with him. Charlus likely had another year or two of his apprenticeship to go, but he'd fully qualified as a solicitor in his own right last year before becoming Griffin's particular apprentice. Not the fastest to do so, but solidly respectable.

Now Griffin had to lay out the meat of it. He - and Antimony - knew it had to begin here. He briefly, but with proper attention to detail, walked people through what they'd observed, adding a number of benchmarks and necessary notations. Griffin called out specific points where everyone in the room knew there had been a bobble. It was, as they'd asked around, strongest in the inheritance court, but there were examples in every other courtroom as well. Nothing that was precisely a problem, yet, but keeping it solely in the realm of unmet potential was Griffin's job. One of his jobs.

Griffin didn't stand. It would not win him any extra points here, and it wasn't worth the energy it'd take. He was, at least, having a better day today. They'd had three days in a row of stable weather. When he was done, he waited.

"You're sure there isn't some other cause? There was the weather, in the autumn, all that chat about auroral storms." That was Master Willis.

"A cause, possibly, for snow, which we certainly had. But nothing to affect the charms. And honestly, all our records suggest that if it were related, we'd have seen an impact sooner than five months. This appears to be a steady degradation over time, though, of course, we are working from the seasonal testing points." Griffin shifted one of the pages in front of him. "We ran the next one early, of course. That's in the notes in front of you." It had meant three long days in a row, because they couldn't begin until the courts let out for the night.

Henning flicked through the pages to find what she wanted to reference, marked up with her personal charms for indexing. "And it's nothing that's been done there in the past three months. No unusual cases, in terms of the magical effects. A few that were trickier than usual on the judicial front."

"But the truth magics were straightforward enough. We checked around the times of the few cases that might cause a concern, but there are no notes of anything shifting when it shouldn't."

"Captain Orland," Nestor Aplin spoke up. "You believe there's something to this?" There was an unpleasant note in his voice. Griffin wondered, not for the first time, how that sort of thinking blemished everything else Aplin did. Oh, Aplin was an excellent man with the more mechanical sorts of agreements, contract law and the forming of oaths. He was not so much concerned with the truth, the way Griffin was, as with precision properly documented.

Everyone in the room knew this was political posturing, playing to an audience that wasn't present, but who would hear everything about this meeting from at least six people. That would be the current tender of Trellech's land magic, who sat at the top of the pyramid of the Halls of Justice.

Anyone in this room - Charlus included - might request a meeting with the Lord of Trellech's Justice, but some of them had such meetings regularly in their diaries. Lamont Morgan, the current Lord, had a weekly gathering with the senior clerks, the seniors among the magical specialists, and a selection of judges. And, on occasion, a rotation of solicitors and barristers, to get a sense of the current issues. Not that they'd be consulted about this problem, not yet.

Griffin normally met with him every fortnight, with the others concerned with the inheritance court and cases. He knew Harriet and Nestor had the same general arrangements for their courts. Lamont had been scrupulous about not showing any one of them favouritism. He'd also been clever enough not to put the three of them in the same meetings too often, in case the raw edges sharpened into something hard to step back from.

"I am the one who brought it to Magister Pelson's attention." If Aplin were using formality, Antimony could too, and obviously would. And, as they both knew, Griffin did technically rank her when it came to the tables of precedence. Griffin noted he got the title, and Aplin got the brief response. "Without telling him any specifics. He came to the same conclusions after a day's observation, and from there we proceeded as noted."

"The question," Christopher Gregory said, "Is what we do about it, isn't it? Obviously, we can manage for the time being with some thoughtful scheduling. But that won't do for the long-term."

"And we expect there to continue to be complex inheritance cases. Titles passing down far more quickly or unexpectedly, with new heirs being named. The Carillon estate, in '22. The probate of that one was simple enough, but sorting out the death duties was less so. There was that matter with the Hadleys in '25. Or there's the establishment of Lady Martin-Baddock and the complexities around Lionel Baddock's inheritance, given his mother is still living but unlikely to recover. And that mess with the Sisleys in '26. And we had the challenge of the Romleys." Antimony's voice shifted there. She'd been deeply involved and knew the surviving family well now. That last had been tragic, three brothers all killed in succession in the War, two with young wives but no children. The bulk of the estate had ended up passing down to their sister barely out of Schola.

"We could all name a few others, if a little less complex." Antimony held her own there. "The simple deaths, quick to resolve, those have been tended to. It's the complex ones that draw harder on the enchantments and will be coming for years."

Griffin would not have put it quite like that, but everything Antimony said was true. He picked up where she stopped. "We are also looking at the fact that if we were to do significant work, we need to decide what it would look like. I have some ideas on what we might wish to consider. March 1929 or later would be optimal for a long-term solution. Between now and then, we would need to determine what that looks like, gather the materials, and make all the preparations. While also working up a temporary solution that would hold until then."

Gloriana fixed her eyes on Griffin. "And how much do you know about it?"

That was the thing. He was still relatively new in his current position, holder of the Yew Chair Primus, as the Courts labelled it. All the magical specialists of the Courts could trade off expertise and duties, but the inheritance court was now his particular charge.

The problem was that Cleon Howard had only retired last year, handing over the chair to Griffin himself. Griffin knew a lot of things, but he was still new to being Primus, and he knew it. Especially when it came to the finicky nuanced inheritance cases, where it wasn't solely about legal precedent, but about the ways magic twined through families. So much had fallen out of Cleon's head by the end, Griffin had to keep double checking what he thought he knew.

However, Griffin had not spent several late nights in the library this past fortnight for no reason. "Obviously, it needs more study, and naturally a specific proposal. But from the measurements taken, the facts make clear that it is affecting the inheritance court significantly more than the others. In consultation with others with expertise, we should explore resetting the jet used in that courtroom entirely. I don't know if there was some flaw in it, if the increased number of complex cases has worn it down, or what. It is clear from the evidence that this has been building for some time, well before my taking the Yew chair."

There was a chorus - or a discordance, more accurately - of mutters around the table. Griffin gave them a moment before pitching his voice to cut through the chatter. "One at a time, please. Gloriana, would you begin, then Christopher? We'll work clockwise from there." It conveniently put half the table before Griffin would have to say anything on his own account, and let the senior staff with the strongest history and claim go first.

Gloriana huffed, but she couldn't actually take any offence at that. "The expense for one thing, and the problems of having a courtroom entirely out of commission for an extended period. Obviously." After a moment, she added, "You can't imagine it would get approval."

Griffin spread his hands out. "At the moment, I would like us to entertain all ideas, no matter how unlikely. It may be that one of them will lead us to the best choice. My goal for the moment is to lay out the possible proposals for Lamont to weigh in on. Our role here is to ensure those proposals are as complete as possible, and do not neglect any relevant factor." There would be a decision of some kind if he had to force them to the point. Ignoring the problem would not make it go away.

Gloriana frowned, but she nodded to Christopher. "The same concerns, but I agree with Griffin that we should consider all possibilities. If we reset the jet, though, do we also need to consider the other courtrooms, given that we are seeing some related effects? And what of the impact on the seventh hall, above and beyond the scheduling constriction? Don't we also need to consider the jet there, for example?"

Charlus was scribbling down notes furiously in short-hand. Griffin knew he'd get everything in summary. "An excellent question," Griffin agreed. "Harriet?" He nodded to her politely.

In some ways, he found Harriet more difficult to deal with than Nestor. Griffin knew where he stood with Nestor. The man did not care for him, did not think him anything like an equal. He had never been directly rude, but Griffin had been able to see the ripples of Nestor's gossip here and there, the people who kept Griffin at a distance. Despite all those mumblings, Griffin refused to know his place and concede his role as Heir.

Harriet, on the other hand, had been entirely civil, throughout, but it had been a remarkably neutral civil. However, Harriet had shown no signs of wanting to become closer allies. She had never undermined him. She got on with her work and did it well. Griffin couldn't argue with any of that, or with her strategy in navigating the politics, but it did make her a cypher.

She considered for a moment. "Similar concerns as have already been raised. Also, a concern about who might lead this. We're short-staffed as it is. We can't spare anyone to go chasing around for an answer. And yet, if it's not one of our own, the work won't be done properly." Harriet decidedly wasn't volunteering for the work, but he hadn't expected her to. For one thing, she had young children at home, two under seven, and she did not favour late nights at work.

Not that Griffin necessarily did either, but he had a rather more fluid definition of work and the rest of his life than most people. He was the sort who had work-related thoughts in the bath, reliably, and there was no good way to chart that in one column or another. And there was no one at home to want time with him or complain if he came home from work for hours more reading.

Griffin nodded at that, then said, keeping his voice just as pleasant and blessing his Incantation training for the ability to do that, "Nestor?" Exquisite politeness in all directions was the answer here. People might not like it, but they couldn't argue with it, not without looking like fools.

"I don't agree it needs doing. We can manage until '29." That was shortsighted, and he very much hoped both Gloriana and Christopher made note of it and passed that along as well. It was the sort of thing Lamont should hear as Lord of Trellech. But of course, he wasn't in this meeting, Griffin hadn't considered inviting him. First, Lamont Morgan was an exceedingly busy man - he kept up his own duties with the Courts as well as the Lord's. But second, and more important, if he sat in on discussions like this, it put all the weight on his decisions, unbalancing the process. But he'd be asking Gloriana and Christopher for their take on the meeting. Griffin was sure of it. Likely others but absolutely them.

Griffin just nodded. "Noted. Master Willis?" From there, it went round the table more or less predictably until it came to Mistress Henning. Griffin had kept his own comments brief, noting that he felt they needed a solution before 1929. He acknowledged that a long-term solution might take that long to arrange, citing several cases from previous centuries for precedent, though only one involved the inheritance courts directly.

Mistress Henning took her time. She had more than enough status to make everyone wait on her, and Griffin certainly had more sense than to rush. He hadn't been sure which way she was leaning. She had an excellent face for bets at cards, if she played. She looked around the table. "Master Pelson and Captain Orland know their work. Their documentation is up to my standards." That got a soft chuckle from near everyone there. "I believe we should take some action. Beginning, perhaps, with investigating what options are viable, a research project, before planning actual renovations." Then she glanced over at Christopher and Gloriana. "Perhaps we might put one to Lamont at our weekly meeting? Master Pelson, if you were to make a proposal for investigation, what would you recommend?"

Griffin swallowed. That was cutting through several Gordian knots. Not that he hadn't given quite a lot of thought to it. "If it is the jet that is the concern, it seems to me we need an expert on jet. That means Whitby, either going there or persuading someone there to come down to us. There are only a handful of carvers the courts have worked with previously, and I do not know their current status. I would begin there, see about some investigatory conversations, and determine what might be most usefully done to evaluate the options going forward. Ideally three or four options, so we could consider efficacy, cost, available staff, expertise, time to completion, and so on." He might not have gone to Dunwich, but he'd lived through four expansions of his father's store, and had picked up more than a bit of the necessary project planning in the process.

Mistress Henning nodded approvingly. "Sensible, yes." She then nodded at Rollings. "Your Honour?"

He was chuckling. "I have, it seems, little left to me to say. Naturally, I would agree with that, yes. I would willingly swear that the court feels different, in ways that are less suitable for proper justice. I see a great benefit in tending that sooner than later. And as someone who also sometimes hears cases in the criminal court, there are excellent reasons to make sure the effect does not expand." That was more support than Griffin had expected from Rollings, and he gave a slight nod of respect at it.

Magistra Follett was nodding along, though she kept her comments far briefer. "The same in all parts as what my honourable colleague has said."

With that, well, the way forward seemed clear enough. Griffin paused just for a moment, not to seem too hasty. "We will have the notes from this meeting tomorrow, as stated. Mistress Henning, Master Willis, Gloriana, Christopher, would it be of help for me to put together proposals for Monday?" They met on Wednesdays, routinely, the most senior staff and a few chosen others. It would mean Griffin working through Saturday and Sunday, but he could do that.

There were nods from all of them. "Monday by noon, then, to allow time for duplication and any questions. Any last comments before we adjourn?" There were none, and this time Griffin stood, waiting for the others to file out, talking. Antimony went with Captain Donovan. They clearly had more to discuss. When everyone was gone, Griffin sank back into the wheelchair.

Charlus cleared his throat. "So, when should I be here on Saturday?"

"You don't need to." Griffin said it automatically. This was his choice. He wouldn't demand Charlus match him. But then he watched Charlus's face and smiled, softening it. "I could use your help. The library, at ten. I'll likely be there from nine." The library was upstairs. It would mean hoping the lift behaved, or taking his time with the crutches on the stairs, but he'd just factor that in. "Sunday, possibly at my flat, depends how much of the research we get done."

"It'll go faster with two." Charlus sounded rather pleased, actually. "I'll go see to writing up the notes. Meet you in your office before end of day."

Griffin nodded. Charlus went off in search of his type-writer. Griffin gave everyone else a minute to clear out of the hallways before wheeling himself back to his own office and into the ordinary and substantial pile of work waiting for him.

CHAPTER 3

MARCH 1ST IN WHITBY, YORKSHIRE

Annice was making her way slowly along the beach. It had been a bad day for jet. Near everything she'd turned up had been coal - tempting at first glance and wrong at a second. Worse, the weather felt unsettled. She probably should have opened up the shop, in hopes of a customer or two. But it was March, it was chilly, and experience told her no one would buy. At least if she was looking for jet, she was doing something that might, eventually, be useful.

So she'd made the trek - all five and a half miles - down this morning, by foot. She'd go back by the portal, as much because of the hills as the distance itself. But walking one way saved her some coin, and that mattered.

The beach at Bay Town, what people elsewhere called Robin Hood's Bay, had been quiet, with few people out. It was March, after all, scarcely a time even for hardy Yorkshire bathers. She'd been out for a good two hours - she had maybe another before the tide caught up with her.

But then she caught a motion up ahead of her, a man in

a billowing oilskin. The light was behind him. Then she got a better angle. "Bill." She waved.

He hesitated for just a second, and then she knew what was wrong. What else was wrong, to add to a long list? He gestured at one of the massive boulders, up against the cliff face, a bit out of sight. "Miss."

Annice picked her way over, carefully. The last thing she needed was to twist her ankle, and she made a quick gesture, averting bad luck. Or more bad luck. Not that she felt it worked, given the number of things in her life that had not been averted at all. When she was perched on the rock, she nodded. "Bill."

"Been meaning to come see you, Annice." Bill Askey was well into his sixties, the generation between Grandad and Dad. Annice nodded, not wanting him to go on, but better to get this over with. "I can't be bringing you more jet."

Annice did her best to keep tight composure. "There any reason I can do something about?"

"Nah. People are talking, that's the thing. Saying you're the one going to be carving it, you have to be. And that's no good, right? The custom being as it is." Bill did not look happy to be saying this.

She wished she could tell custom to go hang, but she couldn't. For one thing, she'd have to convince all the remaining jet carvers in town, magical and non-magical alike, and that was a hopeless cause. And then she'd have to convince everyone who'd mention one workshop over another, not that there was all that much of that going on these days. A decade ago had been the War. A decade before that, when she'd been apprenticing, people had still bought freely.

Now Annice nodded slowly. "Not even in private?"

"Now, Annice. You know word will get round." He hesitated. There might be a fragment there. "No one can stop you looking. And if I find a big piece, unusual big, I could give you first look at it. But on the regular? No."

It was as good an offer as she was going to get. And for the moment, she wasn't desperately in need of more jet. Grandad had built up quite a collection, and carving that up would take her a good bit. She could do her own looking.

"Sure." Annice swallowed. "Ta for at least telling me."

"Ah, pet." Bill looked a bit shattered. "Other people, just turning their backs, then? Hadn't known it had got so bad."

"Expected it." Annice curled her arms around herself. "Thought it'd be faster if it happened, though."

She'd always been a bit on the outside from the time she was born. Her mam and da spoke like educated folk. Mam had been a schoolteacher before she married, a year's apprenticeship down south that taught her about more than Whitby. And Da had gone to Alethorpe, one of the five schools, before coming north. She'd grown up with some of Yorkshire's burr in her voice, and some of the crispness of Da's careful words. She was of Whitby, generations back, centuries, even. And she was different in ways that made everything impossible some days.

Bill shrugged. "People gave you the chance. Who knows, might have met a man who'd pick it up."

"Like Da did." Annice had grown up loving that story. Her mam had been the only child of her grandad and nan. She'd been whisked off her feet by Da, when he'd taken a position as a junior apothecary. He'd fallen for jet, like any sensible man might, just a hair slower than he'd fallen for Mam. "I didn't. Not likely to now, either."

She might have had a chance if there'd been more men. That was the thing. She wasn't a great beauty, the sort who turned up in songs. But she might have made the sort of wife a man would think of fondly while he was at sea, wanting to come home to. It was a realistic sort of hope. Not that she'd appeal much right now, with her hair in a braid down her back, her dress darned in a couple of places, and faded all over.

But the thing was, there weren't men. Not in her generation. They'd been calling it surplus women. Surplus to what, that had been Annice's question since she heard it named. She could bloody well make her own life and do something good with it. Or she could have, if what she wanted was anything other than carving jet. Because whether there were men to do it or not, there were customs about jet carving. They had no room for her.

She might be able to make her life, but she did not know how. And she wasn't a respectable sort of widow. At least then she might have taken in boarders or something. Annice could see it coming. She'd keep trying, until the money ran out, and then the hope, and she'd pack up and leave Whitby and take a position somewhere. Matron in a school, she could keep house well enough and keep track of things. Maybe a secretary or clerk or something, but they probably wanted someone with better handwriting and less of her odd sort of accent. Too educated for Whitby, too Northern for a proper office.

Bill had gone quiet. That was the thing. He might be Grandad's age, but there wasn't much he could do to help. There were lines of class and need and it made her head hurt. Finally, she swallowed. "See you around, I guess." It sounded feeble - it was feeble - but it was the gesture.

He nodded, touching his cap, and let her go. She turned to go back down the beach, away from him. She kept her walking stick handy to poke at the bunches of seaweed. Jet often washed up with them - well, jet and everything that pretended to be jet, it seemed. Sea coal and regular coal and black rocks from the cliff and who knew what else.

Annice made it a good half mile down to the end of the beach, down where the shore dropped off into cliff and ocean, with the farms above. She hadn't spotted anything coming south. She stood there, staring out into the ocean for a good twenty minutes, until the wind got to be too much. Some people might decide, then and there, that it would be easier and faster to just jump into the ocean and be done with it. But that was letting the world win, and more to the point, someone might see her and send the lifeboat men out after her. That wouldn't do anyone any good.

In the end, she turned back, keeping her eyes on the ground. This time, maybe to make things worse, she found jet. More than one piece, and more than something tiny. There was a piece a third the size of her palm, not the largest she'd seen unworked, but up there. And then along it, mostly buried under seaweed and debris, there were half a dozen smaller pieces. Each of them would make a pendant, two might make a matched set of earrings. She double checked them. After all these years, she could tell coal from jet from bitumen, the way they felt in her hands. But she always tested on a bit of porcelain. No sense hauling the wrong thing up the hill. And there was even less sense in getting her hope up.

It was all jet, and she walked back now, pausing twice more for smaller pieces. She bought a pint at the pub, as the price of entry to the back courtyard where the portal was. Twenty minutes later, she was coming out at the portal in Whitby proper. She pulled her coat around her as she walked into the wind, and then finally up to the shop and the flat above.

The shop was, of course, entirely quiet. Everything was still in its place. There was no reason it shouldn't be. There was no one here to make the place feel alive. Annice certainly didn't manage that most days. And whatever else happened, the people in town had respect. They respected Grandad and Nan. They'd leave the shop alone even if they disapproved of Annice herself. Big cities had to worry about things, vandalism or people making free. Here, all her neighbours knew her, for better and for worse.

A few minutes later, she was staring at the keep-cold cupboard, pulling out a bit of bread and cheese. Enough to keep her going for a bit. She didn't want to wait for the kettle, instead eating standing up at the counter before washing up the plate, then her hands. She dried them properly. Annice didn't want her hands to slip. Then she changed into a working dress, something that wouldn't be harmed more by dust and grime.

She climbed the stairs to the attic workshop, lighting the charmlight over the bench, pulling on her apron, and then settling down. Annice had a half-finished piece, working with the hand tools. She'd already shaped it using the long row of cutting wheels and grindstones down the other side of the workshop, working bit by bit.

Now she was working on a rose, shifting her tools to coax petal after petal out of the surface without chipping the jet off. Grandad had taught her the charms for it, besides the manual tools, that gave them a bit of an edge. She wasn't feeling it, though, and after a couple of minutes, she shifted over to the hand drill and its foot pedal. She got it spinning smoothly before picking up the drill and beginning again.

The jet worked its magic, as it nearly always did. Within a minute or two, Annice was lost in what she was doing.

There was nothing else but the piece in front of her, the angle of the light, the way the petals were beginning to take a sheen and polish. More of that would come later. When she finally came to a stop, her neck and back were aching. Her hands - and face, not that she could see it - were coated with brownish-black dust, thick enough in some places to crack off as she shifted. And the light outside the attic had gone from afternoon to twilight well into night.

Not like she had to keep to anyone else's schedule. That was the thing. Slowly, Annice uncurled herself, putting the rose in progress in the box on the centre of the table before she did anything else. She didn't need to drop it, maybe break it, or have to scrabble under the workbench for it. Then, just as carefully, she stood up, stepping back so she wouldn't dislodge any of the tools if she got clumsy.

Then, step by step, she made her way out of the workshop, dismissing the charmlight as she closed the door behind her. Washing up took forever, and left her shivering, because she hadn't bothered to heat the water up more than the bare minimum. She couldn't spare the magic for it and didn't want to spend for the fuel or time it'd take to do it the other way round. She'd warm up, eventually.

Back in the kitchen, she heated a bit of soup to go with the last heel of bread. Annice ate quickly, feeling the exhaustion overwhelm her. She could feel everything falling away as soon as she'd got into bed, unable to keep her eyes open. It'd be one of those nights, at least. Not one of the ones where she was awake for what had to be hours, staring at the ceiling in the dark.

CHAPTER 4
MARCH 3RD IN WHITBY

Two days later, Annice had the shop open. She'd arranged things pleasantly enough, and the light coming in through the shop windows lent a warmth to things that seemed hopeful. It had been a quiet day, but she'd expected that. It was barely into March, and the tourist trade wouldn't pick up until May. But there were always some people there to take the sea air, at least that was consistent, even if there weren't many of them.

She'd had a slow trickle. A couple of the wives from down the street had stopped in to see how she was doing. That was kind, though she never knew what to say to them. Yes, she was fine. She wasn't, but not in a way that fit into the social niceties. She accepted an invitation to tea later in the week from Mrs Watts. They were non-magical, so there were even more things Annice couldn't explain or talk about. But the Watts were doing well enough that Annice didn't feel like she was taking food the family needed if she said yes.

Mrs Allen, the woman with her, she would have. They were a family with more mouths than money, and that was a hard path, no matter what sort of face she put on it. And while fishing paid well when there were fish, it was a risky trade. Not just in the fishing, though that was a big part of it, but in whether it paid much in the way of a catch.

It gave Annice something, no matter how small, to look forward to late in the week. Then there had been a number of people going by and waving from the outside, but not coming in. That was the thing about having the shop open. Back before, a year ago, or two or five, Nan would have been the one sitting down here, chatting away. And Annice and Grandad would have been up in the attic, making pieces to sell.

Annice couldn't do both at once. No magic she'd ever heard of let someone be in two places, doing two different things entirely, all in the same moment. So even if she wanted to sell her carving, she'd have to make them at times no one wanted the shop. Evenings, Sundays - it helped she wasn't religious much at all, though she made a proper show of going to church. If she didn't, people talked.

The door opened, and Annice looked up. No one she knew, which meant visitors, not town folk. "Good morning." Annice kept her voice cheerful. "Come in, please. I'd be glad to show you pieces up close."

"Oh, we're just visiting." That was a younger woman, though not exactly young, maybe a bit older than Annice herself. The other two women were older, plump, and not, Annice thought, the sort to favour jet jewellery. They weren't dressed in the latest fashions, of course, but they wore brighter colours, the ones in the fashion plates. "But the shop looked interesting."

"I'd be glad to tell you a bit about jet, perhaps? Even if you don't want to buy, we are famous for it. It would be something to tell your friends later?" Annice made herself smile again. She'd done this lecture before, hundreds of times, and Nan had always been much better at it. She kept hearing her grandmother's voice whenever she tried, the way Nan would pause, get people laughing and smiling. Sometimes those laughs had turned into a letter, later, asking to buy this thing or that, if arrangements could be made.

She did have a slight advantage over Nan. Mam had been a schoolteacher for a little, and she'd picked up and kept the sort of elocution that people from outside Yorkshire found easier to make sense of. And she'd taught it to Annice, of course. And of course Da had it naturally, from his own people and the school he'd gone to. It set her apart in town, even though she could and did speak both ways when it was called for.

The women hesitated, then the younger one, the daughter, nodded. "We have a few minutes, perhaps. And need a little breather before tackling the steps."

"Ah, you want to climb up to the abbey? That does take a bit of effort!" The hundred ninety-nine steps that led up to the now ruined abbey above were worth climbing. The view was stunning, but the hike didn't seem the sort of thing these women were entirely used to. "Here, let me pull out a stool or two. You can sit while we talk." A minute or two later, they were settled on broad stools. Annice had shared out cups of tea, and they were agreeably inclined to listen.

Annice went through the talk about how they'd found jet buried as grave goods, going back thousands of years. She leaned heavily on the fact it was like amber. It had come from something that had been living, once, long ago. Mighty trees in vast forests had fallen, been buried, and a combination of time and pressure and minerals had turned the wood from wood into something far better.

She let her love for it show. There was a chance these women would laugh at her about it. Of course, some did. But if they did, they'd be out of the store and gone a few minutes from now. When Annice made a sale, it was almost always because she'd caught someone's imagination. Once she'd laid out the older history, she said, "Now, of course, Whitby became famous because of Queen Victoria. When her beloved Prince Albert died, she declared jet to be the court stone for mourning, and she wore it for the rest of her life. Jet - the best quality jet, we think - is found only in a stretch of perhaps seven miles along this coast. It washes up. It was mined for years, though not these days. And we take it and make something beautiful. And - well." Her voice got a little softer. This was personal. "Heavy enough to remind us of our grief, and light enough to wear every day. I've thought about that more and more, the last few years."

There was a small silence before the oldest of the women said gently, "Lost someone dear, then?"

"My father, in the War, my mother a year after. And then, in the last year, my grandad and my nan." The term confused them. They were not Yorkshire folk or northern-ers. "My grandmother, a common term around here." Annice gestured at the shop. "My grandad was one of the best known jet carvers. My father had a love for it. He learned it after he let his love for my mother keep him here. And now I have the pieces they worked on to find a home for."

It was all true, and it was also an ideal shift into the fact this was a shop. She tilted her head, not pushing at it. "I could bring out a few things for you to look at? Some of the older traditional pieces, and some of the newer?"

That got a small round of nods. The oldest woman considered, then pulled something out of her bag. "I have a set from my grandmother." She pronounced it precisely, definitely from somewhere well south and more posh. "One earring is missing."

"I'd be glad to look. Sometimes it's possible to have a match made." It only took Annice a minute to pull out a small table. She set it comfortably where all three women could look at it, and a cloth to set the jet on. "Here, that will let me see it to the best advantage."

As soon as the woman pulled a necklace out, Annice knew it wasn't jet at all, but some sort of simulant. Not vulcanite. That would be browning by now, if it were as old as the woman had suggested. The earring, though, that was jet, or seemed likely to be. Now Annice would have to go delicately.

"This is a lovely earring. And I could likely make a copy myself." She added, because these women probably would find it amusing. "There's a tradition that women carving jet is unlucky, but my da and grandad didn't think so. Or if you'd prefer someone else, I could recommend someone reliable."

"Oh, you seem much nicer." That was the youngest of the women. "You really could?"

The oldest woman smiled benevolently. "I've told Alexandra they're to come to her, or at least the single earring was. If you'd like it done here, I suppose that's fine."

"Annice Matthewman," Annice offered. "That's my name. I can give you a card." She wanted to press on to the business arrangement. "There's one thing I should tell you first, though. I'm afraid this necklace, here, the centre pendant isn't jet. I think it's likely some sort of horn, dyed. Can I bring out a few pieces so you can compare them?"

Annice kept her voice pleasant. The oldest woman froze for a second, and there was a moment when Annice was sure all three of them were going to be out the door. It was the youngest woman, again, who was a help. "Let us hear Miss - it is Miss? - Matthewman out, Grandmama."

It gave Annice a chance to explain, at least. She gave them a moment, going to pull several pendants of the same size out of the display, and then one that was of slate, not jet. "Here, sometimes it's easiest to feel. Jet is very light comparatively. If something feels heavier than that, it's possibly glass, or it might be vulcanite. You can do some lovely jewellery with both, but if what you want is jet, obviously, that matters."

"And this?" The oldest woman touched her finger to it.

"May I?" Annice didn't dare touch it without permission.

The woman waved a hand. "Go ahead. We're right here."

Annice picked it up carefully, considering. "It's easier to tell with a brooch - you can't put screws for a backing into jet, it will fracture. If you see that, it's almost certainly horn or vulcanite. But this is an older piece, you said, ah, see here. If you look along the edge, you can see how it's flaking a bit, and those flakes are translucent? That's horn. It's well made, but it's horn."

Something in it intrigued them, and that got the middle woman, presumably the daughter, between grandmother and granddaughter, asking how else you could tell. After five minutes of it, she laughed in delight. "I'm going to have a grand time asking people to bring out their pieces and telling them. Is there a pamphlet or something of the kind, do you know?"

"Not that I know of, ma'am, but I could write something up, given a couple of days. I don't know how long you're staying in town, but I could send it through the post." Annice liked the thought of that, some woman in some town or city somewhere south, telling her friends about jet.

"We're here for four more days." The grandmother tilted her head. "If Alexandra still wishes it, would you be able to do the earring by then?"

"May I take a closer look?" At the woman's nod, Annice pulled a proper jeweller's loupe out of her pocket and used it to inspect the piece, moving over into the light coming through the window. The part that was a trick would be matching the long oval shape, but she had a couple of pieces upstairs that would likely do.

"I'd need to do some precise measurements and see what pieces I have that would work, but I think so. I could tell you for certain in a couple of hours. Perhaps I could bring a note to your hotel?"

"Oh, the White Horse & Griffin, just around the corner." Alexandra beamed. "Would you? And we want to look at some of your other pieces, definitely. Perhaps we might look now and make some decisions when we come back for the earring?"

It would make a nice bit of a sale, if Annice could manage it. She smiled - an entirely honest smile - and nodded. "Let me write up a few notes, your names and all that, and then I can bring over some more pieces for you to look at."

CHAPTER 5

MARCH 3RD IN TRELLECH

"Sir?" There was a knock on the door, the particular two then three that meant it was Charlus, even if the door muffled his voice.

Griffin called out, "Come in, please." He considered his options for this conversation for the fifth time today.

His office was not the location he'd prefer for what would be, of necessity, a somewhat more personal discussion. But he had work he needed to do that evening, and he was not up to going home and back. Also, it was raining, and he decidedly wasn't up for dealing with the way the wheels kicked up mud if he so much as looked at a puddle wrong. Whatever else happened today, Griffin did not much want to add changing his trousers twice to his list of tasks.

Charlus came in, looking decidedly windblown, which made the decision even easier. He'd have come back from Portal Square, so about twenty minutes walk. Griffin appreciated his gift for managing not to get soaked. It wasn't the easiest charm set to learn, even if it came in very handy in the average month in Albion.

"Put the kettle on, please. It's still brisk out there, isn't it?"

"Yes, sir. But I was hoping to make it back while you were still in the office, so you could have all the information you needed." Charlus took a moment to take off his hat and hang up his bag on the hook by the door.

"Oh, I'm here for a bit. We're going to look at the courtrooms tonight and see what else we want to consider. Take advantage of the new moon alignments. But I'm glad you came back. A little more time to marshal my arguments never hurts."

Charlus snorted. "Sir." He settled down after he turned the kettle on to boil, letting out a long breath. "The warding?"

"The warding." Griffin agreed with that, and brought it up with a gesture, feeling it settle into place. Charlus let out a longer sigh. That was curious information indeed. Now Griffin waited. When he'd been training as a solicitor, that had been a big part of it. He'd learned how to give someone space for something they were finding challenging. It made it easier to get at what they needed and at the truth, both. Then, he'd had to keep an eye on the clock, and here he didn't have to, other than being ready in two hours for the evening's work.

Finally, Charlus looked up. "Someone wants to prove that you can't do this, sir."

Griffin's mouth quirked up. "More than one someone, yes." He considered. "At least two, it might be four or five. I don't have a good angle on some information that would help. What makes you say that?"

"It's not a town terribly conducive to a wheelchair, sir. I think you can make it work. I'll get to that in a second, from what you told me, but I have a few questions. But the whole thing's built into the side of two cliffs. There are those steps up to the Abbey, cliff faces on the side streets. And near every hotel or lodging house I checked has stairs."

"But not every." Griffin had caught that, and it got him a lopsided smile from Charlus. "Do you want a bit more of the explanation than I've given you, then? I'm sorry to bring you into it like this, mind."

When Charlus had apprenticed with him last year, it had been all about what Griffin could teach. Griffin had gone to school with Charlus's aunt, and she had agitated for the apprenticeship. Certainly, Griffin had come out well from the agreement - the money didn't hurt, though he wasn't dependent on it. He found Charlus was attentive to detail, responsive, quick to pick up techniques, and in every other way a model apprentice. He was patient with the forms and formalities, some of which were ridiculous, and he was developing the necessary knack for when to go around those forms.

But Griffin had not then or since particularly explained why he used the chair. He'd left it at explaining it was an injury during the War, which was true enough. He'd only explained the parts that applied to their work. Charlus was never to touch or push his chair unless requested. It was, in fact, a help for someone else to get the door, all of that. Charlus hadn't asked, which was probably his good manners, and Griffin hadn't offered. It was an awkward sort of conversation, but now it was necessary. And to his credit, Charlus had been exemplary in keeping to what Griffin had asked, in the chair as with everything else.

Now Charlus nodded. "Whatever you feel you wish to tell me, sir." Just then, the kettle sang, so there were a few moments of fussing with that and the teapot to let Griffin decide how to begin, where to begin.

Once Charlus was seated again, Griffin swallowed. "Long story short, partway through my service in the Great War, I was assigned to a mining company. Someone saw the Monmouthshire address, I suspect, and assumed I knew mining. I was an officer. I knew enough about how to manage a project, of course."

"You'd been well through your apprenticeship then, sir," Charlus said, pausing to do the maths.

"That too. I'd been named as one of the three potential Heirs before the War, but of course that didn't matter to my orders. They were mining deep tunnels to get under the enemy. Near Messines, in France. That part went well enough, or at least as well and as badly as that sort of thing ever does. I wasn't entirely comfortable with it, the impact on the land and the land magic, and all that, but I couldn't actually speak up about it. I just kept my head down, took care of my men as best I could."

Griffin stopped, as he always had to when he talked about this. "When the explosion happened, I remember it. There was fire shooting up terribly far into the sky. But it was the earth shaking that I remember most. And then I don't remember much for a fortnight. By that point, I was back at the Temple of Healing, and had been for at least a week. I'd been lucid on and off, apparently, but keeping confidences even then."

Charlus didn't seem sure how to take this, but after a moment offered a comment, trusting it would be all right. "You kept to your training, then, sir. The training here."

"Exactly." Griffin rewarded that with a smile. Charlus had certainly earned it. "The rest of my recovery was slow and complex. Long story short, as I mentioned when you began, I have some issues with balance and with weakness in my legs. We're not entirely sure why, still, just that it's been stable for years. The chair lets me do more, far more reliably. And most of the time, my life is arranged so that it's not a bother. You've seen my flat."

"Everything you need on the ground floor, sir. Even if you have a spare room upstairs, as well." Charlus hesitated.

"Go on, ask your question. It's not something I bring up often. You might as well." Griffin didn't much like talking about it - it was somewhere between awkward and just plain boring at this point. But Charlus would, Griffin hoped, not be awful about it. The precedent so far certainly seemed encouraging on that point.

"Pardon, sir. I was wondering if, um. If it's painful?" The young man's voice cracked a little.

"Not terribly often. Some aches, and such, especially when the weather's foul or changing. But less, on average, than my mother, and she blames that on age. Mostly, it's tedious, when it's a bother. Shops and such. The house-keeper who sees to me is a treasure, thankfully, she knows how things work for me. Or days like this, when the wet makes everything even worse. I'm right at the best height to get a puddle across my chest if someone doesn't watch where they're driving."

It visibly wasn't something Charlus had put together, and he snorted at the image before looking abashed. "It isn't funny at all, sir, just..."

"It's a hilarious image, and remember, I told you we'd have truth here, as much as we can." Humans could not, in fact, bear unending truth, but that was a challenge for people to aspire to live up to. Certainly Griffin aspired to it. "Anyway. I manage well enough when I visit my parents up north. Or a little travel, but that's mostly been London for the theatre, and with a friend."

Griffin considered that this was probably as good a time to mention the rest of it. There were all the political considerations and Charlus was about to see more of those. "But it took a while to make sure that whatever it was that was causing the problem would not get worse. I spent some time in the Temple of Healing, then at a care home that specialises in magical injury. And in helping people figure out the next thing they're going to do." He shrugged. "And eventually I came back here. I was lucky enough to meet someone who makes a much better wheelchair than I started with."

"Huh. There are - I mean, I've seen there are different kinds." Charlus asked it a little uncertainly. "And you said yours was better on hills than some."

"It is. Magic's a great help, actually. The man who made it has a good friend - chosen brother, friend since Schola, all that - who's paralysed. Seth mostly makes furniture, but he got into wheelchairs as a sideline, ones that suit someone." Griffin considered. "You had Professor Wain at Schola. Her brother."

Charlus took a moment to chew on that. "How does the magic help, then? Do you mind my asking?" That was a good sign, that he was curious about that. Griffin had hoped this was how he'd take it, rather than asking about what Griffin couldn't do.

"If you'd like, I'll arrange a chance for you to ask Seth and Ponyard - that's the engineer he works with - when they're in town. Magic makes it more comfortable and helps stabilise it, it helps reduce the amount of maintenance I have to do. And it gives me more tools than sheer mechanics for turning and braking and all that. Or a little more leverage, going up a steeper hill. I don't exactly enjoy going down those, either, but I'm not at risk of rushing down or tipping over the same way I would without the magic. Out in public, somewhere like Whitby, there are limits to that, of course. Can't push the bounds of the Pact and do something that could only happen with magic."

Of all the oaths that ran his life, that was one of the most basic. Only, living in Trellech, where everyone was magical and had made the Pact, it was also one of the easiest to manage. Travel would change all of that, and it had been years since he'd had to consider that for more than a day or two at a time.

"And that's why you asked if I'd come up with you. Right, sir, I think I understand better with what you told me before." Charlus paused to pour the tea from pot to cup, then handed Griffin his. "Some hills are very steep, but there are people who go there to take the sea air, and I saw several people using chairs - the older kind, the basket chairs someone has to push."

"That's not a bad sign. I suppose there are cobble-stones." Not Griffin's favourite, and there were entire streets in Trellech that he avoided unless he was in the mood to bump up and down. The cushioning charms only went so far, and there was always a stone every so often that was particularly difficult.

"There are." Charlus looked down at his notes. "The main inn won't do. The hallways are tight, the whole thing's cramped, and there are no ground floor rooms at all."

"I can get myself upstairs with canes or crutches, if needed, but it's having somewhere to leave the chair that's a problem, yes. But you said there was something that might work," Griffin said.

"There are a whole set of little courtyards, with homes off them. They're called ghaults, I gather, by the locals. I found one - a former stables - redone as a cottage for rental. One bedroom above and a boxroom, but there's a bedroom on the ground floor. And a sitting room and a small kitchen. I put down a deposit for it, like you suggested, for next week. I've a diagram here, and the measurements you asked for. And it's not booked now, or until the middle of April. Not much call for rentals this time of year, she just needs a day or two to tidy and dust." He rummaged in his notebook and passed a folded sheet over to Griffin.

The whole thing was as Charlus said, and the measurements were neatly added. The sketch wasn't quite to scale, but well, Charlus was a solicitor and working on being a specialist in the judicial magics, not an architect. Griffin wouldn't insult him by asking if the measurements were accurate. The key thing was that there was space in the entry for the chair, and likely also a reasonable angle into the bedroom. There was also the main bath on the ground floor, and Griffin hadn't been sure that would be an option.

"Well spotted. And yes, that will do, if you'd write and confirm? I'll want at least a week, I expect, possibly longer. Call it a fortnight, if she's willing to adjust on a few days' notice, and ask about the possibility of extending." Griffin was considering the options. "Where is it?"

"The east side, sir, which is where the jet shops are, the few that remain. And I checked with the pubs along there. A couple have more amenable spaces, and the inn - it's um, called the White Horse & Griffin, actually - said they'd be glad to make up meals for takeaway, in the circumstances. We'll be right around the corner. That won't be a bother."

Griffin swallowed, suddenly. Then he looked up. "I'm

glad you're willing to come with me. It will make things much easier, at least to get started. If I need to be gone longer than a week, we can see about swapping out with someone else. Lucy said she'd be glad to. She just can't get clear next week." Lucy had been his preferred clerk and assistant before Charlus. She was always a delight. But also it would be a bit more of a scandal to have her staying in the same small cottage, by non-magical standards. That was a fuss he didn't need. "Magical cottage or no?"

"No, but I had time to test the hot water and such, and it'd take charms well enough." Charlus glanced at his notes again. "And the portal's not far from there, and fairly level. There are carters and such if you want to hire someone to go further, too. The woman who owns the cottage said she'd put together a list. She mentioned a nephew or something of the kind that does that sort of work."

"Good." It occurred to Griffin then that they hadn't actually talked about Charlus and his observation. That was a key conversation, and frankly, also more interesting than Griffin's physical limits.

He leaned back a little. "I didn't explain why I'm not surprised you think someone wants me to fail. There are people here, in our department, who don't think I'm fit for service."

"And you won't name names, sir." It wasn't a question. That was Charlus confirming that Griffin wouldn't.

"No. No sense in biassing you unduly. If you have a cause for concern, something you think is against our oaths and codes of practice, you should let me know. Or one of the senior staff, whoever you feel you can talk to."

"Mistress Henning, probably." Charlus said. She was an excellent choice, really. She did not approve of problems that impeded the work of the Courts. Charlus nodded.

Charlus considered, and then asked, "How are people, erm, a barrier, sir?"

"They can't argue with me continuing as I am. They've tried, Lamont was having none of it. But they think I ought to give up any idea of being Heir, or of taking over the land magic in due course. And of course, not any other sort of promotion either. They grumbled over me becoming Yew Primus, but we didn't have a lot of other choice there. I'm meant to just go along like this for the rest of my life until I retire. And that's not an awful life, but I refuse to be hemmed into it by other people's assumptions."

Charlus opened his mouth, closed it, and then leaned forward a little. "I can't see you taking that sitting down, no, sir." Again, he was venturing a bit of bravery.

Griffin grinned, then started laughing, warm chuckles. "Just so. Fighting them head-on isn't any good, so I have to pick my battles. But if they expect me to fail, and I don't, well. That's a good thing for me, I suspect."

Charlus went quiet for a little, fifteen seconds. Then he said, carefully, not quite making oath on it, but the weight of that was behind his words. "I hope you know, sir, that you've been a grand apprentice master for me, and that I'll do what I can to help you. Now, and in the future."

Griffin inclined his head, because that deserved proper acknowledgement. "I am glad of the former, and you don't owe me anything other than your good work. But I am very pleased to have your support, your attention to detail." He tapped the diagram with his index finger. "And your ideas. Also your humour, when we're in private or with friends and allies, mind."

That got a broader smile from Charlus. Griffin gave him a moment to settle, then said, "If you're able to stick around tonight, I could use your help now, too. Shall we talk through what we have in mind for the evaluation?"

That led them smoothly into the complexities of the magical design, and the different techniques for evaluating the courtroom enchantments. It kept them busy until someone knocked on his door to let them know the courts had all let out for the evening and they could begin.

CHAPTER 6
MARCH 10TH IN WHITBY

Annice put on her best face for this. She'd already put on one of the best dresses for the purpose, sensible and a little sober, without being ghastly. It was a muted grey that rather went with the spring clouds and threatened drizzle. She had errands to do, and they would not get any easier if she put them off.

First she went to the grocer, then there was a line at the fishmonger.

No one actually ignored her, not really. Whatever her other failings were - like wanting to carve jet for herself, in a rapidly dying industry that was superstitious about that - she was still of Whitby, through and through. Everyone in the shop had known her grandparents and her parents and her. Their parents had known her great-grandparents, and so on. That mattered here, no matter what happened in other places and other towns and especially cities.

Eventually, one matron coughed. "Didn't expect to see you out here, Miss Matthewman. You had your shop open yesterday, didn't you?"

"Oh, I had to do the shopping, of course. I'll be opening

up this afternoon, if you know someone who'd like to come by. I've still got a number of Grandad's pieces for sale, of course."

"A nice girl like you ought to find a place for yourself. I suppose you're getting on a bit for a family of your own, but they always need another matron or pair of hands at the children's home, up the cliff."

Annice forced her expression to something pleasantly neutral. "You're so kind to think of it, but I'm hoping to figure out something else. Do tell me, how's your daughter doing? She's due any time now, isn't she?"

At least three-quarters of living in Whitby was knowing the safe topic to deflect to. Da had said that was the trick to any insular town, and he'd had to learn Whitby's ways himself. At least the deflection got Mrs Summerby off on her daughter, the second grandbaby-to-be, the nonsense they were considering for names. By the time she was halfway through that, she was at the front of the line and had to give in her order.

Annice waited her turn patiently enough, got her own order in, and then went along to the baker for the last of what she needed. She could make bread, and usually did, but the last two times had turned out soggy and shrunken, and she wanted a decent loaf for once. She wasn't even sure why the bread wasn't behaving; the yeast was still foaming like it ought.

Finally, she brought her food back to the kitchen, going in through the back door, up the stairs to the kitchen and the flat, and then putting everything away. She wanted to go up to the workroom and do something that felt right, and she knew she couldn't. There was a chance, a small but real one, that someone might come and want to buy. She'd work on the matching earring for the lovely women from yesterday tonight.

Part of her knew she should probably go make the rounds of the other jet carvers who might still talk to her, but that was exhausting. She knew what they'd say or not say. They might offer a smile, but they wouldn't share any information. There wasn't that much work to go around, so it wasn't like they'd pass along a referral for someone who wanted something they didn't want to do. And while Annice had her own style, it wasn't very much in fashion the past couple of years. It was another thing the War had broken.

She'd always been interested not just in a single piece, but in how it connected to all the others. Her necklaces had sometimes tended to the ornate, each bead carved to balance the one on the other side. The ones she'd loved most, it wasn't a matched line of perfect pairs. Instead, it was complementary ones, where each shape was a little different, fitting into some larger construction of the whole necklace.

Back a couple of years ago, before everything went worse, she'd wondered if she'd be able to get more training in how to work the metal as well. She could do simple settings, but not yet complex ones. That would have let her do something, play with something, more like the new Art Déco styles. It might make jet into something ancient and modern, all at once, that would catch the eye and the heart and the soul.

But that took money, and it definitely took knowing the right people. None of that was on offer. And she didn't have enough jet pieces to afford to take risks with them. She'd need to stick to shapes that she could hope would sell. Those were not dreams she could indulge, and she set them aside as gently as she put the food away. Each thing in its place: cupboard, counter, table, or pantry.

Once that was done, she washed her hands to get the dust off, then went back down to the shop. She set up the lights and then raised the blinds and flipped the sign on the door to say open. She didn't expect to be busy - there weren't that many people out on the street - but she could make the attempt.

Annice sat for an hour, nearly two, before there was anyone at the door. It was a man, maybe a little older than she was, accompanying an older woman. "Good afternoon, ma'am, sir." Annice stood behind the counter. "Welcome to the shop. I'd be glad to show you anything you're interested in."

The woman glanced around. "Oh, my. You have a more pleasant shop than that other place we were in, Bernard. Don't you agree?" Her voice was high-pitched, the sort of voice that made Annice think of loudly chattering birds outside the window when she was trying to sleep.

"I'm glad you think so, ma'am. I do like to show the pieces to best advantage. Are you here in Whitby to visit family, or perhaps to take in the sea air? So good for the health, everyone always says so." Annice could amiably chatter with the best of them. It was absolutely a survival skill. It got them through a round of the woman dithering about which pieces she'd like to see first. They began with the beaded necklaces, then the pendants, then the necklaces again, but the smaller ones.

"Is it just you here, dear?" The woman suddenly looked up, sharply.

"Oh, it's my grandfather's and my father's work." She used the more formal terms, as she always did when selling. People might say they liked the novelty of a Yorkshire accent. They didn't actually mean it most of the time, they'd stare blankly. "Unfortunately, they both have passed away, now. But I keep wanting their work to find a home, someone who will appreciate it."

That brought on a bit more commentary, looking at half a dozen pieces in rotation. The man - the woman's son, she was pretty sure now - stood behind, more or less patiently. Eventually, the woman was dithering between two. "Now, this is me being nosy. All my friends at home say I'm just the worst. But surely a young woman like yourself could find someone who can keep up the shop."

Annice might have heard it dozens - hundreds - of times now, but that didn't make it all that much easier to answer. "Oh, I suppose that would solve quite a few problems, yes." It might well also create quite a few more, since then there would be two mouths to feed and not a lot of savings. And it wasn't like she was that far away from sharing a wall or a back courtyard with others. She was always hearing the ways men got awful when they'd had too much to drink to go with too much despair about the future. Or - though a bit more understandably - when their War snuck up on them and terrified them out of all reason.

Marriage would, in short, be a way out of her current troubles. And it would quite possibly plunge her into a whole set she was even less able to deal with. That whole proverb about frying pans and fires definitely applied. So instead, she managed a smile. "Did you want to see the pendants again?"

Finally, the woman made her choices - a beaded necklace, not very funereal, and a pendant polished to a high shine, apparently for an older sister. Annice wrapped them up carefully, tucking them into a cardboard box to travel safely. She added a bit of cotton wool for padding and a bit of thin bright ribbon to keep the lid on. The woman seemed delighted, and the two of them went off, leaving Annice with a bit of extra cash she hadn't expected that day.

There were a couple of other shoppers that afternoon, browsing. No one bought anything. Annice was almost ready to close up when the door opened again, and the man - Bernard - came in. "Mother's such a bother, but you handled her really rather well."

It was decidedly abrupt as an opening statement. Annice ducked her chin. "She was a pleasure to talk to. And people want to get the right piece, that's not something to rush."

"Still." Bernard considered. "She was right. You could marry."

That was vastly more abrupt. Annice considered her options, and coming over offended had some risks. "I wasn't looking to. I'm well on the shelf."

Bernard - she didn't even know his last name - shrugged. "I've a cousin, injured in the War. Not good for much now, but he's got a bit of a pension and maybe he could take up something crafting. Like this. Here. You think about it. If you like the idea, we could introduce you by letter."

Oh, Annice could figure that one out. The man was likely tucked into some relative's house. They'd be delighted to get him out of it, put all the burden of whatever his care was on someone else. She wasn't utterly opposed to the idea of marriage. But if she wanted to tend to a stranger's needs, she could go get a job doing it. That way, she'd get paid for it and go home at the end of the day. Tending to someone she loved - like she had with her grandad and nan - that was different.

"You think about it." Bernard glanced around the shop.

"You've some nice pieces here, but I'm guessing not a lot of business."

"You're very kind to think of me, sir. And I have the card. I promise I'll think about it. Now, though, I'm afraid I need to lock up. I promised a friend I'd help with something tonight. I need to get on."

His mouth quirked up to one side, as if he could tell the white lie. Then he shrugged. "We're staying at the White Horse & Griffin a few more days. Come round and ask if you want to know more."

She just nodded. He did leave, promptly and without a fuss. Annice went through the routine of locking up, pulling the curtains across first. Next, she checked the locks and the warding before taking the cases of the finished pieces and putting them all back in the safe in the back room. She didn't always, but while that conversation hadn't made her think he was intending a spot of light burglary exactly, she wanted to know where everything was. And, of course, she had a bit of magic to help her.

He didn't. She was pretty sure of that, though how she knew was hard to say. Not one of her people, neither of Whitby nor of Albion, and she could feel those currents well enough. Finally, when everything was in place, she turned and went upstairs to make something for supper that would let her get to the workbench and those earrings quickly.

CHAPTER 7
MARCH 11TH IN WHITBY

"Where did you want to start, sir?" Charlus was perched on the chair in the sitting room. Their sitting room, at least for the duration. "I have the map. Would that be a help?"

"Please." Griffin stretched a little, considering the options. They'd arrived ninety minutes ago, before luncheon. Charlus had arranged for the basic groceries - bread, eggs, makings for sandwiches. They'd brought a hamper with them, and a keep-cold box besides, so there were some other things as well. Better yet, there were pubs and such along Church Street for an evening meal, and they could sort out options from those. "How far are the two shops you thought we might start with?"

Charlus set the map out on the low table in front of the sofa. He glanced around and grabbed two small decorative metal objects, likely related to fishing somehow, on the two ends. "We're here, of course." He tapped the courtyard on the map, tucked into the maze of courtyards and alleys east of Church Street. "One shop is here, one shop is there. The main inn is here, if you wanted to try it for supper and perhaps a little local gossip."

Griffin considered it. He was doing the maths on two different parts, of course, he always had to. One was the strategy of the project, and the other was on how far his legs might reasonably carry him. He'd been sensible, anticipating the demands of this trip, and he'd done his best to rest in advance. However, it was always a coin toss whether portal travel would make things a bit more wobbly. So far, that toss seemed to be on his side, and the two shops seemed to be close, with the hotel - and this cottage - between them. "Any thoughts on which to try first, from what you heard on your earlier visits?"

"No, sir. Both are well-established, both do magical work, but there wasn't much to decide between them without asking more detailed questions than you wanted me to. One does a fair bit with, what's the word? Ammonites, too. Polishing them up. There was a bit of a fad for them a couple of years ago for certain kinds of simple talisman work, and apparently it's still a steady trade."

"Huh. I remember that." Griffin nodded. "I'll use the crutches, we'll start there, and see how I feel after. I'd like to see how bad the chair will be overall." It would, no matter what, be easier on crutches than in the chair. Coming up from the portal had been tedious enough, the paving stones led to bump after bump.

"Of course." Then he hesitated. "May I ask, sir, about the crutches? They're not a type I've seen as often."

"Ah." Griffin considered. "This form is fairly new. 1917, I think, at least in terms of being available for sale. I find them more comfortable and more stable. My forearm goes down between the curved pieces, it's a straight line to my hand, I can use all the strength of my arms. The more common kind, it puts all the weight under the arm, and I find it makes me ache much faster. The forearm crutches are also a titch more flexible, if I need to adjust what's taking the most pressure. And magically, the wood's chosen to work best with my magic, it has some charms that help with comfort and such."

"Being able to adjust would be the same sort of things you keep mentioning about the ritual work, sir. Leaving space where we can to adapt to the needs of the day or the space." Griffin nodded, delighted that Charlus had put that together himself. Now Charlus straightened up. "What manner do you want me to take in public?"

"In magical conversation, let me take the lead. Otherwise, let's see. If I am a solicitor, that implies some sort of case, and I don't want that sort of gossip. Such a bother to deal with, both for us and whoever we end up talking to. Are you willing to be my assistant, up here while I take the air, getting out of the city fogs? Something, something business unspecified."

"Implying London, then." Charlus was quick. Griffin was grateful for that all over again. "Sure, I can do that. From near the family townhouse in Bedford Square, if that works?"

"That would suit nicely. I'll come up with something tediously boring before we need it. You just need to nod tolerantly. It will explain your presence, and if there is some reason for you to be away, also explain that. And hopefully no one will bother us with legal questions. You don't mind?"

"Of course not, sir." Charlus considered. "Let me go adjust my tie, perhaps. I'll just be a minute." Griffin nodded. By the time Charlus came back, Griffin was ready to go. He was wearing the narrow striped teal and black tie that signalled his own Seal House in school, just as Griffin's gold stripes on black signalled Salmon House. Both of them were in suitable suits for the afternoon, neither too formal nor too casual. Men of means.

Getting to the first shop was not terribly difficult. Griffin didn't rush. There was no reason to, and every reason to take it steadily. For one thing, he wanted to measure out his stamina today. And for the other, being seen would help their long-term goals, or so he very much hoped. Charlus got the door for him - having someone to do that was a considerable help - and Griffin went up the two steps into the shop. He could feel the magic here immediately, though it wasn't terribly strong in the space, more an echo from some pieces.

There was a woman behind the counter, trays of carved jet pieces out. She opened her mouth, then caught the ties, and more visibly, the meaning of the ties. Griffin nodded, pleasantly. "Good afternoon, ma'am. I was wondering about a conversation with the carver here, about a private commission. I'd like to know if he might be capable of what I have in mind." He leaned just a hair on the 'capable', with the slight pulse of magic that would make it clear he meant he was also magical.

"Oh, pardon, yes, sir. Let me see, sir." She fluttered away, first turning the sign in the door to show the shop was closed, then into the back room. They heard her going up the stairs, a pause, and then two sets of steps coming down. A larger man, bulky around the shoulders and through the stomach, came through, then pulled himself up straight. "Sirs. We're quite private, if you wish to confirm."

That was an interesting reaction, indeed. Griffin let his magic reach out, to get a feel for the space, and there were well-set wards there. Not the man's own, Griffin thought, though it would be rude to press enough to make certain of that. But someone skilled had done the work, and they'd been reliably maintained. That wasn't what he'd expected. After a moment, he heard the woman ask, "Should I bring out a chair, sir?"

Griffin could sit, but sitting when others stood did such odd things to the balance of power. Griffin could, if he had to, play that off as a man who made everyone else stand, waiting to jump to his commands. Something like a king of old or magnate or something of the kind. But he did not care for that mode, nor for how it made him feel. Now he shook his head. "I'm fine, but thank you for the thought, Mistress. Your shop has an excellent reputation, sir. I am from the Halls of Justice in Trellech, and we are looking for someone for a particular commission."

"Courts, eh?" The man nodded. "I'm Robert Carey. M'wife, Bess." He looked neither awed nor surprised that someone from the courts had turned up here. "Something the matter there, then?"

"We're looking to refurbish the inheritance court entirely. It's worn down. We believe it needs thorough renewal, possibly entire replacement."

"Well, I'm not your man. Booked solid, I am, for two years out. Nah, three." His wife had been about to say something. "Even for the courts."

Griffin blinked, suddenly entirely grateful he was balanced on four points and not two. "Beg pardon?"

"Man can't sit around waiting for Trellech to take notice, can he? No way to make a living. I make the pieces here. I do work for a number of the Great Families. Protections, mostly, not that I'm the one setting them, just the stonework and medallions and all. I disappear, all of them up and down the street think I've gone off on some boat for the fishing. All tidy." Robert shrugged. "Them's pay a sight better than the courts, too."

That, well, Griffin couldn't entirely argue with. He took a breath, sorting through the options. "You're the senior crafter of that type, I gather?" Griffin made a small nod at Charlus. "My apprentice made some initial inquiries."

"These days, aye." Robert shrugged. "You can ask down at Cliff Hudson's. He's a decent carver, wife's a bit of a muchness. Don't know what he's busy with these days. We don't talk, so you'd say."

Any solicitor worth a few pence could read between those lines, some standing feud, but a personal one. Not the sort of professional one that would lead to no kind of recommendation at all. "That's the shop at the other end of Church Street, where it turns up the steps."

"Aye." Robert shrugged. "Bloody bright blue storefront. That be all, then?"

It made Griffin suddenly certain Robert - and perhaps his wife, she'd slunk behind him - was hiding something. But he certainly wasn't the man to try to get it out, not without a great deal more cause. "Thank you for your time. And the pointer. We'll be off, then." He nodded politely, rather than fumble to lift his hat to Bess. Charlus got the door with no commentary, and Griffin made his way out.

Charlus waited until they were going back past the alley to their cottage, the sidewalk beginning to climb up a bit before the street twisted up the hill. "Not the reception I expected, sir."

"Nor I. Wonder if we can find out who he's doing work for. What did you find out about this Hudson?"

"Younger - up and coming, or at least middle-aged, to Carey's seniority. The shop was closed up when I was here, though." Charlus gestured at the awning. The whole wood frame of the shop was indeed a striking blue, the shade that would echo the sea on a clear sunny day. Whenever Whitby got those, and Griffin wasn't sure of that sort of weather, actually. It seemed more cheerful overall than Carey's shop. Again, Charlus got the door, but this time, there were no steps. The entire thing was flush with the path outside.

They went through the process again, the woman behind the counter recognising the ties, the 'capable' that indicated magical awareness, and absolutely the slight pulse of magic. She was younger than Bess Carey had been, by perhaps two decades. This was the sort of woman who'd likely started out stunningly beautiful and was ageing into a distinct form of attractiveness.

She also offered the chair first, two easy chairs near the window, to take advantage of the light. Because there were two - with stools nearby and a low wood bench - Griffin took the offer, along with her explicit request to test the warding. He settled into the chair, leaning the crutches between his knee and the arm of the chair so they wouldn't topple. It took her slightly longer to come back than Bess Carey, though he thought the two women had gone up two flights each, possibly to some attic workspace. It would be a practical arrangement for this sort of work. There would be the shop on the ground floor, living space above, and the workshop on the second floor, where the light might be most direct.

When she came back, her husband let her come through first. He was a striking man, rather Heathcliff in his looks and manner, with dark hair waving down past his collar. He was in shirtsleeves and braces, though if he'd been at work, he must have worn some sort of smock, because his clothing was impeccably clean. Griffin looked up and nodded. "Cliff Hudson, I presume?"

"Aye, and my wife Maud. I gather you're needing something of magic, then?"

Griffin nodded. "We've spoken to Robert Carey. His name and yours were the ones we had. He can't take on the work, and it was clear he didn't want to consider it." Then he laid out what they needed again, in a bit more detail this time. He was intrigued to realise it was Maud who was tracking all the details. Hudson had pulled the bench over, and she was on a stool, just beside him.

"Aye, we could do the work, but not for a good while. A year, at least. I'm committed elsewhere, aye? Talisman work. Someone had a big commission, I'm doing the carving. Bigger than the Courts, even, and steadier work. You all only need us every so often."

"I'm a shopkeeper's son," Griffin said, amiably. "I do understand that. Steady client base wins out over the flash. Is there anyone at all you could recommend we consider? A former apprentice, someone who's had some training? We'd pay for your consulting time, if it came to that sort of arrangement."

The couple hmmed and murmured back and forth several times, falling into a Yorkshire brogue thick enough Griffin couldn't follow it easily. After a good minute, Maud said, far more clearly. "It's a pity Jack Chapman isn't still alive. He'd have done the work, and done it well."

Hudson glanced at his wife. "There's a tradition, strong one, here, that women don't work the jet. But he's got a granddaughter, still living. Shop around the corner, up the hill just a hair. She might know someone, at the least."

Griffin was fairly sure there were several things they weren't telling him, but again, he was in no position to press. "That's a place to start. Is there a good time to catch her at home or whatever?"

"Oh, she keeps the shop open a fair bit." Maud flicked through something mentally. Griffin knew that expression very well. "Not today or tomorrow, probably, but try in two days. Or if it rains 'nough to make the pavement shine."

That was an elliptical sort of comment, but it was at least one Griffin could follow as a guide. "I appreciate your time, then. Perhaps I might look at a few pieces while we're here?" He had relatives to buy presents for, he always did. And he knew Charlus did, though Charlus's relatives were the sort who wouldn't consider jet fashionable these days.

The half-hour that took solidified his impression of the two. Cliff Hudson had a creative spark to him that Griffin rather liked, both in his carving and how he went about deciding what he was going to make. His wife, though, seemed to be the business mind of the bunch, and she was the one who'd guided Hudson into working with ammonites and a few other local specimens as well as jet.

None of it had even begun to solve their actual need, but at the very least, they had weeded out two possibilities.

CHAPTER 8
MARCH 14TH

Annice came back home, feeling utterly drained. The day had, for once, not been entirely made of tension. The three women had come round for the earring, and they'd made an afternoon of it. One of them - the middle of the three, Alexandra's mother - had asked about having tea in, perhaps from one of the nearby places. She'd disappeared and then come back twenty minutes later with a hamper full of food.

It had meant Annice could lock up the shop, not worry about who might overhear, or any of the other dozen worries that normally flew around her, like flies. They'd been generous, too, not just with the tea, but with their purchases, each of them picking up a piece. It was enough to keep Annice in groceries for at least a few weeks longer without dipping into Grandad's savings again.

But when they finally left, for a promised supper of fresh-caught fish, back at the inn, Annice had felt deflated. She wasn't really hungry; she didn't feel steady enough to try carving, so instead she went up to the workshop to tidy up. There were still more than a few cupboards that hadn't been properly cleared out in years, in the eaves by the stairs, and they would not sort themselves.

Annice was in the middle of the second one when she moved several books and a pile of ancient newspapers that crumbled in her hands. Underneath, she found a large flat cardboard box, tied shut with string. She set it in her lap, picked at the knot with her fingers until it gave way, then removed the lid. What was inside startled her, badly.

It was the width of her palm, and about half the length high. It was big enough to have made a significant brooch or hair ornament or something of the kind, and wasn't anything like that. This pulsed with magic. When she turned it over, there were tiny engravings on the back, which had a shallow curve to it. It was meant to sit on something, maybe even spin or move lightly. Even with her jeweller's loupe, she couldn't make sense of the markings. They weren't any kind of magic she'd seen, never mind been taught.

Carefully, she set it back in the box, and the paper on the box, and the books on the paper, feeling like one of the counting folksongs in reverse. She closed the cupboard carefully, as if she might wake something up. Then she sat there, trying to catch her breath.

It could have been Da's work. He'd had proper magical training. But she hadn't thought he did things like that. It wasn't like she could ask him now, and she didn't think he'd kept more than routine business records. Certainly she hadn't yet found anything like a working journal.

The only thing Annice could think to do was have tea. The tea was decent, but it turned out not to solve any of her many questions. Finally, she considered. If she went round to Aunt Sarah's, maybe one of the cousins could talk it through with her, at least. That meant a trek across the bridge, to the west side of the port, but the weather was just cloudy, not raining, and not that unpleasant.

The house was, as usual, complete chaos. Uncle Donald was off on a fishing trip, as were the male cousins. But that still left Nan's sister's daughter Aunt Sarah, two of her daughters, two daughters-in-law, and a dozen children including the three babies. They were all crammed into two houses next door to each other. It took a good hour to get through all the pleasantries, and for Annice to agree to a cup of tea and a scone, but not more food. For one thing, she knew they were more skint than she was, if only by virtue of more mouths to feed, and more growing little ones.

Finally, though, she and Ruth, the cousin she was closest to, ended up on the back steps. They sat looking out on the bare little plot of earth that didn't really justify being called a garden, though come a bit later in the spring, it would have some hardy plants growing again. Aunt Sarah usually got a couple of things that flowered in there, for a bit of pretty, as she said.

"You've not been round." Ruth laid it out, point by point. "Mam was thinking you wouldn't."

Annice's chin came up. "Been busy." Her shoulders came up too, defensively. "She put out?"

"You know she worries you think you're better'n us, and it's no good." Ruth shrugged. "Good you came. Also good you didn't need feeding. Mostly."

Annice let out a hollow noise. "Client fed me tea today. Not that common, not like I'd turn it down. I came to see if Aunt Sarah knew anything, but not if she's..." Not if she wasn't sure if Annice was still part of the family. Or was ready to do her part helping the family, or whatever. If any of the boys had showed any sign of wanting to learn jet carving, she'd have taught them long since. But they preferred the fishing boats, even though that was dangerous work. Not that jet carving couldn't be, if you didn't have a touch of magic to catch the dust. They all knew far too many people who'd died of a black cough.

Ruth stared out across the yard, at a point somewhere near the middle of the rickety fence. "You ask. She'd rather." Ruth's voice got flatter, the broad vowels coming out more.

"Will you get her to come out when she's got a minute, then? You too, if you like." Annice offered it as a peace offering of sorts.

"Aye." Ruth pushed upright and disappeared into the house. There was a burst of sound through the open door until it swung closed. It sounded like bedtime was even more unwelcome than usual. After a few minutes, Aunt Sarah came out, drying her hands on a dingy apron. "What's tha, then?"

"Hoping you might know about something, Aunt Sarah." There, she'd make it proper. "It'd be a help. And checking in, too."

"Eh." Her aunt settled down next to her. "We're in a fuss, Ruth wanting t'get married, but where would we put her Sam, that's what I want to know. And there's nawt for space at his."

It was, in fact, a knotty problem on both ends. Ruth and Sam had been sweet on each other for ages. He'd had steady work fishing, but it wasn't enough to afford their own flat, never mind a house. Annice knew that one solution was to ask Ruth and Sam to live in Grandad's and Nan's house with her. She was rattling around. It was true. She didn't need all that space.

But she hadn't been able to figure out how to make it work with the shop. She loved Ruth - and liked Sam - but they were noisy as anything, even on their own and not needing to shout over their brothers and sisters and cousins and all. Sound muffling charms weren't a magic she knew, and even if she did, they wouldn't work well with either the shop or the workshop. She needed to hear other things in the house. Instead, Annice just made a soft, uncommitted noise.

Her aunt let it sit there for thirty seconds before snorting. "Stubborn, thou awt." It had a fair bit of affection to it, the countryside twist to the words. "Had somewhat to ask?"

"I found something in a box, buried under other things. No one's touched it in years. This big." She gestured, drawing the line of it against her hand. She remembered the cool oddly light feel of it, the way jet looked like stone and wasn't really stone at all. It made a soul remember it had been wood and still had some quality of it.

"Ah." Aunt Sarah looked off toward the back of the fence too. It was a favourite staring spot. Someone really ought to hang something decorative there. "Your da. Don't know much about it, mind. Just that he thought it'd bring, dunno. Good. Keep out what wasn't.'"

Protection, then, or some combination of protection and attraction. "Where'd he learn it?"

"Dunno. Saw it once or twice. Not like anything else. Then they put it away. Wouldn't talk 'bout it. After the boat went down with your uncles." Fishing was dangerous, storms were more so, and two of her uncles had drowned when Annice was little. From the stories she'd heard later, people missed the way they were sober, and not the way they were drunk, and no one talked about that, either. Annice nodded slowly. "You don't know anyone who'd know?"

"Think on't." Aunt Sarah shrugged. "Should go see to the littles."

"Thank you." Annice meant it, trying to put that in her voice. Aunt Sarah patted her absently on the shoulder, and then used that same shoulder to lever herself upright, leaving Annice and Ruth on the step. There was silence, well past when the door closed and they could hear themselves think again.

"You know what she wants. Thinks you ought t'offer." Ruth whispered it. "Can't tell her otherwise, me either."

Annice's chin came up. "You don't want to?"

"Not unless you're actually willing. And you're not, so." Ruth shrugged. "We'll figure something, I don't know. Sometime. Somehow." She sounded both determined and resigned, all at once, and Annice wanted to make it better, without seeing any way to.

"Come up for tea sometime? Both of you. I don't know. I really don't. But tea, at least. Away from the chaos."

"Mmm." Ruth bumped Annice's arm with hers, companionably. "Can." Then she leaned back on her other hand. "You lonely, there?"

Yes. No. She liked the quiet, it turned out. Though Nan and Grandad hadn't been very noisy most of the time. Just the sounds of them moving around. "Some. The quiet would be fine if I could make more jet pieces and sell them. Bill told me he can't gather for me anymore. Too many people spotted it, y'know? Caused trouble for him, too." Ruth made a grumble deep in her chest, disapproving, but Annice shook her head. "He's got to do what he needs. No good otherwise."

"He owed your grandad somewhat. Don't know what it was. Just that he did." Ruth laid it out, like she bartered at the fishmonger, cutting the deal as finely as anyone could. "What're you going to do?"

"Dunno." That was the truth. "One day at a time, yeah? And that stone, I don't know what it's meant for. Maybe I could find someone to buy it."

"Doesn't solve all of it," Ruth pointed out. "You need a man to keep carving. Cover for your work. Someone the others would accept. Or the family." Her shoulder twitched, and she glanced over behind her at the door. "And that's not a simple thing."

Annice grimaced. "No." Then she stood. "You're all up early. I should get back."

"Come again, aye? I'll make your goodbyes to Mam." Then Ruth was standing, coming to open the side gate, so Annice could slip out without causing even more chaos by saying goodnight. The walk back was harder, somehow, like everything was grey and the life and light was getting sucked out of the world even more than it had.

CHAPTER 9
MARCH 15TH

It had taken several days to find Mistress Matthewman in, and the shop open. That had given Griffin and Charlus plenty of time to ask around at every other jet worker they could find, but they'd got the same answer everywhere. Or rather, it had been two variations.

Either the shops weren't magical, or if they were, they wouldn't do that sort of work. Half the magical folk had the sort of reaction that made Griffin suspect they were neck deep in smuggling. It was no use trying to explain he didn't care about that if the crafter could do the work, the two were distinct. But he also didn't blame someone in the midst of smuggling from wanting to avoid anything to do with the Halls of Justice. Or especially anyone familiar with the truth magics. That was neither fair nor sensible.

Fortunately, one part of it had gone smoothly enough. It had been a long time since Griffin had shared living space with anyone - not since he'd been at the Gospatrick Home in the last stages of his rehabilitation healing. He'd hoped it would be all right, from how Charlus was in the office, and he'd been correct.

His apprentice had been agreeable. He didn't talk too much in the morning before either of them had properly woken up. And most importantly, he was careful about whether he moved furniture. The cottage they were renting had some narrow pathways to navigate with a chair, but as long as the sitting room chairs were in their particular best places, it was manageable.

And Charlus had been quite willing to go pick up take-away, or scout ahead for which of their options for an evening meal would be the easiest to manage. And which would work even if Griffin used his crutches instead of the chair because of a handful of stairs up or down. It meant this trip was exhausting - Griffin was sleeping fairly well every night, even though he also had some aches from an unfamiliar bed and a decided lack of pillows. But it was not overwhelmingly so.

Finally, though, the shop had been open. And there were no stairs to get inside, or so Griffin had thought. Instead, when Charlus opened the door, he stopped. "There's a ledge, sir, and two steps up." Some oddity of the buildings, then, or how to get a flat floor at that level, built into a hill.

"Beg pardon?" The voice inside was a pleasant soprano, a mezzo, but with that trill of pitch that Griffin had come to enjoy. His apprentice mistress, whose voice he'd heard often in all its many forms, had been a mezzo.

"Good afternoon, ma'am." Charlus flung himself into full polite mode. "I'm assisting Mister Pelson, here, but he's in a wheeled chair. We could come back..."

"Oh." There was a silence through the open door.

"Come round the back, the path at the right. There's a ramp." Not something Griffin had expected, but not something he was going to turn down. The tiny path through a creaky door in a wood fence turned out into a non-existent lot. But there was a small ramp, as if someone had intended to wheel heavy loads up to the house. The voice - or rather the person attached to the voice - was opening the door, peering at both of them out of the shadow of the interior.

Griffin touched the brim of his hat. "Ma'am. More than one person suggested we speak to you. We're looking for someone capable of a particular commission. I'm Griffin Pelson, based in Trellech." That would give him away as magical, absolutely.

The woman stepped forward, a bit more into the light. She was near enough Griffin's age, perhaps a little younger, with dark hair pulled back from her face. A bit of a wave and whatever one called the poufiness, so it wasn't a severe effect. And she wore a grey frock with an apron around her waist. "I'm not sure what I can do for you, but come in." She stepped back to hold the door, and Charlus went ahead. Griffin backed up a hair to give himself a little more movement to work with to get up the incline, but the charms on the chair made that much easier.

They made a little procession in through a hallway just wide enough that Griffin wasn't in fear of bruising his knuckles. A small storage room stood at the right with back stairs going up beyond that. Griffin's attention was immediately taken by the shop. There was a feeling of magic here, but not the wards and protections of the other magical shops they'd been in. Or rather, not just those. Once fully into the shop, Griffin slowed himself to a stop and nodded. "We appreciate your time, Mistress."

"You're awfully forward, sir." She turned around to face

him, then considered and pulled up a chair for Charlus, then one for herself, perching on it, rather than ask Griffin to move. "Who recommended me, please?" Then she seemed to remember that she hadn't actually confirmed her name directly. "I am Annice Matthewman. But I suspect you wanted my grandad, and he's - he died several months ago."

"My condolences, Mistress." Griffin kept his voice gentle. "It was Master Cliff Hudson and his wife who mentioned your name - and your recent loss." Something in what he said - or perhaps how he said it - made her stiffen up, and Griffin wasn't sure where he'd gone wrong. "I gather this isn't your usual sort of inquiry. The pieces here are lovely, though. I'd like to look for something for my mother, whatever other business we may or may not manage."

The second half of that got her breathing again, at least, something more normal. She looked up, meeting Griffin's gaze frankly, and that wasn't something Griffin was terribly used to. For one thing, most of the time, people were at the wrong height to make it simple, relative to him. And the rest of the time, they were nervous about what he might see. She didn't have that reason, at least not that he knew about.

"Surely they told you, someone has by now, it's bad luck for a woman to be carving jet." Now there was a different tightness. Three kinds, in as many sentences, and Griffin wasn't entirely sure how to interpret any of them.

Griffin nodded. "And if that's a custom you keep to, I won't argue with you about it. May I lay out what we're looking for, and see if you can offer any suggestions? We're glad to pay for your time, by way of consulting, too."

"Ah, well." Mistress Matthewman leaned back a little. "I

wouldn't turn that down. All right. Go ahead." The way she was responding continued to fascinate Griffin, half like a barrister in court, half something else, a mix of insistent defensiveness and refusal to engage, all at once.

"To begin, I and my apprentice - this is Charlus Edwards - work for the Halls of Justice in Trellech. Formally speaking, Magister Griffin Pelson, Esquire, Senior Solicitor and Keeper of the Courts, Yew Chair Primus. Which is all mostly a lot of nonsense outside our usual environs where everyone already knows it. Please do call me Griffin, or Master Pelson, if you'd rather be more formal."

Mistress Matthewman considered. "Annice. I suppose. Can't be bothered with all those words. We'll be forever. What do I call you, sir?"

That was to Charlus, who promptly replied. "Charlus. Or Master Edwards. I'm still earning my eventual title."

Annice - interesting name, that, and not one Griffin had heard much in his usual work - nodded. "You work for the Courts. Are you here investigating something? You said solicitor in there."

"I am a fully chartered solicitor - so is Charlus - but my key role is helping to maintain the judicial magics of the courts. The part of my title that talks about Yew Chair Primus means I'm the senior member of the staff responsible for cases involving inheritance, though not the only one focused on them."

"Senior? You're my age. That's not senior at anything." It was the first personal comment he'd heard out of her, and it made him snort.

"I'm very good at what I do." He shrugged, palms up, leaving his wrists resting on the arms of the chair. "We are here because I believe the jet in the courtroom dedicated to inheritance cases is wearing out. Our working theory is tricky to test, we don't have a proper control. But we believe that the difficulty of a number of the cases since the War has weakened the magical resonances significantly faster than expected."

"And you're here why?" Annice frowned then looked around the shop. "The jet? I don't do that kind of work. You want Cliff Hudson or maybe Rob Carey."

"Both of them are booked up for years, they say. So are the other people we've asked, while we were finding a time your shop was open." Griffin said it as neutrally as he could, and it wasn't enough. She stiffened up again. "And I admit, while I've studied the records of the previous stonework, I do not fully understand the process."

"Well, no." Annice frowned. "Do you do anything with your hands? Make anything?" She gestured, vaguely.

"Someone taught me knitting, but I'm not very good at it," Griffin said amiably. "I was in hospital for rather a long time, the end of the War. Mostly, I enjoy reading and organising things, but I've done a bit of miniature making. I've nieces with an extravagant sort of dollhouse, my sister's children." And he'd watched Seth work on his chair for probably days worth of time. Griffin would hand over tools on request, but that wasn't something he was prepared to discuss at the moment.

It visibly wasn't what she'd expected, but she gathered herself up. "The process, from what Grandad told me, is much the same. You need to carve the jet to fit the spaces in the stonework, for a permanent installation for that. It's delicate work, and jet can go brittle." She obviously thought of something, then some other thought caught her eye. "The courts."

"Yes?" Griffin wasn't sure what she'd thought, but it made her visibly skittish.

"That means the truth magics. How do I know you're not, I mean? Right now."

It was an entirely common sort of fear, and no matter how ridiculous Griffin found it, people would have it. Of course, he knew what the truth was, and they didn't, and that was part of the point of the problem. "I can call the truth magics, but only when I'm in Trellech or a properly prepared courtroom - which would also be in Trellech. Or potentially, I haven't actually tried this one for years - in a soc-and-sac court established by the local Lord or Lady of the land. I'm not actually on best speaking terms with Lord and Lady Hutton, so not likely I'd be doing it in this part of Yorkshire."

Several things in that apparently seemed implausible to her. Her eyebrows went up and kept going. Griffin was increasingly fascinated by her expressiveness, far beyond what he was used to in Trellech where everyone - him included - guarded that sort of thing. "How do I know you're telling me the truth?"

"Q.E.D., I can't call the truth magics on myself. Not here. I'll make oath on my magic, if it pleases you. I'm quite competent for that, as well. It's a regular part of our work."

She stood, suddenly, the sort of abrupt movement that Griffin appreciated all the more now that it was largely beyond him. She turned away, looking out the window to the street beyond. "I don't know what to think about your asking. Would you like to look at something for your mother now and come back in a few days?"

"I can do that." Griffin would like to have a nice tidy solution for his problem, but it had already become clear that wasn't on offer. There were no cases in the Courts right now, since they were on the Equinox break. Then it'd be another two weeks before anything actually came to trial or needed the courtroom magics. And he'd been told in the strongest possible terms that finding some solution was his focus for the time being. "Should I call again in a few days, or would you prefer to send a message round?"

"I can send a message." Annice crossed her arms, turning back. Griffin nodded at Charlus, who produced a notecard from his pocket and a pen, writing out their current address. Griffin didn't offer the journals by way of contact. He was fairly sure this woman wouldn't have one, given what he'd seen of the building. Nothing was in horrible repair, but nothing was new, either, and that meant the cost of a journal was likely beyond her.

"Excellent. We'll find something to amuse ourselves, I'm sure. I brought books. Now, my mother's got an eye for the unusual, not the staid Victorian drops. Something with a natural feel to it, that might do nicely. She has a sometimes excessive fondness for the Arts and Crafts style."

As he hoped, it startled Annice out of her protective stance. "Excessive, sir?"

"I don't know about you, but I find a bath tiled in beautiful ceramics of disapproving maidens processing along the opposite wall to be a little disarming. Beautiful, the colours are very striking, but they seem to see right through one."

She made a noise that Griffin couldn't begin to interpret at all. It might have been anything from amusement to annoyance. Then she brought out several pieces. After a brief consideration, he picked up one of an unfurling rose, which had a delicacy to the petals Griffin found quite charming. He suspected there were at least three different makers of the pieces, but he wasn't enough of a craftsman to know for sure. That settled, he paid up for both the piece and her time, using the higher end of the acceptable scale as the Courts' accountants had it.

Then they were led back out through the faded hallway, to the outside, and left to their own devices again.

CHAPTER 10
MARCH 16TH

Annice made her way down the beach, walking carefully. The last tide had brought up more battered bits of wood and good-size rocks than usual, the rising spring tides did that sometimes. Not much of it was any use to her, however, though she'd been almost fooled by five pieces of coal so far.

She'd made it well away from the harbour proper when she heard someone behind her. She turned around to see Bill coming up, a little out of breath. "Bill." Annice had no reason to take her mood out on him.

"Wondered if I'd see you." Bill took off his cap, ran his hand through what was left of his hair, and tugged it back on. "Heard there was someone asking 'bout you. Wanted to give you a word."

"Oh, he found me. The man in the wheelchair, yeah?" Annice had been trying not to think about that conversation, though of course that meant it was all she could think of unless she was absorbed by something else. Two days, and she couldn't get him out of her head, or what he'd asked. Offered. She didn't even know what to call it.

"Him." Bill hesitated, and that wasn't like him. One thing she liked about Bill is that she knew what to expect, straightforward honesty. Not this hesitation.

"Did you talk to him?" Annice glanced around and found a bit of a boulder where they could both sit comfortably enough. They'd done it before.

"Aye." Bill said nothing more until he'd sat and chewed on it for a minute. "Odd chair. Odd man. And the one with him. Right quiet. I was in Edgar's when they came in. Though he had the crutches then. Odd." Bill pronounced it. "Ought to be one or t'other, you'd think. And that's a sort of crutch I've never seen b'fore."

Annice tried to figure out what to say to that, and it wasn't like she'd had Griffin Pelson's medical history explained to her. Or any of his other history, actually, other than that baffling title. "He didn't say much about it. They had to come round the back, though. He had the chair when he came to see me."

"You want I should warn him off?" Bill was big, he was burly, he could certainly be plenty intimidating to both Griffin and what was the name? Charles. Charlus.

Annice hesitated, but then she shook her head. "They were polite. And they bought something. Well. Mister Pelson did." She had to think and put the non-magical title on it. She also didn't know how she felt about the fact he'd bought one of her pieces, the rose she'd only just finished. He'd looked at all the others, he'd complimented Grandad's work, and Da's, and all. But he'd bought hers. Definitely not something she was going to talk about with anyone. Maybe Ruth, but probably not Ruth either. Ruth didn't entirely approve of her breaking with tradition and doing her own carving.

"Huh." Bill leaned back, staring out at the ocean. "They

asked a knot of questions. Who did jet carving, who'd done inlay, if anyone had. Not usual."

Annice nodded. "I didn't tell them much." The hell of it was, she didn't know if she could actually do the work. She could do the carving fine, but she did not know about the rest of it. Grandad had taught her, like he'd taught her the rest of it. But she'd never had a chance to practise. Which was the other part. Surely someone had set it the last time it needed setting, but who had done that? It was a mystery, because she didn't think it had been anyone from Whitby. Or if it had, they'd kept it very much under their hat.

Not that she could talk to Bill about that. He knew jet, the raw material, not the magic of it, and Annice kept the Pact. Everyone did, when speaking of magic to someone who didn't have it. The oaths against it brought them smack up against their worst fears. Now she swallowed. "What did you think of him? Them?" Though mostly him, because the other man, Charlus, had been in the background.

"Don't know as I trust a man who..." Bill wriggled a hand. "Chair, crutches, no explanation. Or what he asked, not being clear."

Annice was caught up with the same frustration, if from a very different angle. On one hand, Griffin had answered the questions put to him readily enough. He'd given her chapter and verse about what he did. Even about the truth charms, which made her very uncomfortable indeed. There was something about him that was almost compelling, and she didn't trust that at all. Lots of people could be compelling, and at least half of them were angry drunks and worse, if someone didn't do what they wanted the way they wanted.

Lots of men had reason to drown their sorrows, and lots

of women too. But taking it out on other people, that was a problem Annice refused to deal with, at least up close. It made the way Griffin drew her attention - exactly the way jet did - make her squirm. Finally, she swallowed. "What did he ask Edgar? Was he looking for jet, or a carver, or what?"

"Both. Aye. Both. More the jet itself, though. He knew a bit about it, mind. More than some," Bill considered. "Wasn't too rude for posh."

Annice snorted. "Posh is supposed to have manners. Whether or not they use them on us."

It made Bill laugh. That was something. "Heard you had some custom, too?" Bill was cautious about this.

"Three women - grandmother, daughter, granddaughter, here for the sea air. The grandmother had an earring gone missing, and I made her a copy." It wasn't quite in the same category as making new pieces, and therefore not the same flavour of unlucky.

"Ah. Wish there were more of that. It'd cause less trouble for you. But they were happy?"

"Mmhmm. And bought one of Da's pieces, too." She hated selling them. But on the other hand, he'd made them to be worn and to be sold. And to feed the people he loved and keep the house warm in the winter. And she'd liked those three women. It hurt less to have one of Da's pieces there than a lot of places. Annice swallowed, wanting to change the subject. "Bill, did Grandad ever talk about having pieces he didn't talk about? This big, polished." She held her hands out, making the curve of the shape.

Bill was silent again, long enough Annice thought he wouldn't answer at all. "He bought some big pieces from me, like that. Don't know what he did with them. Over the years. Not that many to be found. And a few came from the mines, inland, before they got shut down. Back when. Before." Before the crafting peaked and then dropped off, before a flood of Spanish jet came on the market to fill the gaps from the mines being shut down.

"So it wouldn't surprise you that he had some."

"Nah. You found one?" Bill glanced over at her. "I could have a look."

Not that one, he couldn't. She wasn't sure what the magic in it would do, and it certainly looked like magic, even if he couldn't make sense of the actual purpose. She didn't want to risk him like that, or herself. "Nah. But I'm cleaning out cupboards. You know where he might have kept blanks?"

There was another long silence. "Heard he stuck them away, somewhere. Dunno where. House, maybe. Shed, maybe."

"Ta." Annice swallowed. "Good hunting?" she offered. "Ought to get back up the hill and open the shop." She didn't expect it'd do any good, but it wouldn't do any harm. And she could be confused about what to do next up there, with a cup of tea and a bit of warmth, as well as think here. Or if not warm, at least not so much of a wind.

Bill nodded. "You be careful." It was the sort of thing elders said, and just like with Griffin two days ago, she was at a loss at how to interpret this.

She made her way back along the beach, picking her way over stones, and finding three modest pieces of jet for her trouble. They'd been covered by seaweed from the other direction. She left two others for Bill to spot, sizes that she'd have a harder time selling. Then she went up the harbour, and up to the house and shop. Twenty minutes later, she had a mug of tea, the stool she perched on by the counter, and no customers. Nor any sign of them.

Annice cupped her hands around the mug. Bill hadn't told her anything terribly new. If Grandad had one big piece of jet, he might have had more. She could unbury every cupboard and check. She probably ought to, and do a proper inventory of the house, anyway. And she might find some clothes from Nan she could make over or sell. Maybe she'd find something else useful.

No one came in all afternoon, and so she turned the sign around, locked up, and looked longingly up the stairs at the workshop. Her fingers itched to get working on the pieces she'd found today. One had a curve that suggested a selkie, perhaps. But that wouldn't get anything sorted in the cupboards. She found scrap paper to write on, and a stub of pencil, and promised herself that after she'd inventoried two cupboards, she could go up to the workroom.

The two cupboards took much longer than she'd expected, and by the time she was done, she was starving and her back ached. She heated up a little soup, not wanting to cook more, but then at least she got an hour in the workroom, sketching and then beginning to prepare one of the other pieces for something decorative, the arc of a leaf.

CHAPTER II
MARCH 16TH

T alking to the jet workers hadn't got Griffin very far. And he'd meant it when he said Lord and Lady Hutton weren't particularly in favour of him. Just before the War, he'd been the one to point out some factors in an inheritance case for Lady Hutton that hadn't gone the way she wanted. Fortunately, Charlus knew the family, and had got hold of a contact or two within the magical community in Whitby for a conversation.

It meant they were ensconced in an exceedingly ornate parlour that hadn't been redone since perhaps 1870. Griffin had set the crutches to one side, but it was the sort of place that didn't like to admit furniture had legs, never mind people. Everything was covered by pleats of patterned fabric and doilies in an excess of fabric decoration. Mistress Hemworthy certainly extended the theme. She was wearing unfashionably long skirts by modern standards, her ankles tucked back under the chair she was settled in.

"I don't know what you young men think you'll manage, coming here. Whitby is beautiful, but she is insular. Particular about who is welcome, and who isn't."

Mistress Hemworthy sipped at her tea. "I married in, but it took me, oh, two decades to have any acceptance at all. And that was with my dear Simon smoothing my way, every step. And my own poor skills, of course."

"Mistress Hemworthy, word of your skills has spread far and wide." Griffin wasn't exactly lying, but he was laying it on thicker than he usually did. She did a particular kind of porcelain painting. It was a genteel lady's art of the previous century. Hers had a touch of magic to bring a little protection to the cup and well-being to the drinker. Like the cups they were using now, and Griffin felt he could use as much of the latter as was on offer. "But we would be most grateful - myself, my apprentice, and my colleagues back in Trellech - for any assistance you might provide on how best to approach things."

"Grateful, is it?" Mistress Hemworthy let that hang there for a moment.

It wasn't a bribe. First, this woman would not be so crude, and second, it wasn't actually the sort of thing bribes worked on. Griffin took a moment to consider his options. "You mentioned you make it down to Trellech every so often. The Courts would be glad to include you as a guest to one of the Temple of Healing garden parties in the summer. Or I believe there's an opening for an exhibit at the museum, Chinese porcelain and such, coming in..." He let his voice trail off.

Charlus cleared his throat. "August, sir. Magistra Hollings mentioned she thought it should be a spectacular show. She has quite an interest herself. A number of pieces from private collections, and so on."

This sort of thing was the usual way to spread goodwill. Griffin would never touch it for something dealing with a specific case, but when it came to the other business of the

Courts, how to keep them running smoothly, he knew the parameters of what he could offer on his own. Neither of those would be difficult to arrange. The Courts got extra tickets for just such a reason.

Mistress Hemworthy sniffed, then nodded. "The museum. If you could arrange tickets, that would be a delight."

Charlus nodded. "I'll check into the arrangements and confirm the dates, mistress. There may be a possibility for a private tour." Very polite, almost demure. Charlus carried that off well.

"As to your question," Mistress Hemworthy turned her attention fully to Griffin. "No one knows what to make of you, of course. You are not from here. You are asking complicated questions. And your, your..." She gestured at the crutches. "We're not used to that sort of thing. A few people in town use a wheelchair, a few use crutches, but not both."

Griffin caught Charlus stiffening a bit beside him, but he kept his tone light. "It's always an awkward thing to handle. People will make assumptions, and of course if someone sees me across the street or some such, they can't even ask the polite questions." He wouldn't say - not here and now - how often the questions were something far from politeness. She wasn't a stupid woman, she could figure it out. "I was injured in the War. The way the Temple of Healing put it, when they were sorting out what happened, was that sometimes my head and my feet don't talk to each other very well. Like seeing the bottom of a muddy pond, one of my Healers said. You know it's there, you can feel it, but you might mistake a rock for a turtle."

"Well, my." Mistress Hemworthy considered him, looking him up and down like some exhibit. "Well, it's really quite inspiring, working like you do, with such limitations. Not like so many others we see, hurt during the War, poor things." The mix of fawning toward him and pity toward others wasn't something Griffin heard often these days, not directly. But it always grated. Other people disabled by the War hadn't had his resources and existing standing, for one thing. And for another, he was here to keep the Courts working as they ought, not to be anyone's inspiration. Same as he had been before the War.

Beside him, Griffin could tell Charlus had frozen, unsure how to act. Griffin shrugged slightly. "I care a great deal about the work of the Courts. But my work relies on my mind, not my feet, fortunately. I'll never be a grand dancer, but I wasn't much of one before the War, so it's no great loss."

It provoked Mistress Hemworthy into a small snort. That was a very human reaction. Griffin went on. "Sometimes I trip - and a fall can be quite painful." Worse, he'd broken his wrist once, and that had him out of commission entirely for a week, even with quick access to healing magic. "More my balance than the strength of my legs." Though the nastier falls were usually the latter, he wasn't going to get into that. "But a lot of places aren't set up well for a chair, so while I prefer it when I can, sometimes the crutches are easiest." Like here, where there had been a set of stairs up to the front door.

"I suppose that you have had practice making it sound sensible." Mistress Hemworthy sounded dubious. "If people ask, what should I say?"

Griffin had a great deal of practice being sensible about it, but again, he was not going to have that argument today. It wouldn't do any good. "That it's a War injury, that it's about my balance rather than whether my legs work. That's usually what I say in brief. Most of us, I think, know some older relative who needs a cane for balance. Mine's just a bit more so."

There was another little sniff, but she let it drop, changing topics a bit abruptly. "The other part, of course, is you're from Trellech. And the people here - the fishing folk, the crafters, the people who make up much of the town - they don't know what to do about that. We pay our fees and taxes, of course, to Trellech. Some of our folk go to one of the Five Schools, though far more often Forvie than any of the others, for the fishing. A few went to Alethorpe. Our former apothecary, of course, and the current one. Frederick Matthewman, that was, poor man, but of course he wasn't born here, just married in. John Whiting, he was born here, a respectable family." That first name caught Griffin's attention immediately, but he just nodded.

"That's normal, of course, even expected. Even with the portals - and there's some history, isn't there, that there are two within a few miles, and a road between them?" Griffin asked.

It got a louder sound, not quite a chuckle, but definitely heading that direction. "Oh, the answer's easy. Smugglers. I don't recall which portal came first, but there are the two, and easy enough to pass goods from the one to the other, depending which direction is needed."

"Ah." That put an interesting complexion on it. "I'd thought most of that was earlier in time? Not contemporary."

"I'm certainly not the sort of person who would know," Mistress Hemworthy said. Though she was certainly the sort of person who would buy a thing that had been smuggled. Especially if it put a bit of luxury on her table or in her wardrobe. That wasn't Griffin's to investigate, and so long as no one rubbed his nose in it, he wouldn't.

Griffin let the silence linger for a hair longer, just to see if it made her uncomfortable. She moved a little, the sort of tell that Griffin had learned to notice very early, helping behind the counter in the department store. Once he was sure of it, he cleared his throat. "Who would you recommend talking with, about finding someone who might be a help with matters in Trellech? We seem to have exhausted the jet carvers, but it may be there's a crafter or someone who does pieces here and there, who might consult?"

That got him an extended discussion of the notable magical families in town. From what Mistress Hemworthy said, they tended to be larger clans. There would be multiple generations in the same line of work: grandparents, children, grandchildren, so it was more getting a sense for the family lines. There were a couple who might be promising, if he could get into a conversation with them in the first place.

After two cups of tea, they made their proper farewells. Fortunately, they weren't too far up on the west side of the river and harbour. Getting back to their rented cottage did not take as long as Griffin was afraid of, though certainly longer than he'd wanted. There had been a number of stares in the process and comments that picked up after they went past.

Once they were back in the cottage, Charlus said, too-brightly, "I'll put the kettle on, then?"

Griffin didn't argue, settling into the half the sofa he'd claimed as his preferred spot and putting his feet up. The matter of the tea kept Charlus busy for several minutes, and he was busy writing in his journal while waiting for the kettle. When he brought the mugs over, Griffin looked up.

"The conversation bothered you." It wasn't a question, it wasn't supposed to be a question.

Charlus paused for a moment. "Yes. Does it bother you? I can't tell." Then he ran his free hand through his hair and sat down with a bit of an ungraceful thump. "And you don't talk about it, usually. You didn't to me until we were coming here."

"Like I said, it's mostly boring. To me, anyway. And I hope to other people, when they get over their own feelings about someone using either chair or crutches. It's a tool, like the journals or a potion from the apothecary or dozens of other things." Griffin considered the next part. "I know people talk. It's not talk about the chair that bothers me, actually. It's the other assumptions. That I must be slightly dim, or significantly dim. That I can't handle my own needs, or my own shopping, or my own home. I have a housekeeper. But every single other senior member of the Court staff has at least a housekeeper at home. Half of us have rather more than that in the way of household staff, even since the War." Griffin shrugged.

"And, sir? That's not the only part." The trouble with having intelligent and observant apprentices was that they noticed things.

Griffin grimaced. "It's that people can't see around their own snap judgements. That offends me on a professional level, more than a personal one. If we're aiming at something like the truth, how can we do that if people are so hidebound they can't see other ways of being in the world?"

"Related to, um, the larger questions with the Courts?" Charlus was feeling his way with this more. "Like you spoke about."

"Just so. Lamont is a far-seeing man. He's not remotely stupid. I'm quite aware that this particular task is very much a demonstration of my real skills. The methods I'd hoped to use aren't working. We're going to need to get creative. In ways that permit our success, of course, but we need to set aside our own assumptions."

"Like about who we're asking?" Charlus asked. "What have you thought so far, sir?"

"If it were just the jet working, Whitby obviously has people, but there are answers to that. We might even - with a sufficient fee - get Carey or Hudson to take on the commission. Or at least long enough to look over the work and make up a proposal and tell us what set of skills were needed. A skilled materia worker, a gem cutter used to other materials, they might well be able to do the actual fitting. I know several of those, but the initial consultations with them said they deferred to people who knew jet."

"Only that's also complicated, I suppose. And leaning on, um. National feeling, that's not the right word, will not work." Charlus was putting it together promptly, that was excellent.

"As Mistress Hemworthy said, Trellech is a long way away, both physically and emotionally. They don't feel any real sense of loyalty there, necessarily. That won't move them. And the, oh, the symbolic benefit of truth and the Courts probably won't. They have other priorities."

Charlus leaned forward now. "And that doesn't bother you?"

"It is what it is. Seeing the truth of that matters. We're not going to change people - hundreds of people we don't know, actually thousands - by wishing them different. And honestly, a lot of their priorities are sensible. They care about a roof over their head, food on the table, a bit of heat in the winter, that the fishing boats come home safe. I can't argue with that, and I'm not going to."

Griffin looked up, and said, after a moment, "When I was little, my father's shop was much smaller. Small enough he'd know who was having a hard week or month or year. He'd give them a break. A discount, or let them know when something was about to go on sale the next day. It taught me a lot about what people focus on, to get by, even though we were comfortable then." More so later, but Charlus knew that part himself.

There was a long silence, then Charlus nodded. "Thank you, sir. That's given me a lot to think about. Shall I go out and pick up something for supper and bring it back?"

"Please. Whatever looks best, and if they have some bread for the morning, that'd be lovely." Griffin stretched, considered getting up, then reconsidered it. "And if I fall asleep where I'm sitting, wake me up when you get back, please."

"Sir." Charlus grinned and then got up. "Back in a few." Griffin watched him go, glad of the chance to be alone with his thoughts for a little and sort things out more about their next steps.

CHAPTER 12
MARCH 18TH

Annice hadn't meant to run into Griffin and his assistant over lunch. She hadn't meant to be in the pub for lunch at all, actually. But she'd discovered the sort of mould through her last bit of bread that wasn't at all good to eat or easy to cut around. Spending a bit of coin wasn't impossible, and she knew what the cheapest filling things on the White Horse & Griffin's menu were, always. Fish, at the moment.

She'd wondered if she could get in and out without them noticing, but in the end, something pulled her over to their table. Likely her desire to have a bit more coin in her pocket. Another consultation, that would be something. She told herself that was most of it.

"Pardon." She cleared her throat. "Sirs. I had a thought about the question you'd asked about Grandad's work. Perhaps you might come round when it's convenient?"

"This afternoon?" Griffin gestured at his half-eaten meal. "After you've had time for your own luncheon?"

She hadn't meant that early at all, but there was no help for it. She'd have to follow through with talking to them now. She'd been the one to make the offer. Better to do it sooner than later, at least that way it wouldn't be hanging over her. "An hour. Would that be all right?"

"An hour. Excellent." Griffin smiled at her. "Until then." He didn't add the 'Mistress' on the end, not out among folks without magic, but she heard what he didn't say. All the bits of respect and consideration. And she thought he seemed pleased about it, more than just whatever progress it meant on his project. That didn't seem right, but she couldn't get the idea out of her head. It wasn't anything he'd done. It was more what he hadn't done.

He had been nothing like that man looking for some poor nursemaid to marry his cousin. It hadn't been like the other handful of not quite offers she'd got. She wasn't any sort of beauty. Her hands were rough and scarred in places from not just the jet carving and a knife or stylus slipping, but the ordinary cleaning when magic wasn't on offer.

She went and picked up her order, taking it back to the shop and the backroom, perching at the little table by the stairs to eat. She went back and forth, throughout the meal, about whether to tell him - them - about that big odd stone, with the carvings. They'd had a proper education at Schola, they must have, they'd know more about that sort of thing. But what if the stone was something bad or wrong, the sort of thing people like her weren't meant to have? They were also tied right into the Courts, surely they had to report wrong things.

Maybe she'd have to decide in the moment. The last fifteen minutes before she expected them, she spent tidying up the shop. She set up space for Griffin's chair. Then she pulled out more comfortable chairs from the kitchen for herself and Charlus. She added a table to put things on, and she selected a handful of pieces that showed the skills she might want to talk about.

They were indeed precisely on time. That was taking some getting used to. She was used to people turning up on a schedule that made sense with the sun or the tides. Or how many people they'd stopped to chat with on their way through town. That sort of precision to a clock was unnatural. They immediately went round to the back, without needing to be told, and she let them in. "Good afternoon. Come through? Would you like tea? I can put the kettle on."

"Please, if you think the conversation will be a little. And do put Charlus to work carrying things, if you like. He won't mind." Griffin was smiling, looking comfortable even though it must be an odd situation for him too, an unfamiliar one.

Charlus grinned, looking much younger suddenly. "I don't mind, and I almost never drop anything." That had the sound of being a joke of some kind.

"If you'd like. Let me put the kettle on and set out the tray, and show you where that is." There was a little fussing with that, but Charlus stood well back and didn't get in her way. She got the kettle on and set out the tray. It wasn't as if there was a lot of choice in teas on offer.

By the time they came back to the main room of the shop, Griffin had a notebook out. It was balanced on a little sliding table that somehow fitted onto the chair itself, at a bit of an angle. He had a pen out and resting on the open page. "Quite handy for notes," he said, as if she hadn't been staring at it rudely.

Annice coughed, then sat down, perching on the chair. "I looked through some of Grandad's notes. Can you tell me a little more about, um? What's been done with the space since 1900?"

Griffin pulled over a small notebook, but Annice rather thought he didn't actually need whatever notes there were. "The last time the stone was reset was late 1902 - the work was done in October and November, as Saturn went direct again. I was in my apprenticeship, but not very involved with that specific process. I was still focused on getting chartered as a solicitor."

He tapped his fingers on the notebook, as if checking an aspect. "Historically, we aim for refurbishment roughly every seven and a half years, but we adjust based on whether we can get a transit or alignment that's reasonable. That's a magical process, primarily, though sometimes individual stones are replaced. Only, they had to do a short-term fix in 1919. I wasn't back in the Courts yet, but I have notes from it. Then again in 1921, and in 1924, but the charms feel like they're fading fast. And the next time we renew the stones would normally be 1929."

Annice frowned at that. "And you don't think you can wait that long."

"No." Griffin's voice was sharp for a moment, then he swallowed. "I do beg your pardon. I have had to argue that point with a number of colleagues. We might patch something together, but I'm concerned about the damage to the alternate room, and at the impact of degrading charmwork in the Courts as a whole. You might think of them, perhaps, as beads in a necklace. They are all distinct, but part of a larger whole, and if any of them is cracked or shattering, the others might also be affected. Certainly, the piece might become unwearable without mending." Then he looked up, suddenly earnest. "That's likely a bad analogy. I don't know your line of work nearly well enough."

That he'd said anything of the kind startled her, rather a lot. She swallowed again, then was saved momentarily by the kettle singing. Charlus got up without more than a murmured comment and went off to put the tray together. It left Annice to look down at her hands until he'd set things out. He poured, too, which felt very odd, but she certainly didn't feel trustworthy with hot liquids right now. Charlus left the cup where she could reach it.

It meant Annice had to say something. "So the last time the stone was reset, replaced, that was 1902. That wasn't Grandad. He talks about doing it in 1875. And I can tell, besides the date, he talks about being away from Yorkshire during the mine disaster, he knew people who knew people there." When both men looked blank, she added, "The Swaith Maine Colliery explosion. December 6th, 1875. A hundred and forty-three men and boys died." Whitby people weren't miners, mostly, but plenty of them had family who were from other parts of Yorkshire.

"I'm so sorry." Griffin seemed like he almost meant it, and that didn't make sense either. He paused, taking a sip from the teacup by his free hand, then cleared his throat. "So someone else did it in 1902. Do you think your grandfather would have known, if it were someone in Whitby?"

"Probably. Do you have any notes about it?" Annice wasn't sure what records they kept.

"The name's blurred on the copies we could find, which is not how things ought to be done. I have one of the clerks looking back in the records - payments, that sort of thing, that might have more information. Can you explain the process a bit more? Most of our notes just say the jet is set in places in the floor and the walls - I can show you those sketches - but not the details."

"Grandad talks about the stones needing to be prepared a certain way. There's some amount of markings, carving, to help with alignment, but then, yes, set into something.

In an ideal world, I suppose you'd have an entire line of it, making a channel all around the room, whatever the proper shape is? But you can do it with single pieces, and link them together. I know some of that. It goes into certain kinds of jewellery, pieces that have an affinity."

"Huh." Griffin considered that. "So you'd need, do I have this right, not just pieces that could be the right size and shape, but that also, I don't know, got along with each other?"

"You don't think that's nonsense?" It burst out of her before she could think better of it, or of her tone.

He shrugged. "I've certainly come across odder things. Modes of talking about it. And it makes sense, honestly, with some of what I know. But I'm not a Materia specialist, or a Sympathetic magic specialist, and this is a bit of both, isn't it? The materials and how they relate. And how they relate to that space and location and all that. So add in a Locational magic specialist to the pot."

It should have sounded flippant, somehow, but it didn't. It sounded like he meant it. "Can I ask, um, what you do? Not your title." Which still didn't make sense, and which certainly hadn't been explained.

Something about the question made him smile a little, leaning back in his chair. "I'm a solicitor, as I said, which means I'm qualified to work with clients in all sorts of legal ways, bar representing them in court. Which I wouldn't do anyway, because maintaining the court is my job. My training is in Incantation, primarily. That's fairly common for people in our line of work. Schola, then a long apprenticeship, ours runs six or seven years on average. We train as a solicitor first, then in the judicial magics. Charlus has been doing the second part for going on a year now." Charlus nodded once.

"Oh." Annice looked down for a long moment. "That's nothing like what I know."

Griffin was looking at her, his head slightly tilted. It made her a little uncomfortable, like he was seeing things in her she wasn't sure about. But he was also paying attention in a way no one had since Grandad died, even her cousins and aunt and uncles. Then, he said as if it were the most normal thing in the world. "Would this be an easier conversation if Charlus weren't here? Two on one seems unfair."

Annice had been brought up with old-fashioned manners and a certain dubiousness about unrelated men and women being alone in the same room. But this was, in fact, a new world, the tail end of a vastly different decade. And while she didn't understand Griffin, she was almost certain she had nothing to fear from him, not exactly. Almost. Finally, slowly, she nodded.

"Charlus, would you mind heading back to the cottage, then? I'll write in the journal if I need a hand getting back, but I should be able to manage if Annice will hold the gate for me."

Charlus was immediately standing up, unbothered by the request. "Sir, of course. Later. Thank you for your hospitality and information, Mistress." Having him be so polite almost made everything worse. He set his teacup back on the tray for tidiness, and then he was out the door, closing it behind him and leaving her alone with Griffin.

CHAPTER 13
MARCH 18TH

Of course, what Griffin hadn't explained about his training was that a great deal of it had to do with observing people. It was at the heart of handling the human aspects of the Courts and their work, for one thing. For all he found Annice difficult to read, he could tell that she was feeling unsure how to explain things to both of them, how to measure it out. Since there was, in fact, a simple solution to that particular problem, he would take it. And likely come back to the cottage to find all their working notes fully indexed, summarised, and in order, which wouldn't hurt anything.

Now Griffin leaned back and said, "Before I ask more questions about the jet, can I ask a bit about your background, your family - in terms of your training? It might help me explain better." One of things that had been puzzling him was that. She spoke well, with less of the local dialect than a lot of people around. Not that he was foolish enough to object. People spoke how they spoke. He was the visitor, he certainly didn't get to object.

"Mam was Grandad's daughter. Grew up in this house. I

have what was her bedroom." Annice gestured upstairs with her chin, then flushed, as if talking about anything that personal was exposing something tender. Which, well, talking about her bedroom and her family both probably were. "Mam trained up as a schoolteacher, before I was born. Learned to speak proper. There were new laws about education, about primary education being required for everyone. None of us went to the Five Schools, Grandad had apprenticed. But Mam had no interest in the carving, not in the making it - she hated the way it made her hands feel, the dust?"

Griffin nodded, hopefully in an encouraging way. "And your father?"

"He went to Alethorpe. Came up here as an apothecary, fell in love with the carving. Grandad took a liking to him. They'd been talking in the pub, that's the story they told, and Grandad brought him home, gave him a place to sleep, and he just - stayed. And he and Mam were grand together." She'd wished for that sort of romantic story herself, but no one was going to bring a man home from the pub for her, now, were they?

"I'm, um." Griffin had a sense of the gaping hole in this household. "I'm sorry for their losses. May I ask when?"

Annice pulled back, her eyes wide and startled. Griffin held up a hand. "Pardon. Just. It's obvious you love them, but in a way where you haven't been able to tell them directly for a bit. One of the things I learned in my training."

"Odd sort of training." She said it as a murmur, but loud enough he could hear it. "Da got called up, the end of the War. And he didn't come home. Mam - six months after we got the notice. She just wasted away. If he'd made it another couple of months, it'd have all been different. And then it was Grandad and Nan and I, until a year ago, and just me and Grandad until last November."

"I am sorry." Griffin swallowed. He still had both parents, he had a sister and nieces and a nephew. If he wanted a bustling, noisy, friendly home, he could go visit, whenever he liked. And Annice had lost all of that, drawn out over time. "And especially about your father. That was the worst of it, for me, knowing the people who didn't come home, and for all sorts of stupid, badly chosen reasons they didn't have any say in."

He saw the flicker in her face, something complicated, and again something he didn't know how to interpret. Normally, he kept that particular unpopular opinion to himself, unless he was around other veterans. And mostly the ones who'd been hurt down to the bone, in their own ways. Seth and Golshan, a few of the others he'd met through their mutual support groups. But Annice deserved to know it was a tragedy and a shame, and that if people had managed the War better, her father might not be dead. Or her mother.

Annice twisted away, to pour herself more tea, one of the reliable markers of someone who needed a little space. She was brave enough, though, to ask a question, and he wasn't entirely surprised by what it was. "You, um. Served?" Then she flushed again.

"I did. It's how I was hurt." He didn't want to go into it, not right now. He was sure something would show that would unsettle her more. "Not as visible as some men, except the chair is, of course." He took a breath, considering his words. "I spend a fair bit of my free time, such as it is, with men who were hurt worse. I was lucky, I could come home, I can do a job I love and am good at. Far too many didn't get that."

She cupped her hands around her teacup, frozen in place for a moment, then she just nodded. Then it was as if something had unlocked for her but it came out of her slowly. Griffin held himself quiet, not wanting to startle her out of the moment. "I told you it's unlucky for women to carve jet. But Grandad taught me. Is there really no one else who can even look at it?"

"Not that I know about," Griffin said. "That's the trick of it. And I'm very confused about why we don't have better records, or more people who can work it. A single point of failure is absolutely no good for a supply chain." The phrasing of it made her chin come up. Griffin half-smiled. "My dad started as a shop-keeper. It teaches you a lot about where things come from, and how far in advance you need to plan to have them available."

"Oh." Annice looked up again, meeting his eyes briefly. "You, um. Shop-keeper? And you didn't go to Dunwich if you went somewhere?"

"I am, as I said when we first met, very good at what I do. And by the time I was actually born, Dad had a small department store, then a bigger one. Now he's sold it off and retired. And some of my mother's people had gone to Schola. They could help me prepare for the exams. I enjoy reading, so it was mostly pointing me at the right things to read and letting me alone to do it."

Annice blinked again. "Not like that round here." She said, finally. "Though Mam liked a book, and Grandad read the papers all through, every day of his life he could."

Griffin nodded. "Books are grand. Not the same thing as doing something, but - oh, well. Here's an example. I read books, before we came up here, about the history of jet, as a magical stone. Everything from them being in grave goods, to being used for talismanic purposes.

Apotropaic, if you want the formal term for a lot of it, keeping evil away."

"There's a word for that? A whole word?"

Griffin let himself smile a little. "There is. A lot of what I do is about the words, but the things exist. Evil, bad luck, whatever we want to call it, it's out there in the world. I think people from the beginning of time, from the first people, wanted the same things we want. A bit of good luck, for the evil luck to go somewhere else, protection from the cruelties of the world. And also hope things might be a bit better." He let himself gesture. "We're just coming to the Equinox now, there's more sun. That's a bit more hope, in some ways of thinking."

She froze again, and Griffin cursed himself for that lack of control. "Pardon. I do get going."

There was a tiny gesture, more or less a shrug. "Do you know anything about talismans, then? I mean, pieces for that sort of whatever?"

"Some. I'm not an expert in them, but they come up in the Courts fairly often. I know the basics." He thought about asking if she had some specific reason, but better to keep it more firmly in a professional mode.

"Oh. I came across..." Her voice cut off suddenly, then she cleared her throat. "I honestly don't know if I can help. I don't know any of the, I don't know. Complicated magical bits."

"Do you use magic at all for the carving you do?" Griffin kept his voice even.

Annice looked at him, without blinking, for a long moment. "The one you bought, the rose. That's one of mine. Magic makes it easier to do the delicate bits. Shape the petals so they won't shatter. Jet's fragile, oddly fragile. And some things like lines for the carving, that won't stay once you release the charm, Grandad taught me those. Some things to make cleaning up and managing the workshop better."

"You made that?" Griffin let himself smile warmly. He hadn't been at all sure. He wasn't trained in art, but he'd thought there was something particular about that, the way she'd handled the piece. "My mother will like it all the more for that, then. She enjoys knowing the history of a thing, where it came from, who made it. And it's lovely. A proper rose, both delicate and persistent."

Annice ducked her chin and looked away. "If you say so."

Griffin repressed his desire to talk over it, to fill the silence. Instead, he took a couple of steadying breaths. "Look, perhaps I might let you get back to your afternoon now. Would you think about something, though? We'd be glad to bring someone to consult in Trellech, even if that's looking at the stones, figuring out what our next steps might include. We'd pay for your time, of course, and also your expenses. The Ministry preferred inn isn't luxurious, but it's clean and comfortable. With the portals here, you might only need to be gone overnight."

That was too much. He could see it immediately. He went on. "Now I'll get out of your hair. If you could let me out and get the gate. Or I can ask Charlus to come back."

"No. That." She stood, her hand twisting in the fold of her apron for a moment. "Some time to think, thank you. I'll send a note. If you'll be - um." Suddenly she shifted, peering at him. "You're not going back?"

"Not just yet. I might still learn something useful. And I brought reference material with me. I can read that as easily here as at home. Pop into a couple of the other jet shops, ask questions in general. I've only been responsible for the inheritance courts for about five years. And senior for only a year. Before that, it was other things, so while I know the more recent material, I haven't read through all the archives yet." Now he was blithering on. That wasn't likely to help. But it seemed to have settled her, to know he would not disappear through the portal in a puff of magic.

"Oh. A day or two, then. Probably." Annice took a couple of steps, and then went on more deliberately ahead of him to get the door. Griffin took a moment to put the desk back where it folded away, along one side of the chair, and followed her out. He remembered at the last minute - when she was getting the gate - that there was one other detail.

"Are you sure you don't need to wait for Charlus?" Annice asked it a bit nervously.

"Oh, I can manage. Here, though, I can't forget this." If he had, he would have had to push himself back up the hill and call plaintively from outside her door to pay her. That didn't appeal at all for about six reasons, especially the part that had him imitating a lost kitten. "Your hand?" He pulled out the coins from his inner jacket pocket, dropping them neatly in her palm. "Thank you for your time."

Then he pushed himself along, out to the street. When he glanced back, she was standing at the gate. Her thumb was running over them in the practised gesture of someone who relied on coin in hand for their living, and could count them by touch and weight as easy as sight. Then Griffin had to keep moving or it would be even more awkward. He was moving down the hill, focusing on making sure he didn't end up going too fast for comfort.

CHAPTER 14
LATER THAT AFTERNOON

Annice hadn't been able to settle down after she let Griffin out. Her mind wouldn't settle, her hands wouldn't settle. In the end, she went back upstairs, working her way through all the cupboards she could think of that might have something in them that might matter.

When she was done, she had four boxes. The one she knew about, with the talismanic stone in it, two other empty boxes of the same size, and a box with a pile of papers and notes in it. She brought those down to the kitchen. There was more table space than the workshop. Annice was staring at them when she heard a knock on the door frame. "You at home?"

"Ruth." Annice pushed back from the table, half standing. "Come in?"

Ruth waved her into her chair. "I'll put the kettle on. Mam sent me round to ask if you're coming to Sunday supper. Or, I guess. Warn you if you were planning not."

Annice laughed, a little hollow. "Sure. Anything I can bring?"

"Nah. She's a bit worried, y'ken?" Ruth shrugged, as if unsure how to put any of what anyone felt into a suitable dish.

Annice figured that meant there was going to be Yorkshire pudding to go with whatever meat, so offering to bring bread wouldn't be much use, and bread was what Annice usually brought. She wasn't usually bad at making bread, though the rest of her cooking was good plain fare. But Aunt Sarah wouldn't want one more person in her kitchen getting in the way. Hauling anything else down and across the bridge wasn't great, even with magic to keep it warm. "Sure."

"What's all this, then?" Ruth turned to get the kettle going, then gestured at the papers as she pulled the other chair out.

"There was a man here." Annice tried to remember what she'd said. "Um. A client. Sort of. He bought one of my pieces." And she still didn't entirely know what she felt about that. She'd made it for buying, that was the point of it, but he was going to give it to his mam, and. She pulled her thoughts back. "Let me try again."

"Best, yeah. That didn't make no sense." Ruth leaned back a little, watching her.

"There's a man. He works in Trellech for the courts. He's been asking jet carvers for help, something in the courtroom? I don't understand all of it, though I could maybe do some of what he's needing. Maybe." Annice took a breath, and then it came spilling out. "He said he'd pay for me to go down to Trellech and have a look. My time, a room, food, all that, everything."

"And you're thinking of saying yes? That's the way bad things go in novels. Serials. You know that. Girl goes off, girl disappears, someone else has a mystery t'solve." Ruth had a point, but it wasn't like that. At least Annice was pretty sure it wasn't like that. She didn't know how to explain why. She couldn't explain it to herself, after all.

"Told him I had to think about it, I mean. But it'd be a fair bit of coin. And I could use that. And I don't know. He's not finding much help anywhere else."

Ruth shrugged. "Should fix their own things, shouldn't they? What does Trellech do for us? Portal Keeper, sure, they're decent folks. Don't mind paying the portal fee, even. Healers, there's a point in Healers, when we see one. Trellech? Nah."

Annice didn't have an argument for that. Though she supposed someone had to keep track of where people were, so there were portals and Healers. And there were trials for things, even if she didn't know most of it. Maybe she should pick up the subscription to the Trellech Moon again, even if the morning edition didn't get to Whitby addresses until the evening post. She shrugged. "Anyway." She swallowed. "He makes me feel odd. Not bad. Just. Odd."

Ruth peered at her, long enough to make Annice squirm. The kettle finally sang, and Ruth got up to fiddle with the teapot and leaves and pouring the water. When she brought the pot and mugs back to the table she asked, "What's the man like then?"

"He, um." Annice paused. "He's in a wheelchair. There's someone with him, an apprentice. The apprentice didn't say much, but he helped with the tea earlier? Not stuck up, I thought he would be. He sounds posh."

"And the other one?" Ruth leaned back. "Your client?"

"His name's Griffin Pelson. He's, um. He knows a lot of things I didn't even know were things to know? But he's not as posh, I think. Not to start. His da was a shop-keeper, then made good." Annice looked down at the table, in between where her hands were resting. "He was in the War. He came back hurt. I don't know how, but he can walk a little? That doesn't make sense. And I don't know how I feel about him. Not scared, it's not like that, but it's not comfortable, either?" She then looked up, hoping to find words, and didn't.

Ruth tilted her head, opened her mouth, then closed it. "You let me know if you need Sam to come be about. In case. Or one of the others." Whatever else was scant in their lives, there were a number of burly weatherbeaten men who could loom in the background. "You're going to talk to him again, then."

Annice looked down at the table once more. "Aye. Because maybe I can help." She then shifted, brushing one of the boxes. "I told you about what I found, that stone. There's two more empty boxes, the same size and shape, and some pencil markings I don't understand. And this box of papers. Maybe Griffin could explain a little of what they mean. The papers."

Ruth pursed her lips. "You think there're more stones?"

"Maybe. Dunno. Or what the one I have does. Maybe it does something we don't need. Don't want."

Ruth nodded. "You could go round and ask Carrey and Hudson. Or whoever."

"Don't want to. I will." Annice shrugged. "Give me a little to work up to it."

Ruth laughed, and then changed the subject, which was at least something. The boys were being boys. When they'd caught up, Annice promised to be round for Sunday supper in a day and a half.

Which meant Saturday was for going round to the Careys' shop. She waited until there was a lull, making awkward small talk with Bess Carey. Bess and Rob were both Whitby through and through, and Da hadn't been, and, well. It meant it was all awkward. Finally, the shop was quiet, and Annice cleared her throat. "Pardon, Rob. But I found something in a cupboard, and I'm not sure about it. I made a sketch."

She pushed it over the counter toward Rob, who peered at it. "Some sort of talisman. Not my sort, don't know what it does. Do you have it?"

Annice didn't want to admit to it. "Know where it might be. I wondered if you knew who'd made it. Or if there might be others. There were some sketches, some empty boxes."

Rob stared at her, and well, it was a good example of things that made her uncomfortable in ways she didn't want at all. "Nah." He pushed the notes back to her. "You given any more thought to your shop? Bess has a nephew, looking for work. You could meet him. Maybe make a match of it. You could do the carving, he'd give you cover for it."

She could do the carving and the cooking and the cleaning and run the shop. She was pretty sure the nephew would sit around on his backside and never do anything. "Thank you, no. People keep trying to marry me off." That was the problem with having grown up on her parents and their romance. Nothing else had that shine to it. It was all coal, no jet. "Ta for your time." Before they could say anything else, she tucked the papers away and went out the door to the Hudsons.

That, at least, was a more comfortable conversation. People gossiped - a lot - about Maud. On the magical side, people gossipped about love potions. On the non-magical, about her getting above herself. But Cliff seemed more than happy. Maud had been good to Grandad and Nan, coming round to check if the three of them needed anything. Or when she got extra eggs from a sister with a farm. Not the sort of person to lean on for more personal things, but more friendly than not.

Annice went through the same explanation as soon as she got a moment. Cliff peered at it for longer. "You were down at the Careys?"

"Seniority," Annice agreed. She didn't know what had caused the problem between the Hudsons and the Careys. She was pretty sure it was before she was born, or at least before she'd have noticed anything. Annice had no idea how to ask now. But one thing she liked about Cliff was that he understood how other people dealt with it.

"Guessing they didn't tell you anything useful." Cliff glanced at her, and she shook her head. "Right. I think you're right, there's more than one. Now, I heard your Da talk about it, but theory, not the thing itself, you ken?"

Annice nodded again. "I didn't ever hear of it. My Aunt Sarah, she remembered it coming up, but then my uncles drowned. No one talked about it again."

"Ah, that makes some sense. Protection's a funny thing. Sometimes it's a wall, and sometimes it is a net, see? Jet can do both. Now, I don't know all of it - you'd need someone went to Schola for that, specialised in it." Which Annice had, if she could take the risk of talking to him about it. Even if Griffin didn't know, he probably knew who else to talk to. Not that whoever it was would talk to her. So she could just forget the whole idea now.

"But you don't have any idea where the other piece - pieces? - would be?" Annice asked.

"You have one of them?" This time Annice did nod, rather than ducking the question. "They might be different locations, to make a shape, between them? Three would give you a triangle. One where you are, one, I don't know, down this end of the beach. One down the bay, I don't know. Safety while looking for the jet, maybe." There were plenty of things that could go wrong on the beach, and all three of them knew it. Anyone could slip, there could be a sudden wave. Maybe coming upon a smuggler at the wrong time, or someone with a grudge taking a chance at ending it. "Where'd your Grandad spend time, north or south?"

"Robin Hood's Bay. He had a hut there, fishing and all. Old fishing boat, too, though he didn't take it out much by the time I was old enough to help."

"Maybe down there, then. You might look at a map, think about if he knew anyone might have held one for him. Friend or somewhat. Just a thought. You let us know if you could use a hand looking." Annice hesitated, then nodded. Then Cliff said, "That man from Trellech talk to you, then?"

"He did. Offered to have me come look at the courtroom, at least, see if I could figure anything out. But I don't know that kind of work. And I don't know if it's, I mean." She glanced at Maud, who at least might understand the basic problem.

Cliff snorted. "I asked round about him, some of my clients. He's got a good reputation. Sharp, but not unkind, yeah? Few people ended up on the wrong side of decisions he was part of. They didn't like that. But they admitted it was fair. Maybe a little too fair, y'know?"

That was an interesting way to put it. "And you wouldn't go?" Annice asked. "You know a lot more about that sort of thing."

"Booked up, like I told him. And I don't know as much more than you do as you think. You've got a good feel for the jet. Tell you what, though. If you go, bring your notes back. I'm glad to talk them through with you if I'm not working elsewhere. If there is something I could do, maybe

I could make the time for the doing. Just not for the mucking around before and after and all that."

Annice knew he made good money - even better than what was on offer - with some of his clients. That made sense, probably. She nodded, slowly. "No promises. I don't know what I'm going to do. But thanks."

Cliff shrugged, and then shifted to ask her about something he'd been working on, taking advantage of a natural groove in the jet to form the shape. He honestly wanted her opinion, it seemed, and that kept them talking until a customer came in and Annice slipped out.

CHAPTER 15
MARCH 19TH

"Look, you have family rites for the equinox. You should go home for them." Griffin was on the sofa in the sitting room, settling in to be persuasive.

Charlus looked exceptionally dubious. "I don't need to. Sir." That last was pointed. "I'm needed here."

"For the moment, what I'm doing is research and getting things into my head. And yes, it's a help for you to make sure there's food, and move stacks of books from one location to another, but it's not actually essential." Griffin was, in fact, curious whether Charlus would catch on to the other reasons on his own.

Charlus dropped into the chair. "You have a plan in mind."

"Several plans. And also, several that are on hold for various reasons," Griffin agreed. "Care to name them?"

"On hold, whatever happens with Annice Matthewman. No note today, probably not tomorrow, it being Sunday, and who knows about when." Charlus ticked it off on his finger. "And possibly some progress with one of the others, but that's slow."

"Just so. What else?" Griffin shifted slightly, to take the strain off his hip.

There was silence for a good twenty seconds. "The Courts. People in the courts, specifically." Griffin beamed and gestured with one hand for Charlus to continue. "Politics." Charlus said the word with some distaste.

"And you being at the equinox rites with your family might turn up some interesting information, don't you think?" Griffin flicked his fingers. "You know they gossip. Well, most people gossip. It's just a question of who they gossip with and to and about."

"The factions, you mean. If anyone is being pointed about your absence, your success or failure. But if I'm there, won't they shut up?" Charlus asked.

"To your face, yes. To one of your relatives? Maybe not. Not everyone actually keeps track of the familial relationships as much as they ought. Anyway. You might hear something. If you don't, you don't, you should still get a few days with your family." There were other people, former apprentices, where Griffin would not have pushed that, because he'd known things with their family were touchy. That wasn't the case with Charlus, who cheerfully chattered about seeing cousins or aunts or uncles when he got a chance, as well as his parents.

Charlus nodded. "All right." He let out a long sigh. "I feel like I'm letting you down."

"I'm telling you to go. Look, you can go round and collect groceries for me. I'm perfectly competent to make a sandwich or heat some soup. You can come check on me - say Tuesday or Wednesday." Equinox was the Monday. "And I can make it down to the White Horse & Griffin on the crutches just fine, and I will, so long as it's not actually pelting with rain."

That got him a little snort. "And the rest of the work?"

"You don't like the idea of politics, do you?" Griffin said, pressing on that point.

Charlus shook his head. "It's naïve of me, I know, sir, but I'd rather hoped the Courts were above that. The pursuit of truth and justice."

"Ah, but truth often has a certain aspect of perspective. Certainly, there are a variety of approaches. I don't care for some of the people who don't care for me, but I do, on the whole, think they're competent at what they're doing." Griffin left it there to see what Charlus would do with that.

"But not perhaps - may I speak freely, sir?" Charlus looked up, a little wary now.

"Please. I would like you to." That was promising, and this was one thing people had to come to in their own way and their own time. It was part of apprenticing, but it wasn't one that could be listed out as something to be mastered, not without changing how people learned.

"You might not want that the others should, for example, be named Heir. Should rise to a different position. At least as things are." Charlus took a deep breath. "Nestor Aplin, for one. And, um. Ulrich Moore, or Neave Williams. And I wouldn't trust Tess Manfred as a clerk, exactly."

That last one was an interesting piece of information. That was new to Griffin. Though generally he preferred Lucy or one of the other clerks he knew well, and Tess was still relatively junior. "Nestor, indeed. He has not been subtle about it to me, though I haven't heard anything new in a while. And I was aware of Moore and Williams, but not Manfred."

"I heard her gossiping a couple of weeks ago. With someone outside the Courts - she was a table or two over at supper." Charlus considered. "It wasn't anything against the confidentiality oaths, not about specific cases. I didn't report it, but it got closer to that line than I would have thought judicious."

"Did she know you were there?" Griffin asked.

"Yes, she'd nodded at me when they were seated." Charlus bit his lip. "Is there a way to mention it informally?"

"There is. You could have a word with Mistress Henning or Master Willis or Master Osgood." He oversaw the clerks. "They can keep an eye out, and if there are other reports, they can act on the aggregate, even if no single incident quite steps over the line."

"I'll do that, then. When I get back to Trellech. You're sure you'll be fine here? There isn't anything besides the groceries I can set up while I'm gone?"

"Me, my books, and some tea." Griffin grinned. "You'd be bored, anyway. If you feel you need to keep busy, you know what to be studying."

"Would it help if I went round the Courts, besides that report? There won't be anyone there, of course, bar a handful of people." Charlus offered it a little tentatively. "Um. Harriet Wilson?" He made it a query, not just about her likely presence over the recess, but also the politics.

"Harriet's a cypher, honestly, in several ways. I work well with her, we both think we'd do an excellent job as Heir. We're both likely right, but the Court would do different things with her. I don't worry about politics from her end near as much, because..." Griffin hesitated, trying to figure out how to put it.

"It has seemed to me, sir, that she wants to prove what she can do. Not prove what you can't." Charlus was a little cautious, but he said it, and Griffin was tremendously proud of the trust and also the analytical sense it showed.

"That's an excellent description, thank you. She's likely to be around a bit. Feel free to offer your help if she has anything you can lend a hand with. I'm curious what that might shake loose."

"Sir." Charlus looked pleased to have a little more context. "And the rest of it?"

"Let me think about it, and I'll journal with what to look for. Tonight or tomorrow." Griffin shrugged. "And I thought I might arrange a carter to take me up to the Abbey ruins on the equinox before you fuss about my being inside the whole time."

"Sir." Again it was amused. Then Charlus seemed to think of something else. "You also think it's likely people might talk to you differently if I'm not here. Is that part of it?"

"It is." Griffin beamed. "Well spotted. You have been exceedingly helpful, but I want to see if anything happens if people see me on my own. Sometimes it does. People make assumptions about the chair, what it means. Like I said before, most of them are wrong, but it's hard to argue with an assumption, or something stuck in someone's head."

"You said people treated you like you were dim. I can't imagine that lasting much beyond someone actually talking to you." Charlus nodded. "All right. Let me put together a list of what to make sure you've got for food and that the laundry's put out, and all that."

After all that, Charlus left via the portal on Sunday, leaving Griffin in anticipated peace for a couple of days. Annice did not send a note or anything of the kind, but Griffin honestly hadn't expected that. On the Monday, their landlady had made arrangements for a carter to pick Griffin up. The cart had been decidedly rustic and bumpy, and the carter had eyed the crutches with distaste. Griffin had spent the ride on a bench in the back, along with several bags of grain and some smaller crates, looking out at the scenery.

Getting to the Abbey was an interesting geometric problem, actually. They were staying down near the harbour, on the east bank of the Esk. The abbey overlooked the harbour, nominally right above them, up the famous hundred ninety-nine steps. To get to the top of the cliff involved the carter going well north before turning east and up a long sloping hill. It wasn't terribly far, in absolute terms - Griffin thought it maybe a mile and a half, maybe two - but it took the better part of an hour. The man let him out with a grunt. "Have deliveries. Back in an hour, m'be two."

"Fairly sure I can occupy myself for two." He had a guidebook, and besides, what he was actually interested in was time in the space. "Back out here, then?" He dug out coins with a bit extra, dropping them into the man's hand. The carter nodded, then wheeled horse and cart around in a big circle, and disappeared back out to the road.

Griffin turned his attention to the abbey. There were legends about the place, and that was some of why he'd wanted to come up, seeing as how he was in Whitby with some free time. But it wasn't just the current ruins that interested him. First, there was the way Saint Hild had administered her abbey. And second, there was the whole question of an abbey not just as a religious structure, but as one which shaped boundaries and the law and the way the laws worked for the people.

He slowly made his way along the dirt path, taking his time. He didn't want the crutches to catch on something uneven in the ground, a dip, hollow, or stone. He had no need to rush, anyway. There were a number of papers in more recent centuries, since the Pact, about whether Saint

Hild had had magic of her own. She was certainly an aristo-crat, raised in the court of Northumbria after her father's murder. One tale came from her infancy, about her mother dreaming about a necklace of such light that it filled - so the Venerable Bede had said - all Britain with the glory of its brilliance.

She'd come to being a nun later, not until she was thirty-three. Griffin always rather liked the stories of people who changed courses in the middle of their life, they were often far more interesting. She'd become a nun, then abbess elsewhere, before founding a double monastery at Whitby around 657. It had been home to both men and women, though living separately. It had even hosted the synod where the dates of Easter were established. Griffin found a grounding and peace in the religion, but he absolutely appreciated the effort it took to sort out that kind of system when there were many different adherents and preferences.

On one hand, the calculations weren't terribly complex, as chronological magics went: the first Sunday after the first full moon after the Spring Equinox. The problem came when people were using different definitions for every part of that phrase - when Sunday began, how the lunar months fell, and even the date of the equinox. At one point, it meant that the Northumbrian court celebrated Easter on different dates, depending on if they were aligned with the king or the queen, with all the complexities of fasting and feasting that meant. Saint Hild had argued for the more Celtic calcu-lation, using tables that ran for eighty-four years before repeating, but the Roman method had won out. As a legal-istic argument, Griffin appreciated the points in favour of the Roman dating system, but it had been a bitter argu-ment, and it had lessened Saint Hild's influence.

Though it had not shaken her place in legend. There

were tales about the area being beset by snakes. One version of the story had it that she had gone to God in prayer, and with several suggestions. That part always made Griffin laugh, because it was sensible. She'd suggested that the snakes lose their heads, so they could not bite. When that did not stop the distressing wriggling coils of snakes all over the ground, she suggested they be turned to stone. The stones - now people knew they were ammonite fossils - were abundant in the cliffs around Whitby. Griffin had seen plenty polished up in the shops.

The abbey, though, had been a triumph. Hild had run the entire place, with a number of the monks becoming bishops, and one coming to be a poet. The first poet whose name was known, in fact, Caedmon. Griffin had learned of the surviving verse, though in translation, and bits of it had rolled around in his head ever since. This was not the abbey that Hild had known, nor Caedmon had known, but it evoked the verse brilliantly. "Hail now the holder of the Heavens' realm, that architect's might, his mind many ways, Lord forever and father of glory, Ultimate crafter of all wonders." That was the face of the divine that Griffin had always found most intriguing, ever since he'd first heard of it.

Making his way into the ruined abbey, that image was made material. Hild's abbey had been destroyed by raids from the Danish. Not long after the Conquest, though, there had been a Benedictine monastery established, then built out into the Romanesque style, then in the Gothic. Alas, it had fallen into ruin with Henry VIII and the dissolution of the monasteries. There were soaring arches, though the vault itself was long gone, and there'd been further damage from German bombardment from the water during the War.

What Griffin had wanted most, though, was the feel of the place. And that was where a bit of quiet - a mist had come up, chill enough he had the place entirely to himself - did wonders. He could feel the structure of it, the way the architecture was its own magic. The place had been infused with intention and determination and lines of magic that lingered still, even though it had been centuries since it had been used for its intended purpose. He made his way along, walking slowly, step by step, leaning on the crutches. Now and then he'd pull his arm out of one, to press his palm to the stone, and feel what the place was telling him.

It wasn't like the Courts, not exactly. But they had something of the same lineage, making a place for a particular purpose, and reaching toward something better than mere utility or necessity or individual benefit. And like so many ancient buildings, there had been repairs - work done on the West transept, the part that had been hit worst in 1914 - to mend and stabilise it. That was from the guidebook, of course. Griffin knew someone had called it a waste of money, but the place was beautiful, and it was a landmark for ships on the ocean besides.

He'd kept an eye on the time, coming out far enough to see if the carter had come back periodically. At an hour, no. At ninety minutes, no. At two hours, his legs were giving out, and he came out to sit on a bit of wall. Time passed until it had been three and a quarter hours. Griffin could feel his hunger - not a risk, not yet, but balance in all things had to be his watchword now about his body.

He gave it another half hour and then had to concede that the carter wasn't coming. If he wanted to get back somewhere with warmth and food, well, he'd have to do it himself. There wasn't anyone around to ask. He had his journal, but he wasn't sure if Charlus would see it promptly, given the day, and the same with anyone else he could reasonably ask in Trellech. The Guards he knew would either be busy or off-duty with their own celebrations. His parents would be at his sister's.

Griffin was at the top of the steps. Going downhill was easier than going up. There were probably places he could sit along the way. And he might well find more people on the steps. He thought the railing ran along a line of houses. Slowly, carefully, he began picking his way down, counting the steps because that way, he could measure his progress.

He'd only got to seventy-seven when he had to give up and sit.

CHAPTER 16
MARCH 21ST

Annice had given up on anyone buying anything in the shop around two in the afternoon. She was feeling restless - more than restless. After a bit of useless tidying in the kitchen, she decided to go up and at least put a flower or two on Grandad and Nan's grave, and Mam and Da's, too. It was too early for most flowers, of course, but one of the shops had some early wildflowers, and she bought one small nosegay.

She set off up the stairs, of course. That was tradition. Not just the burying of the dead, but a number of the old families kept to that for visiting them, remembering them. Nan had been clear about that mattering, so long as Annice could. It was a lot of stairs, but not too many to manage. She'd made it up past the halfway mark, to where the stairs curved, and there was someone sitting there. At first, the mist made it hard to focus, before she realised it was Griffin.

Who was sitting there, looking like he hadn't moved in a bit, crutches off to the edge nearest the hill. He was looking at her, a little wide-eyed, as if she'd startled him.

"What on God's green and pleasant land are you doing?" The phrase - very much Nan's and her Mam's - came out of her without thinking. "Are you all right?"

The corner of his mouth twitched up. "Sitting. This bit is not, however, terribly green."

It was not Whitby at her most pleasant, either, really, between the mist leaning into becoming a drizzle and a bit of a breeze. Annice put her hands on her hips. "You know what I meant."

Griffin lifted a hand. "I got a carter to bring me up this morning. He never came back." He then shifted to gesture at the crutches. "I'll be all right in a bit, enough to get back down."

"And how long have you been sitting there already?" Annice, well, Annice could understand why someone might go up to the Abbey. But this was foolish. Didn't he know it was foolish? He didn't answer, so then she asked, "Who was the carter?"

"Mrs Urwin - my landlady - arranged it. A nephew of hers, I think? I have been contemplating what to say or not say to her." Griffin shrugged it off, as if this problem was something he hadn't expected, but had experience with.

"He'll lig, soon as anything." Annice snorted. "She ought to have known better."

"Lig?" Griffin blinked at her.

"Um. Laze about." Annice waved a hand. "I— look. It's not right, you out here on your own." He shrugged, and even more than usual, she did not know how to interpret that. "I was going to leave some flowers. The cemetery. I won't be long. Then we can see about getting you back down sensibly." It wasn't like she could carry him. He probably knew the charms to make things lighter, same as she did. But there was no way someone like her - lightly built, six inches shorter, probably - could carry him and have it pass. But if he couldn't move, she could go fetch someone to help, or something.

Griffin took a breath, then nodded. "Of course." He hesitated, and then asked, now very cautiously. "A particular anniversary? The reason?"

It took her a moment, but then she shook her head. "Just the equinox. I wasn't going to, only." She half turned away. "Half an hour, maybe, at most. Probably less."

"Take the time." He pulled one of his feet in closer, and aimed his attention out toward the water, away from her. She waited a moment to see if he was going to say something else, and when he didn't, she kept going up the stairs. A little faster than usual, like some of her didn't want to waste unnecessary time.

She didn't hurry the flowers, though. She put them down on the graves and ran through all the things she wanted to talk to them about, all the things she wished she could, as it came out in phrases and scattered words. Words made the way she carved tiny shapes out of the jet. Her faith wasn't like Nan's or Mam's or even Grandad's, but that didn't matter. She felt better for saying it. When she was done, and done with a proper prayer that could have been said in church with everyone listening, she took a couple of breaths and turned back for the stairs.

Griffin was still right where she'd left him. "There's a bench further down. Just around the bend." She wouldn't tell him it was a coffin bench, there for the pallbearers bringing coffins up the steps to their final home, meant to give a bit more dignity.

"Give me a little more, and I'll try further. Just." There was a resignation in his voice. "You needn't stay."

Oh, now she wanted to call him a name or two. But all

the ones she could think of were local words, and it was right foolish to call him names he wouldn't understand. "Can I sit?"

"Sure. Not my steps, are they?" He pulled his coat a bit more tightly around him. Then he took a breath and let it out. "Sorry. I should have planned better."

It made her cock her head and frown. "You had a plan. It's Hannah's wazzock of a nephew who's the problem. Bet he took your money and went to gamble. Or drink. Probably gamble." Then she swallowed. "Can I help somehow? Go fetch someone? Give you an arm?"

Griffin turned his head, looking at her, then he blinked. "You do mean that." He sounded startled.

"Charlus helps you. Why isn't he here, actually?" That had finally caught up with her.

"I sent him off to spend time with his family. I've been doing research. There's only so much he can do to help with that." Griffin shrugged. "And an arm's not much good when I need both hands for the crutches."

She couldn't argue with that. She didn't know enough about it, and she certainly didn't know how to ask for more details. Or dare asking and mess things up more. "What were you going to do if no one came along?"

"Maybe send a note by journal. But everyone I'd ask - I do ask people for help, just, you know. Friends. Family. Charlus, who's obligated to it, but also quite willing." Now he sounded defensive, the way Annice got when other people offered to help her, and that was an uncomfortable mirror right there. "They've got their own plans for the equinox, and I don't want to drag them away if I can manage?"

"And this is what managing looks like?" Annice's voice came out sharper than she meant to. Immediately, before she could think better of it she added, "Are you sure you're not using truth magic on me?" She got the words out, which meant there really wasn't anyone nearby, because the magic of the Pact would have warned her if someone was.

Something in it made him chuckle. "I told you, it won't work for me here. Trellech, now, that's another story." There was a little purr to his voice, saying the name, the way novels wrote about someone talking about a lover. She'd never heard it like that in person before, though she'd heard all sorts of other ways love came out in someone's voice.

"It's awfully uncomfortable. Being truthful. Thinking about being truthful like that." Annice curled her own arms around her.

"They're not meant for all the time. But I..." He considered, looking away from her. "Do you want to hear about it? Most people find my theories about it tedious."

"How long will it take for you to be ready to keep going, try for it, anyway? And how long are the theories?" Annice put it to him like that.

"Short version of the theory, then, and then yes, I will try some more steps. I do appreciate your company, actually. Both, um." He stopped, and she was sure he'd been meaning to say something else. Instead he went on, "If I tumble or something, it's good to know someone would know right away."

"Any decent person would want to help," Annice said firmly. "Theory?"

Griffin took a breath, adjusting how he was sitting a little to twist toward her. "Leaving out a lot of background that's long, I've been fascinated by the judicial magics for ages. Since I knew they existed, I think. My dad had a case in the Courts when I was nine. Nothing he'd done badly wrong, but he had to go and give formal evidence. Mum had to come with him, and they couldn't leave me alone - my sister's a bit older. She was away at school."

Annice nodded cautiously. "That part almost makes sense."

It got a laugh out of him, a warm one, and she liked the sound of it. Not that it mattered if she liked it. But he was talking, and she thought that was probably good for him. "Anyway. I went to Schola, and then straight into apprenticeship. Not something anyone in my family had done, but I loved it. Still love it. But I think that if you're spending your life in the courts, in those particular kinds of magic, you have to think about how it shapes you. Not everyone agrees with me. Some of them are even quite successful and accomplished, professionally speaking." Annice was fairly sure there was some particular person he was thinking of, speaking with the excruciating politeness someone might well use with someone he hated. The way Rob and Cliff talked about each other when they had to.

"And so you, um." She tried to figure out how to put this. "You're always thinking about the shape of it. Like when I'm carving. Everything goes into making the shape."

Griffin nodded. "Exactly. And I built myself around it. Making that shape." He gestured up toward the abbey behind them. "Like that, in miniscule. I think a lot about how the spaces we're in shape us, shape what we do, what is more or less possible."

"A life isn't small. Not over the length of it," Annice pointed out. "You went to the War. You came back. What would, um." She considered. "Were you an officer?"

"A captain, before I was injured." Now his voice was more cautious, with spaces between the words.

"What would your men have said about you?" Men like her da, that would have been. Or from somewhere else, thrown into a war that didn't make sense, with not enough of anything.

"I tried to live so they'd think I took care of them, as best I could. It worked better with some than others. And then I was gone." Griffin looked away abruptly. "I didn't quite break any promises, but it felt like I had. They felt like I had, I think."

"Did they tell you that?" Annice asked. "With words? Directly?"

Griffin kept looking away. "Most of them weren't magical. There was so much I couldn't talk about." Then, suddenly, he pushed himself with his hands, rocking upward. He got the crutch under one arm, his forearm in the curved piece, his hand braced on the handle at the bottom, then the other. "Let's give the stairs a try. Don't foul the crutch, that'd be bad, but if you could keep an eye out, anything uneven or that might catch me up."

She wasn't going to argue. And honestly, she was worried about him sitting out in the cold, even without how the last bit of talking had gone. "Sure." Annice stood, brushing her hands off on her skirt. "A step or two ahead."

CHAPTER 17
MARCH 21ST

Griffin forced himself to moderation. He hated the in-between stage, when he knew he'd done too much. It hadn't quite caught up to him yet, but he also wasn't back somewhere where he could rest and take all the masks of coping off. Annice did what he'd asked her to, keeping far enough ahead that he wasn't worried about her skirt catching on one crutch or something worse. Hemlines were trending shorter this year, so his various contacts who cared about fashion had mentioned, but of course Annice wouldn't follow that.

It was an absorbing question, actually, or at least a distracting one. She made beautiful things, given the opportunity, but her clothing was decidedly neutral. Some of that might well be a quiet mourning, and Griffin approved of that. He'd seen so many people in all the prismatic stages of grief come through the inheritance courts. The ones who took their time almost always had the right idea. The ones who didn't hurry into what their life should look like now, or shove every bit of missing someone down and away.

But outside of that, when there was space for it, was she the sort of person who'd like to keep up with fashion trends for herself, given the chance? Or was all of her attention focused on the jet carving, with whatever she wore as a neutral craftswoman's uniform? Griffin couldn't actually throw stones. He had a wardrobe full of appropriate and unexciting suits, with a few minor alterations from his tailor to make them more comfortable when seated all day. There were no seams where he sat that might rub or cause hot spots. But beyond that, he looked like every other man of his profession. And since he was no barrister and certainly not a judge, he didn't get the traditional flowing robes in court.

That set of thoughts kept Griffin occupied most of the way down the steps. Annice hesitated for just a second each time they got near a bench, to see if he wanted to stop. But Griffin rather thought that if he did, he wouldn't move again for days. Every time he just shook his head minutely, and she kept going. At least she wasn't arguing with him.

Finally, they got to the bottom of the steps, near to Annice's shop. Griffin half-expected her to stop there, but she glanced at him again. "Cottage, then." She had the address. He'd given it to her in case of sending a message, so now she just went onward. She ducked through the alley between two buildings into the courtyard, then stopped by the door. That meant he had to fumble for the key. It was clipped into the satchel over his shoulder. As always, it had fallen down into the bottom, and even the key strap he'd attached it to wasn't a great deal of help.

Once he got the door open, she let him go first, hovering on the doorstep. He didn't turn around, just said, "Come in, if you want. Or if you need to get back to something, I'll be fine." Precision - and truthfulness - meant he couldn't say he was fine now. He'd be fine. In a day, maybe three, depending on how much of that cold had affected things. Or sitting out in it.

"Can I put the kettle on for you?" Annice's voice was a little tentative, as if she weren't sure he'd accept.

Griffin nodded. "Please." Then he considered his options. The sofa would be more comfortable, but the chair meant less moving around later. He had just enough space to wheel it into the bedroom, or to leave it right outside the loo. A moment later he settled into the wheelchair. Griffin let habit guide him into tucking the crutches where they'd be held in place with a touch of magic, for when he needed them later. Then he wheeled himself over to the low table by the sofa, so he could put the satchel down and rummage for the pill he really ought to take.

Behind him, he could hear the sounds of the kettle filling, then beginning to heat. Without looking, he said, "Thank you for keeping me company." Then that didn't sound like enough. It was curt. He didn't want to be curt. She hadn't done anything wrong, not in the least. "And I'm sorry I was abrupt. I don't talk much about the War, not with other people who weren't there."

"That means you talk about it with someone who was." Annice's voice was neutral, and moving to see her face would be very obvious. "We're near strangers. Why would you talk to me, anyway?"

That sentence, though, made him turn, the twist of the wheels that brought him halfway around so he could see her. "You're lonely here, aren't you?" Then he swallowed. "That was terribly rude of me."

"It's true." Her mouth twitched, then Annice spread out

her hands. "I'm fighting the tide. Not much trade in jet, not anymore. Not much chance of marrying at my age. Old house, just me in it, and my aunt and cousins on my nan's side. They could use the space. Barely making ends meet with the carving, and that's not likely to get better, because too many people think women shouldn't carve jet. But... where else would I be?"

He heard it, then, the note that was all about how he loved Trellech. Griffin considered. "I don't have answers for you. I don't know enough about the way things are here. But look. Would you make tea, and there are some sandwiches and things in the keep-cold? Charmed to keep. Charlus left me well stocked." He saw her hesitate, and added, "Or if you'd like something hot, I'd be glad to pay for you to pick up something at one of the pubs or inns or whatever."

"That, if you don't mind." Annice straightened up.

Griffin rummaged for his coins and turned over what he thought ought to cover it. "That enough? I eat most things, but something hot sounds good. Fish or whatever."

"Fish and chips? Easy and fast." She flicked her fingers over the coins. "I'll bring you the change. And leave the kettle 'til I'm back." Griffin nodded, and without saying anything else, she slipped out the door again.

She was gone long enough for him to wheel to outside the loo, make use of it, wash his hands, snag a jumper from the bedroom, and return to the sitting room. He was very pleased he hadn't fallen over doing any of it, though he was definitely going to be regretting several recent choices soon. Annice came in bearing a basket, and then said, "You eat there?" pointing at the lower table. "Or, no, your chair has a thing."

"It does. Wherever you'd like to eat. The kitchen table's

fine if you'd rather." Annice shook her head. She efficiently set out two packets of fish and chips, poured hot water into the teapot to steep, and had everything out on the low table by the sofa, where Griffin could reach it well enough. When he had a free hand, she held out hers with the change. He wanted to tell her to keep it - he wouldn't miss it - but that would be an insult, so he took it back.

Once she sat, they both spent a couple of minutes inhaling half their respective food. Then the tea was ready, and she poured it out into the sturdy mugs that had come with the cottage. Griffin cupped his hands around it, letting the heat warm his fingers. "The fish and chips are grand."

"My favourite place. Grandad loved them." Annice wiped her mouth with her hand. "You wanted to know about the town?"

"What you love about it." Griffin shrugged. "I love Trellech. I know Trellech, a way I'm never going to know anywhere else. But right now I'm here, and I'd like to know more about it. The way someone who loves a place can tell it."

"You're sure I do." It wasn't a question. She didn't make it into a question. "I'm not arguing. Just. How do you know that?"

Griffin shrugged, setting the mug on his little ledge of a table so he could go back to nibbling at the chips with appropriate appreciation while listening. "I spend a lot of time listening to people talk about what they care about. Sometimes they say it outright. Most of my work is with the inheritance court. It brings out explicit things people want or are upset they're not getting. But often, they want something, and they maybe can't admit to it. That's the hardest part. It's so tricky to help someone feel like they can say the difficult bits out loud. Sometimes that's because of family -

someone else will be angry if they speak up, or disappointed. Disappointed is somehow worse, I think."

Annice opened her mouth, closed it, then took a bit of a chip. Then, carefully - and oh, he could read volumes in that - she said, "Oh?"

He chose his words carefully, but also went to some pains to cover that. "If someone's angry with you, you can argue with them. Stand up to them, resist them, whatever that looks like for you in that situation. Mostly my people don't run to anger. I get along well with my Mum and Dad and sister and her husband. And my nieces and nephew are lovely. Sometimes very loud and messy, but they're an age where that's expected. Ordinary. But I've heard it enough. A few times at school, more since. Plenty, in the Army."

Annice nodded, and that was what he'd wanted, to give her examples where she could see what he meant. For probably the millionth time in his life, he blessed the training he'd had in rhetoric, going back to Schola, and everything since. "But disappointment?"

She was quick. And he'd set that up, deliberately, but that didn't mean it didn't make him flinch a little, and that he let her see it. It was honest. It was truthful, and it was also a touch manipulative. "That too. Oh, my parents were plenty proud of me. But once I got into Schola, there were a lot of expectations. And I am, truth, excellent at my job. It is a highly specialised job. Other people can do it, but not that many people actually want to and are capable of it. Like a lot of other specialist jobs. And the path there isn't very direct, sometimes."

Now, there was a whole steep cliff piled with things he wasn't saying. Some of them were about how what he wanted was to hold the land magic for Trellech, and what that would mean. Others were about how he'd be forever disappointed in himself if he didn't try as long and as much and as well as he could. But that some part of him was bracing for that inevitable loss. "But you can't, um. Disappointment is a fog, not a mirror. You can't argue with it, you can't straighten it out, you can't get a grip on it at all. It slides right off. And that's hard to live with, isn't it?" Then, before he could stop himself, he added, "Especially when I'm disappointed in myself."

Annice was quiet long enough to eat two chips and a bit more of her well-vinegared fish. "They train you how to see things like that?"

"Yes. Though honestly, I was like this as a kid." Griffin spread his hands, making sure not to send his mug flying. "I'd apologise, but I meant to do it. And I can't just turn off the skill. Just like I bet you can't walk down the beach and not look for jet. Or start thinking about what you'd do with it when you got it home."

She snorted, a definite sound of admitting that was also the truth.

"Anyway. You asked how I know you love Whitby, and it's all of that. When people love a place - really love a place, I can hear it. And again, I hear about this in inheritance, who wants a family property because they adore it, and who sees what they could sell it for, sometimes - it comes out in all sorts of ways. And people who love a place know things about it. Not the things in whatever books there are, or the local newspaper..."

He gestured at the paper that had been wrapped around the fish and chips. "Or even the local gossip, though that's a bit closer. But what makes the place itself? The smell that one day, when it's suddenly properly spring. The glimpse you get through buildings, onto something different. The feel of it under your feet. The changes in the air. I could probably navigate Trellech just by smell now, bakery to pub to restaurant to the Ministry canteen or the Guard refractory." He found himself half-smiling. "All right, though these days, it's faster to tell by the ground under the wheels. But the smells are mostly much more fun. Fewer cobblestones in a smell."

CHAPTER 18
THAT AFTERNOON

Annice looked up at that, watching Griffin. "I've only been to Trellech twice, really briefly, and when I was little. It's much, um. Much more? Isn't it?"

"Oh, if you get me going about that, I'll be going on for hours. And I'm likely boring." But his eyes lit up, even just at the idea of that conversation. Annice still did not understand him, not remotely. She didn't understand some of his references, certainly not how he looked at the world. There was an optimism there out of season, as well as the stubbornness that had absolutely been on display this afternoon.

Now, she considered. "If I tell you about Whitby, will you tell me a bit more about Trellech?"

"Of course. If you'd like. Tell me to stop when it gets too much." He considered. "Beer, to go with your fish and chips? It's chilled. No, you stay, I can get it." Before she could do more than nod, he set his food back on the table, apparently so it wouldn't fly off. He leaned back slightly, getting the chair to near enough pivot. He opened a trunk up against one side of the room, to one side of the window.

Out came two bottles, and he was setting them to rest against the side of his chair and his leg as he came back. He opened one with a flourish of a charm and handed it to her.

Annice curled her hand around the cool glass, and wondered about a lot of things. For one thing, he used his magic easily. That must be living in Trellech. He was used to not having to hide it all the time, not in school, not in the shops, not on the street. For another, the beer was the right kind of cool, and he'd been able to grab it without any fussing. That meant all sorts of planning, the kind she'd learned to do taking care of Grandad and Nan, having things in the right place so half her day wasn't taken up running up and downstairs.

Now she lifted it as he opened his own. "Thank you. You're very generous. That's not like here, for one thing. Not for people who aren't from here."

"Nets of families, I'm sure. Everyone's got history with each other, if you've been here for a while. And I'm guessing some of it is where you live - east side of the river and west?"

Annice couldn't stop herself from laughing. "Aye. My cousins, they're on the other side of the Esk. More of the jet workers were here. The other side's the fishing, and all the things that go into that. But also some jet. Can't escape the jet." She was feeling a little odd now, giddy with having done something complicated, unexpectedly complicated. And the way he was smiling at her, encouraging her, not laughing at her or expecting her to keep quiet. Then she took one more swallow of her beer and thought about how to talk about Whitby.

"You've seen one of our legends. And if you did much reading, you know about St Hild and the ammonites." Griffin nodded at that. "I've got a few good ones, polished, in the shop. One that opalised, it's gorgeous." Then she considered. "And if you've read the guidebooks, you know a bit about Dracula and about Captain Cook."

"Both of those. Though I'm more interested in Cook, he actually lived here. I mean, the atmospheric lurking is all well and good, but it's not the same as knowing a place. Leaving from a place that's been home." Griffin's voice took on a deeper note, something that made Annice frown. "Something the matter?"

"The way you talk about being from a place." Annice said it before she could think better of it.

"Going overseas nearly did me in. Not the actual Army or the fighting, but not being in Trellech. Knowing I would not get back to Trellech for ages. And when I did wake up there - I was in the Temple of Healing for, mmm, eight days, ten, before I came back to myself? The first thing I remember was knowing I was home, down to my bones. Which were objecting to a lot of other things at the time."

He'd bristled immediately when she'd asked earlier. And besides, she'd heard aunties and nans and all asking people how they'd got hurt, as if there were some test of approved injuries that counted and nothing else did. That was rude, and it wasn't kind, and it certainly wasn't helpful. She refused to do that. Carefully, she said, "What's it like there? You hear about the gardens?"

"With good reason. There are plenty of healing plants, things they use in salves and potions and just plain in tisanes. But there are also a lot of flowers for beauty. It was different during the War - everyone was working flat out, including the VADs, helping the nurses. But now there are people who come around and bring you flowers and all that. And a little cart with books to choose from. But besides the gardens, there are the baths, below the temple, all sorts of different ones. Most are consecrated to a deity, there are people who help you pick which one might help. Sometimes that's the cause of how you got hurt, or who suits your, I don't know, soul." He added after a moment. "We went with the second, for me. I'm Christian. My parents were, and there's a lot about the idea of a great architect I find interesting."

Annice blinked, because at least two-thirds of that was nothing like what she'd expected. "Did it help, then?"

"It helped me feel like I could keep going, so yes. Keep figuring out what my life looked like now. Did it heal me? No. Nothing like 'throw aside your crutches and walk', obviously." Griffin looked away, to the side. "It confuses people, really."

Annice cocked her head, considering him like he was some piece of jet. Oh, he wasn't wearing black at the moment, though his tweed suit had more than a bit of the brown mark that true jet made when tested. She was thinking more about the angles and the way he was carved. People were vastly more complicated, of course. For one thing, they kept moving. "It doesn't confuse you. Not now?" That last bit, her voice arced up, more uncertain than she'd meant to sound.

"Not now. I know what I can do, what's at the edges, what I really can't. And I am a solicitor. I am very good at understanding not only the lines but the implications. Like I said about architecture, earlier. That's why I went up to the Abbey in the first place. I wanted to get a sense of the space, how it went together."

That, at least, she could understand. "Whitby's a little like that. Only it's not static. There are rhythms, like I guess the Abbey would have had, back when. Bells to call the hours. But we have the tides, and when the fishing boats go out, and when they come back, and what it looks like when there's a storm coming in. How the Esk sounds, on a clear day and in the rain. All of that." She gestured at the table. "Where to get the best fish and chips in town."

That reminded him, apparently, that he should finish eating, and he got his portion back onto his little side tray. That was still brilliant, and she was rather envious of how flexible it seemed to be in where he could put it. He nibbled on a chip or two, then said, thoughtfully, "And the jet's right here."

"Seven miles or a bit more, down the coast from here. When I go looking, it's usually at Robin Hood's Bay. Fewer people, though the hill's a lot." She hesitated, then added. "There's a portal, most of the way down, in the pub. I know some reliable carters near there. If you wanted to see it sometime."

He froze, went entirely still, as if every bit of him was taken up with thinking. Then he took a breath, deliberately. "Not for a couple of days, but if we get a - um. What are the good conditions for being on the beach and not slipping?"

"Sun. Timing it right against the tides. Going carefully and letting me go first? It's easy to turn an ankle if you're not careful, even hit your head, but it's not all loose stone and gravel. Not good for the chair, obviously."

"No." Griffin looked away again. "Ask me in a few days, then. If you think the weather will hold."

Annice hesitated. "You think you'll be here then? I haven't said I'd help. Or anyone else, right?"

"No one else. You are, in fact, my hope for this." Griffin looked back at her. "And you don't understand why I think that at all, do you?"

She tried to hold on to her dignity. "It's not something people have said to me. As a class of things to say."

"It seems to me that most people - your Grandad and Nan and Da and Mam excepted, I think - don't have much understanding of your skill, and certainly not enough respect."

"I can't actually argue with that. You're very annoying that way, did you know?" She suddenly wondered if he had a wife or had had a wife, or something. He hadn't said anything about it. He didn't wear a ring, but some people didn't. "Do people tell you that?"

It made him smile, which was entirely unreasonable. "Sometimes." It made him look charming, and she didn't need him to look charming. This was already complicated enough.

Now Annice swallowed. "Look, give me another day to think something over. Can you come to the shop tomorrow? Or do you have other plans?"

A cloud went across his expression, in a way she'd seen in Grandad a couple of times. "There's a decent chance I won't be up for moving much tomorrow. You're welcome to come here."

Oh. She rubbed her mouth, trying to hide her expression. "Are you going to be all right? Should you be writing to someone? Or get a Healer? I could meet someone at the portal." That last made his eyes widen. But surely he was the sort of person who could get a Healer to come out without too much trouble. Whitby didn't have their own, and besides, whatever had happened to him didn't seem entirely the sort of thing any random Healer might know. He must be like carving jet, instead of other lapidary work, where jet was so much softer, so much easier to carve, the work could barely use the same tools.

Now he was leaning back, looking at her. "You know, I really appreciate how much you aren't fussing, actually. A lot of people would be covering me in blankets and mugs of hot tea - not that that wasn't the right thing when we got in. Or insisting I go to bed. I don't need a Healer. If I do, I promise I'll write Charlus and make him deal with it. Or someone else who can come out. And I will see if Charlus can come by tomorrow, just in case I need something. Does that reassure?"

It didn't tell her much about what he was going to do, and even less about what he might be feeling now, or expecting. But it wasn't her place to pry. She swallowed, and then managed, "I'm glad I didn't overstep. Can I set anything out in the kitchen for you, so it's easy?"

"A small pot on the stove, for heating soup, and making sure the sandwiches are easy to get to in the keep-cold box? It's on the counter. Charlus set it up." He flicked his fingers at the trunk where he'd got the beer. "That one's mostly fine, but every so often it gives up for no reason, and that's fine for beer and not good for sandwiches."

She snorted. "No. All right. Are you done with your paper and all?" He nodded, and she set about tidying that much up. She dropped the old newsprint in the garbage, washing the ink off her hands, and then checked that things were easy to reach in the kitchen. She added a wooden spoon and a bowl to the counter next to the stove, then checked the sandwiches.

The keep-cold box wasn't too different from the one at home, and so she fed it a little more magic, so it would go at least another couple of days without needing more. Then she turned around, drying her hands off one last time. He'd shifted the wheelchair just slightly, so it angled to face the kitchen area, and he'd put the little tray table away, wher- ever it went.

"I really am grateful you came along today. I maybe

haven't said that enough. I appreciate your kindness, no end."

She ducked her chin. "And now I'll get out of your hair, so you can do whatever's next for you." She didn't quite turn and flee, but it was a near thing. "I hope you have a good evening?"

"I hope you do. And I'll do my best." She thought that was as good an answer as she was going to get, and so she went out the door, making sure to close it properly behind her. It wasn't as if she could see through the curtains, but she looked back once, as she got to the alley to the street.

CHAPTER 19
MARCH 22ND

Griffin heard the knock on the door from the sofa at about three in the afternoon. No position he'd tried was quite working, but he also didn't want to move. The knock was almost certainly Charlus, unless someone had picked up his particular pattern. Griffin was glad he'd packed a pair of loose trousers. With that and smoking jacket and a collarless shirt, he was presentable enough if it wasn't Charlus. "Come in."

The door opened carefully, and then Charlus peered around the door before coming all the way in. "Sir." He had a basket in his hand. "Need me to fetch anything right off?"

Griffin shook his head. "Not at the moment. Come in, put the kettle on, sit." Charlus took the hint, and set the basket on the low table by the sofa. First he shrugged out of his coat and hung up his hat, then put the kettle on to boil. That was a particular need met, at least. Griffin had been wanting tea for an hour, and hadn't quite managed to motivate himself to make it happen. And unlike his office or his own kitchen at home, the kettle wasn't handy unless he was standing.

From there, Charlus came over and began unpacking the basket he'd brought. "Morning and evening papers. Your mail. Captain Orland insisted I bring these along to you with her compliments." He set a small cardboard box down. "And a number of notes to discuss. There are also several meals from your housekeeper, from your kitchen."

"Ah, bless." That was a fairly comprehensive haul. "If you'd put the meals in the keep-cold box, please." He hesitated, then added, trusting that it wouldn't foul things, "And if you'd do me a favour and bring the potion case from my bedside table. The one that's carved wood, long and narrow, has the paler wood inlay on it."

Charlus raised an eyebrow at it. But he didn't say anything until he'd done those things, going last into Griffin's bedroom at the end of the hall and bringing it back, setting it where Griffin could reach it.

He ought to sit up properly, but having his legs up felt better, and changing anything seemed like a bad idea. Instead, he twisted - gently, he'd been reminded of what the alternative felt like that morning - and opened the case. It was also of Seth's making, beautifully designed both to securely hold a selection of potion vials and have space for three pill cases.

There was one for morning, one for night, and the third for when he needed something specific. He considered, drawing out the next to last of the vials - the others were stoppered and empty - and then drained it quickly, before he took out two of the pills. "If you'd put it back, when you get a moment, please?" He slipped the empty stoppered vial into place and closed the lid.

Charlus still didn't comment, but Griffin had been deliberately obvious about it, making a benefit out of the fact he couldn't bring himself to move. Hopefully, the potion would ease a bit of the aching, and the pill would manage some of the tension of overwork that was running through his forearms still. The routine daily ones were to help keep some of the symptoms easier to manage, sorted out through some trial and error and now made up by his apothecary to be easiest to take and have handy wherever he was.

The kettle was making the little hopeful noise it made before it started singing properly. Charlus had heard it, too. He went to stand and wait there while it fully came to a boil, setting up the teapot and mugs on a tray. Griffin leaned over and pulled the box from Antimony over with one finger, then nudged it open. "Ah, bliss. You have to try these. They're from one of my favourite bakeries, and Antimony knows it."

"Sir?" Charlus paused for a moment, as the kettle sang properly, and he poured boiling water into the teapot, then brought the whole thing over.

"Welsh cakes. Not quite like Mum makes, but handier, and they do a range of flavours. Not at all traditional, but there's a combination of spices and some orange peel." He didn't bother giving the Welsh, Charlus wouldn't know it. "And oh, she put in a couple of currant, that's the most traditional." Then he looked up. "What brought that on, that she sent them along?"

Charlus snorted quietly, pulling up the other easy chair to the other side of the table. "I might have looked a trifle worried this morning. She caught me checking things in your office and told me to wait until she came back." Then he cleared his throat. "I would like to calibrate my worry, please."

"Did she ask you to let her know when you had more information, then?" Charlus flushed, and Griffin lifted his hand. "I'm not upset with you. Or her. Give me a minute, though. Well. A minute and a bit of cake."

The cake was, actually, quite restorative, more than he'd expected. Something about the sweet and the tart and the spice hit exactly the right spot. He took his time eating it, licking the last of the caster sugar that had dusted it off his index finger. Charlus was eating his own, his eyes widening. "Told you," Griffin said. "I'll give you the address. It's a bit out of my usual route."

"Sir." That was approving. "Glad to go fetch more for you, then, as relevant. And for me."

Griffin chuckled. "Another proper convert. Antimony will be pleased." He shifted a bit to adjust how he was leaning against the arm of the sofa. "To answer your worries, I'll be back to normal in a day or maybe three. Not good for much - magically or otherwise - today, but people are always telling me I ought to take a day off, and I didn't on Saturday or Sunday."

Charlus looked unconvinced. And to be entirely fair, Griffin had sliced the truth on that set of comments a little fine for his own liking. He took a breath, then added. "Right now, a lot of me aches or is otherwise complaining, but it's not a sign of new harm or anything. I overdid it yesterday. I should apparently not have trusted our landlady's nephew to be reliable as a carter in both directions."

"You were thinking of going up to the Abbey, sir." Charlus blinked, his eyes widening. "What happened?"

"The man got me there quickly enough, but he didn't come back. Eventually, when that was clear, I made my way down the steps. I was sitting on one of them, maybe a third of the way down, not quite half, when Annice came up in the other direction. She was going to leave flowers in the cemetery."

Charlus considered that, falling silent for several minutes. "You didn't write to me."

"I didn't. I thought about it while I was sitting there. But I knew you'd be busy, and so would the other people I might write. And I was working myself up to keep going. Annice talked with me a little and then walked down with me. And went out and got fish and chips. There's a place she favours with good reason. Comparative to the cakes, here, in its own class."

"Huh." Charlus coughed. "You let her help, sir?"

Ah, that was the rub of it. He'd only recently told Charlus much of that, of course, and here he was, letting Annice help on a week's acquaintanceship. Three conversations, and while three might be a number of power and magic, that was not many at all when it came to knowing someone. It ought to be seven, at least, really. More than that. Griffin was about to say something. Then he felt that fleeting tug of where the truth lay. "I don't understand her, but I trust her. Odd, I know. I do also trust you, but you weren't here. And you should have time with your family."

And it was easier to trust Annice, in some ways. He didn't have obligations to Annice, ongoing professional connections, beyond the project of the moment. It made it easier to be vulnerable than with Charlus, with all the ties of apprenticeship. And decades in the future of professional collaboration, too.

Charlus considered. "May I ask a personal question, please?"

There were a number that might come from this conversation. "Go ahead and ask. I might not answer, but you've earned a fair number of answers now."

"You've lived on your own since the War?" Ah. That would be delicate in multiple directions, then.

Griffin nodded. "Split another cake in half? I should eat something more solid, too, in a bit. I did have lunch. The sandwiches were handy." Then he considered his answer. "By the time I was back in the Courts, my father was thinking about retiring. It took him several more years, but the house I grew up in was stairs all over. Mum found me my flat, and we refitted it a bit to make it work better for me. As to the more personal..." He shrugged. "I walked out with someone before the War. She married while I was gone. There's no harm in that. I hope she's happy." She had not loved Trellech, particularly, and that might have broken them apart anyway. "And since, there's been work, and I haven't..."

He paused, because he certainly hadn't talked about this with almost anyone. "I won't live with pity or someone who thinks they're doing a selfless, noble thing by being my nursemaid. That's a way to poison whatever love we might have had to start, and quickly. More than that, I work all the time, I haven't met anyone who might suit. Also, working all the time is in fact bad for romance, unless it's with someone you work with, and I have more sense. Let that be a caution to you."

Charlus listened attentively, and Griffin was glad for that skill. He knew Charlus would be analysing this, what he'd heard, but also that he'd remember it. "You're usually very self-sufficient." Then his voice caught, as if he'd put two different things together suddenly.

"That would be the gossip, then?" Griffin asked, as gently as he could manage. He broke one of the cakes in half and nudged the other half over to Charlus.

Again, Charlus flushed. Not much, but it was enough of a tell that they should talk about it sometime. Normally, Charlus had quite good control, but this was more personal, something that more directly involved him. "Several pieces of it. Um, sir, I assume you're aware that Nestor Aplin doesn't care for you at all. You said, last time we discussed him, you hadn't heard anything new. Some of this might be?"

"Oh, yes," Griffin said. "Though I gather from you saying so that I have been reasonably adept at hiding that the feeling is mutual so far."

It made Charlus chuckle softly. "One of my aunts is married to one of his cousins. She doesn't like him much, and we got to talking. He's been talking against you. Not in the Halls of Justice, but in other places. She didn't know about - or understand - that you're in consideration for the same thing."

"Still. And that decidedly annoys Nestor. Harriet's more even-tempered about it. She thinks it ought to be her, most of the time, but she wouldn't take it personally if Lamont picked me. Or Nestor, for that matter." Griffin considered. "Nestor has thought I should give up on it since before I came back. Before he was put in as the third candidate after Horace died in 1919. I do miss Horace." Griffin sighed a little with it. "What sort of nastiness? I'd rather know the truth."

Charlus did know, enough that he echoed the last three words, a fraction of a beat behind Griffin. "I couldn't get all the details out of my aunt, but it sounded unreasonably nasty. Undermining you, professionally, several ways round. That you're not fit for duty, that you've been letting things slip," Charlus considered. "That you should have fixed the problems years earlier."

"Ah. That's an entirely different political problem. You started with me right as Cleon retired. The rub of it is that he ought to have retired three or four years before he did. Enough time for me to get established again, to have a year working in the inheritance courts in specific, and then take over for him. That didn't happen. And he kept tight hold of his part of things until finally, he had that fall, and eventually agreed that coming into work was too much to do regularly." Griffin hesitated, then added, "It wasn't a physical infirmity, though, as much as a mental one. Memory. He'd forget when he was."

Then Griffin had a horrible thought, and he said it before he could bury it deep. "Now I'm wondering if whatever affected the courtroom, the jet, had to do with that. I don't think so - surely someone else would have noticed. Or worse, had symptoms. Or one of the diagnostics would have caught something."

Charlus was open-mouthed. Then he swallowed. "Should I get another round of testing set in motion?"

"Please, though for right now, can you just check on materia for it and see if we're low on anything? I'll need to write up a proposal for Lamont and for Gloriana and Christopher. One of the architectural specialists, and someone good with odd magic and ritual workings. I might see privately if Cy - Council Member Smythe-Clive is available for a look. He's seen some of our other work." Other people might reasonably ask the Penelopes, but it was complicated since they often had to give evidence in those spaces one way or another.

"You're familiar with him, then?" Charlus came from the sort of family that didn't have a landed title, but had in the past, and would probably marry into one again sooner than later.

"His sister runs the baths at the Temple of Healing, and she arranged for him to help evaluate where my skills were when I was newly back. We've kept up a light correspondence since. You know the sort of thing. I'd copy something out of the legal journals and publications, he'd send back an article from outside Albion that might be relevant. Council Member Landry's also quite skilled at ritual work, but I don't know him nearly as well. And he was after your time at Schola, so that won't work, though I could ask Seth to ask his sister." Griffin waved a hand. "Chains of interconnection. We'll try the shorter one first. And if Cyrus isn't willing, he might know who to suggest."

"I begin to see why you work all the time, sir," Charlus said after a moment. "You're always thinking about the consequences. How one thing leads onward."

"That's the pursuit of truth and justice for you. Even if they're not always the same thing." It was also the infirmity. He always had to think of the possibilities several steps out, to stand a chance of keeping going with what he wanted to get done. But he wasn't going to mention that now. "Anyway, I will work on that as soon as I can, but to be honest, likely tomorrow." He flicked his fingers. "The potion does rather horrid things to my ability to write neatly, and I didn't bring the typewriter. Was there other gossip?"

"A couple of other things. Like there are factions, lines of preference, in the Courts. Which I knew, but perhaps you could lay that out more sometime, sir? Not today, though, if you'd rather not."

Griffin took a breath, considering it, then thought better of it. "It will almost certainly make more sense if we wait. You were going to go back, yes?"

"If you don't need me to stay, sir. I'm glad to, of course." Charlus glanced over at the stairs. "Most of my things are still in my room here."

"No, I'd rather you go work on getting the materia together. And being around the place, seeing who wants to talk to you when I'm not there. Don't tell them any details about how things are going. You can say I've told you not to, if you like. Or you can say I haven't told you all of what I'm working on. Both of which are true, of course."

"Of course," Charlus said, and now he looked amused. Then he hesitated. "May I ask something, sir? A touch more personal, about how you approach the gossip?"

"Please." Griffin rearranged himself.

"Why don't you say something about it? More openly? Mostly, it seems to me you just let them insinuate things."

"Oh, several reasons. First, perhaps most importantly, I'd rather spend my time on other things. But second, it's like arguing with the tides or the moon or the sun rising. I'm not going to change their opinions by arguing. Especially Nestor's, he's also a solicitor. We both know how arguments are crafted. If he brought it out in the open, I could address it. So he won't let me get that advantage. Instead, I'm going to do my best work - like I've been doing all along. And hopefully, that will speak for itself. It gets tiring, mind. Every time I do make a minor slip, the sort everyone human does, I wonder how much more this one will count against me than it would for someone else. But that's a known sort of maths these days. And I'm lucky enough to have excellent support and advice. Antimony, a few of the other Guards, various people in the Courts. You."

Charlus ducked his chin. "Thank you, sir. I suspect I'll be thinking about that part, when it's worth arguing and when it isn't, for some time. Let me go make sure you've got things handy, then, and I'll go off." He took a moment to finish the half cake in front of him, then Griffin could hear him moving around. A couple of minutes of checking in the kitchen later, Charlus said, "You should be good for milk until Thursday. I'll plan to come back then? And there are fresh towels out in the bath, all that."

"You're very thoughtful, thank you. And I'll take it easy tonight. I've a book." More to the point, once he'd had supper, he could reasonably retreat to bed and the book, and not have to move much for a bit. Charlus nodded, and then a minute later, he was making his farewells and out the door again. Griffin let out a long breath, because that could have been a great deal more difficult to deal with. And now he had the evening without any expectation of visitors. He could reasonably retire for the night once he'd had a little more food that wasn't cakes.

CHAPTER 20
MARCH 24TH

Annice was waiting nervously. She'd gone round to Griffin's cottage yesterday, both to check on him and to ask him a question. The conversation wasn't helping anything at all in her head. She'd done a lot of thinking, and she still couldn't make sense of half her thoughts. They just kept circling back to the north, like someone following a compass. Or someone out on the water, using the ruined Abbey as a landmark, visible a long way away.

They hadn't talked long yesterday. She'd been able to see he was still recovering. When she'd knocked, he'd been up in the kitchen. He'd been leaning on one crutch, heating up some soup and stirring with the other hand, so that seemed better than it might be. But he'd moved slowly, like everything took thought. Now, he would be here any minute, because she'd asked him to come here.

She kept peering out the window. Finally, there he was, coming up in the chair, with the two crutches tucked however he did that. They ran down behind the back of the seat. That was good because what she wanted to ask him almost certainly involved going upstairs. She hurried around to get the gate, ducking her chin and smiling, not managing more than a few words. "Thank you for coming." It wasn't much, but she felt like it was that or it would be a flood of babble.

Once he was in the front room of the shop, he looked up at her. "You wanted me to look at something? Upstairs, you said." He turned around, threading the crutches out of where they rested between the wheel and the chair, angled up to the back. They held for a moment, then came free, and she was distracted, watching them.

"How do you that? Keep them in place?" Annice gestured with a hand.

"Magic. Though if someone non-magical asks, it's magnets. You can do it with magnets, actually. We did some of the testing that way, but it's a lot more fiddly, and you have to line them up perfectly. And in my case, actual magnets interfere with some things in my day to day work. Otherwise it's a huge bother to have crutches with you and the chair. Some people make a sort of sling, but then it catches on things or bumps into people. This, they slot into that little holder at the bottom, to make sure they don't slip down, then another near the back. There are charms that will grab them and hold them in place."

That was a lot more information than she'd expected, as if a part of the conversation three days ago had unlocked something in him. "That's very clever." It was. She could think of many uses for that kind of sticking something in place. "And you're sure you're all right to come upstairs?"

"It's only two flights, after all. You have, what, twenty-four stairs? Not a hundred ninety-nine. And I know you'll not mind me taking my time." Griffin said it easily, but it hit Annice hard, like a blow to her stomach, knocking the wind out of her. It was true, of course, she wouldn't rush him. But he apparently trusted she wouldn't, and how could he do that?

"Of course not, no rush." She let out her breath. "Look, I said a little yesterday. That there was something I think my Da made, and I don't know enough about it. It's up on the second floor, in the workroom now. But I don't know if there are other things like it in the house. And I don't know what it does."

"So, shall we start in the workroom then? I assume there's somewhere I can sit, once we're there - a chair, a stool, a bench, I can make do with an old crate just fine."

"Stools." Annice ducked her head. "If you'd rather wait a little, rest, that's fine?"

He considered, touching a spot on the chair just above the wheel, then pushed himself upright, settling his arms into the crutches. "Show me, then?"

Griffin was slower than he had been, taking each step carefully, like he wasn't entirely sure what his feet were doing. That must be an odd sensation, not one Annice knew much about, except when she had pins and needles that went away in a few minutes, or perhaps bumped her funny bone and her hand felt queer, all down her arm. He had to stop at the top of the first flight, leaning gently against a wall. He stared at a spot on the floor, rather than any of the angles that would have shown him the kitchen or the nearest bedroom or anything else.

The next flight brought them up into the studio, and this time, she immediately went and pulled out one of the stools, setting it near the door where he could see everything. He said nothing for minutes, but he was looking around here intently, as if he were memorising it all, so he'd never lose it. It made Annice look at the workroom with new eyes, but she waited until he spoke.

"Would you tell me a little about the space? What the tools do?" Griffin's voice was quiet, the way someone ought to speak in church or in the cemetery, like it was something holy. Unexpectedly holy.

"Once, this would have been a proper workshop. More than a few people working, each one doing a specific task. Now, I do them all, just in sequence." It was how things lined up, so they'd flow. "This is the bench, to check the stones over, looking for flaws. Then you chisel the bigger pieces into the size you want to start, as a rough."

He nodded, and that gave her a little more confidence to go on. "The grindstone, here, where you get the piece into a rough shape. It's sandstone, and it can crack if you're not careful, and that's..." She shivered. "Grandad had stories about injuries. Magic helps that one. We can keep the shards from going everywhere."

Griffin glanced at her, his head tilted a little. "I'm clear that this is difficult, skilled work." His voice was still that odd quiet. "What's in those boxes, there?" He gestured at the shallow wood boxes next to the grindstone.

"Sawdust. You have the stones, and you've been using water with the grindstone. You put the pieces in the sawdust until they dry out a little. Ours have charms, again, to help that happen evenly, but sawdust still does most of the work." She should think about replacing the sawdust. Change of season always meant that. "Then the carver's bench. Everyone has their own kind of tools, a lot of us make our own." Annice swallowed hard, because she'd said 'us' out loud, and she normally hid that.

When she managed to look at Griffin, he was still smiling,

encouraging her along with a little wave of his hand. "The stove's for glue, or for making a new milling wheel. You melt lead, pour it in the mould, sharpen it with a file, and then add some carborundum powder. That's for the grooves and lines. I don't use that as much anymore. Most of my work is carving."

"So, you're saying that besides all the skills that go with the jet, you have to manage all these tools, making new milling wheels as you need them. Keep all of your tools in good shape." Annice had never heard someone put it that way, but who else was going to do it if she didn't? She nodded, hesitantly, and Griffin went on. "That's a skill in itself. Plenty of people don't have it. And that?"

"Rouge wheel." This one made her laugh. "Charms definitely help here, too. You heard, maybe, what they call jet workers?"

"Red devil, is that what you're aiming at? It seems a specific sort of term, doesn't it? But no one explained it." Griffin settled back a little on his stool, then moved to lean the crutches against the wall at the edge of his reach.

"There's a reason for that. That's for polishing, the rouge wheel."

"The name does in fact suddenly make sense, yes," Griffin considered. "Jeweller's rouge, of course. Isn't that, um." He looked up at the ceiling, as if searching his memory. "Ferrous, no, ferric oxide."

"That, and then linseed oil, some paraffin, some lamp black. You work it into the stone. But the oil and the paraffin are slick, and that sprays up from the wheel, mixes with the dust, which is that sort of dried blood brown, and then, well. We work with sharp tools. There's often a bit of our blood in there." She held up her own hands, looking at them in a way she didn't usually, all the little nicks and scars and minor injuries. A couple of fresh ones, still healing. Nan had been the one who made the best healing salve, and she'd long since run out of Nan's stock.

Griffin nodded. "There's a line of thinking about crafters that a piece isn't real until it's been blooded. Doesn't take much, but just a drop."

She blinked at him. "How do you know that? How'd you know about ferric oxide? Or any of the things you knew."

He spread out his hands. "You wouldn't believe me if I said that a Schola education can do wonders. Though actually, that is part of it. We don't turn out as many pure crafters as Alethorpe does. Who could?" That had an amusing, teasing note to it, like it was a joke that had run through part of his life. "But the houses, at Schola, we have different things we focus on. I was in Salmon, people who want to be excellent at lots of skills. One of the way to do that is crafting. We had workshops - nothing specifically like this. But a woodworking shop, a little bit of carving, certainly sewing and leather. Some people got very interested in little devices that did things. You picked up a lot, just talking to people. But this is ..."

He nodded, looking around the room, pivoting on the stool to see all of it. "This is elegant. This is a dance. Of course what you make is beautiful. You've set it up so that beauty is the natural result."

Annice felt her jaw drop. She had no idea what to do with that. Again.

Before the silence went on too long, Griffin asked, "What was it you wanted to show me?"

"That worktable, here, with the good light. Can you just move around a little? I'll go get it." Griffin nodded, and she heard the scrape of the stool as she dug the box out of the cabinet down the hall. At least she could do that. When she came back, he was leaning one elbow on the top, looking down that side of the workshop. "Here." She brought the box over, then went to bring over another stool. It put her next to him, a few inches between them, but she could suddenly feel him present in a way he hadn't been before. "I found this. I don't know what it is, or what it does. Rob and Cliff just said it was some sort of talisman."

Then, before she could stall further, it came out in a rush. "Can you help me figure out what this is? If there are others, there are notes. If you can, I'll come look at your, your Trellech, your courtroom." Even though that terrified her, being in the city and people expecting her to know things. Though then she saw him smile, suddenly, at something she'd said, and she had no idea why. "And I'll help you source the jet, at the least, or advise or..."

When she came to a sudden stop, the silence felt so loud. Griffin took a breath. He kept taking his time. But he shifted on the stool, turning to look at her better. "I'd help you without that. You don't have to trade for it. But I would very much like to show you my Trellech, and my courtroom. And whatever you can suggest, I am sure we will be better off for it." He nodded at the stone. "May I touch it? Hold it?"

"Sure? I don't know if that's a problem. I don't know anything about it. It was in that box, at the bottom of a pile of other things, dusty like no one had touched it for years." Annice crossed her arms. Then that felt awkward, so she put her hands in her lap.

Griffin glanced at her, and then he was focusing on the stone, with a sudden intensity that was compelling. He took a moment, just looking at it, then rummaged for a notebook inside his jacket pocket, and a pencil. Then he pulled the stone closer, looking at it, first overall, then focusing on different parts.

It should have been boring, even though she very much wanted to know more about it. It certainly took quite a while. She could see the light shifting, as the sun moved from morning into noon. Then Griffin spoke, still quiet, so it didn't startle her. "It's a talisman, obviously. I'd have to do some research on some of it, or if you're willing, consult with an expert. But I can tell you about some of it."

"Yes?" Annice's voice cracked. "Is it - is it a bad thing?"

"Oh, no." His voice was instantly warmer. "I'm sorry. I should have said that right off. It's for protection, designed for your family. Um. Your specific part of it, your grandad and nan, and da and mam." He used her names for them, like little precise drops of rain falling and then smoothing together to dampen the jet and make it glossy black. "Will you let me guide your hand? I can show you some of it best by touch. You especially, I expect."

Annice swallowed hard. Then, cautiously, she held out her right hand, shifting her stool so the angle was better. His fingers brushed hers, his thumb curling around into place behind hers. His skin was warm, dry, not at all rough like Da's hands had always been, or Grandad's, or her own. "Here. Your index finger, mostly. Do you feel that shape?"

Da and Grandad had taught her like this, back long ago, what the feel of it was like, and it was easy to fall back into that again. "Those lines?"

"Just so, like a compass rose, only it's more in some directions than others? It's marking a particular location, I think. I know a locational magic specialist I can ask, or at least she'll know who would know. And this, here, those are symbols. Blessing here." She felt half a dozen different shapes. "And then it arcs into protection, but not, um." He was close enough she could hear him swallow, the faint puff of warmth from his breath. "Not protection from evil, exactly? But protection from jealousy, from greed, from small heartedness."

Annice let her fingers run across it, thinking about that. "Everyone loved Grandad. And Da, even though he wasn't from here. Do you think they - they were worried they might be small hearted?"

"That's one of the things that would take more research. I can make sense of most of the actual working symbols here, more or less, but the context, what it means that it's in jet, that's a whole other layer. The way they're laid out, if they were copying something, or came up with it themselves. But I think it's lovely. It's like a necklace. It brings different pieces together for an effect by the whole." His fingers moved hers up. "These are, I don't know. Things that are blessings, but about other things. Hope, love, comfort, company. Goodness. A lot of it - there we are. That's one of the symbols for home." She could feel it, under her hands, a crossed circle. "Also earth." Griffin added that. "But I think here it's the physical, homey things."

"Oh." She didn't want to pull her hand away, and he didn't remove it, so there her fingers were, just resting on the stone. "Did it, did it run out of magic? Before Da..." She couldn't say the rest of it.

"I'm not sure. There would be, um. Innate energy in the stone. Maybe quite a lot, because of how jet is. Maybe they didn't know how to renew it, or someone didn't, for good reason." Things had changed after her uncles had drowned. Annice wondered if maybe one of them - more likely Da - had worried that they'd used magic in a way that people ought not to. "And you thought there might be others."

Reluctantly, she pulled back her fingers, because she

had to find the notes. "Here. There are sketches, but they're not all the same symbols."

"Can I make a copy of these?" Griffin paused. "I need to go back to Trellech for a meeting tomorrow. Charlus is coming out to meet me, to make sure the travel all goes smoothly. I should be back in the evening, or if not, Saturday morning."

"You're not, um." The world Annice lived in, that kind of getting called in somewhere usually meant trouble. "Is there a problem?"

"The head of the Courts, more or less my boss, wants to talk to me. On a Friday afternoon when most people won't be around." Griffin shrugged. "There are likely politics in play." Then he turned his head. "I will come back, though. I won't leave you hanging."

Again, she felt like she couldn't quite breathe. "Why? I'm not anyone."

Before she could figure out what was going on, his fingers were on hers again, though this time his left hand, palm to palm. "You're interesting. You make beautiful pieces, you ask excellent questions, you notice entirely different things than I do. And, perhaps just as important, you don't fuss about my chair or my crutches or any of it. That's rather rare. I hope..." He paused, as if he were weighing something rapidly in the moment. "Whatever I can help you with about these stones, I want to. And I hope that after that, we'll still be in touch. Whatever that looks like."

Annice blinked at him. "You have other people." He must. He was posh, he had a fancy job, he kept talking about people he knew. There was a whole entire Charlus. She'd heard them talking and getting on.

"Never as many friends as I'd like." Griffin met her eyes,

then, and she absolutely couldn't make sense of his expression, except that it was like a stone, waiting to be carved. There was strength in there, and a plane on which it might cleave, and others where it might shatter, and she had no idea which she was seeing right now.

"Oh." She took a breath and let it out. He didn't hurry her, of course he didn't hurry her. He was just sitting there, not moving, not twitching. "You're very confusing. Often. But you don't laugh at me. You don't make me feel stupid, all the things I don't know." Then she added, "I don't have so many people wanting to talk to me I should turn any down."

It made him smile, somehow. "Plenty of people can't see what's right in front of them. I try not to do that. I enjoy your company, the way you see things."

There was no possible sensible answer to that, so she just nodded. "And, um. The stones?"

"The stones." His tone shifted, though he kept his hand where he was for a moment. "I'd like to make copies of the sketches - I have paper in my bag downstairs. I can do that with a charm, if you're willing. We can try some charms - they need a bit of preparation. Especially for me being able to go where that might take us. But there are some options I can check on. Can you tell me all the places your Grandad spent time? Or your Da? I'm assuming you've checked all the places in this house, attics and cabinets and whatever's in your cellar?"

"Several times now." But the questions settled her a bit. She talked a little about the houses - her bedroom, the little one. Grandad and Nan's, and Mam and Da's. The kitchen and sitting room were next to them, on the first floor, and where the storage cupboards were. "Grandad had a fishing shack. I haven't been in there. And there are maybe a couple of other places, but I don't know."

"You think about that and make a list. No matter how unreasonable it seems. I think it must have been a place - places, if there are two - he had access to, and that he was confident wouldn't be disturbed. So not the apothecary shop or something like that."

"I'll think about it." They talked through the options for a bit longer until it was well past noon.

Finally, Griffin extracted his hand. "I have some other work to do - a few notes to write, if I want to do some research for you tomorrow, for one thing. And you must want to open up the shop, yes?"

She did. And she didn't. She wanted to stay here all afternoon, in the workshop she loved, with the sunlight pouring in the window and making everything glow, even the dust. And that was a luxury she couldn't have. "You're right. You often are."

It made him grin, and that was something, as he gathered up the crutches and made his way cautiously down the steep stairs. Down in the shop, he made the copies efficiently. Then she was letting him out the back door, through the gate, and staring off after him, entirely unsure what had just happened.

CHAPTER 21

MARCH 25TH IN TRELLECH'S HALLS OF JUSTICE

Precisely at four, Griffin knocked on Lamont's office. He'd taken the last half hour to spruce himself up and make sure all his notes were in order. The proposal was at the top of his portfolio, and that was tucked neatly against the arm of the chair. He'd left the crutches in his office with Charlus, who was working on copies of a few things Griffin hoped he'd continue to need. After the meeting, however long or short it was, Charlus had offered to take him back to the portal. That meant he didn't have to send his case with a change of clothes and a refill on his potions and pills on ahead.

Now, Griffin put on his best professional cheerful face, and at the acknowledgement from inside, opened the door and wheeled himself in. Lamont - or one of his clerks - had thoughtfully removed the chair on this side of Lamont's desk, pulling it to the side. Griffin rarely met with Lamont here. It was far more often in a group in one of the meeting rooms. He couldn't decide what he thought of it now. Or, as he'd said yesterday, what to make of the fact this was at four on a Friday. The building was rapidly emptying of the few people there over the spring recess period.

Lamont himself looked relaxed and dapper. He was in his usual dark suit and gemstone bow tie - today's was a golden amber, with a pocket square to match. Griffin knew he was in his later sixties, and he might be ten years or so from retirement. He'd become Lord of Trellech's Justice rather young, after a short time as Heir, right around when he turned forty. Griffin hadn't started working in the Courts, and Lamont had been well established as Lord when he'd begun his apprenticeship in the autumn of 1901.

History had it he'd named his Heir promptly, back then. But one had died - a regrettable illness, something with his heart. And the other under consideration had declined a few years later. Instead, Lamont had named three potential Heirs before the War, but then had refused to choose between them. There was no use treading that ground again, not right now. Griffin instead pulled his focus to the office, to what had changed since the last time he'd seen it.

The office itself was pleasant. It was, of course, nearly twice the size of Griffin's. There was an adjoining door to the Heir's office and another to the clerk's. The Heir's office was currently empty, as it had been for fourteen years. It was well lit, with a brightness that was glowing rather than brash and artificial. White walls hinted at an ancient temple, but with splashes of jewel-toned colours breaking up the white.

They had a multitude of forms; an art print, an orrery, the very books on the shelves that lined the sides of the room. But they were also matched to each other rather than haphazard. The desk itself was stained dark. It had a strip of beautifully resonant birch wood inlaid along the edge, a reminder of the chair Lamont held as Lord and Head of the Courts.

"Good afternoon, sir. I hope you had a pleasant and blessed equinox?" Lamont kept those rites, and keeping track of who did was something Griffin paid particular attention to.

"Quite restorative, thank you, and an excellent time besides." Lamont nodded as Griffin set his brake so the chair would stay stable. "I appreciate you coming down here this afternoon. I wanted to ask you a bit more about your current project, with fewer people wanting to over-hear." He lifted two fingers. "I should say, before anything else, that you are not in trouble. And I do not expect anything you say today will make me recall you if you think there is more to do."

Griffin let out a breath, trying not to make it too obvi-ous. "I appreciate that, sir." He pulled the portfolio out from one side, then the foldaway table surface. "Where would you like to begin?" The last part was the fountain pen, in case of notes.

"Tell me what you've been doing, would you?" It was certainly a reasonable place to start, and one Griffin had prepared for.

He laid out what he had done so far, passed across the list of what he'd done, who he'd talked to. "Mistress Matthewman has agreed to come and have a look. I'm hoping to make the arrangements for late next week. She has some business to attend to in Whitby first."

Lamont listened attentively. It was, Griffin had long thought, one of his particular gifts. He focused on what was in front of him, but also on how it intersected with all the other things going on. He asked excellent questions, and he thought about the consequences. When Griffin finished laying out everything so far, Lamont nodded. "Very thorough. And if, as you say, Mistress Matthewman is the best choice to bring here, I am glad to approve it. The usual room and expenses. You're competent at doing the forms without six reminders."

Griffin had to smile at that. "Sir." Then he cleared his throat. "You could have asked for this by letter. I'm assuming there's some other reason you wanted to speak."

It earned Griffin a small chuckle. "Of course. I didn't expect that point to slip by you." Lamont considered, resting his fingers on the broad polished wood of the desk. "I was pleased to see you extending yourself on this question. You know there continue to be concerns about your ability to do the work."

Griffin nodded once. It was not a comment that needed a reply.

"I am well aware that I really do need to pick between you, Harriet, and Nestor. And I am under some pressure to do so sooner than later. Or some other Heir, but we all know it will be one of you three." Lamont weighed his words here. "None of you is a simple choice. Nestor, as Fir Primus, would make the administration of the courts run smoothly and precisely, like clockwork."

Griffin certainly knew better than to comment on his colleagues here, especially Nestor. Or his competition, even though he knew it wasn't exactly a competition in the usual way. "And he already oversees three courtrooms to my one." Might as well put it out there himself, seeing as it was the truth.

Lamont raised one finger from the desk. "And Harriet has an eye for the larger view, as Apple Primus. And she is more at home with the ritual magics in some ways than either you or Nestor. Though you needn't bristle, your skills are also refined and solid."

To have that spotted, his reaction, stung a little, but Lamont was as observant as the rest of them. More so, given the amount of practice and high level of politics he swam in on the regular.

"And both of them have something of an advantage of birth over you. Coming from those sorts of families." Griffin's folk were Fourth Families, not part of the Great Families of Albion. People like him had been named Heir before, more than a few times, but it was starting from behind, even if Griffin had gone to Schola.

"I imagine it's a difficult scale to balance, sir," Griffin said, after a moment. "A tradesman's negotiation, this thing for that, based on dozens of factors."

Lamont chuckled again. Whatever else this conversation was, he wasn't strained about it. "Exactly. And I have been weighing those. My concerns about you have not been about your health per se. They have, however, been about the consequences of your health. Since you returned to us, you have sometimes been more cautious than even a man of probity, a solicitor, might normally be. Some have wondered, to me, if you could or would act when needed." Lamont laid it out, deliberately, and now he was watching Griffin carefully.

The thing of it was that Griffin couldn't argue with that, not exactly. He was more cautious now, in dozens of ways every day, because getting something wrong, especially exertion, had a ripple effect for hours or days. He thought that overall, this made him better, long-term, because he thought through the consequences before leaping. But Griffin also couldn't argue with the statement, nor how it was true for him in particular. Now he took a breath and let it out. "That's a fair enough concern, sir."

"Seeing how you have gone about this particular problem, I am no longer so worried. You have been mindful of resources, your own and other people's. You have not rushed a decision or your actions. But you have also pressed when pressing was needed. You have made solid progress given the lack of ideal experts. And you have done so away from home and your usual habits and routines and resources. Being Heir - or Lord - rarely involves leaving Trellech. But it is necessary at times beyond the Council rites or various social gatherings. Demonstrating you can be as effective in Whitby as here in the Halls of Justice has some weight."

That put a somewhat different twist on it than Griffin had been thinking. Enough of one that he was honest now, bringing part of it out in the open. "I assumed, sir, that more than one person thought I'd fail - that the hills or the stairs would make me take a tumble in pride, if not physically."

"Oh, that's also true." Lamont's smile was rather different now, someone waiting for someone else to step into a trap. Not Griffin, Griffin was fairly sure of that. Mostly. "I would, therefore, ask you to continue in your plans, in the way you see best. I will continue to ask you for explanations, as well as the written reports, but I am giving you your head. Make of it what you will."

That put the whole thing in the proper context. Lamont had not created this challenge, but he would use it to refine his own plans. He could have taken this back from Griffin, and instead he was letting Griffin do it his way. It was up to Griffin to make the most of it. Griffin considered, making a couple of notes of things to prioritise, given that remit.

"And the others? If there is opposition? I'm presuming you'd prefer me to handle it through the usual methods, and to let you know if that does not serve."

"Oh, let me know either way, but yes, just so." He glanced at Griffin's notes. "Anything else, then?"

"May I draw on the resources of the Courts? Mistress Matthewman has noted that she doesn't have training, but we suspect there's some talismanic work at play, or that might be helpful. Someone with a focus on stones, gemstones of any kind, by preference. I know someone, but she's a master of her art, and her fees match her skill."

"Oh, I believe we can do something about that, yes. A moment." He touched the bell on his desk. It didn't ring in the office, but thirty seconds later, Griffin felt a shift in the warding of the space, and the door from the clerk's office opened. "Sir?"

"Would you pull the contacts and standing profiles of the talisman workers we contract with, particularly anyone with a focus on gemstones? General pieces, not necessarily the courtroom settings, yes?" He added to Griffin, "Anyone on the list has my approval, usual rates. You had someone in mind, then?"

"Niobe Hall, sir, and I know she's on your list, but I'd like options if she's not available." Griffin replied promptly. "I think taking a step back and looking at other approaches might be beneficial."

There was a brief exchange, more gesture than sound, from Lamont to the clerk, and she disappeared. Griffin knew that would be ready before he left the building. Some messenger would be rounded up to bring it to his office. Once the door closed again, and the warding came back with it, Lamont considered. "I have not asked you, directly, what you want out of things here. Not for some years."

"My answer has not changed much, sir." Griffin wasn't entirely sure why he was bringing this up now. But this was a more direct conversation about who should be Heir than Lamont had had with anyone in a good while. Or so Griffin was fairly sure, because he suspected Nestor wouldn't have hid smugness at it, if he'd been in a similar one. "I love Trellech. I always have. And I find myself drawn in so many ways to the Courts. To the work of the courts, the ideal of justice and fairness and improving things for people who have need of that, properly. But also to the..." Now he ran out of any eloquence. "The shape of them. The spaces we make here, what that makes possible."

"And Trellech? This is the first time you've been away for a while, hasn't it?" Lamont leaned forward now.

"A few days, three times now, with my parents, up in Cambridgeshire. But no, not this long since the War." Griffin thought about how it had felt, coming back through the portal. "Whitby is a beautiful town, with a lot to commend it, and also a lot of struggles. But coming back this morning, I was home and glad to be. And I will be glad to be back when my work in Whitby is done." He let himself shrug. "It is unfashionable to love Trellech for herself, all her odd alleys and corners and ageing streets, but I do."

Lamont leaned back. "I appreciate your answer, and the truth of it. But of course, I know your standards there, and you do not let them slip." That was a particular bit of praise. And Lamont, of anyone, would indeed understand that.

Griffin let himself smile. "Of course, sir. Nothing but, here and now."

"That was the last for the moment, and I'm sure you want to get back to Whitby before it gets too far into the evening. Can you wait for the profiles? I'll also send down a few notes to go with you. It might be an hour?"

"Charlus made us a portal reservation for half-seven, after the evening crush." Griffin said. "I was planning on being in my office until then, no point in going home so briefly."

"Excellent. We'll have that for you as promptly as possible. Let me know if there's anything else that would assist in your project. The notes will include an expanded budget you can spend to, without additional approvals." That was going to be excellent. Griffin had been as careful as any shopkeeper's son should be about expenses, but having more to work with would be a help with additional experts. "A good evening, then."

"And to you, sir." Griffin nodded, waited for a return nod, and then smoothly released the brake. He backed up a little, and turned tightly to wheel himself to the door and open it.

CHAPTER 22
MARCH 26TH IN WHITBY

As arranged, Annice turned up at Griffin's cottage to find Charlus there, finishing up packing a day bag. He was wearing older clothes - so was Griffin, actually, and sturdy boots. Griffin waved a hand from the sofa. "If you don't mind, Charlus thought he'd at least come down with us. If we don't want him on the beach, he can lurk in the pub and be handy in case we need to find another carter."

"Oh, no worries about the carter," Annice said. "So long as he gets paid. It's a friend of one of my cousins. I know his Mam well enough, and she put the fear of everything into him."

"About leaving a cripple?" Griffin said it almost lightly, but there was a sharpness there.

"No. About giving up the coin for the return trip." Annice knew Mrs Gerold would have none of that, not in her household. "He said he'd meet us at the pub. He's got some other deliveries round those parts for the day." Now she watched Griffin relax a little. That had been the right sort of answer. "And Charlus can come with us if you want."

"It's your call, it's your information, your grandad, and all," Griffin countered, and she saw how he must bargain when he actually did. He hadn't with her, that was one thing that unsettled her. She was used to the customers, the tourists, not bargaining, but people in town did with each other all the time. She wondered what it would take for him to bargain with her, to treat her like an equal in that.

She shrugged, leaving the question for the moment. She could decide when they got through the portal to the pub. "Let me check what you've packed, all right? And how was your day in Trellech?" She asked the second part more out of politeness than anything.

Charlus opened up the bag he'd been packing. He had a wool cloak, two flasks, probably with tea, and a couple of pasties, though not with any shape or baker's mark from around these parts. She nodded. "That'll do. And a healing kit? Scrapes and bumps and whatever." She didn't say - she didn't know how to ask - if Griffin needed anything specific.

It was then he spoke up behind her. "The conversation with Lamont was interesting, but he's given me my head in solving this. And a larger budget to apply to the problem, which is an additional sign of trust."

Charlus snorted. "Not that you spend for work without everything documented in triplicate."

"I beg your pardon, I make five proper copies, like anyone sensible ought." Griffin's sounded mock-insulted. Then he was almost laughing as he added, "Annice, there's one clerk who no one has the heart to fire, but certain receipts and forms end up on her desk, and they don't move until quarter end. The sensible among us send one copy to her, and one copy to the next step, and eventually they get clipped together."

She turned around. "That seems very practical. And she doesn't get in trouble?"

Griffin shrugged, but now she could see him. He seemed in a more relaxed mood in general. "She's very good at other parts of her work. And it's a large system. Sometimes you put up with a snag like that to keep the whole thing going. Do you have everything to be comfortable? If it gets chilly, I'm decent at warming charms."

"We're back to me wondering if there are any magic things you can't do, at least a bit?" Annice asked.

It made him laugh. "I was never much of a duellist, and I'm less of one now. Though I got better at some of the protective and martial magics in the War. Seeing as how they were rather immediately of interest." His voice went a little hollow at the end, before he picked up again. "I am in something of a mood. I apologise in advance. If I tease in ways you don't like, tell me and I'll aim it all at Charlus."

Charlus glanced back, then shrugged. He seemed used to this problem, at least, so it wasn't something new and strange to him. "I'm here to fetch and carry. But we're ready when you are. Tea before you go, or no?"

"No, I'm fine." She considered. She had on her own sturdy boots, a basket for the jet, lined in cloth so no small bits would fall out or get lost, and a warm jacket. "We can go to the portal here whenever you like. Coming back, it's a drink in the pub first, but I suspect you've got the right sort of coin for that."

"We do. Both of us, in case Charlus needs to go do something. And I've got your fee for today, if you want it now, or later." Griffin hesitated, then added, "And I'd like to arrange for when you come to Trellech. Later in the week, if today goes well, perhaps starting going down Thursday?"

Annice was nervous about it - still, again, both words applied - but she had said she would. "If that makes sense. Stay overnight. Come back Friday?"

"Something like that. Or rather, we'll make those arrangements, and if something else suits, there's no difficulty with the inn." Griffin shrugged, and then he pushed up from the sofa. He got his hands into the forearm crutches, considering for a moment, and checking the balance. There was something a little different about the bottom, a bigger base. He caught her looking. "Different tips. Better on rough ground, and also a little easier on my hands, more cushioning. Same on the grips." He opened one hand to show that there was something around the grip now that looked like cloth, but apparently had charms or something of the kind doing the work. "Charlus, the door?"

Charlus obligingly opened the door, letting Annice go out, then Griffin behind her, then locking up. They made an agreeable enough procession down to the back pub that had the portal here, down a little ghault with just a few buildings. They knew this one, of course, but let Annice open it to the other portal. There were three default settings, for Robin Hood's Bay, for Trellech, and for York itself, as the nearest big city. Anything else people had to know how to set themselves, or get Harry, the pub keep, to set for them. He had a little book tucked away for it.

She went first, mostly to make sure the space was clear around the other end. No one was in the back room, thankfully, and she took a step or two back. Griffin came first, then Charlus, looking around. A rather weatherbeaten pub wasn't his usual setting. She was pretty sure of that, even without the posh way he spoke and moved.

Once they were out in the main room, she immediately spotted her target. "Bobs!" She called it out, pitching to carry over the usual Saturday morning chatter. Bobs looked up. He was too young to have been in the War, but he'd picked up as a carter in the last years of it, doing his bit to keep his Mam and brothers fed and a roof over their head. She jerked her chin to show he should come out, and he promptly drained his beer. He'd been quick about it; the pub had only been open a quarter hour. Once they were out in the courtyard - where the donkey and cart were amiably waiting - she nodded. "Mister Pelson, Mister Edwards, this is Bobs Matson, who'll take us the rest of the way down." It was all formality, because that was the right show here.

Charlus helped Griffin up into the cart, and then they bumped along, sitting on benches on either side, with Annice craning her neck as the road turned. They moved from where she could see through to the ocean. Then they wound on a steep descent around through the village, before the sudden turn at the end that brought them right to the beach level. She heard Griffin gasp and then chuckle. Annice glanced at him.

"I said to someone yesterday that Whitby had a number of charms and surprises. And this is one more." He waved a hand. "That's delightful. But I would not want to walk it, no. Bobs, when do we expect you back?"

Annice cut in. "We have two choices there. The pub closes at three, and low tide's at two. So either around two, or we wait until half-five to go through. We want to be heading off the beach by five at the latest."

Griffin went quiet for a couple of breaths. "I ought to say two. But half-five sounds better. Meet us here at, mmm.

Half-four? Is that enough time to get back up without straining the donkey?"

"Aye." Bobs was never one for much conversation, though he looked to Annice for confirmation. She supposed they could find a rock to sit on, off the beach, and it didn't look much like a storm was going to change the tides. She nodded, and he confirmed, "Half-four."

"Excellent." Griffin dropped a couple of coins into Charlus's hand. Charlus went around to give them to Bobs. The carter, predictably, tested them in his teeth and looked pleased, then tapped the donkey with the whip softly to get her to walk off.

Charlus asked once he was gone. "Should we be offended? The coin?"

"No." Griffin's voice was firm. "He was testing to make sure it wasn't lead. Or illusion. It's fair. Someone cheated him in the past, Annice?"

"More than one." Annice had heard a few of the stories. "He'll pick up some work along here for the day, and five's giving him more time. Why did you say you should go for two?"

Griffin nodded down at his own feet. "Yesterday had all the travel. I'd be more sensible to stay put today, not go out on the beach, but this is important. And also, I want to. And I am sometimes a small insistent child inside my head, screaming at the top of my lungs that Griffin can do it." He pitched the last very much like some of her younger cousins, and Annice had to laugh at it. She liked that he said that sort of thing, even when it was confusing, because most people wouldn't.

Charlus was considering this, then asked softly. "Another lesson, sir?"

"Oh, that one's at least three." Griffin shrugged. "Anyway, I'm assuming there's somewhere we can sit, or maybe even somewhere we could sit and get food down here, possibly."

"Pub." Annice said. "There's a pub. There's always a pub. Can't get drinks, off-hour, but the one down here will do sandwiches and tea in the snug in the afternoon."

Griffin snorted. "See? There we go. Now, do you want Charlus to stay or go amuse himself elsewhere?"

"You're welcome to come. And we might want someone to go ahead and test the sand some places." She took a breath. "The beach huts, first. I have Grandad's key."

CHAPTER 23
LATER THAT MORNING

Griffin let Annice go first for at least five reasons he could think of off-hand. First, and most important, she actually knew where they were going, and he didn't. Second, he was doing better than he'd been afraid of, after the travel and conversations and research yesterday, but he was not going to push himself more than actually necessary today. Even if rather a lot of it was likely going to be necessary. Third, he was thinking a lot about what Lamont had said. Griffin had been gnawing on it all last night, about being over-cautious. Fourth, having Annice go first gave him a look at the way the ground changed, and that much more information about how to manage. And fifth, well. He enjoyed watching her.

That was another thing that had kept him up last night. He had friends. She had been right about that. He had colleagues whose company he enjoyed, and he was very much looking forward to more conversations as a peer with Charlus when his apprenticeship was done. But he'd been right when he said he could always use more. Or closer. Both.

Lamont's comment, however, had brought it sharply home that he had fenced around the idea of anything like a partner, a romance, even a momentary fling. Not that the fling was likely, given that he refused to court pity. Of course, most people he met now were because of his work, which was fine for a friendship but more complicated for anything else. Certain kinds of overtures weren't appropriate in that setting. They were a kind of bending of authority that turned everything in his magic bitter, an aversion he had no desire to change.

The thing was, he wasn't entirely sure if he were interested in Annice herself, the ways someone properly should be for a romance. It might just be that she was someone new, unlike other people he knew. It had been so long since he'd even let himself consider the question, he was entirely out of practice with it. And to be fair, he had put a good face on the dear John letter during the War, and he honestly wished Madeline well. But it had also hurt, and he was not at all eager for anything like that again. He'd had too much of the hurting and confusion already for one lifetime.

Watching Annice, though, from behind, he kept being drawn to her. They were aiming at a handful of small huts squished in against the rise of the cliff, that looked like an unusually bad storm at high tide would sweep them away. Griffin found himself watching her rather than the brightly painted huts against the cliff that rose sharply up behind them. Her dress was the same muted grey, echoing the greys and black and browns of the beach, but somehow she drew the eye, even without being able to see her face.

Suddenly - enough he nearly overbalanced when he stopped - she turned to a hut down near the end. "This one." There was a bit of fumbling with the key, a creak of a lock that needed a touch of oil, and then the door came open. The hut itself wasn't fancy - a set of cupboards and a workbench along the back, a cot along one side. It had been built in, it looked like, not a creaking camp cot. It was chilly, of course, but with a warming charm, it wouldn't be unpleasant for a night, or at least a nap. There was an old battered wood chair, facing the cot on the other wall, with several crates full of smaller containers beside it.

It wasn't large, which meant there were only so many places that might need to be searched. Griffin counted them out; cupboards across the top of the bench, the ones below, if there were any spaces under the cot or in the crates. Just possibly something in a loose floorboard or a ceiling panel or some such. Griffin cleared his throat. "Do you see anything out of place, or unfamiliar?"

"It looks just like it has." Annice turned, considering. "There's a lantern, and I brought a candle. We do sometimes get people coming this far down the beach." Which meant no magic, not where someone might catch a glimpse of it. It also limited what charmwork Griffin might reasonably do. He nodded. "Is it all right if I sit?" He nodded at the cot and chair.

"Oh, yes. Either. Do you have any idea where to start?" Annice waited a moment, and once Griffin took the cot, she sat in the chair, leaving Charlus to lean against the wall.

"We want to be systematic, I think. And also not fall over each other in the process. Though I think we might solve that by you and Charlus checking various locations and handing me anything that isn't obviously fit for some other purpose?"

"A lot of it is fishing bits and bobs. Do you know about fishing?" Annice was entirely dubious, and that wasn't unreasonable.

"Enough to know when something isn't one. Or to set it

aside and let you look too. Though I admit my fishing experience is rivers, not ocean." He gestured at the back cabinets. "I'm going to suggest starting at the left there, working your way across the top, then the bottom, then the crates. I'm thinking about if there might be something under the cot, or hidden by a floorboard, and the best way to discover without more chaos than necessary."

Annice's expression shifted several times in that, though all she said at the end was, "Thank you." It must be difficult, being here, with people who were still strangers. A moment later, she stood up, then went over to the cupboards, and a moment later, Charlus joined her.

They worked along, about halfway through the top, before he asked a question Griffin had also been wondering. "Pardon, but do you know why there's a portal in an inn?" He kept his voice quiet, but they had the doors open and Griffin was keeping an eye out. Also, he'd added a charm for privacy. People might still look in, but a conversational voice shouldn't carry past the door.

Annice snorted. "Smuggling." She seemed like she was going to leave it there for a moment, but then she went right on. "That's the older one, here. The one in Whitby's younger. There's lore about an even older one, up past the Abbey, but not for centuries, I guess. Anyway. The portal was first. They built the inn around it. Didn't know it was odd?"

"There are a couple I know of in buildings, but mostly courtyards, with some sun and wind and rain." Griffin said. "The banks share one, the Guard has one, both private. But I think those were built up around, too. The roof is the odd thing." He added. "Talk freely, so long as it's this sort of volume."

Annice blinked at him once, then nodded. "Real handy

to be able to pass things up to Whitby, ahead of the customs men. Not quite as much anymore." She added the last bit hurriedly.

"First, that's not why I'm here. Second, it'd be a matter for the Guard, and they mostly care more about whether people might get hurt." Griffin shrugged. "Thus, so long as no one makes me pay attention to it, we're fine."

"Good." Annice turned back to the cabinets, running her hands along the shelf, handing a stack of smaller objects back, and getting on with it. Two hours later, the two of them had worked through all the obvious locations, and Griffin had handed out tea and pasties. Annice looked a little defeated now.

"Do you have a piece of jet on you? Or could you find one easily enough on the beach? It doesn't need to be big, it just needs to be only jet, or maybe jet and metal."

Annice frowned. "Why?" It was a clear question, and he liked how she asked it without hesitation now.

"I can do a trick to find the closest thing that's the same material. I didn't want to try it until we'd checked the obvious places, because, well, there could have been jet here."

Annice sucked her lip between her teeth. "Let me go have a look." She considered. "You want to come see how it's done?"

It was not cautious, it probably was not sensible, but Griffin nodded. "Please." He added to Charlus, "You can stay here, take a breather. I've been sitting this whole time." A moment later, Griffin was standing, and Annice led him out onto the beach, then further down, past the end of the huts.

She was looking down, scanning the ground. "We're

looking for something black and shining with the water, but most of what you think is jet is probably going to be coal. Or maybe bits of tar, but you're observant. You can probably spot that one fast." It was a particular compliment, and Griffin smiled at it. He was following along a step or two behind her, so he could also see how the pebbles shifted as she walked. Then his eyes caught on a patch of seaweed and other washed up muck, but there was a dark gleam.

"Over there, to the right?" Griffin kept his voice even. "Do they look so much alike, then?"

Before she answered, there was a little cry of delight from her, something utterly joyous. She had taken two or three broad steps over to where he'd indicated. She came up with three things in her hands, juggling them into her left while her right thrust down into her pocket. "Here. Let me show you. Can you come ..." Then she took a couple of steps toward him, almost colliding. She looked at his face, her eyes wide, then back down at her hands. One now had an unglazed piece of white porcelain.

"Here. Um. Your hands. Can you get one free, without a bother?" Educationally speaking, he probably ought to suggest they go back to the hut, so Charlus could hear it, and he didn't want to. Instead, he shifted a bit, propping the left crutch to make a better tripod and getting his arm out of the right, holding out his hand. "Feel each one first, all right? Whatever you feel."

She put each stone in his palm, one by one, for long enough he suspected she was counting the seconds. Once she'd gone through once, he asked, "Can I feel the second one again?"

There was a laugh, something he'd said pleased her,

then there it was again. He let out a huff of breath. "I think that's the jet, but I'm not sure?" He thought it was some glimmer of the magical reactions, that it reacted more like materia than the other two. She left it in her palm, making marks on the porcelain with the first one - a black streak - and then the third, which left a pale white scrape. He held his hand steady, for her to take the last piece, and that left a surprisingly pale mark, almost golden.

"The black one is sea coal. The pale one is slate. And the gold, here, or it's much more often brown, that's jet. How could you tell?" Annice was looking up at him again now, searchingly, like the answer mattered.

"It felt more alive." It was the kind of thing he rarely talked about, not with people who weren't materia specialists. Though, to be fair, Annice was in fact a materia specialist, just in a single kind of materia. "Lighter, too. Is that normal?"

Annice dropped the jet in his hand again. "Very. It's one of the best ways to tell when everything's wet, other than the porcelain. Anyway. We have your jet. Shall we go back?"

He didn't want to break away. There was something about this moment on the beach where he felt free in a way he hadn't since before the War. Maybe it was the wide horizon that made things feel more possible, or differently possible. But they had work to do, he had promises to keep. "Please. I can show you what I wanted to try."

They went back across the beach as slowly as they'd come, but it was as much because Annice was searching for more pieces of jet as anything else. She found two other pieces, then demonstrated again to Charlus while Griffin got his kit out of his bag. He didn't carry a full set of working stones like some people did - some of the Guard, all the Penelopes, anyone doing certain kinds of investigation. But he carried a few things, and more importantly, the little neutral cage to hold an item that he could suspend from a bit of silk yarn.

Once he had it set, he cleared his throat. "If I could have the jet? We're going to see if I can shape a resonance between this and things like it in the essential ways. It should pull toward the nearest source. That might be beneath the floor, mind. Or the next hut over or something."

Annice folded her arms, but she didn't ask him questions or say anything at all. Griffin got the jet into the little horn cage, then made sure it was hanging still from his hand before reciting the incantation he used for this. He kept his voice low, but he could see how Annice leaned in a little to hear better. Slowly, the horn sphere started pulling the end of the string toward the cot. Griffin took a breath, then carefully leaned the crutches against the wall, taking the couple of steps to the other side to repeat the incantation again. This time, it pulled forward, along the wall of the hut, at right angles to the previous.

"Charlus, could you see about under the cot, please? Maybe under the mattress?" Griffin considered taking a step forward, then decided that was going to pitch him onto his knees or face-first onto the cot, which wouldn't help anything.

A moment later, Annice cleared her throat. "Can I pass you the crutches? Or the chair?"

Griffin had to stop, breathe, stop himself staring at her. It was the right thing, in the right moment, and he hadn't expected her to ask, not like that. Then he managed to nod. "The crutches, please." Charlus glanced between them, baffled, but then Annice was there, next to him, handing him the right crutch, then the left, before she stepped back to look at the cot. Charlus was doing a fine job rolling the mattress back before coming up triumphantly with another box, resting in a space built into the cot's frame itself.

A minute later, he and Annice had the entire mattress off, but there was nothing else under there, not even very much dust or sand. They spent even more time checking the rest of the hut, but nothing else turned up. Once they'd made the cot back up, Annice opened the box, carefully, as Griffin perched on the cot and watched her face and her hands. She lowered the cardboard box to reveal another broad round piece of jet, carved and shaped like the other had been. "Do we leave it here?" she asked.

"I think bring it back. If I'm right about the other, they might need some care before they could be active again. And if you want someone to look at it in Trellech, or have the option..." He let his voice trail off.

"Right." Annice looked back down at the box.

Charlus cleared his throat. "We're getting on for half-four, sir. Should I see about Bobs?"

Griffin hesitated. The thing he should do was ask Charlus and Annice to come back and talk through the options. But he was feeling on edge, or odd, or something he certainly didn't have words for yet. "Please. And when we get back, I think I'm going to ask you to go back to Trellech. With a couple of people to contact first thing in the morning, if you don't mind?"

"Not at all, sir." Charlus glanced from Griffin to Annice. "I'll go make sure Bobs is handy and tell him you'll both be along in a couple." Charlus packed up his own things promptly. Annice set about putting the hut back in order, tidily making the bed and tucking in all the bedding neatly while Griffin leaned against the wall. Then he made his way out, letting her lock up. They slowly headed back north along the beach, with her continuing to look for jet all the way. The tide had begun to creep in while they were looking at the cot. But there was still plenty of room to walk for a little while yet.

CHAPTER 24
THAT EVENING

By half-six, they were back in Griffin's cottage, and Charlus had disappeared, back to do mysterious things in Trellech. Annice wasn't sure what to do with herself. She didn't want to go back to a dark, quiet house - with not much around to eat. But she didn't want to intrude.

Before she could excuse herself, Griffin was leaning on the table, one hand on it. "Do you want to stay for supper? There are things to heat, or if you didn't mind going out for something, that would be fine, too." He wiggled a hand. "I did like the fish and chips."

"Sure." Annice swallowed, because that had sounded grudging. "If you don't mind."

"Not at all." He rummaged in his satchel, pulling out some coins and handing them over. "If I'm not out in the sitting room when you get back, I'll just be a minute. I'm going to wash up a bit. You're welcome to do the same, now or after."

"When I bring the food." It wasn't exactly drizzling out

there, but since they'd found Bobs and the cart, it had been threatening to, and that would make everything gritty. Annice could go fetch food. She knew how to do that. She might not know a lot else, besides that and finding and carving jet. Annice closed the door behind her.

When she came back twenty minutes later - there hadn't been much of a wait, nor people wanting to gossip with her - there was no one in the sitting room. "I'm back?" Her voice hitched on the second word, and she was sure it made her sound awful.

"Wash up, if you like. I'll be out in a min." Griffin's voice came out remarkably clearly from another room. Probably his bedroom. She went into the loo to find his own kit neatly laid out. Apparently he was the sort of person to use a charm rather than a razor for shaving, because she didn't see one. But there was also soap and a handful of ointments and lotions and such. Of course, she didn't touch anything, but it was right there, and there was that burst of memory of living with Grandad. It wasn't just the masculine scent of the soap, but also the darker colours for whatever bits and bobs he had. And the tidy leather case for it all, the comb and brush made of some dark wood.

He still hadn't appeared when she came out, drying off her hands on her skirt. She set herself to work putting the food out before hesitating. Then she decided to be brave. "Beer to drink or tea?" She pitched her own voice less successfully, but instead of a comment back, she heard him come out. Just one cane, and she didn't know what to make of that. He'd changed into different clothing. Trousers, different trousers, and a smoking jacket, a dark blue lined in a muted dark golden yellow, that should have seemed garish and didn't.

"Beer for me, thank you. Though if you don't mind getting it, that would be grand. But whatever you like for yourself." Griffin made his way steadily but a bit slowly, more slowly than earlier in the day, over to the sofa, sitting down on it. "And sit where you like, of course."

The other easy chair, the one she'd used last time, was across the room. Pulling it over seemed like a lot of fuss, so instead she gathered up two bottles of beer before coming over to sit on the other end of the sofa. Annice glanced over at him, and he took one bottle, opening it with a charm, and then held out his hand for the other one.

"You use magic differently than I do." It came out of her mouth before she could think better of it, and then she could feel herself blushing. "I'm sorry. I didn't mean to be rude."

"Oh, that's not rude. I hear a lot of rude, these days, and I can tell the difference, down to a fine art. Oh, this is just the thing, yes." There was an entirely honest pleasure in his voice, in his distraction at the food, that made her turn to watch him. Annice had expected someone like him to be confusing, and he certainly was, but she'd expected him to hide what he wanted, and he wasn't. Not now, about a decidedly working class batch of fish and chips. Not about hunting in the hut, earlier, and he'd lit up like a lamp on the beach, figuring out the jet.

"People are rude to you?" That was a thing that confused her. Griffin seemed not entirely refusing to talk about it. She could start there.

"My legs. The way some people think, it's terribly rude of me not to be consistent. Sometimes the chair, sometimes the crutches, sometimes the cane. Though mostly not just the cane or canes in public, they take me more concentration. But around the house, it's easier sometimes. Or just a change." He shrugged. "And then many people want to know what happened, like it has some simple answer."

She opened her mouth to ask, because he hadn't explained it, before she closed it. Then she reached for her plate, where she'd dumped out the chips, because if she was eating one, she wouldn't be saying something awful.

Griffin chuckled enough to make her look up. "You're not asking, and that's lovely of you. If you want to know, I'll tell you. I don't tell most people. I didn't tell Charlus until this trip, actually."

"That's just more confusing," Annice said. "I mean, you work with him."

"I told him the parts that applied to the work. That I need the chair or crutches or whatever handy, where they live when I'm in my office, that I can't be the one to run upstairs. There is a lift in the building, but it's not terribly reliable, and going up and down is hard. Worse, when it's busy, because as you've seen, I'm definitely not fast."

That made her half-smile. "Very determined, though." She focused on her food again, looking away.

His voice got quieter, not quite like whispering a secret, but not in the clear way he usually spoke. "Usually, I just say it was the War. Which it was, but the Healers aren't entirely sure what happened. Some combination of an explosion, the local magic, my magic, my sensitivity to the land magic, even if we were in France. Anyway, my head and my feet don't always talk to each other reliably. Or my leg goes weak. Usually not both at once, not these days, but I can take a bad tumble if I'm not careful. And that's defi-nitely worse on the stairs. And with a chance of taking me out of doing anything on my own. I broke my wrist once, and that was the worst. I couldn't write, even reading was hard, and I couldn't go anywhere without the chair and someone to push it, because I couldn't trust my legs with only one cane."

Annice risked a glance at him to find him watching her. She swallowed, thinking through what to say. "You seem like you've sorted out what works."

That got her a sudden smile, something glowing like amber or sparkling in the depths like the few opals she'd seen up close. "Enough. I have many good things in my life, some I'm still sorting out. But that's like everyone, isn't it?"

Annice felt like she was far more about failing to sort anything out, but there were the good moments. There was making jewellery, talking with Ruth, even today's outing, which had felt good even if it had been only partially successful. "I, um." She swallowed. "I envy you that. The good parts. The— you know things I don't."

"It's not just you. I know things a lot of people don't. And I don't know things other people do." Griffin took a few bites of his fish, the batter crumbling off into the chips as he did. "You know things I don't. The jet, for one."

"Finding the talisman, though." Annice fumbled through trying to find words for it. "I've heard about that, but never seen anyone do that."

"Do you want to learn? I could teach you in an hour or so." Annice's chin came up immediately; she'd never really considered that might be an option. Finding the jet, searching the beaches for it, could take hours, normally. A charm like that would change everything.

Only, it wouldn't really now. Not with the demand for jet dropping more every year. Twenty years ago, forty, it would have set up a family for life. Now, it would just torture her with what she didn't have. Family. Stability. An idea of what her future looked like. But magic didn't actually fix much of anything, maybe.

If all of that showed on her face, Griffin didn't comment on it. He cleared his throat after a brief silence. "Though I suppose we ought to figure out how we're spending our time, and you coming to Trellech." He seemed distracted by that. "Charlus was arranging for a room at the inn. They're used to all sorts of people there, working with the Ministry, if you're worried about it."

Now Annice was looking at her plate again. Without moving, though she could feel her hand twitch. "I've never stayed in one. Never been out of Whitby or nearby. Yorkshire, anyway."

"Ah." Griffin considered. "Would an explanation help? Or would you rather not have it from me?" He then leaned forward, taking a bite of his food again.

Before she could stop herself, it burst out of her. "Why do you keep just thinking I could learn it? I know jet. I can't see how to keep making a living with it, but I know it. I understand it. It's, it's." She lost the word for a moment, then found it again. "It's conchoidal fractures, that's what it's called. Straight lines don't make sense, and you think in straight lines. Mostly."

"Most people accuse solicitors and barristers of thinking in twists." Now he was laughing, and that was both confusing, and made her look at him again. He didn't quite have that same glow as earlier, but he was relaxed. He took another bite of his food, then considered. "You showed me your workshop. There are so many parts to it. I know from seeing that you can sequence things. You can decide when it is time to move to the next step. You can take safety precautions, and understand the ones that don't matter most of the time, but absolutely do sometimes." His shoulder shifted just a little. "And I was thinking about something else today."

Annice didn't know what to say to that, but she also didn't want him to stop talking. "Oh? About, about what? Your work?"

"About my meeting yesterday. That was with Lamont Morgan, who is head of the Courts, and also Lord for Trellech." Griffin almost seemed about to say something else. Then he went on. "We were talking about this project, of course, but he also said he'd been watching me because he was concerned that I was, mmm. Being conservative is probably more accurate, but he said cautious, with myself. With how far I reached." He coughed. "Pardon, I'm not good at talking about some of this, entirely not in practice."

"I— if you'd rather not, I don't mind." She did want to know. But here they were, back earlier in the evening, like making a spiral loop around a bit of jet, not quite coming back to where they started.

"I rather think I'd like to make a try with you. If you don't mind." Griffin's voice had gone softer again. "Lamont suggested - the way people we look up to do, really - that I had been overly cautious. Not extending myself, because of my injuries and recovery. That there were concerns about whether I would be quick enough to act as needed."

"That's unfair!" It came bursting out of her. "Judging like that."

"That is, in fact, what we do. Make judgments, discern what needs doing and how it is best done. I don't blame him for that." Griffin hesitated, his voice a little uneven, but he went on as Annice twisted to look at him better. "There's a particular thing he's thinking about. But I have been thinking about it since yesterday. Rather late last night, actually, the sort of staring up at the ceiling thinking."

"And you think he's right?"

"I think he's not wrong about how it's perceived by

others. And." Griffin leaned forward slightly. "I got on to thinking about you a bit. You have a space you know, one you understand, one where you are very skilled. But as you've said, you don't know where you go from here. You could keep on as you are, for a little, but probably not all your life, not unless there's some new grand fashion for jet and less superstition."

"Or I marry someone who can carry the public face of it." Annice felt herself grimacing. "I don't want that."

"Don't want marriage, or don't want to hide your skills?" Griffin held up his fingers. "They're two distinct problems."

"Don't want to pretend my skills aren't mine. That feels wrong to me. Lying, repeatedly, and every time, it chips away a bit more of me until there won't be anything left." Then she shrugged, looking down at an angle at the table. The fish and chips, the remains of them, would not react to what she said. "The only offers of marriage I've had the past decade are about being someone's nursemaid, or taking on someone who can't make good in anything else. Marrying someone who did their part, that's one thing. Taking on all that burden, and then lying? No."

When she managed to glance at him again, he'd done that thing with his head, cocked a little to the side, as if he were listening to something. Griffin gave it a moment, that caution that she could see now he'd named it. "If, when you were in Trellech, I introduced you to a couple of people who do similar kinds of work, carving stones, working with jewellery, would you be interested? You know some skills already, I'm fairly sure you could learn the others. There are some programs for training fees and such."

She blinked. "Why would you even do that?" Then, suddenly, she stood. "Thank you for supper and thank you for helping today. I just realised something I have to do. Um. Later. Tomorrow. Something." She heard him almost say something, the pitch of it before a word. Then she was rummaging for her cloak, not sure what she was doing, but sure she couldn't keep being there.

CHAPTER 25
MARCH 27TH

Griffin worried the next day. He hadn't wanted to stop Annice, anything but. Even if he'd wanted to - distasteful as it was - he wasn't able to fling himself in front of her or change her mind. Especially not after an exhausting day. For all those reasons, and a lot more, he'd let her go.

But it didn't stop him from carefully going and leaving her a note. It said, in his more casual handwriting, that he'd be at the cottage all day, doing some research. And he'd be at the White Horse & Griffin for supper starting around half-five. He hoped that suggesting somewhere public might be a little of a help. They knew him there well enough now.

The only problem was, there was no sign of her. He nodded and chatted briefly with a few people who recognised him, startling every time the door opened. It wasn't Annice, over and over again. Griffin had made it through his meal, just poking at the last few bits of a beef stew, when the door opened, closed, and then she was standing there.

He saw her dress first, the way it draped and folded, the place on the hem it had been mended, before he looked up at her.

"Miss Matthewman." He was careful. They were in public. "Good evening. Will you join me? Can I buy you something?"

Annice shook her head, just once. "I wanted to talk business with you. Would this evening be convenient?" He did not know how to read her tone. She was closed in and her voice had almost no intonation.

"Of course. Just let me pay up." Griffin did that as quickly as he could, leaving the change on the table. He let Annice go first, waiting until they were outside on the street with no one too nearby to ask, "Where would you prefer?"

She looked him up and down, considering. "Yours." It was closer, and he was grateful he had the forearm crutches rather than try to figure out getting the chair in the pub. When they got through the ghault, he unlocked the door, and then let her in.

"Is there something that would be a help right now? Tea? Beer? Calming potion?"

"Do you have one of those?" Her voice shivered on it.

"I do. If you'd trust one of my stock. Comes from my usual apothecary in Trellech, I go to Postlethwaite's for most things these days. Not that that means much to you, I suppose. They're properly certified. You can see the stamp and all. Moment, it's in my room." Without waiting for an answer, he went off to fetch it, bringing the whole case back in the satchel over his shoulder. He handed over the vial, letting her check it, and focused his own attention on his evening doses.

When he looked back up, she opened it, then swallowed

it in one gulp. He could see the slight fading shimmer of her checking the charms on the bottle, so she was being reasonably sensible. Or, for some reason, even when she couldn't talk to him, she still trusted him that far. Then she waited for it to take effect, and he saw the moment where whatever she'd been feeling settled out a bit. Not all the way, not dangerously calm, but enough she could act more deliberately. He gestured at the sofa or the chair. "Where you'd like."

"What did you mean last night? About helping me. It's got to come with strings, doesn't it?" Annice's voice was still pitched high, strained a little. Griffin was listening for every clue he could get and then some.

"No strings. No commitment on your part, other than having a look at our stones in the Court, but that's a business transaction. The rest of it is..." Griffin turned his hand up. "Like I said, Lamont named something in me that's true. And if you've got the same sort of problem, and I can help, that feels good. Or if I can help in some other way, but you'd need to tell me what's actually helpful."

She sat down with a thump that rocked the sofa. Griffin could feel it jarring a little through his hips. Then she winced. "Sorry. But you know the Courts. Not other things?"

"I know a number of experts, and how to get introductions to a fair number more. Crafters, some of them. Talisman makers. I don't think I know a jeweller proper offhand, but I know someone who does, and who'd be glad to arrange an introduction. What you do with it at that point is up to you."

She looked away from him, across the room. "You were right last night. That's what hurt. That I could make something work for a little longer, here, but not forever. Sooner or later, if I live more than a couple of years, I'd have to figure something out. Unless the stones, the two we have, do something really big. Powerful magic. And I - they're not that, are they?"

"I think - again, I'm not an expert here - they're meant as a family magic. Keeping your family safe, as they're defined by the makers. Not a big magic, but a long-term one. And it worked pretty well for a long time, from what you've said. Your family were happy, and safe. Your grandad and da were doing skilled work that kept everything together and then some. You own your house outright, right?"

"Yes." Annice said. "And that's an argument in the family. I've cousins who could use the space."

Griffin nodded. "Look, what I'm offering is a chance to see what else you might like. I will not tell you what to do. But I have connections in Trellech, all sorts of people. I'm glad to put you up at the inn, or if you felt comfortable, my flat has a spare bedroom and another bath and loo upstairs. Nothing fancy, but private. And I'd not bother you up there." He flicked his hand at the crutches where they were propped up.

Her mouth twitched. "And the stones? I was thinking, um. Maybe I could sell them."

"We can find someone to ask. We will find someone, whatever else you want, if you're willing. But I think they're personal. Meant for this place. Though they're lovely big pieces of jet, and I suppose that has some value, if you ground it down smooth again." She flinched, maybe at the idea, and he went on hurriedly. "Learn more about them, then, before you decide. But it's probably not a windfall. Not enough of one."

"And you don't mind, um. Putting me up. Introducing me?" Now her voice had the quaver in it. Annice leaned forward a little, her arms around her stomach a bit hunched over.

"I would be delighted to. And the money's not a bother for me. I make a solid salary." Griffin considered, then added, "Maybe this helps. I've thought a lot about what would happen, if I couldn't continue in the Courts, even in an administrative role rather than a magical one. I'm still a trained solicitor, I still have other skills. I love what I do, but I also like knowing I have options. That I'm not hemmed in to just one thing. And that's the bit I'd like to help you with. You could come back here, and keep going, but at least you'd know more about what else might or might not work."

She was quiet for a long time, minutes. Griffin watched her carefully for the first minute, then leaned back, letting his eyes mostly close, summoning all the patience he could. He just waited. Then, almost in a whisper, she asked, "How do I know what to choose?"

This was something Griffin knew. The question of legacy came up a great deal in his work of the past five years. "What do you want for others? What do you want to preserve? Keep safe, make sure that thing continues, however you want to put it." He began watching her again, mostly her hands where they lay in her lap, twisting her skirt once or twice.

"The house. Grandad and Da's work. Things Nan and Mam made. I don't know. The house." Then Annice looked over at him. "And that needs money. And me. And I don't know."

"Can you get someone to keep an eye on it for a week or two? Longer if you like, you're welcome to stay longer. You might figure more out when you're not right in the middle of it."

There was another silence, but much shorter this time. When she looked up again, he asked another question. "You said you have other family, your cousins? Could they keep an eye on it?"

"Aye." Annice swallowed hard. "Can I get a beer? Can I get you a beer?" The two questions, one after the other, said so much about her. That she needed a bit, that she thought to ask him about it.

"Please. Both, I mean." She stood, and Griffin watched her cross to the chest with the beer in it, the way she was deliberate about her movements. She brought it back, and held it out, and he opened it with a charm, then his own.

It wasn't until she was sitting again, her hands curled around the bottle, that she spoke. "Why do you want to help me, in particular? I mean, there must be lots of people to help."

Now was where it got delicate, and also, he would tell her the truth. "I— I keep watching you, and I'm trying to figure you out. You confuse me a lot, but not in a bad way. A way I want to understand." Griffin twisted a little on the sofa, to better face her. "You make beautiful jewellery, you have clever fingers, you care about what you do, and I like all of that. I don't understand why, sometimes, but I know I do."

She looked at him, searchingly, then down at her lap. "I told you, I don't want to marry. And I definitely don't want that kind of trouble."

"To be entirely fair, you can outrun me without breaking out of a walk." His own voice cracked a little at the end, getting her to look at him again. "I'm glad to swear on my magic that I won't do anything you don't want, if that would make you feel safer trusting me. Or whatever else of that kind. I just..." Griffin swallowed, hard. "I want to understand you more. If you'll let me."

"And you want me to come to Trellech? Stay a bit. Besides the actual agreement."

"I'm committed to Trellech. I know you love Whitby, but I want to show you what I love there. So many people just walk by it, and don't notice, and I think you'd notice. You'd care about what you saw. And getting to show you that? That'd be great fun."

Finally, slowly, she nodded. "I'll come down and look at your courts and your rooms and your jet. And then we'll see. I'll ask Ruth to keep an eye on the house. What sort of things should I pack?"

"Something you can work in, clean and well mended, for the Courts. If you'd rather pick up a few new things in Trellech, before we go to the Courts, I know where to take you for a bit of shopping. Fair prices, decently made - the people who took over my father's store, a couple of others."

"Discounts?" The way she thought about that made him laugh.

"Possibly, yes. They do good solid blouses and skirts, good material, magical dyes for a bit more colour fastness. That sort of thing. And some comfortable shoes, whatever personal things you want for your hair and soap and all. I'll set up the inn, and you can decide how you enjoy being there."

They talked a fair bit from there, and then she asked if he'd talk a little about the Courts. He didn't think he'd been that long-winded. But he looked up after a couple of minutes, to realise she'd fallen asleep on the sofa, her feet curled up to the side. Griffin considered waking her, but she was sleeping deeply enough that she didn't stir when he tried her name. Instead, he found a blanket from the linens, draping it over her one-handed without being too clumsy, and left her to sleep. He read in bed for a bit, but didn't hear any sounds, certainly didn't feel any shift in the warding, before he drifted off himself.

CHAPTER 26
MARCH 28TH

Annice woke up the next morning, unsure where she was. Then her eyes snapped open, and she realised that first, she was on Griffin's sofa, and second, it was definitely morning. There was light coming through the curtains, she could hear some sounds from the courtyard. She was nestled on her side, back to the back of the sofa, with a blanket draped over her.

He must have done that. She didn't remember anything about a blanket, anyway. But she also didn't remember even realising she was falling asleep, or him going to whatever it was he was doing. Annice pushed herself upright, contemplating the feel of her mouth - and the taste. And then what to do. Politeness, caution, sense, they all suggested leaving. Only she knew he set wards, and she wasn't sure how to undo them. And while it might be horrible to still be here when he woke up, it was even more horrible to wake him up by setting them off.

In the end, she got up and went to the loo, doing her best to comb her hair with her fingers. She rinsed her mouth out and got herself together, washing up a little.

Once that was done, she found herself with nothing to do. She was hungry. He'd need to eat something. Presumably, everything in the cottage was things he was willing to eat or knew were here. She could make something.

Investigation found her bread for toast, eggs, and butter. That would do. And some cream, of course, though not a lot, and probably meant mostly for tea. And there were some sausages there, in butcher paper. She set to work figuring out where the pans were, and then getting started. She knew how to keep a meal warm with a charm, so no reason not to have it ready.

Before she had got started properly, there was a sound from the hall to the bedroom. "That you, Annice?"

"Who else would it be?" It was rather rude, as a response, and she swallowed, then added. "Good morning?"

"I'll be out in a minute. Morning!" He sounded remarkably bright; not someone who hated mornings, then. She was about to do something about the eggs in the rendered fat from the sausages when she heard the loo flushing. Then he was wheeling himself out in the chair. "That smells excellent. Did you sleep all right? You were deeply asleep when I tried to wake you."

"Surprisingly comfortable sofa." That was true. Both the comfort and the surprise. "You don't mind that I started cooking?"

"Goodness, no. First, I'm starving, second, it smells grand. And third, I'm glad you felt like you could." Then he tilted his head. "And fourth, were you worried about the wards?"

She hesitated, then nodded.

"Oh, well. Fair. I'd be glad to tie you into them, if you like. Though I suppose if we're going to be in Trellech in the next day or two, it's a bit silly." Then he looked at her again, like he was reconsidering. "No, I'll show you after breakfast. And besides, that's good practice, making sure you can get out of a place."

Annice did not know what to do with that, and so she went back to focusing on the eggs. A minute or two later, she slid the fried eggs onto the plates waiting with the sausage and toast, a little butter melting on each slice. "Is there jam somewhere?" She had the tea, too, in comfortable mugs, nice and strong to get going with.

"There's a jar in the cupboard. Strawberry, my house-keeper makes it."

Annice found the jar. She loaded up a tray to bring things over to the table, and after a moment Griffin pushed away from where he'd been by the sofa to join her. She set the plates out, then went back for forks and knives. As she handed him his, her fingers brushed his, and she twitched.

Griffin let her sit down - and have a bit of tea and a bit of toast and egg - before he spoke again. "I am glad you felt safe enough to fall asleep here." There was something curious there, as if he were puzzling through things as much as she was.

"I didn't mean to, just. It was warm and comfortable and I didn't mean to be rude." She looked up, then saw his face, which was honestly open and smiling. Not hiding anything. "What do we need to do today?"

"There's still the question of at least one more stone. Can you tell me where else your grandad and da might have put it?" That conversation took a fair bit of breakfast to work through.

She came back, in the end, to the same answer she'd had. "I asked my aunt. She doesn't remember anything of the kind, but I can't think where else it might be. Everything got cleared out from the apothecary when Da stopped working there and focused on the carving, I'm sure of it."

"Would they mind if you had a look round? Coal cellar, or shed, or attic, I don't know what spots might not have been bothered." Griffin leaned forward now, elbows resting on the edge of the table, his forearms flat, making a triangle. It reminded her of what Da had explained about a triangle of manifestation, a magical thing she hadn't really understood until now, how it was about implied movement. For all Griffin was sitting still, he was aimed at something.

She ducked her chin. "Probably not. Do you want to come?" Annice looked up. "It'd need the crutches. Not much space, and there are steps everywhere."

"As well as what your relatives might think of me. It's your choice. Do you want to explain me and what I'm doing there, or would you rather not?" He spoke easily, and she could tell he meant it. He looked earnest, honest, the way she'd learned to read when it came to trade and business. She did not know what to answer.

It fought inside her head. She wanted him to see things, but she didn't want him to see the sort of chaos her extended family lived in. He probably wouldn't make fun of it, but he wasn't someone who seemed like he'd tolerate shouting and babies toddling around, and the casual references to all sorts of things that weren't entirely legal. Finally, she shook her head. "Maybe better not. Will you be here when I get done?"

"Of course. I have plenty to keep me busy. Notes and all." He gestured at the room. "Books, if I run out of things to work on. A nap, possibly." He considered. "Though not if I'm expecting you. That's unkind."

Annice still had no idea what to say to that. "I'll go

down there, then. Change, put together something to take with me. I'll be back, I don't know. Mid-afternoon?"

Griffin nodded. From there, he asked her a bit more about the west side of the Esk, and what sorts of things were along there. He didn't seem particularly interested in going and exploring, but she supposed exploring could be exhausting. And they'd been down on the beach yesterday. After a few minutes of that, she asked, carefully, "Are you all right after yesterday?"

"A bit achy, but that's more reason not to go out today. I'll do some of my exercises and stretches here, and likely have a soaking bath. I'm not..." He hesitated, then tilted his head, as if weighing something. "There's a difference between being fragile and having limited resources, if you see the distinction. A bit like jet, I suppose. Hit me on the right cleavage plane, and things shatter. Drop me on the ground, and there's a decent chance I won't take much harm. But once you've carved bits out of me, they don't come back quickly." Then he laughed. "This metaphor got away from me, didn't it."

She nodded, then she couldn't help smiling, because he was so bemused by it. "And yesterday was, um, a carving sort of day and not a shattering sort of one?"

"Exactly. So I'll be a little more careful today, not push myself, do the things that often help, and get on with what I can." He shrugged. "Whenever you want to go off, I'll be fine. You needn't stick around on my account. Though breakfast was lovely, thank you. More than I usually manage in the morning, but the sort of thing I wish I had more often. If you could bring the dishes over to the sink, that'd be grand, but I can do the washing up."

It gave her a cue, anyway. Annice smiled and went to bring the dishes back. When she was done, Griffin had settled onto the sofa, his feet up, a book in his lap. She nodded. "Back sometime." After he explained how to let herself out of the wards, she did that. Her first stop was to her house to make sure all was well - it was - and to change and find a warmer shawl.

Once she was down at Aunt Sarah's, it was just about as much chaos as she'd expected. The most energetic children were in fact in school, but that left the babies and the two cousins who'd left school and who hadn't found work for the day. She chivvied them into helping her search. She got them to do most of the climbing into the eaves of the shed, checking the attic, and then getting down into the coal cellar. There wasn't much coal, which was good for searching, but worrisome for Aunt Sarah. It was getting on for the end of March, but there would still be a few chilly nights.

When they had no luck, Annice accepted a mug of tea and sat down to drink it with Ruth. Ruth was eyeing her, warily. "Had them all over the place today." Her cousin sounded aggrieved.

"Sorry. But it matters." Annice stared at her mug. "Ruth, would you keep an eye on the house? For, I don't know. A few days, maybe longer?"

"That Trellech man?" Ruth asked. "Griffin. Like the pub."

That made Annice smile, because yes it was. "He's paying for a room at an inn, and a fee for consulting and all that. You don't need to sleep there or anything, I haven't set up a room for that, anyway, but would you come by? Every day or two, check all's good? Open up the shop, if you want, the price lists are there."

"Ah, I'm no good at that. But I'll check on the place. Maybe use your kitchen for some baking, instead of fighting for space here?" Ruth asked that tentatively.

"The kitchen's fine," Annice agreed. "I'm near out of flour, but I'll pay you back if you buy some?" It seemed equitable. She felt, more than anything else, a sense of relief, like there was a rough edge on a stone that she'd worked smooth the proper way.

Ruth nodded, got up, and patted her on the shoulder, now thinking hard. But Ruth was taking her thinking somewhere else, on purpose, and Annice wouldn't fuss at her. Annice was still sitting at the table when Aunt Sarah came back from the shops. "No luck, then?"

Annice shook her head, pouring the rest of the pot out in the waiting mug. "You can't think of anywhere?"

"Did think of one thing. Didn't look. Let me have m'tea, and we'll go upstairs." Aunt Sarah looked resolute about it. "What'll you do with it?"

"Figure out what it does. If we want it to keep doing that. We need to see it to be sure, though." That was the truth, though she didn't mention they'd found the second, and she wasn't going to if no one asked. When Aunt Sarah finished the tea, she went off through the house, calling out "Coming?" behind her.

Annice trailed up to the first floor, then the second, into the attic. It was probably a good thing Griffin hadn't come along. "We looked here." They had, she could see the dust marks on where they'd moved boxes and crates, and some of the dust still in the air. She sneezed.

"Not this un." Aunt Sarah went to the far end of the attic, moving several things, like a badger digging out a burrow. At the bottom of the pile - and no, they hadn't touched it - was a long sea chest. The sides sloped in a little in all directions from the base, a flat top, worn rope handles on either end. "My granda's," Aunt Sarah said. She took the lid off, leaning it on one end against the eaves. "Haven't been in here in an age." She pulled out one bit of carefully folded cloth, then another and another, before finally, there was a cardboard box that was all too familiar.

Annice leaned forward, blinking.

"You take it." Aunt Sarah said it roughly. "Leave me be with this."

"Yes, Aunt Sarah." It was the only possible thing to say. She took the box, said, "Should I let Ruth know you'll be down in a bit?"

"Or one of the boys." Her aunt turned away from her and didn't say anything else. Annice climbed down the twisting stairs, then to the ground floor, and found Roger in the kitchen. She told him Aunt Sarah would be a bit and ducked out before anyone could ask her for more information. It was now well into mid-afternoon, and she ought to go find out what was in the box.

CHAPTER 27
MARCH 28TH

Griffin spent the day restless. Oh, he got plenty of things done, most of the ones he'd hoped for. He'd even caught a nap for an hour. But there was something twitchy in him, and not just that he'd exerted himself more than he really ought to the day before. He managed enough time upright to wash up the dishes and put them away, and to make his own lunch.

But by the time Annice reappeared around four, he was definitely ready for more information. And to see more of her. He'd said it out loud, that morning, but the way she'd trusted him, to sleep comfortably, that was something he treasured. It didn't go into words easily, for all it was true. She didn't trust many people, he thought, and she had good reason for that.

Now, he waved a hand at the wards, letting her in, and unlatching the door at the same time. She was blinking at it, and he offered. "Afternoon. I've applied myself to particularly handy magical skills, as you can see." Then he saw how tired she looked and waved a hand. "Sit, please. Tea? Beer? I can get it. You've obviously been on your feet."

Annice didn't argue, not one bit, which was definitely a sign he was reading her accurately. "Beer. And, um. Would something to eat be a bother?"

"Of course not." Griffin considered his current options, both in food and in cooking, and said, "Soup and sandwiches? I have some I can heat."

"That's fine. Something warm sounds great. And the beer." She sat down, and he got her the beer first thing.

It took most of Griffin's focus to get the food put together. He got the sandwiches made while the soup started heating. He brought them over to the sofa one at a time, using the left crutch to make sure he kept his balance. She looked up. "Do you need a hand with the soup?"

"If you don't mind. Anything that can spill is a little trickier. The tray's clean, if you like." He went back to the kitchen, stirring the soup, to find her watching him.

"Do you not cook much?" Annice had her head tilted, as if she were trying to do maths and it wasn't working.

"More in my kitchen at home, though I'm not a terribly deft cook. But that's set up with counters I can use in the chair, and it's not far from the stove to the kitchen table. That sort of thing. Here, well." He shrugged. "More awkward. The actual cooking? I have a housekeeper, she leaves me things, I can manage an egg or some basic soup. But there are plenty of places for takeaway near me, and they're used to me, if I want something different. Or half the time I'm working late, and Charlus or one of the clerks will do a run for food. We can eat from the Guard refectory, though I admit their food is nourishing but not necessarily exciting."

"Feeding a lot of people, then." Annice seemed intrigued by that part.

"Feeding many people on irregular schedules, or who

need to grab something fast. Stasis magic helps a lot, but also things that can just sit there and keep warm. Hearty stews and soups, pasties, that sort of thing." Griffin considered and then judged she'd be all right with a more personal question. "You enjoy cooking? Beyond what you need to do?"

She made a delightful grimace at the question, the way he'd deliberately asked it. She wasn't insulted, that was obvious, but she was also visibly baffled by it. "I cook because that's the way food happens." Then Annice paused. "All right. Maybe I do actually like some of it. Bread. Rolls. Yorkshire pudding. Baking things, mostly." Before he could ask anything else, she added on her own, "Sometimes it feels like the inverse of carving. Instead of removing things to show what's inside the stone, you're adding things to expand and make a new shape. I suppose that's silly."

"Not silly at all. Here, though, the soup's ready. Do you mind?" He backed up into the far end of the kitchen space. That let her grab the bowls he'd set out, then shifted to pour out the rest into something for storage and rinse the pot. Once they were settled again, he kept the conversation on simpler things until they were both done eating. A question here or there about what would make her feel more comfortable staying at the inn, what kinds of places might she want to know about. Explaining the options filled up the time nicely.

Finally, Annice swallowed and looked up. "I found something. Or my Aunt Sarah did." She gestured at the bag she'd brought in with her. "Should I clear the dishes and bring it out?"

"Absolutely. Let me grab my notes. That will help." While she took the dishes off and washed them quickly, he pulled out his notes. Tonight, he settled himself squarely on the sofa, with space for her and space on the table for the object. Once she came back, she glanced at him, then brought out the cardboard box, placing it on the table.

Griffin nodded. "When you're ready."

Annice swallowed, and he could see her hands shaking for just a moment. Then she lifted the lid, then removed the stone inside and slipped the box out of the way. "Is it - it has to be, right?"

"Here are the sketches." Griffin kept his voice deliberately relaxed, lower pitched and a hair slow. "There, yes. See, the angle on this one is different, the way it was supposed to move." He pulled out a copy of the map he'd been using, adding an angle to the map itself. "A triangle, getting a fair bit of the coastline. The parts where you look for jet, particularly, right? All along here."

Annice leaned over and peered at the map, then ran her finger along it. "Like that. A bit up the coast, but that's probably the way the lines run, right?"

"Exactly. If there were more points, he could have done something more nuanced. Three points, you get a triangle."

"Did it do us any good?" There was a sudden echo in her voice. He suspected she might be on the verge of tears. Part of Griffin - actually, a lot of Griffin - wanted to touch her, give her whatever human comfort he could. And for all she'd slept peacefully last night, he wasn't at all sure she'd accept it.

Instead, he took a breath. "Can you talk to me about it? Why you wonder?"

"We did all right. Not wonderfully. Not so much money we never had to think about what food we were buying. But we could buy the potions we needed at the apothecary, and shoes, things like that. Tools for the workshop. We had enough. A bit more than enough, almost to comfortable."

She waved a hand down toward where the bridge ran, and the other side of the river. "My cousins, they're not like that. It's part of why I didn't want you to come today." Her breath hitched. "Besides the stairs. The stairs would be a lot. And things on the floors. Babies. Scrap wood. All sorts of things someone meant to do something with. It's chaos, and I don't think you like chaos. You wouldn't like that."

Wouldn't like her, in that environment, if he saw her in that. She didn't say it out loud, but Griffin certainly heard it. Before he could think better of it, Griffin shifted, touching the top of her hand with his fingers. "And you feel different to them, and not different, all at the same time."

Annice didn't jerk her hand away. "Aye. Don't speak like them. Got teased for it, speaking proper. Because of Da being from elsewhere, and Mam being a teacher long enough." She shrugged with her other shoulder. "You wouldn't understand."

"Try me." Griffin kept his voice as even as he could, but it was a struggle. When she looked at him again, she focused, blinked, then he added, "I work in the Courts. I've seen the worst of people, sometimes. And a lot of people who are in a mess, and couldn't see a way out, or where things kept going wrong."

It made her mouth twitch. She looked away, at the table, but she was talking again. That was good. "Not enough money to get to the next time there'll be fish or a bit of day labour or whatever. Never enough. Always a lot of mouths to feed, not enough rooms to sleep in, someone having a problem or an injury or a baby or a cough that won't go away. Even with magic. Magic helps, don't get me wrong, fewer of us die. But it doesn't make there be food on the table or coal in the cellar or anything like."

Griffin found himself watching her intently now, the

way she was speaking, the way she moved. It hit him then that he wasn't just curious about her, interested in a life he hadn't lived. It was something far more personal and far more complicated than that. She blinked once, then turned to look him square on. "Why are you looking at me like that?"

He bit his lip. "Do you want to know? I'll tell you the truth, you know that."

Annice almost drew back, but then she deliberately let out a breath, her hand and her body where they'd started. "I do know. Why?"

Griffin swallowed just the once. "I was thinking that, um." Words failed him, they never failed him, they weren't like his legs. Only now they were not there when he needed them. He tried again. "I like you. As a person. If I thought you'd permit it, I'd be asking to take you out, the way a man takes a woman out. We are working together, but you're a consultant. There are ways to ease that." Then he flushed. He could feel it. "Of course I'll tell you the truth. There's no other way to do this."

He expected her to push away, to stand up, to leave the room. She had a few days ago, when they'd touched on places just as sensitive. To Griffin's surprise - and he suspected also to hers - she stayed. Her fingers were trembling under his. "You can't mean that. I'm nothing like you."

"You're curious like I am. You care like I do. Like I want to, anyway. You see things - such glorious tiny things like a flashing bit of jet in a beach full of stones and dark black pebbles and coal. You pay attention. Why wouldn't I be interested in that?" Then, some imp of the perverse added. "I also promise I am not at all interested in a nursemaid.

And I like to think I've proven I'm good at managing for myself, professionally and otherwise."

That last part helped, actually, because she actually smiled at it. "That part's true enough." Annice let out a long breath, and Griffin gave her the space for it. He could be patient. She was watching his face intently now, like she was studying something to carve, maybe. "What does that mean? Given, um."

"It doesn't affect the consulting arrangement. If you'd feel more comfortable having the formal arrangement with someone else, Charlus could take it over, or I could see about one of the clerks. Maybe Antimony." At her confusion, he added, "One of the Guards, she does a lot of work in inheritance cases. A friend, but she's made all the Guard oaths. You can rely on that."

"Huh." Annice let out a breath. "And if I don't? Don't want to make a change, I mean."

"Then I will show you a bit of Trellech. And show you the courtroom, and you can have a room at the inn that's on your own, as long as you like. And if you needed more time, I'd be glad to keep the room for a bit." He considered something. "My family's well off now, enough that if I couldn't work, I wouldn't have to worry about all the things my War pension wouldn't cover. But I make good money, I don't spend a lot, and I am comfortable. The sort of comfortable that doesn't fuss over what I spend on food, or paying my housekeeper well. Putting you up for a week isn't a bother. A month or two, even. Though I hope we'd figure out something else in there. The inns aren't terribly comfortable for a long period." He added after a moment, "Not as much privacy as I like."

That got her to blush charmingly, he thought. He might, in hindsight, have been having feelings for her for a bit now, actually. "Oh." Annice looked up. "And what does that mean?"

"It means, right now, I like this. Sitting close." Griffin considered, wanted a promise that she'd understand was real. "I will check with you, I promise, about doing new things, about if they're something you want. But I like your company, I would very much enjoy more of it, in ways we both desire. You. Just as you are, and all that you are, and being who you are and where you're from." He should, he realised, talk to her about Trellech, about being Heir, but that was a long conversation, and if she couldn't deal with Trellech, well. Maybe she should see the city first.

Now, she considered, then carefully twisted her hand in his. "And if I don't like something, I can outrun you. On feet, anyway." She glanced at the chair, where it stood in the corner. "Maybe not in the chair. It'd depend on the hill, aye?"

That got him chuckling. "Probably. But I'll only chase you as much as you wish. Tell me to stop, and I will. Do you want my oath on it?"

"No." Annice swallowed. "I mean. Thank you for offering. Um. Could you talk more about the stone? Me just sitting here, like we were doing?"

"Of course." Something more ordinary, if talking about an unusual talisman she'd only just discovered existed were ordinary. Griffin settled back into that, until half an hour later, Annice shifted against his side.

"You want to get home?" Griffin asked, carefully.

"I need to pack. I did some, but, um." She'd been on his sofa all night, and then out most of the day. Of course she'd want to put things to rights.

"Charlus is going to be here at nine, and I can have him come around to your shop and carry your bags. Or he'll have a cart, probably. We have to bring the trunk here back, and all. Tomorrow."

She leaned forward then, kissing him on the cheek and getting up before he could do anything in response other than smile. "Tomorrow." she agreed, gathering up the stone, its box and lid, and her bag. Annice hesitated by the door, waving once at him before she let herself out. He let her go with no further comment, but he watched through the angle of the window until she completely disappeared from sight.

CHAPTER 28
MARCH 30TH IN TRELLECH

Annice didn't know where to look. The morning had started out smoothly enough, if by smoothly, she meant Charlus turning up with a luggage cart and taking care of her battered suitcase and carpet bag. Then he'd reloaded everything at Griffin's cottage, and gone trotting off to make the last payment to their landlady, while Griffin finished making sure he'd packed everything. Annice had stood there, not sure what to do. Finally, they'd gone out, and along to the ghault with the portal, tucked away a few more alleys east from the White Horse & Griffin.

It was coming through into Trellech that had floored her. She had wanted to stop dead, but she knew she couldn't. There were people coming through behind her. Specifically, Charlus, with that loaded cart. Griffin had wheeled off to one side, out of the way, waiting as Annice looked around. Sheep were coming through one portal, herded into some fencing. As she looked around more, she could see that Portal Square wasn't any such thing. She'd known that it was a triangle, but it definitely felt angular, standing in it. The far point had lines of people.

"That's the international portal. People waiting for customs and such. Those buildings there, on each side, people can wait there. The ones closer to us are for domestic travel. If you've booked a portal and have to wait for it, for example, or you're meeting someone. Not a problem here." Then he looked up behind Annice. "Charlus, can you see about getting our luggage in the proper places? Meet you at the court when you're done. Annice, do you have everything you need for the afternoon? Whatever tools?" Annice nodded. She had several measuring tools and her notes and all with her.

"Certainly, sir. It'll be half an hour, maybe a little longer." Charlus nodded at Annice and then went off with the handcart.

"He's got a carter waiting. It's mostly how busy your inn is. I thought we'd go back through town, let you see a bit of it. I'm glad to go the long way round. Let you have a look at the shops."

Her face did something, she wasn't sure what, but he grinned. There was something joyful about him here, something she definitely didn't understand. He added, encouragingly, "Long way round is fine for me. Stick to the main streets, you might as well get a tour."

"You're sure?" Annice did sort of want a look, even if everything was a whole lot.

"About two miles. I have my chair, and I won't have too far to go home after. It's sunny, it's not market day, and it's all reasonable pavement, the way I'm thinking." He was still smiling, earnest in all the ways she thought he could be. "Tell me if it's too much, but..."

"But you want to show me." Annice swallowed. "All right."

Griffin leaned a little so he could twist the chair around. "This way. We're going up the side of the Temple of Healing so you can see the front. Then we'll turn west, come south down the main high street - glorious things in the windows. And then down toward the Ministry Quarter and the Courts. Not quite three sides of a square."

The street they took got a lot quieter. There were tall stone walls lining one side, with ivy and other plants growing down them, an occasional tree visible from the other side. "That's the Temple of Healing gardens. We can go in, if you like, but I'd need to schedule it. Or the baths, if you want to try that. They have some open for general, what's the word? Renewal, as well as the more specific ones, focused on particular healing. I've done both."

"I. Um. have nothing to wear for that." Annice said, blushing. She hadn't thought about packing swimming gear or even paddling. It was still March, and they weren't terribly near any other water.

"Oh, there are options for that, too. But we can talk about that later, if you like." It wasn't a conversation for a public street, absolutely. Then they came up into another square, this one smaller and less full of sheep. They got part way across when Griffin stopped and turned. "There. That's the Temple of Healing, the front of it."

The front of the building rose up, four, five, six storeys, a massive glorious shape. It was like the Whitby Abbey had been, only not the same at all in other ways. It had all its stained glass, for one thing, and was gleaming white, the way stone was when people took care of it. Though now she thought about that, there was less smoke here.

Griffin was just grinning, ear to ear, but he then said, "Question?"

"The air's better here. Even though we're inland." She waved a hand. "The stone's clean, too."

"They do scrub it regularly. But much less coal here. A lot of the heating in Trellech's magical. Hypocaust systems, some of it - especially the bigger buildings. I know a little about it, but if you're curious, I know a few people who know a lot more."

"You always know someone." She said this fondly, and he smiled even bigger. She hadn't known that was possible. Annice had thought Griffin cheerful in Whitby, but this was something else. "And you - you like being back?"

"Oh, yes. Coming home. And showing you the city, that's a grand thing too. Let's keep going. The inside is worth its own trip. And I admit, I'm probably not entirely up to that today." It made her realise he must have spent a fair bit of time there. He'd gestured at it, now and again in conversations. Of course, it probably wasn't an entirely comfortable memory.

"Please. You said there were shops?" She more or less understood shops.

Griffin nodded and set off again. "Now, we're going to be starting at the exceedingly posh end. A couple of the extravagant sorts of jewellers, for one thing, and the most elite fashion and such. But then it will get more ordinary, all right?"

She was glad he'd warned her. The first few shops as they turned south weren't overwhelming - a cigar shop, somewhere that sold paper goods. But then they came to somewhere with clothing in the windows. One was far more a costume than a frock, made of layers of near translucent fabric, building up shades of blues and greens and ocean greys like an undine out of legend. The neckline and cuffs of the long sleeves glittered with tiny shimmering beads. It was hours of work - hundreds, maybe more - and she couldn't stop looking at it. Not that she wanted to wear it - she was sure she'd ruin it first thing. But she hadn't known that was a thing people really did.

Griffin had stopped, waiting. "There are other places further down. This is - well. I said high end." He tilted his head, considering it. "That's the sort of thing someone protective of her person would wear to a gala ball. The skin that's covered, you see? Protection charms against potions or dusts or whatever that might influence her."

"Ugh." Annice didn't like the thought of that. "Do you go to things like that ever? Though I suppose the clothing is easier for men."

"Sometimes. Not very often at the moment, maybe more later. Which is another conversation to have when we're not standing on the street." This time, unusually for him, he was definitely ducking something. Annice made a note of that, but just nodded for now.

"What next?" They kept going. He did give her a good ten minutes to stand staring at the jeweller's windows. She took in not just the flash and glow of the gems there, but how they were set. He didn't suggest they go in - for one thing, she could see there were several steps leading into the shop proper. But she couldn't have had a conversation about it. There were rubies there, glowing a deep red, and gorgeous emeralds, no shadows to the colour, and a sapphire in the shade of the ocean on a perfect summer day. The settings were all brilliant, too, making the stones shimmer without overwhelming them.

Once she was able to tear herself away, they continued down past the market square. She lost another ten minutes staring at the toy shop nearly opposite the market space. One side of the shop window had a vast play set, wooden blocks that shone in different colours, with a scene of a castle. Dolls, big enough to be interesting, too small to cuddle at night - dotted the space. There was a princess in a flowing dress, a knight in armour, a village down below, with people doing all sorts of things. A king and queen stood on the ramparts of the castle. And of course there was a dragon, who twisted its head back and forth, very nearly like it was going to breathe fire at any moment. It wasn't just the way it moved that fascinated her. It was the shine on the scales, a prismatic flow of colour that must have been hard to manage, even with magical paints.

Again, Griffin let her take her time. "They also make excellent dolls and stuffed animals, mind." He nodded at the door. "And it's where I get some things for making furniture for my nieces. Their dolls, in their doll house, are about that size. Big enough to have fun dressing."

"I was thinking they weren't much to cuddle with, but they're lovely to look at." He was right, the further window - once she got there - was nearly as compelling, with dolls with glowing porcelain faces and plush velvet frocks and cloaks. There were a set all in historical clothing, others in the latest fashion, and if she'd been younger, she would never have taken her nose away from the glass.

Finally, though, she had to move on. Griffin kept an easy pace - she was finding that what he was choosing was comfortable for her to walk with, more than she'd expected. When they were waiting to cross one street, she was distracted by a notice, or rather a series of notices. They were posters for upcoming performances. Most of them had some sort of illusion work, so that the figures moved - some waved, some went through five seconds of some scene. On the vaudeville posters, there were acrobats or dancers kicking up their skirts in a flurry of ruffles.

She completely missed the cart pulling away and the street clearing, and Griffin must have realised she hadn't moved, because he came around to her right side. "We could go to the theatre, if you like. I know people at the New Ricardian, and a couple of their boxes are accessible by their wheelchair lift."

"Of course you know someone." She glanced down at him, and he spread his hands, then she tilted her head. "Someone else with a chair?"

"I mentioned Seth made mine? And a friend of his. The friend who lives with them, he's paralysed. Different thing. I met the New Ricardian folks because of a case, and then they introduced me to Golshan and to Seth, and my life got a lot easier. Vastly better design, easier to move. I would not have suggested taking the long way in the chair I started with. Bulky thing, and a lot heavier over distance. Golshan used to work for the New Ricardian, before the War, they wanted him to be able to come visit. Anyway. Tickets for Friday or maybe Saturday? Do you want to think about it?"

She ought to think about it. That presumed she'd still be here. But then she glanced at the playbills again. "Are they good? The actors?"

"I think so. And this play's got excellent reviews. I've not had a chance to see it. Opened while I was in Whitby."

Annice took a breath. He wanted to show her things. And she suspected that whatever needed work in the Courts was going to be more than a day. Maybe she could end her visit with the theatre and go away on Saturday, and consider it all an exceptionally dizzying dream. "If you'd like."

"Grand. I'll sort that once I've got my journal out. Here

we go. It's about to get less interesting." Griffin set off again, across the street, through one last section of shops, then angled down a street. "The right side is Club Row. The Schola houses all have a club there, a couple of posh ones, various of the societies, a couple of particular interests."

"Solicitors or Ministry, or anything like that?" Annice wasn't sure she entirely understood how clubs worked.

"Oh, no. We have a pub, though. Well, two pubs. People take sides about it. I stop in at the Stream - that's the Salmon House club - sometimes. And more often in the Veterans than the Arthur, which is the officer's club." He said it easily, unlike whatever that had been outside the Temple of Healing. "Ah, here we are. I wanted you to see the front first, but we'll need to go round the back for the ramp."

The front of the building was immensely imposing, broad steps leading up to an arched front, with great stone pillars on either side. Above were the scales of justice, and a dozen other symbols, only some of which made sense to her. The white rose, of course, though the entire building was white stone, but there was a sword, there were scrolls rather than books, a feather.

"Where I spend most of my time." Griffin said it fondly. Like Da had talked about Mam, the way a person might talk about someone he loved. Even if it was a building. Annice had no idea how to answer that.

After a moment, she asked, "Where's your flat from here? And, um, we didn't pass your da's store? Where it is, was?"

"Is and was. No, it's on the corner on the other side of the market. Nice big corner shop, plenty of windows to display dry goods and all. And my flat's, well. Roughly four blocks that way, if you cut through the smaller streets in Club Row and across into the residential streets."

Annice glanced around. "Huh. Thank you for taking me the long way. It's— it's a lot more than I expected. All the different things going on, the magic?" Seeing it out in the open, the way everyone here could be out in the open, would take some getting used to.

"There will probably be some performers out this evening, if you want to ask the inn. Musicians, illusionists, all that. There are usually a couple on Club Row in good weather and often not as good. Oh, right. The inn is just over there, up toward the market again. Not very far. Mostly Ministry folks and consultants. Other people stay up north of the market, there's a cluster of inns and restaurants. But you have to go through all the chaos to get here, and on market days that can be a bother if you've somewhere to be on time."

"Market day everywhere, I suppose. Though probably fewer fish here?" Annice offered it, hoping he'd find it amusing.

"Fewer fish, yes. A lot of sheep. Anyway, shall we go around? This way, to the left." When she nodded, he took off down a narrow but reasonably clean alley to the left of the massive building.

CHAPTER 29

MARCH 31ST

I t felt wonderful to be home. Showing Annice the Court, though, felt immense and weighty, like when the judicial magics were in play. Only, of course, they were, and they weren't. The whole building was infused with that magic. Griffin knew that as well as anyone else who worked here. Better than most, even.

But what he was feeling wasn't institutional, it wasn't about infrastructure or walls or floors. It was absolutely personal. Annice had been so cautious - so dubious - about the truth magics. And she had good reason. They made a lot of people nervous. If Griffin wasn't nervous about them, it was more that he had specific skills, had trained for years to be around them. Like a snake handler might have, or someone who trained horses, or any other delicate, risky, skilled work.

Now, Griffin got up to the small platform by the back door. Annice joined him, still looking around everywhere, though this corner of the building was not the most scenic, just solid and barely ornamented stone. "If you come by yourself, you'll want to come through the front doors and ask someone to show you to my office - there's always someone on duty at the front. Me, though, I'm tied into the warding." He moved his hand to the plate by the door, feeling the magic beneath his fingers. Then he used a bit more magic to pull the door open. "This way. My office, and leave whatever you don't need, first?"

His office contained Charlus, a fairly large stack of paperwork in his in tray, and a minor assortment of other mail and matters to tend to. Charlus stood as soon as they entered, and Griffin waved Annice inside. "Make free of anything that's out - the private things get locked and warded when I'm not in the room or not using them right that moment. Charlus can let you in as easily as I can if you need something. Leave your coat, certainly. Everything all set with the luggage, I assume?"

Charlus nodded. "Yes, sir. And they confirmed your note at the inn. Your bags are at your flat."

"Much appreciated." He hoped Annice would also appreciate the note he'd sent round. That was the point, but that was for later today.

Annice glanced around, then cleared her throat. "Could I wash up somewhere? Before handling the stones."

"Of course. Charlus, could you show her where, and where the other staff are? You do need an escort in the staff areas, Annice. But there are always people at the front desk who can help, even when the Courts aren't in session, like the next week. There are people coming and going throughout. Give me a minute to take a quick look at my pile of mail while you wash."

He had needed, it turned out, nearer ten minutes than five to sort through everything. Most of it was routine and could wait a bit longer. But there were three notes, sealed in the thick expensive envelopes that indicated a number of things about the sender's status and position. He set all of those aside for the moment, and then sorted through the rest of the pile for what needed prompt attention. About ten of the notes had seals from other people in the Courts. Three others were from people he considered allies, if not friends, all on sensible but not ostentatious stationery. Griffin popped the resulting pile into his portfolio and tucked it between his thigh and the arm of the chair. He then checked his tie by feel, just as Charlus was getting the door for Annice.

They made a little procession down the hall toward the courtrooms, with Griffin pointing out the other spaces. The inheritance court was tucked down at the end, since it was one of the smallest. Charlus got the door, and Griffin wheeled himself in, inhaling the air. There was the faint scent of the yew, nothing strong, but he could tell immediately which courtroom he was in by that alone. The magic, though, that was trickier. It looked much like he'd left it, but the feeling that something was off was even stronger for his absence, and he frowned, immediately.

Annice glanced down at him. "Something the matter?"

"I think it's only got worse. And there's been no cases here since I came to Whitby. Maybe it's just not being here. Absence makes things clearer. But would you have a look, and Charlus and I can see about running our usual benchmarking tests sooner than I'd planned."

"What's the goal for today?" Annice asked, a little uncertain.

"It depends on how much time you're willing to grant to the problem. But I thought that today, you'd get a look. We'd get whatever measurements you think would be helpful about the current state, and then we'd see what you thought for the next steps. If that's popping some stones out of the inlay work or the casing points, we can do that, but it might take overnight to prepare."

"So I should go look. And take as long as I need?" He was delighted she asked it that way, and he was nodding.

"Just as long as you need. Charlus can fetch and carry for you if you need supplies. And I'll set up at the table here, and work through the paperwork from my absence. You can interrupt me any time. It's nothing fussy." Griffin had figured that she'd do better without him hovering over her.

He'd expected she was going to be some time about it, and he was right. First, she did a full circuit of the room, to see how the various lines of metal and stonework connected. That included peering behind a table here or there to confirm the alignments. Around noon, there was a brief pause in his office for sandwiches - not terribly good ones, in an absolute sense - before they went back to the courtroom. This time, she worked far more slowly, both with a jeweller's loupe and without. Griffin got through a fair bit of his accumulated paperwork and reports.

It wasn't until he'd got through the official business that he turned his attention to those notes. Four of the six said basically the same thing, though in varied language: there had been politics afoot in his absence. Did he wish to discuss privately at some point? The fifth was from Harriet, and was about an ordinary piece of business, but it might have been an excuse for a private conversation. And the sixth was Lamont, who didn't gesture at any of the gossip, but who did wish for a report when Griffin had a little more to share.

The four notes sat there while Griffin considered them. Three of them got replies saying that he was working closely with a consultant for at least the next day or two, but schedule some time. The fourth was Antimony. She got a comment in her journal saying he was back in Trellech. He wasn't sure about his evening plans, but if she were free, drop a note in the journal and he'd write back if he was. After a moment, he added that he wanted to make sure Annice was settled in for the evening and didn't need anything. Antimony was a clever woman. She'd read several things into that correctly.

Two and a half hours after they'd started, Annice came over and stood in front of the table he was using. "I don't have answers for you, but I think I maybe know part of why it's happening. But I don't know how to test, not without taking things apart and damaging the jet."

Griffin looked up, blinking, then grinning. "That's a lot further than we'd got. What do you need to test?"

Annice looked down at the table, her hand fiddling with the fold of her skirt. "Is there a way to make sure of what the material is? I don't think it's a jet simulant, but I think it might be jet that's not from Whitby. I can't tell without some destructive testing, though, so is there a way to test it that isn't?"

"Oh." Griffin leaned back, needing to brace against the back of his chair. "That's an interesting problem, yes. There is other jet, I suppose."

"The most likely is Spanish, probably." She winced. "It's what helped take down Whitby's jet carvers. But there are other options. I don't suppose anyone found more records of what happened in 1902?"

Griffin shook his head. "A couple of notes from people who might have more, but no details in the piles of paper. I can check with people tomorrow." He leaned back, tapping his fingers and thinking through the logistics. "The Penelopes have ways to test origins of materials, if they have samples to work with. I don't have any idea what they have for jet. It's not a destructive test for what you're iden-tifying, and it can, I think, be done in situ, but they might need a day to set up." He looked up. "Charlus, can you take a note over to them? I think we need Penelope Mason, or maybe Penelope Witt, but tell them to read the note and assign whoever makes sense on their end."

Annice was blinking at him. "Penelopes? Oh. Wait."

"They solve problems. Often rather creatively. More people I know, though they're more commonly working with criminal cases and some civil ones. Sorting out the accuracy of evidence, that sort of thing. Also making sure alchemy labs are safe after someone's done something fool-ish. Ditto ritual spaces, or basically any other time people get creative with magic without good sense to go along with it." He'd heard a few stories here and there, when everyone had a moment to swap stories rather than get back to work. "If they do what I think they will, they'll need some time to set up."

"Oh. More than a day or, um. Tomorrow's Thursday. More than Friday?" Annice shifted from foot to foot.

"You're welcome to stay at the inn - and if you wanted the theatre, Saturday would be grand. They set two tickets aside. Not as much chance of Friday, but I'm on the wait list if people cancel." Griffin did not look up at Charlus, because Charlus might have thoughts about that, and Griffin was not ready to see them. "If you decide to go back to Whitby until Monday, though, you could also do that."

"Do I need to decide now?" Annice's voice had gone a hair breathy, the sort of thing that was nerves, Griffin thought.

"Oh, no. We'll send Charlus round with a note and get more information, and then you can decide from there, all right? Or do more investigating yourself tomorrow and then decide, if you like. And I wanted to introduce you to someone for your project. Of course, we've an appointment tomorrow afternoon." He'd mentioned that already, but he suspected it had slipped out of her head.

"Right. Yes. Um. Do we stay here?" Annice glanced around the court, which was pleasant, but not exactly comfortable.

"If you're willing, you could come round to my flat. My housekeeper got things ready. I've cream to go with the tea, apparently, and also scones. And other food, but it's getting on for tea time. We could start with that." Griffin shrugged. "And then I could take you round to the inn. Charlus, can you journal when you have an answer?"

"Of course, sir." There was a current of something in his voice, but it was all covered by amiable willingness to help. "And I can come round and show Mistress Matthewman to the inn if you decide you'd rather stay put for the evening."

That would do well enough and give options. Annice wrinkled up her nose. "Do you have to be formal?"

"We are in formal spaces. It does rather become habit," Griffin said, chuckling. "Does that suit?"

"If it's not a bother. And, um. I could use a cuppa and a scone. Is it far?"

"Not very. Especially if we cut through the side streets. Ten minutes, maybe, once we get our things from the office."

She nodded once. "Yes."

"Right. Charlus, let me write that note, then we'll be off at the flat. Journal when you get an answer, but I don't expect that'll be immediate unless we're very lucky and all the relevant people are actually handy in the office."

Charlus nodded and went to go tidy up what he'd been working on. Griffin dashed off a polite but explanatory note. He added that Charlus could answer further questions or that Griffin would be available by journal. Finally, he pulled out his sealing wax and slipped his signet ring off his finger. Once it was sealed by wax and charm, he handed it off to Charlus. "There we go. Now for tea."

It was, in fact, a delightful excuse to get her to see his flat. He certainly wasn't going to give up a bit more time with her, and somewhere outside of work.

CHAPTER 30
THAT MORNING

Annice kept looking around. This time, Griffin was being far more direct. First, they went out again, down the ramp, across the street from the Courts, and then cut through a narrow street into Club Row. Griffin gestured at a couple of the buildings, the clubs he went to now and again. Annice had heard about the Schola House clubs, as most people had, but they were entirely mysterious to her, of course. No one she'd talked to at any length had been in one. Well, except Griffin, and presumably also Charlus.

Then they were cutting through another small side street, Griffin veering around a cart that was parked awkwardly on one side of the street. One more crossing, this time one of the major streets, and he was rolling off to the left, a residential street that curved around. They were coming up on the back side of the houses. None of them were large, but they were detached, the way more posh houses were in Whitby, not row houses separated only by narrow alleys and paths at best.

He took a sudden sharp right into the back of one

house, and she found herself facing what must have been a barn. There was a large door on the front, filled in with newer stonework around a smaller sliding door. Griffin came to a stop in front of it, then glanced up at her. "Previously the stables for the couple of houses along here, with some staff rooms over. Fully made over before I moved in, of course." He did something to the door, presumably the warding, and then gestured, and the door slid smoothly to one side, like any stable door. Well, with rather a lot less noise than the average stable door.

Griffin gestured. "Go ahead. I'll get the door behind us."

Annice stepped in to find a space that was simultaneously rather warm and welcoming, and yet oddly sparse. The first thing she noticed was that there was nothing in the way of furniture near her. And then, a moment later, that the floor was all tile, but no rugs of any kind. She glanced back as Griffin closed the door. He pulled up beside her. "You can get out, whenever you'd like, from this side. And I'm glad to tie you into the warding if you'd like to be able to come and go. Needn't decide now." Then he went on without waiting for her answer. "The loo's that door further down on the left. Let me just sort a few things in my bedroom. If you want to wash up, do that, and then I'll see about putting tea together."

That at least seemed sensible, and she nodded, keeping her carpetbag with her. The bathroom was ridiculously big, with a large copper tub along the shorter side, a sink, all the modern magical conveniences, some of which she'd only heard about. The only odd bit was that there were hand holds mounted in multiple places on the wall by the tub. She found the water from the tap was hot almost right away, once whatever was in the pipes had come out.

When she came out again, Griffin was leaning against

the frame of the door on the other side, to the right of where they'd come in. He'd left the chair somewhere - his bedroom, maybe, she didn't see it - and had a cane leaning against his hip. "Everything you needed there?"

"Um. Yes. Though it's..." She stopped, because she wasn't at all sure what she actually wanted to say.

"Mum complains about the lack of rugs. They catch on the chair, though, and also the cane or crutches. And the heat comes up through the floor. That's a nice magical touch, brilliant of the folks who sorted it out. Rugs make it a little harder to stabilise." Griffin waved a hand. "And I keep thinking about some sort of dining table or something of the kind, but then I want to cut across spaces in the chair. I'd have to keep going around at awkward angles, and so I don't get a table."

Annice considered before venturing. "But not the chair here and now?" There was something more relaxed about him here.

"Not for the moment. Easier to manage in the kitchen for what I have in mind." He considered, then gestured. "Besides the wide open space, there's the kitchen here. The stairs upstairs are at the back, but I'm rarely up there. If you decide you want to stay longer, that's where the guest room is, and another loo and bath and storage. My bedroom." He nodded across the room. "Sitting room by the fireplace." There was a large sofa there, a broad teal-blue of plush fabric, with a cosy looking blanket folded neatly across the top. "And then my study and bookshelves off to the right. By which I mean a desk and a couple of reading chairs."

She snorted. "You seem to read a lot." Not that she didn't like a bit, but she thought Griffin did a lot more, and not just for work. "Tea?"

"Tea." He pushed forward, swinging the cane into place.

There was a slight wobble as he did before he rebalanced. "Sit at the table if you like. You've had a long day working."

He had too, but she wasn't going to argue. First, he was right about her having had a long day. Second, she was fairly sure that being a solicitor meant he was much better at arguing than she was. And third, she wanted to watch how he was in his own space. She could learn a lot from that, and she needed to.

Watching was actually both informative and also somehow lovely. Griffin obviously knew exactly where everything was, and he shifted from task to task with an elegance of movement that meant he didn't have to take many steps. The kettle had been filled with water and put on the stove. Then he was drawing scones out of a stasis box on the counter, plates from a cupboard, a butter dish. "Tea in here, or would you rather by the fireplace?"

The chair she was sitting in was perfectly reasonable, but it was a wood kitchen chair, and that sofa had looked deliberately comfortable. "Sofa?" she suggested. "Do you need me to carry anything?"

He grinned over his shoulder. "Not this time, no, but thank you. The kettle should be done any minute." He loaded the various bits onto a tray. "I'm assuming you'll want a proper meal later. The inn has a kitchen. They can do all sorts of ordinary things, or send out for something else. I am assuming you'll want an early night and some time on your own to sort out the day."

Her mouth twitched, then she was smiling. "Do you read minds or something? Yes. I am enjoying this, actually, but there's been a lot, and I'm still thinking about your actual problem, and, um. Everything." And she knew she was likely going to be staying in Trellech more than just overnight. She wanted to see the theatre. And she wanted -

this was something she had no right to ask for - to see Griffin being this kind of cheerful.

Before she could get lost in her own thoughts, and before Griffin could reply, the kettle sang out. He turned around then, busily pouring hot water into the teapot, then pulling a small rolling cart with a flat top out from next to the stove. It had handles just about at his shoulder width, and he was leaning on them just a little. He hooked the cane over one wrist. "Take your pick on the sofa. Though if you wanted to pull over one of the side tables for more space, feel free."

It meant she got to go along to the sofa, which faced a pleasant fireplace - unlit, of course, but the room was comfortably warm already. The mantle had a series of what looked like watercolours of what she suspected were all places in Trellech. Some of them looked like places they'd walked by. One was the front of the Courts, and there was one of a massive garden that might be the Temple of Healing. He took a little longer, but then he was sliding the cart into place and murmuring a charm. "That will keep it steady. Here we go. Scone? Or there are some biscuits. And shall I pour, or would you rather? There's cream and sugar, there."

"Attentive housekeeper, then? With how long you were gone?" Annice was still trying to make sense of the space, honestly, but it felt alive with Griffin here, and maybe it hadn't otherwise.

"She's very good. And she doesn't fuss at me. It's part of why we get on well." Griffin shrugged, and then poured without asking again, handing her a ceramic mug, a sturdy one, of tea and letting her add her own cream and sugar. She cupped her hands around the mug, not sure what to say. Once he had his own tea, he settled back into the sofa and let out a contented sigh.

Annice shifted a little. "You like things to be comfortable, don't you? And also, um." There wasn't an elegant way to say this, she was fairly sure. "You seem to really, what's the word, light up being here? Like charms and illusions, only real." She wanted to hide. That had been incredibly clumsy and likely also rude.

To make it worse, he almost glowed. "I do. Though that's something we should talk about, actually. If you don't mind? There's a thing I haven't mentioned, and it's relevant to both our current work and, well, me."

"That seems like a serious sort of thing to leave out?" Annice was fairly sure now that he wouldn't be offended, but she didn't know what else to say.

Griffin half-smiled. Then he was looking at the fireplace - above it, at those prints, as if he were gathering up words like he'd gathered up the tea things. Purposefully, with efficiency, but with his great attention to detail. "You know how the Lords - and some Ladies - hold the land magic, yes? And how the heads of school do for the Five Schools?"

It was an odd place to begin a conversation, but she nodded. "The basics of it, aye."

"Trellech works a little differently. So does London, but London is its own place." Griffin took a breath, let it out, and she realised suddenly he was actually nervous. She was fairly sure she'd never seen him be nervous.

Annice set her mug down on the cart and twisted to face him. "Go on?"

"The land magic in Trellech is passed down from person to person. But it's always someone who works in the Courts. Who does the work I do, tending the magic of the Courts. Because that's the heart of Trellech, keeping things running fairly and smoothly, tending to the people and the needs that come up." His breath hitched. He glanced at her, then down at his hands, then back at her face. "Right now there are three potential Heirs, and I'm one of them. I've been one of them since before the War."

"Oh." Annice inhaled, then let it out sharply. "What does that actually mean, please?"

CHAPTER 31
THAT AFTERNOON

Griffin took a breath. Annice's question was an entirely reasonable one, from anyone, but even more so from her, if he and she were to have anything of the more personal sort. The problem was that Griffin still had no idea how to talk about this, even though he'd been rehearsing it in his head for a couple of days.

He glanced around, and it wasn't as if anything would save him from this particular conversation. He didn't exactly want saving, but he did want to do this kindly and smoothly, and he didn't know how to get through to that part. "Do you mind a little more light?" Asking the question let Griffin take a moment.

Annice blinked, then shrugged. Griffin twisted a little, calling out the charm that cast a light in the back of the fireplace. It was an intriguing bit of illusion work, linked to a stable talisman mounted in the fireback. It brought up a warm light, flickering just enough to be pleasant, and Annice blinked, then looked back at Griffin.

"I don't always want to bother with lighting the fire." He then let out a breath. "I am stalling on answering your question. It's not something I talk about that often, and most only with people who already know the context."

"I thought that normally there's only one Heir at a time?" Annice said, cautiously. "Is that a place to start?"

Griffin could start there, yes. "You're right, that normally there's only one. Lamont - that's Lamont Morgan. Lamont, as I mentioned when I came to Trellech for the day, is more or less my boss. Ordinarily, there are two or three potential Heirs, perhaps for a few years, and the Lord picks one. Only in our case, we've been potential for over a decade, and he hasn't picked. He won't discuss his reasons, just that he will in due course."

Annice tilted her head, looking more confused than upset. That was a reasonable start. "And you don't know why?" She leaned a little, so she could look more directly at Griffin. "What does it mean for you? If he picked you? Would you have to, I don't know, live somewhere different, or do something different, or - um. Is it even something you want?"

Griffin felt the breath escape him. "I want it very much." He couldn't keep looking at her at the end of that. Now he was staring at her knee, more or less. Then he felt her fingers touching his chin, and nudging it up. Griffin half-closed his eyes, then made himself look at her. She was looking straight back, deliberate and not ducking the complexity.

She left her fingers there, speaking carefully. "Tell me about that, then."

Griffin just let himself begin. He couldn't make his thoughts line up and be orderly. He knew that. "I love Trellech. I've always loved Trellech, from the time I knew where I lived. Before that, I just loved it without knowing, I suspect. Not just the visible gems, though those too, but the way the alleys twist, and the streets change, and how I can walk through and figure out when things were built and rebuilt, by the shapes of the building, the paving, all sorts of little cues. The way the scents change, as you walk through different parts of the crafting quarter, or the way the magic shifts, when you're nearer the Guard Hall or the Courts. How that's different than the far reaches of the Ministry quarter and their offices. The way the different clubs along Club Row decorate for holidays or special occasions. Which ones are restrained and which ones are pure delight, a chaos of colour and illusion work and charmlights."

He took a breath, and Annice let her hand drop loosely into her lap. Now she kept watching him. "And what does being Heir mean to you? Or Lord?"

"For me?" She nodded once. "It means knowing the city, and taking care of the city. Tending it, stewarding it. From what I understand, the way the land magics run here are different. We're not agricultural, beyond people's gardens, that's all outside the walls. We have a substantial cemetery, these days, and that needs tending, unique from other land. There was an incredible row about it, after the War, how to deal with some of the magical implications."

Annice blinked. "I'm not sure I want to ask."

"Oh, not, um, things that would be about moving graves. But some people, they're more remembered than others, people visit them more often. Some of that's ordinary - more recent burials, people who loved them. But strong personalities, people who had a sort of outsize influence, those sorts of people. It can affect the wards and protections, warp them. I don't know the details. I know it took about twenty specialists to work it out, and some of them still aren't talking to each other."

It made Annice snort, and she relaxed a bit. "And what

does it mean for you as a person? Would you still live here? Would you have a lot of other duties?"

"It would mean more fussy social events. The Council rites, twice a year, of course. That's part of it, but other things, too. Being a presence in Trellech. Some amount of formal, I don't know, opening of new things, usually Lamont opens up the Guild mumming plays the first night. There's a procession for May Day. A lot of them I'd be at, anyway. Because it's my city, and I love her."

"That part you seem clear about." Annice tilted her head. "You said you'd ask me before doing anything. What would that mean for me?"

"As things are now? Entirely a private matter between us. As Heir, probably the same. Unlike all the landed titles, procreation is not a strongly implied obligation. It's not as if we're passing the land magic down the bloodline. There have been Lords here, though sometimes they get called Steward, who weren't married. At least once a confirmed bachelor, and no one inquired in any detail about his private living arrangements. Lamont is married. His wife only comes to the most formal things, usually." Griffin watched her reactions now, carefully. "It's why I had to tell you now. I couldn't get the words to start up right before. Not that I'm doing very well at the moment, anyway."

"You're answering my questions well enough." Annice said it thoughtfully. "And that's why you wanted me to come here."

"That's the thing." Griffin let out a huff of breath. "I can't move somewhere else. I mean, even if I were willing to do the daily portal trip for work, which would be trickier for me, I need to be living here. If Lamont chooses me."

"Why do you think he hasn't chosen anyone? And what are the others like? You must know them." Annice hesitated, then she set her fingers on his. "Still thinking about the locations."

"You don't have to decide now. Just. Knowing you know, that's a thing I can't bend around." Griffin paused, just feeling her touch. "I think he's looking for something specific. And all three of us, we have virtues - in terms of the role - and challenges. Harriet is very adept, but a little more by distance than by feeling, if you see the distinction? She holds the Apple Chair. That's the court of equity, larger questions that we need some sort of answer to as a community. But she has young children at home, and she doesn't care much for the social fuss. I get on much better with her than with Nestor."

"You seem to get on with many people," Annice said, and then her fingers curled through his. "What's different about Nestor?"

"The three of us have different roles - it's part of why I got shifted to the Yew chair some years ago. Nestor's in the Civil courts, Fir Primus. He's got two secondaries under him. Harriet and I each just have the one, because there are three actual courtrooms. And there's someone over the Criminal Courts. We're not limited just to cases involving our courtrooms, mind, just that we're responsible for specific things."

Griffin was stalling again, and he knew Annice realised that. "He thinks about profit and business and contracts. All transactional, and there are some ways in which - done well - that's fair. And there are some ways it's desperately unfair. It's sometimes, too often, about who has more power in setting the terms, and who can get them enforced. We have precautions about that, in how we handle things, but they're not perfect."

Annice snorted. "You really don't like him, is what you're saying."

"No." It made Griffin smile. "About as much as your two senior jet workers dislike each other. Though I try to be more like Cliff when I can."

That got a laugh from her, a full-throated one. "Fair. So why hasn't Lamont named you?"

"There's been a lot of worry about whether I'm competent. Because I need the chair or the crutches, because it's visible. The thing is, we've had, oh, half a dozen cases in my time in the Courts, of people who should have retired earlier than they did. It is possible that my condition will change. Though it's been stable for most of a decade, since I got care that helped more. And as I've pointed out, several times, ageing comes for us all." Griffin swallowed. "Your hand, may I?"

Annice blinked, but then she nodded, and Griffin shifted a little to get a touch closer to her and take her hand in both of his more comfortably. Then he went on. "I keep doing my best, over and over again, and it keeps not changing anything. Except I'd have done my best anyway. People deserve that. People who are tangled up by grief, especially."

She squeezed his fingers, suddenly, and then she was moving faster than he could make sense of. A moment later, she was pressed against his thigh, her other hand coming up to cup his cheek, and she was kissing him. Tentatively, at first, and with both his hands holding her other one, he couldn't get an arm around her properly. Neither of them were balanced well. They almost bumped noses. Absolutely none of it mattered. When she pulled back, she was blinking, and her eyes were shining. Not quite crying, but he'd seen that on so many people, enough to spot it in an instant. "I should have asked..." Now she was the one looking down.

Griffin freed one of his hands, moving it to touch her leg. "Was I not enthusiastic enough for you?" He was grinning now, with the way she'd gone after what she wanted. This was what she was like when she let her desire actually show rather than shoving it away into politeness. "We could do that a bit more. Practice. Skills do benefit from it."

Now she was giggling, and he felt he'd done something wonderful there. "How, um. What's comfortable for you? That's the part I should have asked. If there's something to avoid."

"Oh, if you want to sit on my lap, in any particular fashion, you won't hurt me. My legs, it's not, um. Fragility. It's the way they don't always do what I tell them." Then he paused. "It's been a while for me. I've never been inclined to the more casual sort of fling. I work entirely too much to meet people most of the time, and - well. The chair doesn't help, really."

"But here we are, we met because of your work, and the chair doesn't bother me. I might have more questions in a bit. About what it's..." Her voice faded. "And is this casual?"

"If you need it to be casual, we can take it as you wish." His voice caught on the last part of that. "But I would, if I could, prefer to see it as what we're learning together, doing together, about seeing if we could have something lasting. No promises now, not yet, but open to the idea that we might, if everything goes well."

"And if it doesn't, you've shown me a city you love." Annice nodded once, decisively. "I, um. Haven't been with anyone for a while. No one who was both magical and fine with my skills, and then there was Grandad and Nan needing someone handy most of the time."

"Well. Then we will just have to see what happens when we've some incentive to brush up." Griffin considered. "A bit more, then, and then I'll take you to the inn, so you can have some time on your own tonight. How's that."

"I— yes." Her voice shifted, and now she was considering. "You meant it about your lap?"

Griffin nodded once, and a moment later she was rearranging herself, sitting sideways across his legs, which put her in a much better position. He got a hand solidly round her back, to help support her. She had one hand on his shoulder, and then she was leaning in to kiss him again. It was better this time. They weren't struggling for balance or breath the same way. He let her take the lead, and she explored the way she touched jewellery, delicately at first, then with more certainty.

When they both had to come up for air, she was much more relaxed. Then she squeezed his shoulder. "Strong, through here. Like you worked on one of the fishing boats, all in the shoulders."

"It is how I get about," Griffin agreed. Then his stomach rumbled, and hers, and he laughed. "That's a cue to get you to the inn, I think. Shall we?"

"And tomorrow?"

"Tomorrow I have people to introduce you to. And we can sort out a bit more of ourselves after. Saturday, there's the theatre."

"Saturday." She said it like it was a gift, when she was the one giving to him. "Things to look forward to." Then she carefully wriggled off his lap, and waited for him to sort himself out, without fussing over him, or insisting on offering him a hand up.

CHAPTER 32
APRIL 1ST

Annice woke up unsure of where she was for a minute. Everything felt slightly unreal, though not at all in a bad way. The bed underneath her was cushioned, not the sort of soft that she had sunk into, like some fairy tale, but the sort of soft that supported. She stretched out on her back, trying to sort out her thoughts.

Last night, Griffin had shown her to the inn, and then stayed for supper. He'd checked, of course, that she wouldn't rather be on her own. Having him there had been a help. He knew how to talk to the staff. Well, he'd known at least half of them by name. He'd asked after brothers, parents, aunts, cheerfully, introducing her as a specialist who was helping out in the courts, as Mistress Matthewman.

When he'd left her, one of the staff, a woman, had taken her upstairs to her room. It was twice the size of her room at home - not like that was terribly hard. It had its own bathing room and loo, plenty of space for clothing, a desk. And on that desk, there had been a basket of things to eat. The woman had pointed out the cold box, and noted it was stocked with beer and cheese and cream for the tea. Then she'd indicated where the kettle and teapot were.

Annice had investigated the basket cautiously when she'd been left on her own, and she'd found tea she liked. The beer was a local brewery, not one she knew, but it was exactly the sort of thing she'd mentioned liking. And a note from Griffin, in what she knew was his handwriting, saying it was in case she was peckish.

Attention to detail. Annice stared up at the ceiling. There was a lot she found lovely about Griffin. A lot she didn't understand, still, but a great deal she liked. Yesterday, how was that just yesterday, she'd wanted to kiss him because he cared about the grief, because he wanted to do what small things he could to ease that. Possibly also big ones, because people probably didn't end up needing his help in detail if things went smoothly.

But this morning, she found herself dwelling on his attention to the small things. He'd been paying attention to her, to what she liked and didn't like, and it showed in every bit of what he did. The basket, but also making sure she wasn't left on her own in a strange place, not sure how to act or what would be rude. And today, he was going to introduce her to someone who could help.

She took her time getting ready - he'd said he had some business at the Courts first thing in the morning. That meant a pleasant breakfast in the inn's morning room. The handful of other guests were all busy reading papers or books, and she read through the Trellech Moon as she ate. Then she tidied herself up, hoping she looked like she knew a bit about what she was about. She had a clean blouse, the better of her blue skirts, a cardigan, and she'd put up her hair properly. It would have to do.

Griffin had explained this to her. That Annice was going

to meet someone who worked in gemstones, all sorts of stones, and that she made talismans out of them. Not like the jet pieces that Annice had packed, but tiny things, intricate, a kind of magic she didn't even know how to think about. Magistra Hall was in her late seventies, apparently the sort of woman who kept working because she enjoyed her work, but who didn't need to anymore. Annice had no idea what that would feel like, either.

What she knew was that they were going to a workshop in the crafting quarter of Trellech. And Annice wanted to make a good impression. Griffin thought well of Magistra Hall, and she didn't want to embarrass him. He'd said that if they got on, Magistra Hall might be willing to work with Annice longer than a few days. Annice had no idea how to think about that, it seemed terribly unlikely to her in several dimensions. Why would someone like that want to work with her? All she knew was jet. On the other hand, she was determined to be polite and learn what she could.

Once she was done with breakfast, she went outside a little early, because she didn't see the point in making Griffin fuss with getting the ramp at the side door if he didn't need to. He wheeled up, perfectly on time. "Morning."

Annice let out a breath, then it all came out in a rush. "You really thought of everything, thank you. It made me feel comfortable. And they've been lovely."

He lit up, just delighted, and she wanted to keep doing that. Annice was beginning to suspect that not enough people noticed all the things he was quietly doing to make things work. She could at least notice and let him know she had. "Oh, good. Not that I had any doubts. The inn does very well with people who are reasonable."

"Some people aren't reasonable?" They set off, with

Griffin telling her stories he'd heard, about various people who were in fact not at all reasonable. They had been banished to the inns near the market, who both charged rates fit for putting up with the nonsense, and who employed specialist staff to make sure it didn't bother other guests. They crossed a fair bit of the city centre, though on different streets than the day before. Annice thought the route a bit more efficient, before Griffin turned into an alley. It opened into a courtyard, and Griffin was reaching for his crutches before Annice could think to ask where they were going.

"Is the chair all right here?" He must know what he was doing. He turned over his shoulder and grinned. "See the pavement? Actually, here, take three steps back toward the arch, then come here again. Pay attention to how it feels."

She did, moving from a smoothly tiled courtyard to larger pieces of what looked like slate, set in hexagonal shapes. Annice could feel the difference. Now she was concentrating on it, but it was subtle. Griffin took a step or two away from the chair. "And now try to move the chair."

"You're sure?" Annice hadn't wanted to interfere with it, though she'd seen Charlus help him with it a few times.

"Just try to move it a little, from the back. You won't hurt it." He was grinning broadly, the kind of grin that meant she could give him a gift by going along with it. She stepped up behind it, pushing gently. The wheels moved a tiny amount, maybe an inch, but then the chair rocked back against her hands.

"Not brakes." She looked down at her feet. "Warding?"

"A very specific warding. Any object on the property can only be moved by the properly designated owner, or by the owner of the property. I trust her, it's not raining, we're fine to leave the chair here. It's a little cramped inside."

That proved to be true. Griffin got the door, then half propped it open with his shoulder to let her come through. Annice stepped into a shop that had a small space at the front with a counter. There were all sorts of ceramic and stone pieces hanging from the ceiling, on cords, and then carved stones set in rings and pendants under glass at the counter. There was a woman seated behind the counter, knitting, with grey hair pulled back in an old-fashioned plain bun. She was dressed well. That was the kind of fabric that would have Annice suggesting the nicer pieces, the ones that had taken more work and bigger stones, but she wore it comfortably. Annice wasn't very used to judging age among the magical, but she wouldn't have thought this woman in her later seventies, maybe late sixties.

"Magistra Niobe Hall, this is Mistress Annice Matthewman. Annice, this is Niobe, a shining light among Albion's crafters." He held up two fingers. "I remember how you scolded me last time, when I said only Trellech."

The older woman laughed. "You rarely make the same mistake twice. Do come through, Mistress. Or shall we be informal?"

Annice swallowed. "You are welcome to be informal with me, Magistra. I am not entirely sure if I can manage it with you."

That got a longer laugh, easy and good-hearted. "Oh, we're going to do very well together, I suspect. Come along." She hopped off the stool she'd been sitting on, setting her knitting down, and going down the narrow hallway toward the back of the shop. Annice at least knew what to do with that, and she followed, with Griffin behind her.

The hall had a couple of closed doors, and then a set of stairs climbing up in the middle of the building. The workshop was perhaps twice the size of the front, with a wide range of workbenches, and tools that Annice more or less recognised. Not that she'd used all of them - there was a pottery wheel in the corner on one side. "Now, you had something for me to look at? Here, back on this bench, it's clean." The workbench at the back was in fact completely lacking in dust of any kind. After a quick nod from Griffin, Annice set her bag down and brought out the three boxes of the talismans.

"May I touch them?" Niobe had pulled on an apron - or maybe a smock. It had loose sleeves that covered her upper arms. Annice nodded. Griffin pulled up a stool without asking permission. Niobe took quite a long time examining each stone, first looking at all three in quick succession, then going back for details.

Annice shifted uneasily from foot to foot, and she was starting to feel a tad achy, when Niobe turned her head. "I'll need to think about these a bit. A few days, if you're willing. I should be able to fully transcribe what they do and what they were intended to do. And also propose a method for reawakening them, if you wish. I won't guarantee success, not yet - it's not my work, someone else's work is always trickier. But I'll be able to give you more information then."

Whatever Annice had expected, it wasn't that. She opened her mouth, then closed it, not sure what to say. Niobe glanced at her, then shrugged one shoulder. "And you've brought some of what you've made? Can you bring that out, please?"

Griffin had told her to, so she had. Now Annice reached into the bag again, and brought out the dozen pieces she'd packed, showing the range of her skill, all nestled into cotton wool. She opened the box, and set it down, and Niobe asked, just once, "And I may handle these?"

Annice nodded and then went back to uncomfortable shifting. She didn't want to sit, that was the thing, she was all nerves now. After a minute or so, she felt Griffin's hand on her back, just above her waist, steadying, and she leaned into it just a little, the pressure helping, before she glanced over at him. He was just there, patient, waiting, like he was sure what they were going to hear.

This examination was shorter. "This is quite skilled work, and from what Griffin has said, you should be fully able to do whatever carving work you need for the Courts here. I am, hmm." She looked upward for a moment, the way so many crafters did when they were mentally calculating a price. Annice was sure that whatever it was, the price would be both fair and too much for her to pay. "The talismans are about two or three days' work and Griffin has already offered to cover that. If you would like to stay in Trellech for as long as that takes me, I am glad to give you a trial. We can see which of my skills you might want to explore. It would let us discuss a next step after that, if that seemed mutually feasible."

"A next step?" Annice swallowed hard. "Magistra, I— I don't have the resources for that."

"For the next few days, you can put yourself to work helping me keep the place tidy. I'll do my bit, but I am an old woman. I haven't had an apprentice in a few years. I ache in bad weather, and someone to lend a hand with the broom and rag and all that would actually be a help. Also, cleaning is more pleasant in company." Her shoulder twitched. "And if we get on, and you're interested, we could discuss further opportunities at that point. I am fairly certain I can teach you enough to be helpful in preparing blanks fairly quickly. That would let us see what else comes easily to your fingers. And perhaps you'll teach me a bit about jet? I've never worked much with it."

Annice had a lump in her throat, and she looked at Griffin, hoping he'd explain or tell her whether this was fair or all right. He was nodding along. "Usual temporary contract, then, Niobe? I have a copy with me."

Niobe started laughing again, the easy laugh she had. "Of course you do. I wouldn't expect otherwise. Usual terms." She focused on Annice. "That means I provide your raw materials, feed you at least one solid meal a day, and trade you labour for training. Additional hours of labour at a fair wage, and practice time doesn't count against your hours. I'd expect three or four hours of labour cleaning most days and then several hours learning and practising. Anything you make that's sellable, you get half the profit from. I keep the costs for the materials and the other half the profit, and yes, Griffin, a full transparent accounting."

Griffin grinned again and spread his hands. "It's the common arrangement in this case, when people are getting to know each other. Fair, and I trust Niobe to be generous with it. Just like I've told her I am certain you'll work hard and be interesting to teach."

"You think too well of me." It came out of Annice's mouth before she could stop it.

Niobe turned around to face her properly. "I think we'll enjoy finding that out, you and I. All right. Griffin, off you go. I'll make sure she gets back to the inn this evening. You go do whatever it is you do."

"May I walk Griffin out?" Annice wanted a word with him, or rather needed a bit of reassurance.

"Certainly. I've got to find another smock and see about setting up a few things for us to start with. The smock I pulled out will be hanging off the tips of your fingers, that's no good. Five minutes, no more. We'll get started, then lunch upstairs. Off with you, Griffin, don't dawdle." Griffin took that as his cue, and he waved a hand, without saying anything further, then set his arms in his crutches. He led the way down the hall, stopping once he got outside.

"You're— is this real?" Annice took a step out onto the pavement behind him. Her heart was beating fast, and she didn't know what to do with what she'd been offered. It was very sudden, and it didn't feel steady under her feet, but she'd seen that workshop, and she wanted to know more. And then there was Griffin, and falling for him wasn't sensible, but seemed to be happening anyway.

"Quite. Niobe is very good indeed, but she's opinionated. She doesn't need to take apprentices any more, and not everyone gets on with her. You, though, I think you'll do well, if you want. And she needs a few days to figure out your pieces." Griffin was watching her attentively now. "Just remember, you also have skills, all right? Let them know at the inn if you want me round for supper, they can get me a message quickly. If you're worn out and just want to fall into bed, that's fine. I understand that too. Won't be offended. Tomorrow, though, we have supper and theatre tickets."

"You, um." Annice hesitated, then took a step forward, as he was standing in front of the chair, his crutches tucked along the back edges. She kissed him tentatively, then his arm came around her, and he kissed her back.

When he pulled back, he sat down with a slight thump before grinning at her. "Made my knees go weak, you did."

She leaned down to kiss his forehead. "That's not, you said, a particular challenge. Maybe I'll work up to other things. And I'll let you know about supper. And look forward to tomorrow."

"Good. There we go. I won't keep you. Have a wonderful time learning new things." At that, he wheeled around, as if he knew lingering would make her late. Annice watched him go. She didn't know how to get herself from where she was now to that place she could see anything beyond her life in Whitby. It was like looking up at the Abbey at the top of the cliff, and not knowing how to manage the stairs. But now, at the very least, she wanted to give it a try.

CHAPTER 33
APRIL 2ND

Griffin felt the day was going really well. It was Saturday. He did not need to make an appearance in his office, though he'd had plenty to work on at home, checking through more files for any references to what had happened in 1902 to complicate the jet now. They'd scheduled the proper testing for Monday, so at least they should have a bit more information soon.

He hadn't seen Annice on Friday - she had indeed been exhausted from a full day of learning. But she'd gone back for the morning and early afternoon on Saturday, undaunted. From Niobe's brief comments in Griffin's journal, they were getting on well. Annice was picking up a whole set of related skills promptly, as well as being helpful with the cleaning. Griffin got ready for the theatre, smiling every so often, because that was the kind of arrangement that made him happiest, when everyone got something good for them.

Annice was waiting just inside the door when Griffin made it to the inn and she came out immediately. He'd changed into one of his more personal sorts of suits, this one a charcoal grey with a sapphire blue pocket square and bow tie, and a hat to match. Annice came out wearing a blouse and skirt, but she'd done her hair up. Someone had found her a bit of an ornament for it - a fresh flower, charmed to stay that way, if he read the magic correctly. He beamed at her. "You look lovely. Supper, and then the play, yes?"

"You know somewhere, I gather." She was teasing as she said it, and he did. He'd made arrangements with one of the more relaxed restaurants he liked. The family had known his for a generation now. The current owner was someone he'd played with as a boy and his wife was the head chef. Annice was a bit nervous as they settled at their table, but within five minutes, she was relaxing. The food was fantastic, as always. Annice had been willing to try the lamb stew, as one of the local specialities.

Then it was along to the theatre. "This is the New Ricardian, like I mentioned." Griffin nodded at the usher who got the door, and added, "We're in box four. I know the way up."

"As you say, sir." Two minutes later - the lift was ready for them - they were in the box at stage right, not so much in the corner that they couldn't see everything.

Annice leaned forward on the railing, looking around. "Will I understand the play, then? And what should I pay attention to?"

Griffin laughed. "You know your stories, I'm sure? The founding of Albion. They sometimes do a panto version, but the play is much more dramatic. There will be some illusion work lighting things up, shapes in the forest, that sort of thing. And they do quite a lot with a small orchestra and some deftly applied charms." There was a cough behind him, and Griffin twisted. "Ah, Owen. This is my friend, Annice Matthewman. Annice, this is Owen Hubbard, who works backstage, keeping things running smoothly. Anything she ought to look out for? And how's Clara doing? And the little ones?"

"Sir." Owen waved a hand. "She's very well. You ought to go round sometime. She'd love to see you. Same hours, still, there Tuesday to Friday. And our children keep growing out of their shoes, but that's easy enough for me to solve." He made a little half-bow to Annice. "You might see a glimmer from the next box over. We have a theatre ghost, and she rather likes this play, we think. Nothing to worry about, she just leaves a bit of silk flower around when she's happy. Beyond that, well, now. Would you rather know what's coming, or maybe be a little surprised?"

Annice tilted her head. "Today? I'd rather know what's coming. Been a bit of a whirlwind week." Owen took her through the outline of the play in brief. Griffin thought he read Annice's reactions well, letting her know where the scarier parts were, and also where the particularly good acting was likely to come out. Annice asked a few questions, then, about how Owen knew Griffin.

"Oh, a case. A while back now, six years now. He was kind to my wife, when she was nervous about things. We like making sure he can come see a play." Then there was a chime, and Owen's chin went up. "That's my cue to get backstage. Enjoy, and we'll send someone to check on what you want in the interval."

"The other reason for the box," Griffin said. "They do the kindness of making sure we don't have to push and shove at the bar to get a drink or an ice or whatever. And we can eat it here. We are deemed to be unlikely to drip the ice on the seats." It made Annice giggle, as he'd hoped, and they had just a few more minutes to talk about the coming play before the lights dimmed.

The play was everything he'd hoped. Annice fell into the story of it almost immediately. Three scenes in, he felt her take his hand, squeezing it harder when the tension picked up. The interval brought them ices, to be enjoyed in small cups with delicate spoons. That was a treat that Annice obviously hadn't enjoyed often.

"Ices on the beach, of course," she said. "When times were good. But this is different, sitting here like this. What did you think of the woman playing Innogen?" That topic kept them going until the lights dimmed again, since Griffin had seen her in a number of plays now, and quite enjoyed the range of her skill.

When the play finished, they waited a bit for the crowds to thin out. Griffin cleared his throat, a little unsure how she'd take this. "Come back to my place? I thought we might find somewhere comfortable to be for a bit. Together?"

Annice raised an eyebrow, then smiled. "Details to be sorted out when we get there. Certainly." She walked beside him as they left, then twined their way through the streets. It was late enough that the lamplight cast a glow on the stone, especially the redder sandstone that made up a fair number of the buildings.

Griffin let them both in by the door, then stopped there. Annice turned, looking at him, tilting her head. "You're uncertain, all at once. I'm fairly sure of that."

"You're correct." Griffin let out a breath. "I'd rather the bed, if you don't mind. Or me changing into a dressing gown and all. I'm all right for the moment, but it's the sort of night where I might end up exhausted all of a sudden."

"And that's easier if you're already set for bed." Annice sucked in a breath, chewing on her lip. "Go ahead. Can I wash upstairs?"

"Splendid idea. There should be towels there. If not, there's a linen cupboard, erm, to the right of the bathing room. And soap. Five or ten minutes? I'll leave the bedroom door open." She nodded and disappeared toward the kitchen and its stairs. Griffin parked the chair in the bedroom. His hands were shaking a little as he settled onto the stool he kept by the sink in the bathroom to brush his teeth and wash up. Annice gave him more than enough space.

By the time she reappeared, he was in his pyjamas, with a dressing gown firmly over them as a layer. It was not exactly proper, but he was clothed in as many layers as he had been at the theatre, more or less. He'd tried to figure out how best to position himself, ending up more on the left side of the bed, further from the door, with the pillows fluffed.

She'd loosened the neck of her blouse, undoing a couple of buttons. It was enough to expose a V of pale skin, and she'd let her hair down, so it tumbled down her back in a soft coil. "You look a picture." It came out of him breathy and suddenly needy. "You thought about that." The idea that she had, that she wasn't just choosing to stay, but she was choosing how she let herself be seen, that took his words away. Instead of saying more about that, he patted the bed next to him. He'd tucked the chair well out of the way on that side. She sat first, then toed off her shoes beside the bed, bending to nudge them to one side, before she twisted to look at him.

"I'm being very brave." She took a breath, and then flung herself at it, rather like someone might dive off a pier into the ocean water. Her hand came up to cup his cheek. "You've been so kind. No— let me talk." He'd opened his mouth, and her finger tapped it. "Not just kind. You paid attention to all sorts of things. I only noticed because I was so nervous. The inn, the basket of treats."

She took a breath, but it was the short breath before rushing on. "How you found someone for me to talk to, and Niobe is doing at least half the work of convincing me to stay for you. And it hasn't worked yet, not all the way, but there's a good chance it will. Then tonight, it was new, and I've never been to a proper magical theatre. And not so much with going out to eat somewhere other than a pub or fish and chips. And it was all splendid. You made it easy to enjoy it. That there wasn't something that would trip me up." Then she swallowed. "Um. Now you can say things. If you want?"

He did want. Griffin took a moment to choose his words. "I think a lot about tripping these days. Physical and otherwise. The places we snag on an assumption." He turned to look at her square on. "Niobe's being persuasive, then?"

"She doesn't make me feel stupid. She explains things. There's so much I don't know? But she says it like it's ordinary to know some things, and not others. And like she knows I'm a person who wants to learn. Who can learn. You do the same thing. How do you do that? When it's complicated magic, not, I don't know, something any Tom, Dick, and Harry could learn with a bit of practice?" Then she ducked her chin. "What would it look like if I stayed? Not saying I'm deciding yet."

"If things keep going well with Niobe, she'd consider taking you on as an apprentice. Most of her pieces these days are talismans, not just decorative, but she knows all the gem cutting, too. You'd learn to make them, she'd teach you that. She - or I - would maybe find some other people to learn from, how to do the jewellery parts you don't know. Setting different kinds of stones, I know there are multiple techniques."

She snorted, but she leaned forward to kiss his cheek, so that was all right. Griffin let out a breath. "And I hope you and I would find what works for us. I work an awful lot, I get focused on that. But you'd be welcome to stay here - here, this bed, or upstairs. I'd make sure to take a break for dinner. We could refit one room upstairs as a workroom, if you wanted."

"You barely know me." Annice had gone very quiet now, barely whispering.

"True. But the way you kissed me? I think I want to know more. Learn more. Just like you." Griffin rode the line of that arrow of truth, as far as he could bear. Then he closed his eyes, just waiting.

She didn't move much, but he heard her voice, nearly in his ear. "I kissed you because you care. People grieving. That they have the space. People didn't give me that space, they gave me the custom, and the things you say out of politeness, and it wasn't enough. You? You understand that."

"I'm not perfect." Now he could look at her, blinking to get his eyes to focus. "Don't think I am. I get frustrated when my legs won't do what I want. When my body betrays me. Briefly, these days, mostly. And I'm stubborn, and I won't leave Trellech, and I'm aiming at something that will tie me here, in new ways. Still hoping I can have it, despite everything."

Her fingers touched his cheek. "I don't know how I feel about all of that. But I'm not running away from it, all right? Show me what it's really like. What the stone is, under all that, the ways it comes alive in the carving." She sucked in a breath. "Let's see if I make it far enough to see your mother wearing the rose I made."

Now it was Griffin's turn to suck in a breath, and that was such a particular marker of what they might become, a potent one. "Oh, yes. Though I think there might be quite a few steps before that. We could get started exploring those."

"No need to rush. But mm, yes. You suggested your bed. What did you have in mind?" Annice's voice had gone breathy now, and when he shifted his hand to touch her back, he could feel how she was breathing shallowly.

"Here, stretch out. Kissing. Touching a little. Nothing you don't want. And remember you can outrun me, easily, if you decide to." Griffin held his breath until she started rearranging herself, stretching out on her side, facing him. It made it easy to let his hand rest on her back, fingers spread, in hopes of touching other places in a little. Then he was shifting himself, to match her, then to kiss her. It was easier like this, when he didn't have to worry about balancing on the sofa. She was just as responsive now.

They were breathless with it, for a long time. When they had to pause, to rest and recover a little, he murmured in her ear. "You could stay the night if you wanted. They won't mind at the inn."

"Did you think of that, too?" She was blinking at him - he'd dimmed the lights. When he nodded, she laughed, then nuzzled at his shirt. "Mmm. It's very comfortable here. With you. And the bed."

"No reason to move, then." Griffin might have hoped for a bit more of a romp. But it had been a long day for her - and he suspected she'd been using her magic more than she'd realised. After a few more nuzzling kisses, she dropped off to sleep, nestled against his shoulder. He stayed awake for a good long time, until after the faint ring of the midnight bells from the Ministry bell tower. It felt good to lie there just listening to her breathe and feel the way she trusted him.

CHAPTER 34
APRIL 3RD

Annice woke the next morning, again uncertain where she was. Her head, it turned out, was on Griffin's shoulder. He had pulled a blanket over her, but he was under the sheets himself. She carefully moved, considering her options. Making breakfast seemed the most sensible thing once she washed up. And seeing what Griffin said, when he was properly awake.

He slept quite a long time, actually. More than long enough for her to wash. She made a cup of tea, rummaging for a book from the shelves by the door, which seemed to be his more general reading. She'd curled up on the sofa and read into the second chapter when she heard sounds from the bathing room. A couple of minutes later, he wheeled himself into the main room and caught sight of her. "Not a figment of my dreams, then." He followed it promptly by adding, "I hope you were comfortable and that I didn't do anything you didn't want."

"I slept very well. Don't remember a thing until I woke up. I'm, um, sorry I fell asleep on you?"

Griffin wriggled a hand. "I enjoyed it." It was a simple

statement. It was him saying it, so she knew it was true. "Will you stay?"

"Stay now? Stay, um, longer?" Annice wanted him to be clear, because what she wanted was actually rather foggy. Other than that she wanted more of what last night had been, whatever that was.

"Both. Either. Whatever you'll accept. You can have the bedroom upstairs, if you like. Just." Now he looked very much like a plaintive dog. Or like Grandad had, when he wanted something and couldn't quite admit it.

Annice stood, her hands on her hips, considering him. "It's very hard to resist you when you look like that. So you know. Don't take too much advantage of it." Then she let out a breath, slowly, thinking through her options. "I'm thinking I make you breakfast, and then I go and pack up my things and bring them here. If I change my mind, you can get me a room again, right?"

She wasn't ready to commit to anything. Certainly not to promising to share his bed, not yet. Not in the more euphemistic sense. She knew that when she did that, she'd be saying yes to everything else. Or she'd already have said yes. But she could, maybe, try on what it would feel like. Surely the bubble of it would pop and dissolve in a few more days.

"Right." Now Griffin was lit up like a lamp again. "A quiet day today? Make free with my books. I see you have. Or the kitchen, or anything else you need. I thought we might go out for lunch, have supper here, and be ready for tomorrow."

That was, in fact, what they did. Oh, he made sure there was time to curl up together, for kissing and cuddling, but they didn't go any further with it than they'd done the night before. Except, this time, she had a nightgown on, and she was under the covers, and she stayed there. When his alarm went off the next morning, he reached over to turn it off, then immediately nuzzled at the back of her head. "I could get used to this."

She snorted, and went upstairs to go wash, while he did the same downstairs. The thing of it was, she could too. He'd made it so easy to fit into his life in a way she didn't even know how to ask about. Surely that wasn't just for her, the way Griffin did that. Only it felt like it was, like every little detail was a particular choice he was making, with her comfort and happiness in mind.

They left entirely on time by his standards, depositing their coats and bags in his office before continuing down to the courtroom. There were already two women waiting, one in a Guard uniform, one in a black jacket, skirt, and white blouse with a touch of green at the collar. Both were perhaps in their fifties, two decades older than Annice. But it was hard to tell, especially with the second woman, who had light brown skin and black hair that had a few silver strands.

Griffin beamed at them, though to be fair, he'd been beaming pretty continuously all day so far. "Mason, I was hoping you'd be free. And Antimony." He then gestured with one hand as he came to a stop. "This is Penelope Elizabeth Mason. Penelope as a title, of course. And Captain Antimony Orland, one of the Guard who works most closely with inheritance matters. This is Mistress Annice Matthewman, our current expert in jet." She noticed, yet again, how he made sure to give her the title.

Both women nodded, and the Penelope said, amused, "You needn't be formal with us. I'm Mason in general conversation. And Antimony, for some reason, does not actually hate her first name." It appeared to be some sort of old joke, because the other woman, the Guard, just chuckled.

Annice had never actually been in the same room as one of the Penelopes. All she knew about them was what turned up in the Trellech paper, or in gossip, how they knew all sorts of magical things, and investigated some of them. And there was sometimes nastier gossip, how they were more women than men, and how they got above themselves, sticking their noses in many corners and not minding their place. This woman showed no signs of that sort of rudeness, and Annice didn't exactly have room to throw stones about doing things women didn't usually.

"Annice, then. May I ask what you're doing?" Annice folded her hands in front of her, wanting to fidget and not sure how to avoid it.

"Secret and arcane magics." Mason laughed as she finished, as if she couldn't keep her face straight longer. "I've samples of jet from several locations, and I'm going to do a bit of fiddly ritual work, and then see about identifying what's set in the room. And then I'm likely going to have some questions for you. All Penelopes have a working knowledge of gemstones and such, but there are nuances here I don't know. Yet." Then she waved a hand. "All three of you, over there, don't move out of the area I marked off." The space was roughly a square, made by removing one table in the court and drawing out a circle with chalk.

Griffin rolled over it - apparently it was a marking, not a boundary - and Antimony followed him, leaving Annice to come last. Once Annice was seated, Mason turned away, and opened up a case, setting to work doing things that involved slight movements and muttered charms. Nothing Annice could actually hear.

No one said anything for a couple of minutes. Then

Griffin reached out and took Annice's hand. He tilted his head, as if considering, then stayed quiet, apparently so as not to interfere with Mason's concentration. Antimony, the Captain, glanced at them before her mouth twitched, and she half-closed her eyes. Annice glanced at her watch a couple of times. It was nearly forty minutes before Mason spoke more clearly. "All right. I have some information. Annice, would you come have a look?"

Griffin squeezed her hand once before he let it go, and Annice got up, going over to where Mason was standing. She had a small case made of wood, with different compartments in it. There were four different pieces there, and Annice immediately spotted that the one on the right was horn. "Yes'm?"

"So, three kinds of jet here. And what we have in the settings are mostly - but not entirely - Spanish jet. I tested against a piece of Whitby jet, a piece from Asturias, and that one, there, is from France. Bless having friends with well-documented jewellery collections. Now. What I didn't have time to study up on is why that's a problem."

"French is poor quality," Annice said immediately. "And a lot of the Spanish is. But the problem with the Spanish - at least in this case - is that it's softer. More coal-like, is the way it's put in Whitby, but we're people who work the stone, not people who know the proper science. Or the proper magic behind the differences."

"Ah, that gives me some ideas for some further testing. All right, that means that a setting designed for the one would not work as reliably for the other. I think we can posit that much right now." Mason tapped her fingers on the table. "Does that also mean it breaks down more?"

"Softness would imply that, since we're not precisely looking for flexibility in use here." Griffin's voice came up from behind them, and Annice turned around. He'd wheeled himself over. "You said most of the jet here, not all of it?"

"The actual lines of inlay, the parts that are small beads of jet, all lined up, most of those seem to be Whitby. But they're tiny pieces, just shaped enough to fit in the channels, right? And they're not doing as much of the heavy lifting, magically speaking."

Griffin nodded, and Annice echoed it, adding, "The bigger pieces are the ones at the connections. The crossroads, that's how I was thinking of them."

"So if you could replace those pieces - four, at least, ideally all eight - you ought to be able to keep things going until you can reset the whole thing in a couple of years." Mason said. "Or at least that's a working theory. And you could swap out one at a time to keep all the extant connections running."

Annice blinked at her. "How do you know all of that?" It came out sharper than Annice meant, but the other woman just laughed.

"I'm a Penelope. We know many things. But I don't have the skill to work the stone like that, nor the time in my schedule to do it. I'm an artist in two dimensions, not three. That's where you come in. And I expect you'll figure out several other things along the way, and I'd love to talk to you about it as you work."

"If you're ever free for supper, Mason, we could have you round." Griffin said it easily, like it was an ordinary thing to say. "As long as Annice is handy, anyway."

Mason raised an eyebrow at something in that, but she nodded amiably, then she started packing up her box. "Speaking of, I have three places to be today. Keep me informed, would you? And Antimony..."

The Guardswoman laughed. "Tomorrow, yes. Tea, your office, first thing." She stepped back to let Mason out, waiting for the door to close behind her, before she turned to face Griffin more solidly. "Now, do you want the gossip?"

"Please, yes." Griffin let out a sigh. "First, though. Annice, that made sense to you? Do you have things you want to look at here?"

Annice's mind was spinning. "Is that what we're doing? Swapping out the crossroad stones?" She'd wondered about it, since she'd seen the layout, and she'd talked a little about that kind of setting with Niobe, but not in any detail yet.

"Can you take the measurements for it? Do you need a hand? Antimony can help. Or I can, though the positioning's a little more..." Griffin let his voice trail off.

Annice considered. "I'll need someone in a bit, but let me start with detailed measurements in situ." She pulled her bag around, setting it on the table, and rummaging in it for her tools. Besides, Antimony had said something about gossip, and Annice wanted to hear what that meant. Once she had her measuring tools out, she set to work on the piece nearest where they were standing.

Antimony pulled a chair around to sit in, and Griffin had angled himself so he could see where Annice was, as well as talk to Antimony. Antimony set in, immediately, with "Well, first, at least three people mentioned they'd seen you out and about this weekend. In company. Before I got my tea this morning."

"You were on duty from what, six?" Griffin said, amused. "And yes. Theatre on Saturday, supper before, lunch yesterday, and a bit of walking through going other places. Who told you?"

It got him a list of names and then a mention of a

couple of others, before Antimony said, "And I gather Nestor was looking sour, so good work there."

Griffin grunted. "Different problem, that. What did I miss while I was gone?" That turned into a murmur of commentary. It seemed a well organised discussion, and when Annice turned around to swap out tools, Antimony apparently had a set of notes out. Most of it didn't make sense to Annice, she didn't have any context to attach it to. But there'd apparently been a big blowup with one case. There was something going on with a posh family, and a lot of gossip about whether the Guard was investigating someone else. Griffin didn't seem surprised by it, or upset, so Annice kept her focus on her work.

The conversation kept up for a bit, before some of it caught her attention again. She'd measured all the individual pieces in their settings, but she wanted more information about how they related to each other in the space. Griffin said, more clearly, "What I want to do is prove I'm up to the task."

Her chin came up, and she stood, resting her hands on the desk. Griffin looked at her, meeting her eyes, then said, "We were talking about proving I'm as ritually competent as anyone."

"Even though I know you are. Sensible people do." Antimony said, soothingly.

Annice had apparently learned a few things in just a handful of days. There was a thought tickling at the back of her mind, a combination of what they'd been talking about on and off, and about something Niobe had mentioned in passing. Then Annice pulled it together, holding up her hand to show she had something now.

Griffin immediately nodded at her. "Please?"

"Niobe said something, and you were talking yesterday." Annice stopped. "This is coming out badly."

"Antimony's a friend. And I'm listening. Or we could make Antimony go stand in the hall for a few minutes." Griffin offered the second, apparently entirely serious, and it made Annice wince.

"No. Just, I don't have the right words. Let me try." Annice thought about what she felt from Griffin, how he had been making space for her all along. "You've been so thoughtful, making space for me. Checking that things were comfortable, when you knew everything was new and different and I didn't know what to expect or plan for. And we talked about what you liked about the Abbey, the way the space was made for what it did."

Annice grimaced. This wasn't coming out right, then she just let the words come as she could get them out. "This is a courtroom, right? That's one kind of space, but are there others here? For people waiting, or I don't know, conversations that aren't in the courtroom? Besides offices? Or is it all courtrooms and - fancy? What happens if someone from Whitby, or a tiny village, never been to Trellech, never done much with the Guard, is being questioned or helping with something? Or someone who's upset, like you mentioned with inheritance cases."

"That is an excellent question. We have some meeting rooms, but they're not set up to support anything magically, other than privacy." Griffin said, and his hand shifted his chair for just a second, the way she'd seen him do a few times when someone else might pace. He didn't move much, just rocked back and forth, almost in place. "There's a room we could repurpose. Witnesses in complex cases, space when there's a tough decision in the offing, that sort of thing, yes?"

Annice nodded, bobbing her head several times.

"The Guard has a room or two like that for questioning, but that's a different purpose. You could use one here. We've had more than enough cases where it would have been a help. Or a kindness. Both." Antimony nodded, more direct. "It's an excellent idea. And it's a good scope, to prove yourself. You'd need layers of talisman work, though."

Griffin's smile came back, like he'd stopped concentrating as hard on everything in his head. "Good thing I've got reason to stop by Niobe's regularly at the moment. The materia might be a trick, but we could probably work with secondary stones, if we can't get the primaries. It's the combination of effects. And I'll need to consult a couple of other people on the design work. Not my area of particular expertise."

"It's barely anyone's area of specialty," Antimony pointed out. "Should I put the word around to a couple of people that you have an idea, please make time in their diaries for you in the next week?"

"If you would." Then Griffin looked up at Annice, smiling warmly. "That's an excellent thought, and I'm going to be very busy sorting some of it out for a bit. Can we help with your measurements now, before we lose ourselves in that?"

Annice nodded. "Please. This one over here, I'd like to get some distance, and that involves two people to hold the measures, and one to look at them." That process took them a bit, especially finding angles that worked with the fixed furniture. Then it was time to break for lunch. Annice went off to Niobe's for the afternoon. She had several dozen questions about the process of selecting and setting stones for this kind of work, relevant to both herself and Griffin.

CHAPTER 35
APRIL 9TH

The next four days went by in a way Griffin hadn't expected. He and Annice had settled into a comfortable routine with no fuss at all. They shared a bed, companionably but without new forms of intimacy. He'd have been glad enough if they had. It wasn't the standard Christian practice. But Griffin held that one of the reasons for the prohibition against sex outside of marriage was conception. The other was that it created ties - magical as well as emotional - with the person you were with. Magic tended the first, and he wanted the second, if Annice did too.

The quiet intimacy of having someone there, though, was something he leaned toward more and more. When they woke in the morning, Annice usually put things together for breakfast, and they went off to their separate work. On Wednesday, they'd gone to see the Temple of Healing's spaces properly.

The night they'd gone, it had been rather quiet, and they'd been able to take their time walking around with one of the guides to the carvings and stained glass and all the individual shrines tucked along the long walls. Annice had relaxed there, in a way that Griffin hadn't quite expected, and he had been able to just soak in being in a space that was well-designed for purpose. It had given him - or rather one of the shrines had - several new ideas for his current work, too.

Then they'd come home. Home. That was the thing about it. Griffin enjoyed having someone about the place. He'd known, since he was in school, that he was someone who enjoyed having other people around, regularly, predictably. Not always right in his space - he got lost in his own work a bit much for that. But when he came out of it, he liked having someone to talk with over a mug of tea or a biscuit, someone to chat books with. And here and now, someone to share the day with.

He hadn't thought he'd ever get that. There was the chair, though he knew well enough from other people's lives that finding a partner who was fine with it was possible. But as he'd said to Charlus, what seemed like years ago, he worked a great deal. He could be tedious, and his standards around truth weren't always entirely comfortable.

Annice seemed to have thrown herself into her learning. As expected, Niobe had sorted out the talisman stones by Wednesday, and she'd written up detailed specifications. The three were indeed designed for protection, though in ways that Annice hadn't found entirely comfortable. Not that Griffin had pressed her to talk about it. She either would or she wouldn't. Niobe had promptly presented Annice with a contract for additional work, for as long as it took Annice to properly set the courtroom up. As well as the stones for what Griffin was planning. That was not an instant process. Annice had plans to go up to Whitby on Monday, to search for more jet that would suit. She intended to look not only from the beach, but at her grandad's workshop and Rob's and Cliff's discards.

They'd also made time to be sociable, though. Griffin had arranged for supper out with Mason and Witt on Thursday, letting Annice see how the two of them played off each other. Mason was all odd angles and unexpected connections, while Witt was far more logical. After, a bit to his own surprise, he'd invited them back home for drinks. They'd both stopped by a few times over the years, for a case, but they'd never come in and spent time. Seeing them together - and the way they leaned into that difference rather than it causing friction - always made Griffin feel better.

Annice had enjoyed it, too, though not as much, perhaps, as she'd enjoyed meeting Golshan and Seth and Seth's engineer friend, Ponyard. That had been Friday afternoon, when Golshan set up at the Field, the Schola club for Horse House. They'd put in a ramp for him, early on, and also hosted a number of the veterans gatherings in Trellech. Griffin didn't go terribly often - perhaps once a quarter at most - but he somehow needed to know those gatherings and people were there. The Fridays, though, that was just for whoever needed a hand, something outside what the structures and formalities permitted.

On Friday, they'd gone in right as Golshan wrapped that up, and Golshan had lit up to see Griffin. "And this is your friend, then? Mistress Matthewman, I gather you want to know more about how the chairs work?" He showed the various features of his, and let Annice see them side by side. He, of course, didn't get out of his. His injuries and paralysis made that much more of a production, and not easy to do unless he was sliding onto a bed or bit of furniture of the proper height.

Ponyard and Seth, between them, had been glad to explain what they'd done. It tied into what Annice was learning about stones, rather nicely, though they were doing it mostly in wood, and a bit in metal. Both wheel-chairs had copper, more than would normally be used, for the magical conductivity. The woods had been chosen to suit Golshan and Griffin individually, both their magic and their physical needs. Annice had knelt on the ground between the two chairs, asking dozens of questions. She'd asked quite a few Griffin had never thought of, about the wear on the metal and the wood. But of course, she knew a fair bit about fishing vessels and mining machinery, as well as working with gemstones.

Now it was Saturday, and Annice was curled up on the sofa, reading, while Griffin had worked on some notes from a stack of books on his desk. Or rather, while he'd been trying to work on notes. He kept glancing over his shoulder to watch her. After he'd done it, oh, ten or twelve times, she looked up over her book. "You keep doing that? Is some-thing the matter?"

"Something's very good. Just." Griffin swivelled the chair around slightly, wheeling slightly back and twisting to the right, so he could face her better. "How much I like you being there. Didn't mean to interrupt, though."

"You don't seem to have been getting much done. Bedroom?" Annice set her book on the side table and stood up.

Griffin chuckled. "Oh, always, if you're offering." He let her go first, then followed, doing the various bits of getting ready while she ducked into the loo, then switching places with her. He came back out to find her stretched out on the bed, up on one elbow, watching him. "Yes?"

"You haven't, um." She gestured at his side of the bed.

What had become his side of the bed. "You haven't." Now she was blushing. "I like being with you. Maybe more things with you?" Now she was near beet red, and Griffin couldn't help grinning. He reached up to touch her cheek, running his thumb over the arch of her skin.

"I haven't wanted to press you. There have been a lot of new things. And, well. You've been willing to share my bed, but I didn't want to make assumptions about whether you wanted to save some things for marriage or what."

"Marriage." Her nose wrinkled up. Then she was giggling. "A little fast, sir."

"I wasn't suggesting it yet!" He was laughing now too, because honestly, this was a ridiculous conversation, even if it was also utterly lacking in discomfort. They obviously had a thing to talk out. He was confident they'd manage it in good humour and come to some agreeable decision. Granted, part of that was that there were a lot of ways this could go that he'd be fine with. Basically any of the options other than her storming out into the night.

She considered, stretching out on her side, head on one elbow. It meant less distraction, with fewer ways for their hands to wander, and a little more effort to kiss. "I said I'd done some things with other people. Mostly one. We were not really engaged, but we were sort of heading that way."

Griffin considered, then reached with his fingers to touch her hand, where it had settled between them on the bed. "What happened?"

"He found someone else, and also more prospects in York. Further inland. And I couldn't have left Whitby then, either. We went to bed enough times that I missed it. And it wasn't so good that I went out looking for more of it from someone who'd understand the, the, um."

"Living in a community where everyone knows

everyone else's business," Griffin agreed. "I mean, I understand that part, even if Trellech's a bigger place."

"The amount of gossip people pass on, obviously." She had been aware all along that Griffin had been teased about her a number of times in the past fortnight. Most of it was kind enough, but not all of it had been approving.

He let his fingers tighten against Annice's for a moment, looking down at their hands rather than at her face for this part. "I haven't much since I came back. Enough to know I could, but never with the right person. A couple of people wanted to nursemaid me, do everything, assume I couldn't."

"That seems tedious." Annice leaned in slowly to kiss his lips. "I don't do that."

"You don't. I like that we're sharing it. You're faster in the morning. It does take me a bit longer. Sorting out clothing and washing and getting ready. It's nice to come out, and the tea's already steeping and there's breakfast. But I think I do my part."

"More than your part," Annice pointed out. "If I were in Whitby, I'd be doing all the work myself, and the cleaning and all the shopping. And all the laundry. I don't miss that at all, even if the charms help a lot." Here, it disappeared on laundry day, and reappeared the next, all folded. "It feels like a holiday, and it feels like..." Her breath caught, and she stopped, blushing again.

"I hope, very much, you'll be here for a long time. With me. In some form, and maybe that will change." Griffin hesitated for a second. "Would you like a bit more of the physical than we've done?" He hadn't wanted to pressure her, not when she was dealing with so many other new things and figuring out what she might want.

"Now?" She met his eyes, then she nodded once, cautiously. "What sort of things?"

Griffin pushed up a bit more on his right elbow, letting his left hand drift to settle in the dip of her waist and the curve of her hip. "It's Saturday night. We can take our time, not rush in the morning. A good time for a bit of exploration." He let out a breath. "Been a while for me, as I said. My arms are fine, my hips generally are. Anything that takes standing's obviously not a good choice for me. Maybe not being up on my knees, but I don't really know. You could be on top of me, if you like, but I don't know if that makes you shy. We might have to do some experimentation. And of course, I've only the beginnings of an idea about what you like." Her breath caught. He was absolutely close enough to hear it and feel the way it shifted her body. "You tell me what you'd like to try, and we'll go from there."

She shifted, then, onto her back, though one of her hands slipped down to take his, letting them rest on her stomach. "I'm nervous. It's a big step. A lot of other big steps, some of which I'm still not quite ready to think about." Then she was tugging his fingers up toward her chest. "You've been showing me how to love Trellech. Show me how to love you. Bumps and all. Show me what you know about me so far."

Griffin nodded. "A specific landscape, full of treasures." He considered his options, then said the phrase that would dim the lights, just enough for them to see each other comfortably. "So I, erm, know the scope of the explorations. Is there anything I should avoid? Anything you'd particularly like tonight?"

"I take a potion." It came out of her in a bit of a blurt. "Da taught me how to make it. You needn't, um." Then she was blinking at him. "I'd like to see the ways you're strong.

The ways you think about doing this. Feel them. Can we do that?"

Griffin bent to kiss her, the sort of kiss that was gentle nips, then his tongue. He let go of her hand so he could use his better, while getting himself settled so his whole body pressed against her side. She could feel him, he was sure, that the idea of this was certainly arousing. He kept up with that for several minutes, letting his hips rock against hers, before finally she rolled onto her side, again, to get her hand down between them.

Between the kisses - now he was nuzzling more at her neck and the scent of her hair - she got her hand on him. "Do you like me touching you?"

"Oh, yes." It came out as a bit of a grunt. Her fingers closed around him, slipping through his pyjamas just as he started speaking. Her hands were strong as well as skilled. He should have expected that, given all she'd trained them to do. He couldn't think of anything else but the touch for a good dozen breaths. When he could think again, all he wanted to do was get his hands up under her nightgown, fingers touching and stroking. He began with it, then she realised what he was doing, and rolled onto her back, letting him concentrate on that. He pushed his clothes aside and off, glad of his ability to balance on one arm as needed.

Griffin had not forgotten these specific skills, but it was easier with her than he remembered. Annice didn't hide her reactions from him; she didn't cloak them in what was acceptable. She let him see the truth of what she was feeling, and that was perhaps the best compliment he knew. Even when, as he did once, he went a little fast, from two fingers to three, stroking inside her before she was entirely ready.

He took longer at the rest of it, before he pushed up on his right arm. "May I, then? Do you want that?"

Annice's hand came up to rest on his shoulder. She'd lost track of words, he thought, but she nodded, firmly. Then her other hand came up to his hip, nudging him in the right direction. It was only moments later that he was bracing on his arms, reaching to find the right place, and then pushing into her.

The first stroke or three were not simple. She was right that it had been a long time for her. Then she rocked her hips a little, and he found a better angle. Griffin wanted to take his time, but found all too soon that he couldn't. All he could manage was holding back enough to bring her along with him, most of the way. His own need boiled out of him before she quite found her own pleasure. As soon as he could breathe again, before he slipped out of her, he got his fingers between them. He managed to bring her off with her own gasp.

Griffin had just enough conscious thought and grasp of his magic to mutter a cleaning charm before he burrowed in against her, soaking in her warmth and presence. And he slept very, very well indeed.

CHAPTER 36

APRIL 18TH

"Tell me again why tonight?" Annice was walking alongside Griffin. It was ten at night. They were aiming for Griffin's parish church.

"The vigil service." Griffin glanced up at her. She caught a good look at him in the streetlight. "I know it's not as common elsewhere, but it's honestly one of my favourite liturgies. The ritual text has a fair bit of Latin, but they'll do the readings and all the parts you have to agree with in English."

Griffin was, Annice suspected, the sort of person who had a dozen favourite liturgies, all for different reasons. They were absolutely about the structure of the space and how it related to time, in the particular ways that enthralled him nearly as much as truth and fairness did. "Not tomorrow at dawn? That's what we did in Whitby." They'd talked a little about the fact that her experience of Whitby's Anglican parishes was different from his in trellech, but not nearly all the details.

"There's a dawn service at the Temple of Healing

tomorrow. Poor Augustus has to do double duty and get up for it. It's rather impressive, but it's also more than a bit of a crush. All the people who only go to services two or three times a year. I wish them well with it, but I don't need to be there." His shoulder twitched for just a second. "Also, I don't get much of a view. Mostly people's arses. They take the pews out, so everyone's standing the whole time."

They paused for a second before crossing a street, and he gestured. "I like this much more. We start outside, and then we go in, and if you'd hold my candle when we get to that part, I'd be obliged. There's a side entrance with the ramp, and a space for the chair all the way forward on the left."

"Why half-ten?" That was the part Annice hadn't been able to figure out.

"Astronomical twilight. And it means we'll have the Acclamation after midnight. Satisfies both beginning in true dark, and the coming of the light, and means we're not up until dawn on this end."

About at that point, they came up to the small group gathering outside St. Matthew's. It was one of the three Anglican parishes in Trellech. St. David's was further north, and more ardently Welsh in particular ways. Annice could more or less manage the Latin of the service when it was used. But she'd only picked up enough Welsh to make it clear she didn't speak it. It was apparently a common enough tongue among the people who'd grown up in Trellech, which made sense. Saint Hildegard's was apparently the posh parish, deep in the well-off section of Trellech, attended by those with a particular interest in materia and magic along with their religion.

Griffin was immediately welcomed in by a number of

people, though almost no one spoke. Griffin had explained this was more or less picking up in the middle of a service, running from Good Friday through to this evening.

As it got on for half-ten, there was a single toll from the bell tower. The ritual began in darkness and in silence, barely a rustle of clothing. There was a priest there as celebrant - not the usual rector, Annice had met him on previous Sundays - and others, all in plain white vestments for the moment. They formed a loose half-circle around the front porch of the church, with the priests and deacons and acolytes and a choir standing on the steps. The celebrant called fire with his hands and magic into a great shallow metal bowl, and began, his voice carrying clearly into the night. There was a prayer, calling them together and blessing the fire. Then he used it to light a tremendous beeswax pillar, nearly as tall as the men on the steps.

Annice found someone pressing a candle into her hands, then handing one to Griffin. Everyone processed in. Griffin made for the left-hand door, handing his candle to her before he went. He kept pace with the procession, just a little behind where that single tall candle was lit. It stopped each time the deacon with the candle sang, each time "Lumen Christi", the light of Christ.

When the procession reached the front of the church and the altar, he gestured for her to go into a pew. Griffin aligned his chair with the open spot on the end, out of the side aisle. Just as he stopped moving, someone next to her had their lit candle, and she took a breath, lighting hers. Then she handed Griffin his own, and let him light. The room was shimmering now with a hundred, two hundred, tiny candle flames in the darkness, flickering. She couldn't really see the altar, properly - it was so dark there, and there were people in front of it. But she thought it might be entirely empty, as it had been for the last day.

Just at that moment, another person sang, or rather first one person, and then the choir led the response. She did not know this tune, but she did not need to, the people around her carried her along, especially Griffin's voice beside her. It seemed the most magical of services, how the dark played against the candles, and the way the candles held enough hope to get through the hard times.

She had not been prepared for the readings. It wasn't just that there were a lot of them - Griffin had warned her about that. It was what they were. Laid out, in ancient words, were the building blocks. It began with Genesis, and she understood immediately why Griffin liked this service. Each reading built on the others, some of the most known stories and moments, one after another. It didn't matter that it was long. She was enthralled.

Finally, they worked around to baptisms and confirmations, with everyone following on and reaffirming their own oaths. Of course, that would matter here in Trellech, where everyone lived their lives anchored by their oath on the Silence, as well. It had a new weight, one that Annice was going to have to think about a lot. The Silence Oath, the one she'd made at twelve, like everyone in Albion, didn't limit her actions, other than talking about magic with those who didn't have it. It didn't enforce a belief or a cultural custom. Just that one thing. But now, here she was with people who were committing to belief and to practise, and it felt wonderful to be in company as she renewed her own baptismal commitments.

The organ picked up music then, great sound from the pipes at the back, and the choir sang. Annice tried to focus on what was going on at the altar, but she couldn't quite see, rather like there was a fog. Out of the near darkness, as the song faded, came the call "Alleluia, Christ is Risen!" The entire congregation surged to their feet - even Griffin, who had a hand out to balance on the bench back in front of him.

There was a deep bass rumble from the organ, and then all the lights came up, shining as bright as day. They were bright both inside the church and somehow bright enough outside to shine bolts of colour onto the floor from the stained glass. The music broke out into something utterly joyous, full of bells and trumpets, echoing drums, all together in cresting sound.

At first, she was certain the altar was still bare. Then, before her eyes, item after item appeared, as - that must be the bishop - stepped forward, now fully robed. His cope was thick with golden thread and even stones sewn in that caught the light and sparkled. Soon, the altar had everything needed, and there were flowers bursting into bloom around the pillars, filling the air with a living fragrance. That was magic at work, to make all of that happen in an instant, and she had no idea how they managed it.

The service from there was what she was used to, and she felt buoyed by the tradition of it, of knowing what to expect after having so much newness. When they were seated again and the service went on, Griffin reached for her hand, holding it until it was time for them to receive the Eucharist. He managed that with a cane, though they were near enough the front that it at least wasn't a very long walk.

They waited - as they had at the theatre - for most of the congregation to file out, before making their way down the expected line of clergy. Griffin was beaming until they came to the end, and the bishop. Griffin reached out a hand. "Augustus! Happy Easter to you." Then he glanced at Annice. "This is my friend and colleague, Annice Matthewman. Annice, Bishop Augustus Fuller. We won't keep you, Augustus, but perhaps supper sometime, once you've had a bit of a rest?"

"I will look forward to it. A pleasure, Mistress Matthewman. Anyone Griffin knows is worth knowing better." He inclined his head, and they went on, into a small knot of people, calling out to Griffin, wanting to meet Annice. Someone passed around biscuits, and Griffin murmured that they were traditional, and also tasty. She took a bite, and it near crumbled in her mouth, all currant, and orange and sugar and a hint of spice. The conversation continued for a few minutes until people individually made their good nights and went off in different directions.

It wasn't until she and Griffin were on their own, perhaps halfway back home - and yes, it was firmly home tonight - that Annice spoke up. "Of course you know the Bishop. Why did I think you wouldn't?"

Griffin laughed, delighted with her. "Well. To be fair, he baptised me, early in his time as a priest. And second, Trellech is a diocese of three churches. He'd be terrible at his job if he didn't know the regulars. He rotates which parish gets him for vigil every year, besides the Temple of Healing in the morning. Shall we have him round for supper, or would that be too much?"

"What's he like, when he's not..." She gestured at the shape of the mitre.

"He loves interesting food - not necessarily posh, interesting - and good conversation, and people who can talk about things other than their own immediate problems. When he's not on duty. He'd love hearing about Whitby, he did a stint up in Yorkshire as part of his seminary training. Before my time, obviously."

"I can talk about Whitby. Let's, yes, if you'd like it and he'd like it." Annice knew, as she said it, that she was, in fact, committing to something. That she'd already committed to something, sometime in the last days. She'd chosen to stay with Griffin, then to share his bed. And now she was working around to saying yes to far more. She wouldn't take it back, even if there were a lot of details to work out still. She halted, and Griffin stopped a second later. "Don't ask me about beyond that yet? Tonight was amazing, but it was a lot."

"It's a very impressive service, and I'm always amazed that they get all the coordination right. Easier with magic. We use some of the same tools in the courts, when we have to be impressive and sequence things just so. But getting everything ready for the altar, and the additional vestments and all." Griffin grinned. "The set Augustus was wearing go back a hundred and fifty years, and they're charmed to catch the light and reflect it."

That set the tone for the rest of the walk and both of them washing and changing for bed. It wasn't until they were tucked up in bed - which was no longer entirely strange - that Griffin changed the subject. "I loved having you there tonight. As a thing we did together, that we shared." His hand shifted to take hers. "I'm not asking you anything yet. I just want to be sure you know how much I'm enjoying this. Your company, coming home and knowing you'll be here."

"And you only stayed late at work once this week," Annice said, before kissing his nose. "I like you being here and working, though. It's not the working that's the problem."

"The here." Griffin nodded, taking a deep breath, leaning his forehead against hers. "More of the here, then." Then he dimmed the lights, as if he'd be tempted to say more if he didn't, and Annice fell asleep in the dark, listening to his even quiet breaths.

CHAPTER 37
APRIL 22ND

At four on the Friday, Griffin wheeled himself into Lamont's office. "This is becoming a habit, sir." He felt a hair more comfortable teasing, now. It was, in fact, the second time since Griffin had come back from Whitby.

"What would you do if I said I have found finishing the week in a meeting with you sets me up well for the next?" Lamont was fiddling with an inkwell on his desk. Then he nudged it aside. "Tea?" Today's tie was a deep emerald green, and Griffin was beginning to wonder if there was a pattern to the rotation, beyond whatever Lamont - or his man - pulled out.

"Please, if you'd like." Tea - and the offer of it - suggested Griffin might be here for at least half an hour. He settled himself in front of the desk.

"I gather we are no longer paying for Mistress Matthewman's housing." Lamont settled back in his chair after pouring from a waiting teapot and sliding a cup over to where Griffin could reach it easily. "And that her work is going well."

That was certainly a way to put it, and Griffin was also sure Lamont had known it before the most recent fortnight's expenses went into the accounting. "Both are true, yes, sir. The courts are still paying her stipend for meals, and for her time when she's working on our particular problem." Griffin considered his options here. "She is a considerate houseguest, and I enjoy her conversation when we're not working."

It was, of course, an odd conversation to have with Lamont, and yet it was also the truth. Griffin felt this might be an appropriate amount of truth, couched properly, for the moment. Lamont inclined his head once, taking his time with a sip from his own teacup before he set it down. "You've been showing her a fair bit of Trellech, as well."

"Yes, sir. It's a pleasure, and she's soaking it up. Doing excellent work for us, as well. The combination of learning and talking with Niobe seems to be bearing a lot of fruit, in several directions. She's also been a great help with my working through the proposal. As I mentioned in the memo on Tuesday, she believes she'll be ready to reset the jet next week, so we can activate it on the first. After our other commitments, of course."

Lamont inclined his head, his eyes half-lidded. Griffin knew better than to interrupt. Griffin had expected more questions about the courtroom work. Instead, Lamont said, "It has, hmm, how do I put this, illuminated some things for me. To your favour, currently."

The currently suggested that might not always be the case. "Sir?"

"I have not chosen an Heir. I have known that if anything happened to me, unexpectedly, each of the three of you could step forward. And there is a name in my private files, should that come to pass. I do not expect it to. I would like to make a formal announcement before the next Council Rites at the solstice."

That put a fascinating spin on it, indeed. Griffin considered what he'd seen of Nestor and Harriet this week. Or rather, hadn't seen. Nestor had been busy with a number of meetings, and they hadn't been in the Courts or the Guard Hall. Griffin didn't know where for certain. He had fewer connections in the Fox's Den or Wishton's or Bourne's than in many of the clubs. But he suspected those were the sort of meetings with the excellent brandy or port, cigars, and a lot of cheerful bonhomie. The right sorts of people, continuing in the right sorts of power.

Griffin kept his face as neutral as he could. "Is there additional information I might offer that would help in your decision, sir?" There was a moment, a nudge from somewhere deep in his heart, and he added, "You know me, you know my work. I will not change my spots now, even for this."

"That is, in fact, one thing I like about you, Griffin. Your steadiness." Lamont gestured at the chair. "Not on your feet, perhaps, anymore, but in all the other ways. And we both know it's steadiness of the heart, of the mind, and most of all of your magic that counts here."

"Sir." Griffin inclined his head. "But not only that, or you'd have decided years ago."

It won him a snort. Griffin would count that as a point in his favour. "You have your dissenters, as we discussed, those who doubt you. And it is not only the question of what I think, what I have judged to be true, but also what is seen to be true."

That was the problem with their justice system. Albion's law was not fundamentally adversarial, the way

British Common Law was. They had truth magics, which meant their forms of justice were about making sure they asked the right questions at the right point, with evidence to guide them. But it was also about what people understood, what people witnessed, when witnessing mattered.

Griffin nodded. Then he had to close his eyes. He knew his thoughts would show. Because there was a flashing thought there of what it would mean if he could get Lamont under the truth magics for just a minute or two. To know what mattered, if there was anything he could do to argue his case, persuade, narrow that gap between him and what he kept reaching for.

"Tell me what you were thinking. Just now." Lamont's voice came out almost as a purr. It was impossible to forget that Lamont had all the same expertise in Incantation, in rhetoric, in all the gifts that words brought. And decades more experience. It was absolutely an order.

Griffin squared his shoulders. Truth. Truth had to be his byword, for all sorts of reasons. "I was wishing, sir - not that I would ever ask to do it - that I could ask you a handful of questions under the truth magics."

"It is such a temptation at times, isn't it?" Lamont leaned forward. "I give you permission. Three questions, here. No preparation." Ordinarily, calling the charms would have involved at least an hour of sorting out the framing of the questions.

Griffin blinked several times, swallowing hard. Thoughts were now tumbling over themselves in his head. "May I make a few notes, sir, before I begin?"

"That is fair. It will also let me have more of my tea. Don't dawdle." Lamont leaned back, his eyes twinkling.

It was a perfect challenge. What did Griffin want most

to know, filtered by what it was reasonable to ask in this situation, without abusing power? Most of what was rolling around in his head wasn't conducive to a yes or no answer. It was about scope, about whether he had most of Lamont's goals right. He pulled out his notebook, scribbling down the words in free association, then drawing lines. By the time Lamont set his cup down, Griffin looked up. "When you are ready, sir?"

The older man settled himself comfortably in his chair, hands resting in his lap. "As you wish."

Griffin took a breath, calling up the truth magics. They came to him, as they had since he had learned them, like working dogs waiting for the command, or like water rising up and supporting. A bit of both, there was more direction than a pool of water, more flow than a dog. He let the magics swirl for a second, before he settled them around Lamont. He'd called the truth magics plenty of times in training or with a willing participant, as well as in the courtroom or the course of his work. Each time was the same, and each was different. Never the same river twice, as the saying went.

Lamont felt like a tremendous ancient stone statue. Or perhaps not even a statue, something more like a great menhir, a standing stone, weathered and beaten, and lasting far beyond mortal lifespans. Griffin nodded once, then felt the magic smoothing out, the particular resonance and harmony to it he heard and felt when the magic had taken. Lamont wasn't fighting it. If he had, Griffin could not have held it, certainly. Not without a courtroom's magic and architecture and structure to draw on, anyway.

Griffin had not been granted a confirming question, and honestly, part of this challenge was whether Griffin could pull this off without one. Griffin marshalled his thoughts, then asked his first question. "What brings you to name an Heir now, when you have not for so many years?"

"It is well past time, and I am aware of the pressures and tensions caused by not having one." Griffin hesitated for a second, and then leaned into the pressure, just slightly, encouraging a bit more of an answer. Lamont's lips twitched into a smile. "I have delayed because each of you would take the Courts in a different direction. I was not sure which one would serve us best now, and for decades to come. Especially during and after the War."

The long game, of course. Law was, even if the world changed around them. Griffin nodded once, then posed his second question. "If there are matters you have considered asking me or discussing with me, and you have not brought them up previously, what are they?" It was a complex conditional, but Griffin thought that caught the potential thoroughly enough.

Lamont laughed at that, looking pleased. "We might discuss this more in a moment, when we are done with the truth charms, but the gossip about your time with Mistress Matthewman has been informative."

Griffin nodded once more. "We can come back to that." He considered pressing further, but it turned out that was the sort of thing where he would rather not have truth so tangibly present when Lamont answered. Given that there were still things he hoped but did not know for certain. "If you have any concerns about my ability to become Heir and - in due course - into your seat, would you please share them now?"

"My concerns are those I stated recently. Or further back. They have to do, at this point, with how others perceive you and your competence, whether they can have sufficient trust in your ability to do the work." Lamont touched his fingertips to each other, steepling his hands. "I do not have any concerns myself, at this point. Especially now." He flicked one finger, and Griffin promptly let the truth charms fall away, taking a moment to breathe as they receded.

When he looked up again, Lamont was watching him. "You know you are skilled with them. Even when it is me you are calling them to."

"I appreciate you did not resist, sir. And that you expanded the answer you did." Griffin took a breath, measured it with a few heartbeats, and let it out. "Mistress Matthewman?"

"You know people talk." Lamont's voice was very gentle. "Sometimes unkindly. That you have been seen with an appealing and talented woman your age, socially, has caused gossip. Mostly in your favour. She has looked delighted to be with you. And when you have met up with others, she has not looked at them beyond politeness. She has focused on you. People notice."

"Especially extremely observant people, and we know quite a few." Griffin rubbed his face. "You've talked to, oh, half a dozen of those."

"More like a dozen, yes. A couple who came to me to tattle on you. That you were, apparently, skiving off work." Lamont raised a hand. "I know you weren't. You did, however, leave the building at the end of the workday more often than your usual."

"And to be entirely fair, a non-trivial part of my evenings and such have also been spent working. Just at home. With company." Griffin let out a breath. "She and I are still sorting out what that means. I won't press her, even if it matters for ... this. Your timeline. She gets the time she needs."

Lamont nodded. "Perhaps you and she might come and dine with me and my wife? After May Day, I'm afraid I've a dozen commitments between now and then." It was, Griffin suspected, as much of a hint as he was going to get about any actual decision. Either Lamont would let him down privately, kindly, or he would share that Griffin was his choice. Either way, arguing wouldn't change anything.

"Of course, sir. We'd be glad to. I'll check if there's anything she's scheduled that might be a consideration." Griffin hesitated, not sure what else to say.

Lamont was watching him, steadily. "It is not, precisely, that I think you need a partner, though I can also see why some people think so. A married man is, like it or not, seen as more reliable and settled than an unmarried one. People are so often foolish."

"And most people do not see the divorces and marital disagreements that come through our doors," Griffin pointed out.

"No. Indeed." It made Lamont chuckle, then settle. "But the way you have gone about introducing her to Trellech has highlighted, shall we say, the range of people you know. And, perhaps more pointedly, the things you consider important about the city. It has illuminated - along with your actual work - your gifts at forming partnerships, good working relationships, with others. That is certainly one successful and well-proven way to lead the Courts, and to tend the land magic."

"But not the only one." That was the trick of it. Lamont still had only given the tiniest hint of what his preferences were for his successor.

"No." Lamont leaned back. "All right. Walk me through where you are for the room you're preparing. What came out of that meeting you were having on Wednesday, finalising the talismanic work?" The questions Lamont asked from there made it entirely clear he had the full proposal front of mind. He consulted a sheet of notes only for a few of the specific measurement details. By the time Lamont sent him off to enjoy his evening, Griffin felt like he'd sat for an oral exam again, but had come out looking competent.

CHAPTER 38
APRIL 25TH

B y the next Monday, Annice was itching to get back to work. Griffin had come home Friday evening from his conversation with Lamont very thought-ful. It was, however, the sort of thoughtful that wasn't coming out in words, not yet. That's what he'd said, and that was also what Annice had already sorted out. It was like he was staring at the inside of his head, the way she did when she was contemplating carving something unusual. One couldn't rush the process.

She, on the other hand, was still thoroughly in the early stages of learning more about Niobe's craft. For one thing, it was something that took years of study, even if Annice had something of a head start when it came to the stonework. She'd never worked even with semi-precious stones other than jet or with anything like faceting. But she had done smoothing and polishing for the ammonites, and jet needed a delicacy that had set her up well for the current learning.

That morning, she had been handed a piece of blue chalcedony, accompanied by a lecture on its various uses.

There was a piece of lore about Cicero, the Roman orator, wearing it. Niobe had settled in her chair, pulling a tray of stones between them. Some of them had been polished or even cut, others hadn't been. "It's a popular gift for solicitors and barristers, as well as senior Ministry staff. Anyone who makes their living speaking words. Ideally worn at the throat, a cameo or carved piece as a tiepin or a pendant, for example, or a faceted stone."

Annice looked down at the stones, then back up to Niobe. "And you're saying this would make a suitable gift for Griffin?"

"Just so. The stone comes and goes in fashion, and right now these pieces, none of them were terribly expensive by my standards."

Annice said, bemused, "You work in sapphire and emerald and ruby." She'd learned, her second week, the reason for all the protections on the shop. There were many stones that were stored there, even if the bulk of Niobe's uncut stock lived deep in the vaults of one of the Trellech banks, complete with a dragon to guard it.

Niobe waved a hand. "You've been doing good work. We can count this in provided supplies. Enough to make a talisman and a seal or engraved piece, if you like." Niobe smiled. "His name suggests some particular imagery."

"Griffins are a horribly difficult shape to get right," Annice said, promptly. "I've been trying to sketch decent ones for..." She stopped short suddenly, because she'd started just about when they got to Trellech, and she hadn't admitted it to anyone yet.

Niobe raised an eyebrow and then changed the subject. "I've books of art. You could do something like an illumination. There's an appeal to that. And there are charms for taking a sketch and giving you working lines on the stone.

That's a tremendous help. Much more delicate than the physical transfer methods."

Annice nodded, then she looked up at Niobe. "Where do we start, then?" She was the one staying late at work that night, though it was raining, and she'd already told Griffin to meet her at home. As she was pulling on her raincoat and contemplating the umbrella, Niobe cleared her throat. "You could ask Griffin about a journal. If you're willing. There are the much less expensive options that just connect to one other person, or a small number. But I find it terribly helpful in my business, for correspondence with clients, as well as managing my life."

The magical journals were a wonder, but still terribly expensive. As much as an automobile, far more than Annice could spend. It would be terribly convenient - she'd feel much less guilty about Griffin taking her places or waiting on her. Some of that must have shown in her face, because Niobe said, "Ask him. He likely knows some of the less expensive options."

"Griffin seems to know everyone." Annice let out a breath. "I'll think about it. Tomorrow then? I'll try some more sketches tonight while he's busy."

Niobe nodded, and went back down the hall to the workshop and her own work, while Annice forged out into the rain. By the time she got home, she was soaked, and by the time she'd had a hot bath and changed, she'd almost forgotten about the journal question. Griffin had heated up steak and ale pies, and was settled at the kitchen table. He set aside the book he'd been reading as soon as Annice appeared. "Warmer?"

"Much. I appreciate these floors more every day." Even if she'd also put somewhat worn slippers on, it was more for the top of her feet than the bottom. She slipped into the chair on her side of the table, considering for a moment. "I had a thought today. And also Niobe suggested I ask you something."

Griffin looked up. "And you're not sure about either of them."

It would be annoying, but Annice was actually becoming rather comfortable with how Griffin got to the heart of the problem. It was relaxing to know he'd say what he saw with her as accurately as he could. "Yes." She considered her options and went for what was probably the shorter conversation. "She said I should ask you about getting a journal."

"I would be delighted to get you one as a gift," Griffin said, immediately. "They really are quite useful, and it would simplify things. Even just when you're upstairs working and you want to be on your own for a bit, I could let you know that supper's ready without shouting upstairs."

"Or when you're going to be working late," Annice agreed. "I. I shouldn't let you get one for me."

"Look, how about I get in touch with them, and see if there are any that - for whatever reason - are a little less dear? They do now make some by special order, and sometimes people change their minds, or something is a little imperfect in the art of the book. If you're using it with a cover, like I do, that barely matters."

"Of course you know the people who make them." Annice sighed. "Are you going to invite them to dinner?"

"In this case, no. Mostly because they're as busy as we are, and they've a new baby. But we might go round the shop together. I'll write and see when might be convenient. And we might see them on May Day, depending on the crowds."

Annice wanted to come back to May Day, but the way Griffin had answered that made her think of something else. "You know many people in Trellech. But I'm not clear on, erm. Friends? Friendships."

There was a silence, long enough that Annice looked up cautiously. Griffin was sitting, palms flat on the wood. Then he took a breath, deliberate. "I have a few. But mostly they have their own lives, their own places. Or their schedules are chaos. Antimony, for example."

"Who has both a varying schedule and a family. Though mostly grown up now, yes?" Annice had picked up that much, among the various other comments.

"Like that. And people's houses, they have stairs and all. I don't mind dealing with the canes, but it's awkward to have to ask and check, or figure out the best way to get across town. Or whatever. It's solvable, it's just..." He shrugged. "Tedious."

"So, if we set things up to invite people here, a little more often. If we got a table, something we could move out of the way, we could have people over."

Griffin swallowed. "We." Then he nodded. "If you'd like that."

"I thought maybe a circular table. And it could live in the nook with your bookshelves and the chairs, most of the time. You usually use your canes going there. And then two more chairs, match the ones in the kitchen, and two people could come over." She'd been nervous about suggesting it, but Griffin was smiling slowly.

"I like that. You're better with shapes than I am. I kept trying to make something rectangular and big enough fit, but circular would work better. And on wheels, so you could move it on your own? That's the other problem."

"That's a thing we could ask Seth about, right? Either

circular or something that folds up. Um, those ones that have a flap or two that comes out. One of those, with everything folded up, it could go right behind the sofa and not take up much space unless we wanted a table." Now that she was thinking about it properly, she could think of several options. Even for the chairs, which were admittedly complicated to have out of the way. And she could see why he hadn't considered that sort of solution when it was just him. But she could fold and unfold a table easily.

"I'll write to Seth and get him round to do some measurements. And I enjoy giving him business, anyway, for all he's got a lot more steady work these days." Griffin looked very pleased, three ways round.

"And then maybe have him and his wife and Golshan round as the first guests? Since Golshan brings his own chair?" Annice was pressing a little now, but she was doing it for good reason. It made Griffin laugh and just nod, so it was just the right amount, then.

That topic dealt with, Annice poked at one of the bits of steak in her pie, chewing and swallowing before she asked, carefully, "While we're talking about people, what's my part, for May Day? We didn't do anything in Whitby, in public, beyond the ordinary things. The not magical ones, I mean."

"Here, well, the magic's the thing. There's a procession from the Courts and Guard Hall up north, through the streets, through the market, to the front of the Temple of Healing, then through into the gardens. There's music and dancing - well, dancing for other people. I need to be there for the whole thing. Nestor and his wife, Harriet and her family, the other senior staff will all be there. A fair number of the judges process. Many of them like a good procession. You needn't, if you'd rather not. Or we could plan for you to meet up with someone who has less of the pomp and bother. Niobe maybe, or someone she knows." Now he leaned an elbow on the table, and Annice suspected he was working through lists of potential people in his head.

"Are there other things to know about for the summer?" She hesitated. "And, um. I've never asked. When's your birthday? Or have you had one already since I met you?"

"Not yet!" Griffin said it cheerfully. "June thirteenth. I'd be delighted to spend it with you, in whatever form appeals."

Annice blinked. "Mine's June twenty-eighth. All right." Mentally, now, of course, she was wondering if Niobe had known. And whether there was in fact enough time she could finish at least one of the chalcedony pieces as a gift. She could always do something out of jet. She could go back to Whitby and find something to carve, and she'd probably do that too. But the chalcedony kept haunting her. The milky blue had a compelling quality to it, entirely like a ghost made of solid stone.

Griffin was just glowing. "And you'll permit me to plan something you'll enjoy, for the occasion, then? Though, erm." He swallowed, and she found the way he was suddenly cautious about plans that far ahead endearing now. "That's also the Midsummer Faire. You'd enjoy it, I think. I'd need to plan out a bit of how to handle it. It's something that needs the crutches, rather than the chair, unless I barely want to move all day. But we can plan for that."

"Livestock shows, and um, matches?"

"Livestock shows - honestly, I rather like watching the sheep? They're delightfully fluffy and soothing, somehow. Pavo and bohort matches, both, a horse show, a pulling contest. And then all sorts of halls and tents with plants and crafters, others with performances. Dancing and a concert or two every evening, too, and quite a lot of good food and drink. I can get my hands on one of the pamphlets. They have maps and lists of what's going on when."

Annice took a breath and nodded. "Let's make plans for that, then." It was one more step in admitting what she couldn't quite put into words, and what Griffin was carefully not asking her yet. "Um. Something Niobe said today got me thinking. We were talking about the range of properties of stones, the way some of them are fairly consistent, and others vary. I was wondering how you thought about that with the people you work with. Especially Nestor and Harriet."

"Huh." Griffin rubbed his nose. "That's an interesting question." He took a breath. "Lamont - look, I think I'm right when I say he currently favours me, but he didn't actually say it right out. It's complicated, and it's hard to find words for. Even me." He looked rather forlorn at that, and Annice reached over to pat his hand. Griffin went on. "I think maybe he likes me best to talk to, but that's not the thing he should be deciding on."

"If he's got to work closely with you, it's certainly relevant," Annice pointed out. "Can't have someone elbow to elbow in the workshop where you can't stand each other. It'll foul everything up. That's the way people get hurt. And you can't force it. It's a difference between being workmanlike and friendly."

Griffin shook his head, but then he picked up her question. "I like to think I'm adaptable. A range of experiences and skills, and - well. Many people who need a chair or some help, we get good at solving problems, thinking through in advance what the options are, and getting creative."

"Like going to the Faire," Annice said, because he'd just done that. Even if he hadn't spelled out all the pieces he was already thinking about so they could have a good time going together. "Did Nestor fight in the War?" She hadn't thought about it. Of course, she'd never actually seen the man.

"Not at the front. He's enough older he wasn't called up until they expanded the age range in 1918." Griffin looked up suddenly and ducked his chin. "About the same age as your Da, I'd guess."

"Already knew I didn't like him," Annice said, promptly, before she could think better of it. It wasn't exactly that she wanted other people to have gone to War like Da, but it turned out she thought less of people who'd got out of it. "And Harriet's more like your age?"

"I'm forty-five this year, she's, um." Griffin counted off on his fingers. "Just turned forty-three. And people rarely retire from the courts until their seventies."

"And you were all named when? How old?" Annice could feel a shape coming in the carving, but she couldn't see it clearly yet.

"1913. I was 31. Harriet was 29 or so. And Horace was nearer 40. Nestor wasn't named until 1919, after Horace died."

"So, adult and established, but not terribly old." Annice frowned. "And Nestor's, um. Not very flexible. Granite. Something unyielding. Not very ornamental."

That, how she'd put it, got Griffin to relax. His shoulders had been climbing up to his ears. "He's not required to be ornamental. And to give him due credit, he is very good at his work. It's no small thing to keep three courtrooms running smoothly. The scheduling alone gives most people nightmares."

Annice nodded. "And you're more specialised. Did you do something else before that?"

"Before the War, I spent more time in the criminal court. Oak, that one is. And I dabble." Griffin leaned back a little. "So you're thinking, figure out more about what each of us does best, and what that means for the Courts. I mean, I'd considered that. Just as trees, not as stones. Maybe stones would show something up. Do you have that book you borrowed from Niobe still, about some of the lore?"

"I do. Bed or sofa?" Annice pushed back her chair, going to clear both their finished plates and wash up.

"I'll have my bath and meet you in bed. How's that? And we can read for a bit. Both of us."

"I'll be upstairs for a few, then. Take as long as you need. Half an hour?"

"About that." He pulled back his chair to turn and go off to the bathing room, but he stopped by the sink as she started the water running. "Talking it out's a great help. And thank you for bearing with me not being ready for it for a couple of days."

She bent over to kiss his forehead. "Takes time to find what's in the stone."

CHAPTER 39
APRIL 27TH

Griffin had been staring at the papers on his desk for a good hour, and he definitely had a headache growing at the base of his skull. The knock on the door startled it. It wasn't Charlus. For one thing, it was the wrong knock, and for the other, Charlus was on an errand that would take him another half hour, more than likely.

"Who is it?" Griffin called out, pitching his voice to carry.

"Antimony, if you have a minute." She hadn't journaled first, which was unusual. And she hadn't had ordinary business in the Courts today. The inheritance court had been quiet all week.

"Come in." Griffin looked up, trying to read her expression.

She turned around and closed the door, then looked back at him. "Wards, please? Full privacy."

Griffin tilted his head. "Tea? There's some in the pot." He then took a proper moment to settle himself and call up the three layers of wards he rarely bothered with. "Or would you rather do this elsewhere?"

"No, here's good, now it's warded." Antimony poured herself a mug of tea and sat down facing him. "No meeting for half an hour or so?"

"No. And Charlus will check before coming in." Griffin leaned back. "What's going on, and why the..." He waved a hand at the door.

"Gossip. And not the amusing kind, like you showing Mistress Matthewman the city." Antimony considered. "It is good to see you happy, though."

"We will see about having you round for supper, if you ask nicely. Annice had a lovely idea about suitable furniture for purpose," Griffin said, teasing for just a second. "And you may get to know her better. I might even go so far as to leave you in a room together for a bit."

Antimony snorted, then sobered. "More seriously, what have you done to stir up Nestor?"

"Exist? Demonstrate that being sent off to Whitby was some use? Have a plan for moving forward that he could not stall or forbid? I've Lamont's approval, and Christopher and Gloriana both have given their agreement." Griffin turned his hand palm up. "Both parts, the new project and resetting the inheritance court."

"More than that, I think. He's been agitating. I'd have told you sooner, but I only heard the ripples of it Monday, and it took me yesterday and today to track down a bit more." Antimony tapped her fingertips together. "What do you think of him?"

"Antimony, you are my friend. Don't ask me that." Griffin had a rule for himself about not speaking badly about his colleagues, even when it was exceedingly tempting. Not unless it was part of some direct professional inquiry and he had to give a true response. Then he considered and came up with enough of an answer. "I'm clear he doesn't think I'm fit for duty. Personally, I prefer for Lamont to choose me or Harriet over Nestor, and that's not subtle at this point. But from what I have seen, he keeps all the contract cases running smoothly enough, and he's good with the details necessary for that. Even the parts about which rooms specific parties wait in."

"And what will you do if I share information with you that falls into that sort of gossip?" Antimony leaned forward, crossing one leg over the other, which in her always was a sign of being on the hunt.

"I cannot stop you," Griffin said, spreading his hands. "And if there's something you think I need to know, I trust your judgement. You've demonstrated that you are, hmm. How to put this? Not petty."

It made Antimony chuckle. "No. And that's really the problem. There isn't a sign Nestor has done anything wrong, but there are signs of him being petty. More than just you and the chair, or you and your competence. And some of it's taken on a nastier edge. He was complaining Charlus had done a bit of paperwork wrong. Don't worry, Mistress Henning took your apprentice's side promptly and thoroughly, and sent Nestor off with his tail between his legs. Which did not sweeten his temper, or so I heard from one of the staff at Bourne's the next day."

Griffin let out a grunt. Charlus had mentioned a minor fuss, but that he'd done the thing right. Griffin would have to clarify that this was the sort of thing Charlus should report in detail, please, because the pattern mattered as well as whatever Charlus thought about it himself. "I'll talk to them both. Anything else?"

"Most of the rest is the same gossip as before, but more

of it, and a bit sharper. Trying to find people who'll agree with him. He's having a hard time of that, even with people who don't like how decisions came out in the Yew courts. But he's found a few. Several parties you're unlikely to be invited to."

Griffin waved a hand. "They're the sort who host things up loads of stairs, had you ever noticed?" Then he sobered. "I'm sensitive to the political considerations, but there's not much I can do there directly. If people don't like my competence, I'm scarcely going to be incompetent to make them feel better. Even if I were inclined, my magic wouldn't permit."

Antimony raised an eyebrow. "Different oaths than Creon? He certainly fell into incompetence, poor man, and couldn't admit it."

"I don't know what he took. It's not an oath, exactly, it's feeling that my magic would betray me. I've contemplated making it formal with an oath, but it would set an uncomfortable precedent for anyone in the future, and you know how I feel about precedent setting."

Antimony snorted. "I do. You might have declaimed on the topic several times over tea. Anyway. Nestor's been worse. And there are people who notice that. On the other hand, he keeps the paperwork moving, and that keeps people with a lot of money and influence happy on the whole. And wanting to be in his favour. Though right now, I'm wondering how much of that is his clerks. He's had his seat what, seven years?"

"Seven and a half. About six months before I got back here," Griffin said.

"And he wasn't one of the potential Heirs before the War? Even though he's older?" Antimony turned her palm up. "You don't talk about how that's determined."

"The short answer is that it's Lamont's call. Or the Lord or Lady of Trellech's Justice, as it were, to give the full and proper title. Harriet and I already were. Horace died in 1919, and Lamont named Nestor later that year." Griffin shrugged. "We don't have a bloodline to go on. It's more about who might carry things forward. And no, I don't know why Lamont hasn't picked one of us." He hesitated, but Antimony was both a friend and trained in any number of pattern-spotting techniques. "He's given me some indications he's close to a choice. I don't know what he's told the others, if anything."

"I suppose you and Harriet don't compare notes." Antimony tapped her fingers on the wood of the desk. "I'd be curious about her take, honestly. I don't know her well. We've never had much overlap, but she seems competent."

"Competent, if sometimes more concerned by higher philosophy than I can justify," Griffin said, agreeably. "No, she and I get on well enough. Not close friends, but comfortable enough colleagues, if also competitors. Though really, that's the wrong way to think about the whole matter. It's not a competition. One of us can't win it by some unusual push to the end."

"Even if that's what you're doing, your new idea for a room." Antimony cocked her head, challenging that point.

Griffin considered. "I don't talk about it much. But there's a sense that I'm always having to be aware of not just what I'm doing, but how it looks. I was thinking about it in Whitby. Plenty of people are confused by someone who uses a chair who also uses crutches or canes. I know there was more than a bit of gossip - here, too - about whether I'm faking, or looking for sympathy. Or all the other parts of the nonsense, like whether it affected my head."

"I know you better than that. I've seen your work.

Surely that ought to be enough for the people who know what's needed to judge. Nestor included."

Griffin shrugged. "It's not that simple. And the hell of it is, people have reason to be cautious. I was Cleon's successor. I know that better than most. And you saw plenty of that close-up. He ought to have properly retired at least three or four years before he did. Whatever the root of the problem was."

He let out a breath, slowly. "I am, it turns out, all for a system that evaluates everyone for fitness, regularly and also if specific concerns are raised. I am not in favour of a crowd that judges without information. And I am certainly not in favour of an approach that requires me to lay out my personal medical and magical information to all and sundry on demand." His mouth quirked up. "For one thing, most of them aren't qualified to evaluate it sensibly."

"Hence one of the reasons for staging the whole thing. Do you know more about when you'll be ready?" Antimony said, not touching the rest of it yet.

"Three weeks or so," Griffin said. "The current proposal is for Annice to assist along with one of the brand new apprentices, so there can be no question whose skills are in play. And of course, several people monitoring that particular aspect in detail. No chance to cheat, someone will catch it. Not that I would do that, naturally. It'd undermine my point."

"No wiggle room." Antimony considered. "Are you concerned about the work itself?"

"As much as is sensible, given that it's a new design, and I will be very much on stage. I am not that much of a showman, you know that. Am I sure it will work? Yes, so long as no one interferes." Now he grinned, the sort of grin that he got when he was hunting for the truth of something. "Of course, all the precautions against someone assisting me unannounced also make it near impossible for someone to sabotage the process from the outside. I haven't mentioned that, of course."

"Naturally not." Antimony chuckled. "Oh, well played, that part. Almost worth the rest of the fuss." She considered, then added, "It was frustrating for me, working with Cleon. I felt sorry for him. On his good days, he was still very sharp, and his understanding of precedent then was unsurpassed. But that's not a way to run things or keep the system going. And we need to keep that goal at the heart of everything. But it also seems unfair that you be held to different standards than everyone else. The Guards have fitness exams every year. I'm sure someone could work out adaptations easily enough."

"Oh, I've already got notes and proposals. Just haven't had the proper leverage to get them looked at. Lamont knows about them, and Gloriana and Christopher. I've not made a fuss otherwise."

Antimony tilted her head. "Are they at a stage where you could tell me more? I mean." She let out a huff of breath. "If you become Heir, what does that change?"

"That's an excellent question." Griffin could in fact talk this out and Antimony had enough experience of the Courts to understand, without being tangled in the same politics. "Lamont has been talking to me, one on one, more frequently. And I haven't exactly hid my priorities, what I think would help the Courts run more smoothly. There's no point. If he picks me, we need to work together until he retires. That means being honest now."

"And so you've floated your thoughts about what you'd do to avoid problems like Cleon. And to ensure people can't raise concerns about you without some actual cause." Antimony tapped her fingertips together.

"Exactly. But some people don't like that. And of course, there's all the other politics. Being Heir means being visible, in a particular way, that Nestor would very much like. Now, he'd also be good at a number of the administrative tasks. I do not deny that. But there are also ways where someone - as Heir, named as Heir - can angle things their way. Take personal meetings for things that would usually be delegated, so that you're the one holding the connections rather than the office."

"You've thought a lot about this." Antimony tilted her head. "You know many people. Especially here in Trellech itself. Don't deny it."

"I'm not." Griffin snorted. "Besides, Annice keeps pointing it out. But I know a lot of people in all sorts of walks of life. Shoemakers and theatre folk and apothecaries. The nice woman at the cafe on the corner, and people at the inn, and of course a lot of the Temple of Healing folks, and not just the Healers. Still plenty of people because of Dad's store. I mean, they saw me grow up."

"It's not a grasping sort of knowing, the way you do it. And with Nestor, there's that element." Antimony chewed on her lip. "With Nestor, I always wonder what he wants from me, what's going to even the balance on the books. With you - or watching you with other people - it's more about how to get something good for everyone. Especially watching you in the Court, with contentious cases."

"That's the place we need the most even-handed approach, don't you think? I mostly think it's pragmatic, though. If people keep fighting each other - even once the Court decides - it's going to keep hurting everyone in the net of relationships. If the Court can bring them to a resolution they understand, even if it's not the one they wish had been chosen, maybe everyone can get on with being connected still in a year or two." Griffin rubbed his nose. "Well, maybe more than two in some cases."

"The Rowleys," Antimony said. "And basically all the cases that also involve the criminal courts." She shrugged. "I see what you mean, though. And certainly, I approve of the aspiration. That is why we get on."

Griffin waved a hand. "If I get chosen as Heir, Nestor will, presumably, continue running the civil courts efficiently. I'll have a bit more leeway to make sure those under him are treated well."

"Where a bit means more than none." Antimony certainly understood the political limitations. "And he'll still agitate against you."

"Yes. But there's not much he can actually do, short of proving me incompetent. Which would take a lot of effort and evidence. With any luck, he'd settle down to spending his time on improvements to the system. And I'd support that. Even if it comes with more standing around at cocktail parties on his end than I'd choose. Not just because of the standing part."

"And you're not worried about his connections affecting the Courts?" Antimony asked. "I would be."

"Remember, we're under oaths to justice and truth in that form. There are limits - codified and tested over centuries - that restrict that. And we review those regularly to adapt."

"Huh. That's not something you all talk about much. What was a recent one, then? A change?" Antimony leaned back.

"Oh, how to handle ranks when people returned from the War. All of a sudden, we had a lot more people who had held rank as a Captain or Major, and the way the titles play into some oaths. But at the same time, those people were no longer acting in that rank. It took us a bit to sort out, but there's precedent for that kind of thing. We modelled it on the crossover to titles and social status in Britain, where it depends on whether that role is in play in the case in question."

"Huh." Antimony let out a long breath. "All right. You let me know what I can do to support you in your project. I'll tell you if there's particularly nasty or notable gossip. We'll get on with things and let Nestor sort himself out?"

"That," Griffin agreed. "It's the only sensible way to go forward."

She laughed and then stood up. "I'll let you get on with your other work. See you Friday for the morning case."

"Friday." Griffin dropped the warding, waited until the door closed behind her, then brought it back up again. He didn't much want to be bothered for a little, he needed to make some notes.

CHAPTER 40
APRIL 29TH

On Friday night, Annice and Griffin had gone out for a pleasant and leisurely meal at yet another restaurant they hadn't tried together yet. Griffin still had quite a list of those. They hadn't even got halfway through the list of ones where the chair was easy to manage. They'd come back to the flat, companionably continuing the conversation they'd been having since they sat down to eat. It had been all about the lore related to stones and woods, and how accurate some of it was when it came to making lasting objects.

Once they were inside, it was getting on for ten. Griffin took a breath. "Meet you in bed in a few minutes? I've got something I'd very much like to ask you, if you're willing to hear me out?"

Annice had been putting her cloak away, hanging it up on the hook. "Something?"

"If you'd do me the favour of listening." Griffin honestly wasn't at all sure how she'd take it, because he'd been very careful not to put any pressure on her future. And at the same time, she'd been slowly making it clear that she intended to be around for a bit. She'd extended her contract with Niobe again, this time open-ended. She'd claimed a mug of her own, and space by the bathroom sink. And while most of her clothes were in the wardrobe upstairs, some of them were in the bedroom. If she said yes tonight, they could get another wardrobe made to match his. And any number of other things, to make it a shared space, for that matter.

Ten minutes later, they were both in bed, though not under the covers. Griffin had tucked what he needed into his dressing gown pocket, where he could get it readily. Annice twisted sideways, her legs off to her right on the bed. She'd taken over the far side of the bed, by preference, just naturally, without asking. "You had a question?"

"First, um." Griffin felt tongue-tied. "I promised not to ask about the future. May I? Obviously, you needn't give me an answer right now, or until you're ready, whatever it is."

Annice tilted her head, considering him at some length, then she patted his knee. "You're actually nervous." She sounded almost delighted about it. "I didn't know you got nervous like that? You're always so sure of yourself." Probably the only other time she'd seen him this flustered, come to think of it, was back when he was telling her about being Heir. One of the Heirs in potential.

"I have not, in fact, had much practice with this particular conversation." Griffin tried to keep his dignity together, but now her eyes were crinkling up with laughter, and she was waving a hand for him to go on. He swallowed. "I know this is fast and sudden, given we haven't been talking about things beyond the next few days. But will you marry me? Please?"

She tilted her head a little more, and now he could see

and hear the bit of laughter. "First, yes. Second, is this how you are doing this?"

"Getting down on my knees isn't very elegant in my case?" Griffin met her eyes, smiling back at her. "And I don't exactly have a ring. Or rather, I do, but it's a token one." He rummaged in the dressing gown pocket, bringing out the little box, twice the size of an ordinary ring box, and opened it, holding it out to her.

Inside was a narrow golden band, with a sea pattern twining through it, inlaid with chips of blue and green stones, lapis and malachite and aquamarine, so it sparkled like waves. The other side held a sapphire the colour of the ocean when they'd gone to Robin Hood's Bay. Annice took a moment to look down at them, and then her jaw dropped. "This..."

"I thought you'd like to design the ring yourself, or at least cut the stone. Though Niobe said if you'd rather she do it, of course she will. She helped me choose it. You remember that day she was out for the afternoon?"

"You went - where?" Annice was running her finger against the stone, which had only been roughly cut, just enough to give a sense of the colour.

"London, in this case. She has a contact there. She'll bring you next time, introduce you." Griffin took another breath. "It's not rushing you to ask now?"

Annice reached out to touch the stone and then the ring, and Griffin didn't rush her further. When she looked at him over the box, she said, "Would you put the ring on me, then?"

He could do that. He was fairly sure he could do that without fumbling the ring and dropping it on the bed. Though at least if he did, it would be somewhere they could find it again. By charm, if nothing else. He set the box down, working the ring loose from the pillow that held it. Then Annice was holding out her hand, fingers spread, so he could slide it on.

It fit perfectly - he'd trusted Niobe on that, of course. Now, he had to explain. "That one is lapis and malachite and aquamarine, inset, sealed with a charm over them, so they're smooth. Nothing to catch, nothing to get in the cracks." A ring for someone who worked with her hands, and with jet, and jet dust got everywhere given a chance.

"Very thoughtful." She brought her hand up, twisting it back and forth to catch the light. "The design, too, the colours of it. You think of everything." She then tilted her head. "A kiss. And then yes, I'll, um. Answer the implications of the question, or at least make a go at it."

"A kiss." Griffin rearranged himself a little as Annice closed the ring box and tucked it against her leg. She was the one who began the kiss, leaning into it, her hand drifting down to rest on his leg. It wasn't a passionate kiss, but one that was relaxed, trusting that there would be other things to come. They didn't need to rush having it all now.

When she pulled back, Annice ran her thumb along his cheek. "You've been very patient, not asking. I— it's a big change." She gestured with one hand, roughly toward Niobe's shop. "But there isn't a future in Whitby for me. Not now, and maybe not ever. And there is one here. You, but not just you. I love what I'm learning. And I can learn it. That was the part I wasn't sure of."

"I was sure of it. And so was Niobe as soon as you'd been here a day." Griffin said it earnestly, and Annice leaned to kiss the tip of his nose.

"You like to see the best in people. I'm pretty sure it's why you know so many. Besides growing up here, and meeting a lot of people through the Courts." Then she leaned back on one hand. "I need to figure some things out about Whitby. Go up there, for a day, soon. It's. I should have done it weeks ago."

"But it's a big change. And you weren't ready weeks ago to take that leap." Griffin could understand that much.

"Easter helped. Seeing, um." Annice considered, rummaging for words. "Seeing how the community works here. Different communities. That there'd be a place for me, whether you and I made a go of it or not. I mean, that parish might be awkward in that case, but we'd manage. Not that I want to!"

Griffin snorted. "Let's not. I much prefer the idea of going with you, knowing people, maybe eventually children growing up going there, like I did."

Annice flushed a little. "Like that. Living here. Or I don't know, maybe somewhere else eventually. I do like it here, though." She rushed to add that part.

"But it's very much mine, made for me. We can keep our eyes open for something else that would suit. It's finding something with enough ground floor space that's the trick. The magical lifts are slow, and it's awkward, day to day. But one bedroom downstairs, and the family spaces and a study for me, with more upstairs for you, that could work."

Griffin considered. "And for now, we can fit this up as you like. Your own wardrobe, for one, next to mine, rather than your things upstairs. You could set up the bigger room as a workshop, if you want. Keep the smaller as a guest bedroom, though my parents are happy enough to stay in one of the inns if they visit."

"First, I'd like to meet them." Annice considered, then reached to set the ring case on the little bedside table on her side, leaning to tug Griffin down. "Um. Do they know about me?"

"They do. And they'd like to meet you too. Easy enough for them to come down for an afternoon sometime. Not until after May Day, but the seventh or eighth?" Griffin shifted a little to get comfortable. "And I told you, Lamont invited us to supper. He approves of me seeing you. Or at least, he's also aware of how it looks."

"How it looks?" Annice let her hand rest on his hip, the sort of comfortable touch that he was sure she found reassuring. She kept doing it, and he kept loving it, the quiet intimacy of it.

"He made it clear it's not a deciding factor for him, but - some people judge a man who's not married and settled down. Not serious enough, not steady. Or that the job ought to go to someone who has a family to provide for." He shrugged. "And then there's all the other implications that most people are polite enough not to say where I can hear them. That I can't be fit for that purpose, not much of a man."

"But some people are rude. And those?" Annice let her thumb stroke a little on his hip. "I have no complaints so far. Except, perhaps, that we do sometimes have to get out of bed and do other things." Before Griffin could say anything, she went on. "People kept proposing that I marry their brother or cousin or someone, an invalid. People who are much of an invalid than you are. Because you're not very, so long as there aren't stairs. Where I'd spend all my time being their caregiver, no space for anything else."

"Though there are an awful lot of stairs in the world." Griffin nodded. "And you didn't want that. You wanted to have your own life. Are you all right with how things are, then?"

Annice nodded. "Neither of us knows what we'll be like in a year or five or twenty." She took a breath, then let it out, steadying herself. "But you manage your own things. I enjoy helping, it's not that I didn't want to help? But I didn't want to have to help, if you see the difference. Be relied on to always be there, whatever else was going on. But you, either you'll manage, or I'm pretty sure you'd figure out how to hire someone. A nanny, maybe. A full-time housekeeper, if we're both working and there are children and more to deal with. I don't know. But you'd figure it out, we'd figure it out, it wouldn't be all on me to be the one to get up and do the thing, over and over again. Or be the one to figure out how to make it all work. That was the part I really didn't want. Having to do all the work and all the thinking about what work needs doing, that's no fun at all."

"It does seem a trifle unfair. And you can do wonderful things with stones. Most people can't do that. I certainly can't. Each to our strengths, yeah?" Griffin let himself relax back on the bed, on his back, and then felt her snuggle up against him. "And me potentially being Heir and Lord in due course, that doesn't put you off?"

"I think I want a lot more coaching in which fork to use, and whatever else matters like that," Annice said. "We can practise having fancy meals, where there's a grapefruit spoon and what was that tonight, an oyster fork? As opposed to a fish fork. Which we also had."

Griffin chuckled. "We can find plenty of places to practise, I'm sure."

"And..." Annice swallowed. "Not tonight. We should do other things in a minute. But we should talk about money. Rather than you just arranging everything. I'd like to understand what, um. What you have? Is that rude? And I have some from Grandad. Not a lot, but some."

"We can certainly talk about that. Firm believer in sorting that out, actually, and having it documented, so we both know. Saves no end of trouble if there's a problem later." Griffin turned his head to blink at her. "Other things now, though?"

She laughed, and let her hand drift to somewhere rather more intimate. "You know perfectly well what I have in mind. In broad strokes, at least."

"Puns, is it now?" Griffin let out a melodramatic sigh. "Well. Lady's choice tonight, shouldn't it be?" The discussion of what she wanted to choose had them both laughing, mostly because her hands kept moving. Three minutes after that, Griffin was lost in the moment, and not thinking of anything but the pleasure he wanted to give her, and the pleasure she was giving him.

CHAPTER 41

MAY 1ST

For once, Annice had no objections to getting up well before dawn. They'd got up at four in the morning - that was fishing folk time, not crafters, who needed the light to work by. There'd been a quick breakfast, pastries set out the night before. Griffin had spent part of the evening before they went to bed twining decorations through the non-essential parts of his chair, and charming the spokes of the wheels. He hadn't explained what they'd do, just attached a number of small ceramic discs at particular places.

Now, they were waiting outside the Courts, near the head of a forming procession, with people carrying all sorts of decorative staffs, and wearing a fantastical set of clothing. Of course, everyone here knew about magic, knew about May Day, and could bring out their best charms and costumes and illusions. Griffin clearly decided it was time for him to join in, and he brushed one of those little discs he'd attached, and his chair lit up with magical decoration. There were vines twining around the spokes of the chair's wheels. Vibrant new green growth gave way to a rainbow of buds and early blossoms, at least a dozen different flowers.

That same light and magic flowed up the back of the chair, twining around the crutches he'd attached to the back. Annice took a step back, almost bumping into someone, to get a better look. "Can I touch it?" She kept her voice low, though things were about to get loud, apparently.

"They're illusions. Hand goes right through them, but the charmwork keeps them moving as I do." He seemed delighted with the effect. Before he could say anything more, an older man strode into the centre of the street. She was pretty sure this was Lamont Morgan. He was wearing voluminous green silk robes like a judge's robe, with an enormous staff in his hand. It was made of wood, what looked like multiple lengths of different woods, joined together with metalwork twining round, with a great crystal at the top. Maybe quartz, given the size, but she wasn't sure about that in the dim light from torches and lanterns and the way people moved around and cast shadows.

He walked out to the centre of the road, then banged the staff three times. "Hail!"

The crowd - some fifty people, at least, maybe more - roared back, "Hail!"

"We welcome the May!" Once that was echoed again, Lamont thudded the staff three more times, and strode off at an even pace. Immediately, music started picking up. It began simply, a single flute and drum, but block by block, as they went along, more instruments joined in.

By the time they were up by the marketplace, people had begun singing, loud enough that Annice could hear them clearly. She and Griffin were up at the front at the right, near a woman, her husband, and two small children who were entirely unsure about the morning. She thought that might be Harriet. On her other side was a man who was smiling and beaming in a way Annice didn't trust, with a sharp featured woman next to him. If the woman was Harriet, that was Nestor and his wife, then.

The procession picked up a lot more people as they came to the market square, and even more as they wound east, then turned up into the Temple of Healing. Someone flung the doors open, and the entire procession went up and through. Griffin ducked off to the right, where someone stood holding a much smaller door open. Annice followed him, along with a few others who had canes or crutches or chairs. No stairs this way, apparently.

Griffin certainly knew where he was going. Once they had traced along the length of the Temple, they met up with the crowd again in the centre of the gardens. Someone had built a tremendous bonfire in a metal basin, raised up from the ground. It was in the centre where the paths met, a pyramid of wood and tinder that wasn't yet lit.

There were Healers in their bright red robes, nurses in their uniforms and pinafores, patients in a variety of clothing, and then hundreds of people filling the space. Annice saw people in even more finery. Much of it - like her dress - was green. But there were shades of golden yellow and bright red and clear blue, all the elemental colours coming together, and a fair bit of rich earthen brown.

The songs had turned into tumultuous shouts until Lamont said something - it was entirely covered by the singing - and pointed his staff at the bonfire. Light shot out of it, setting the head of the staff aglow as well, golden light spilling out over everything as the tinder caught, and the bonfire began to burn. A cheer went up from the crowd, a delighted sound that rolled on and on, becoming a living thing. The flames licked up to the top of the bonfire. Then the whole thing was dancing with light, as someone tossed in a small pouch of powder that sent illusion birds and flowers cascading out like fireworks.

Once the fire was well and truly going, Griffin nodded at one of the walkways. "There will be dancing. You should dance, if you want! I'll be there." Annice looked from him to the dancing forming up, people taking hands. It was a circle dance, and she might not know the local steps, but she could probably pick them up. He waved her to it, and she found someone taking one of her hands. Harriet on her left, and then a great burly man on her right, who had the hands of a carpenter or blacksmith, all calluses and healed scrapes. The music picked up then, settling into a proper dance and chant, and she found herself twisting and turning around the bonfire, out along one path, circling around the whole of the garden and back.

By the time the dance ended, she was breathless and grinning, and she went to find Griffin and tell him so. Someone had handed him a frame drum in the interim, and he was keeping a respectable beat from his chair. She stood next to him, clapping along. The next dance was a partner dance, though it didn't seem to be romantic. People twisted through different sets, grinning at whoever they partnered briefly, then moving on. About the time that ended, there were carts brought out with vats of something to drink - tea, by the smell - and biscuits.

Perhaps half an hour later, the dancing had settled down into watching teams of dancers, first with handker-chiefs waving, then the sticks came out. Annice had heard about that - Da had known some, though she thought maybe a different style. After they danced three dances, they picked up a different tune, and led a procession snaking out of the grounds. Griffin watched them go. "A small contingent goes down to the Severn to make an offering at the river, a few of the Guard and the Healers and the Crafters. But it's a fair walk, five miles each way, even if they have carts for people who need them. And an offering at the Wye, too. All the rivers we can reach."

"Oh, I'll stay. Is there more here?" Annice felt a bit breathless and lightheaded, and she was fairly sure it wasn't just the dancing. There was magic all over the place. She could feel it dancing around her.

"In a little, we'll break off and see about breakfast somewhere." He was about to say more when Lamont came up, bowing generously. "Excellent omens for the year, I think. Mistress Matthewman, also glad to have a chance to meet you at last. A delight, I do hope Griffin has conveyed that while I've been too busy to enjoy your company."

"Annice, this is Lamont Morgan. Lord of Trellech's Justice, to give him the proper title of the day. Lamont, this is Annice. I agree, it went wonderfully this year."

Annice bobbed her head in turn. "A pleasure, sure." She wasn't actually sure what you called someone who was Lord in this situation, and it didn't help that Griffin had a particular relationship here. Instead, Annice peered at the staff. She couldn't stop herself from looking.

Lamont rested it on his hands to let her have a better look, rolling it slightly. "The seven woods of the Courts, bound by the seven metals of the planets. Or at least, bound by six, and there's a heart of mercury thoroughly encased in the middle there."

Now he said it, she could see the different woods and the metals. There was the warm glow of copper, the shine of silver and gold, the dark solidity of iron, and then the duller silver grey that must be tin and lead. "And the stone, please?"

"Quartz. A grand specimen, found at Caerphilly, maybe two dozen miles from here." He grinned, and Annice suddenly liked him a lot more than she had. She'd been resentful that this man had been keeping Griffin in limbo for years. But the way Griffin was smiling, the way Lamont was smiling, she couldn't keep up that feeling right now. "And it has dozens of charms set into it, of course. Some for show and effect, like just now. Some for one or the other." Then someone called his name behind him, and he bowed again, murmuring an apology before disappearing into the crowd.

Before Annice could say something, Harriet had appeared again, one small boy held firmly by the hand, the other on her hip. Annice immediately said, "Do you need a hand for a minute?" and held out her arms.

The other woman blinked at her and then said. "Please, do you mind? Someone found some jam. I have no idea how." The standing boy was, in fact, smeared with something red and sticky. Annice took the younger one, bouncing him on her hip comfortably enough. Harriet blinked. "Oh, you do know what you're doing. Right." She bent down to do a cleaning charm and added a handkerchief to the process before straightening up. "Give him back when you're ready? And, erm."

"Harriet, this is Annice, Annice, this is Harriet. As I think you've both figured out. And that's Daniel you've got, and Samuel. Hello!" Griffin wriggled his fingers at both of the children cheerfully. "Blessed May, too!"

"Blessed May." Harriet was a little less exuberant. "Look. We should talk about something. Not at the Courts. Do you have plans for breakfast, or time tomorrow?" By now, most of the crowds had moved away. They were, perhaps deliberately on Griffin's part, not terribly near the refreshments. Before Griffin could ask more, she jerked her chin, indicating Nestor, who was in a knot of people who looked very posh indeed.

"Oh." Griffin's voice had changed in tone. "When's good for you?"

"Tea, today? Do you have somewhere that works for you?" Now Harriet sounded less sure. "This afternoon, our nanny will have the children. Less chaos."

"Four, at the Stream? We can have a bit more privacy there. They won't bother us once we're settled. And do you want Annice along, or just me?"

"Oh, both of you, if you like." Harriet's chin came up. "I will not make that decision for you. Not enough idea of the agreements and precedent." Griffin chuckled at that. She'd obviously meant it as a bit of a joke, even if it wasn't a very good one.

"Four, then. Annice, come along? You don't have a lot of prep to do for tomorrow, right?"

"Not much that will take time." She'd decided yesterday what she wanted to do in Whitby, and she had to pick up some more raw jet, anyway.

Harriet nodded. "Four. The Stream. Whatever room they tell me." Then the boy at her feet was tugging her hand, and Annice handed back the toddler she was holding. She'd even managed it without him messing up her frock and cloak, which was rather impressive, given the nature of toddlers. Harriet turned, heading off into the crowd with both children firmly in hand.

"Well. Breakfast, then? I know a place." Griffin glanced up at Annice, as if weighing if she'd had enough.

"You always know a place. Lead on. And tell me about the other traditions here." By now the crowds had thinned enough they could comfortably go side by side, as Griffin settled in to telling her about the local land lore.

CHAPTER 42
MAY 2ND

Monday, mid-morning, Annice made it back to Whitby and to the house about twenty minutes before Ruth knocked. It had been a rush. Tea with Harriet had turned into a long conversation that Annice was still thinking about. From there, they'd gone on to supper with a handful of other people. It had been a long day, full of many things, and dragging herself out of bed had been hard this morning.

But needs must, and she'd let matters drag out in Whitby too long. She wanted to talk to Ruth first, about what she had in mind. Then they could go along for tea with Aunt Sarah and whoever else, and talk the rest of it out. Griffin would be busy all day and then some. He didn't expect her back until mid-evening.

Ruth knocked, then opened the door to find Annice at the downstairs table. "There ye are." Ruth looked not frazzled, exactly, but definitely worn down. "And what have you been doing, then? You look..." Ruth took a step back, considering, before she poured herself some tea from the pot. "You look happy."

"I am happy." Annice couldn't help twisting the ring on her finger, it wasn't as if she'd taken it off. She looked forward to eventually cutting that gorgeous sea-storm of a sapphire, when she felt she could do it justice. But she liked having something that slid smoothly around on her finger, sturdy and even. She took a breath and let it out. "Look, I've got some things to sort out, but I think you'll like what I have in mind. And then we can tell your mam."

Ruth pulled out the chair and sat down, elbows on the table. "And what's that, then?"

"First, um." Annice couldn't help blushing. "I'm engaged. To Griffin. And he's got to be in Trellech, for more than a few reasons. He didn't rush me and we're expecting a longer engagement, time to make sure of it."

"And where are you staying in Trellech, then? That inn?" Ruth had cocked her head now, as if evaluating how good the haul on one of the fishing boats was, calculating a dozen things by eye and practice.

"His flat. Little house. I don't know what you call it. Used to be stables, entirely redone. He's got an upstairs, but he doesn't use that much. I can put a workroom there." She blushed more. She could feel the heat of it. "His bedroom. Ours, I guess, now. Still getting used to that."

"And he can keep that sort of thing up? Not be scrabbling to keep you both together, body and soul?" Ruth still sounded cautious. "Fancy men like that, they don't always..." Her voice trailed off.

Annice held out the ring. "He gave me this. I'm learning to cut other stones, not just carve jet, I can sign a proper apprenticeship contract when I'm ready. Free and clear, whatever happens with us, though I'm hoping there's a lot of us to be going on with. Griffin gave me a stone to set when I'm ready. Sapphire, as blue as the sea here, just the right colour." Annice swallowed. "He thinks about things. How to make them work. How to make that sort of life something I could cope with, bit by bit. But I, I love him."

Had she said that to him, directly? She'd have to make sure to do so when she got home. Not that Annice would swear to what she'd said in the throes of delight or the sated aftermath. She certainly felt it, even if Griffin had been kind enough not to press her until she was ready. Ruth was watching her. "You're not just swept off your feet? Though, how would he'd do that?" It had a dismissive edge to it.

"Don't you go getting any wrong ideas, Ruth. We're having a grand time in the bedroom, thank you. Nothing wrong with the relevant bits of him, and so long as you don't make him stand up, it's fine." She could feel her cheeks heating up again. "Much more than fine."

"Eh." That was a little snort, half amused, half dubious. "And he's got reasonable prospects?"

The way Ruth put that made Annice start laughing and laughing. She had to put down her mug of tea, her hands flat on the table, and then she kept laughing until she could barely breathe. "Not a problem. Let me, um. It's a very Trellech thing?"

Ruth looked even more dubious now, peering down her nose the way Aunt Sarah did when she'd decided something was suspicious.

Annice gathered her thoughts. "He's been working for the Courts in Trellech for ages. Um. 1900, something like that. Long apprenticeship, he's a solicitor too, but mostly he works on the magic of the Courts, keeping things running. There's maybe twenty people like him? Or there should be closer to thirty. Steady work, excellent salary. And he's - well. Up at the top of that. The kind of thing that means I need to learn how to eat with fancy forks and knives and make intelligent comments about the wine, at least one or two. And he's set up an appointment for me for frocks with a dressmaker, one of the ones with a shop along the high street."

"Frocks, is it? For fancy things?" Ruth was definitely dubious. "Not going to get too posh to come see us?"

"That's the thing, Ruth." Annice took a breath. "If I'm not going to be here, there's the house here. I wasn't sure I wanted to share. That's complicated. But would you and Sam come live here? Keep the place going. I'd probably want to move some of the workshop, but not yet."

"And what'd we pay you?"

That was something Annice had chewed on this morning. And some of Saturday, too. It seemed kind not to charge any rent, but there was upkeep on the place to consider, and the long-term. "Here's the deal. Very reasonable rent, and if you or Sam want to do the upkeep yourself, we can talk about that as things come up, in exchange for the rent. But it's just you and Sam and whatever kids you have. Not three cousins and an uncle and whoever's got kicked out of their other place to live. Not for long, anyway. I want - " She let out a breath. "I want to know the place is loved and taken care of. That. Not overcrowded and chipped and cracking."

Ruth considered. "Mam's not going to like it."

"Aunt Sarah's not getting the offer. If you don't want it on those terms, I'll find someone else. It's why I wanted to tell you now, so you could figure out what to say later."

"Huh." Ruth swirled the tea in her mug around a couple of times. "What's the place you're in like?"

"Old stables, like I said. All bare floors, no rugs. It's hard with the chair, I guess. But they're heated. There's magic for you. Sensible sort of magic, I think. And lots of hot water. There's a fireplace, and a bit of a garden. If we wanted somewhere else, we could look for it. It's stairs that are a trick. He made it over when he came back after the War. Got help buying it from his Dad, but I guess it wasn't much to start. Not fancy, but practical? Except for the things like the heat."

"Heat's fancy, plenty of days," Ruth agreed. "And there's other people there, not just him?"

Annice bobbed her head. "He found me a talisman maker. Which is the other thing I should tell you. That first?"

"You seem t'be having a lot." Ruth spread her hands out. "That."

"One of the reasons he wanted me to meet her is we'd found those stones. Three of them. She's told me what they do. If you agree, and Aunt Sarah, we could set them up again."

"Huh. What do they do?" Ruth was leaning forward.

"Protection. That bit, maybe I should explain to her, too, at the same time. It's got a bit of an edge."

Ruth waved a hand again. "Right. People?"

"I swear, Griffin knows near everyone in Trellech. Or it seems like it. People at the Courts and the Ministry, but also the theatre and a lovely apothecary, well, three different ones. And his parish church, and he even knows the Bishop. To talk to. We're having supper with him next week. But just - people. Interesting people. They're being kind to me, explaining things. Asking questions, not the nasty sort."

"La! A bishop." Ruth snorted. "Well. All right. We going down to Mam now, or in a bit? She's expecting us for half three."

"If you've got the time, thought we could go through

things here. I need to hunt out some of the jet we have here for a project. And you might want a look at the bedrooms and all. Pack up some things to take back with me." Griffin had promised to send someone along to help with a trunk. She wasn't worried about getting it to Trellech.

They turned up down at Aunt Sarah's promptly on time, to the expected amount of chaos. Five minutes later, though, Aunt Sarah had shooed everyone else out of the kitchen. They had tea, and Annice had charged ahead with explaining what she was and wasn't offering. Aunt Sarah's lips got tighter and tighter, but finally she nodded. "Not going to budge ye."

"No." Annice said. "I want to help, but I want to know who's living there, and that the place is kept up well. And I'll come visit, too. We can sort out a regular schedule, if you like." She added, a little less aggressively. "If any of the younger ones want to learn something other than fish, Griffin knows people. Grocers, shops, things like that, as well as crafting. If someone shows promise, wants to learn, that's a way we can help." Like as not, if something happened that needed money, she was pretty sure she and Griffin would help with that too, but not on the regular. That was destructive to family, too. Griffin had seen plenty of that.

"Huh." Aunt Sarah set it aside for the moment. "And the other thing?"

"The stones. I know what they do now." She hadn't brought them with her - they still needed more charging. It wasn't the sort of thing that could be done fast. Especially when she was learning so many other things and using her magic in different ways than she was used to. "But they were meant to keep people safe. I think, um." She swallowed. "We're fairly sure the uncles, that - it's part of why the boat went down. Because the uncles were good some-times, good to the people around them. And not so much others."

Aunt Sarah sucked in a breath but said nothing.

"So if you didn't want the stones back, I'd understand. They won't work in other places. Needs to be one in my house, one here, one down at Robin Hood Bay. Keeps a stretch of the shore safer, keeps people in the harbour and the houses safer. Bit of blessing, bit of magic to ease things. Not pinching so many pennies."

"Well. I'll think on it." Aunt Sarah looked out, her eyes unfocused, in the direction of the sea. "Sea's a harsh judge. And I can't say as you're wrong about how they were going. Someone was going to be hurt, sooner than later, and prob-ably not them. The protection, is that more for them as can't help themselves? The little ones, and all?"

Annice nodded. "People who didn't get a choice." That had been a fascinating line of discussion with Niobe. The construction of the thing was rather deliberate. More protection for people who didn't have a choice about being there, who didn't have an option to get away. Then more blessings for people who were doing their part to keep things good. It wasn't an antagonistic stone, as Niobe had put it, it was just dividing the world into people who got its blessings and people who didn't. Adding, perhaps, a tiny press of the thumb weighted against people who would make trouble.

Aunt Sarah nodded. "Bring them back, then. Though maybe I won't explain all of that to the menfolk. Not right away. It's my job to keep the house running and the chil-dren well."

"Soon as they're ready. A fortnight, maybe. I'll send a note and let you know." Now she took a breath. "Now, catch me up on everything I've missed? How's Fred doing?" The chatter from that got easier, rolling out and filling space and time, until Annice needed to get back to meet whoever was carting the trunk. All in all, it was a fine day, setting things up well for a better future.

CHAPTER 43
MAY 16TH IN THE HALLS OF JUSTICE

Griffin was as ready as he was going to be. They'd finished setting the talismans three days ago, giving them enough time to settle into place. He'd laid out the ritual circle markings before anyone was around but Annice, which at least spared his dignity a bit. The angles involved in bending over tended to be particularly tricky for him, and he found it much easier to just sit on the floor and work from there. That did not, however, present an unimpeachably professional appearance to an audience, no matter how much it shouldn't matter.

Now, he was waiting with Annice on one side and Helios Norton on the other, in a regular chair, one cane leaning up against his hip. He'd need one of his hands free for this. That was part of the challenge. Annice smiled at him, though she was a little nervous as well. On his behalf, mostly, or at least she'd sworn so before lunch. Neither of them had been able to eat much.

Helios was nine months into his apprenticeship, working under Gloriana, and had been deemed simultaneously competent enough to assist, but not skilled enough to affect the outcome. The young man had been pleasant enough, and Griffin had been amiable about laying out what he needed. Besides, he'd be relying on Niobe and Annice's work with the stones, and his own magic, for this. Helios was mostly present as an extra set of hands.

The room itself looked and felt quite pleasant. They'd pulled some furniture out of storage, creating a conversational seating area with two sofas and two easy chairs in one half, and a table that would seat six at the other end. There was light coming in from the window, and Griffin had done the incantation work that morning that left a lingering scent of vanilla and cedar in the air, and lent a sense of well-being to the room. They were a shopkeep's tricks, more or less, creating the space that would entice in the right way. Vanilla because so many people responded to it as they did to baked goods, and cedar because it brought a clean and refreshing note. Spices would have gone too far over towards a cosy personal space, and that wasn't what he needed here.

Far above them, the bell chimed, and then the door opened - Charlus was holding it - and a dozen people filed in. "Welcome, welcome, come in. Along that wall and this one here are best, avoiding the centre." Griffin pitched his voice to sound cheerful. "If anyone needs a chair, these here are the easiest, given the ritual layout." He gestured at the other chairs around the table.

Lamont had been first through the door, of course, looking around and nodding. Harriet and Nestor had followed him, then Gloriana and Christopher. The other six besides Charlus were representative of the various departments, including Mistress Henning, who had a notepad ready for shorthand. Antimony slipped in at the end. He hadn't been sure if she'd be free.

He let them get settled, then cleared his throat again. "As you know, I'll be setting this work to create a space which facilitates more ease and comfort than most of the spaces in the Courts. It is a judicially neutral space better suited for witnesses who have had difficult experiences or just recounted them. For example, if a flood of grief overcomes someone, or if someone has a health concern and needs a few minutes of rest. We plan for tea service there, on that cart, and there's a single washroom just across the hall, as you know."

Now he let his voice get a little more full. The pacing on this was the trick and the challenge in every direction. "It was brought to my attention that some were concerned I might be leaning on my assistants as a crutch to my magic. Now, I consider a crutch a useful tool, but I also understand the desire to be sure you know what is my work and what is not. The full details are in the documentation I provided last week. The talismanic stones for the space were carved and enchanted by Magistra Niobe Hall and by Mistress Annice Matthewman, newly her apprentice."

His chin came up. "Also newly my fiancee, as you all know, so I admit I might have some bias about her skills. However, while Annice is a skilled crafter already, she does not have formal training in ritual magic of any kind, and particularly not in the judicial magics. Also assisting, of course, Helios Norton, and my thanks to Gloriana for the loan of his time and attention this week."

Gloriana inclined her head. Nestor lifted his chin. "We know all this, Griffin. Do get on with it."

There was a slight rustle, because whatever everyone's opinion of this was, everyone else in the room respected the process. Griffin shrugged a little. "Before I begin, any questions? Now you've had time to review the plans."

Christopher cleared his throat, and Griffin nodded at him. Christopher said, carefully. "Your notes indicated that there is some expected upkeep, magically. May I ask how you're planning to manage that?"

"The notes, of course, couldn't include the setting of the stones we did on Thursday. I'm now confident that - once the enchantments are laid - anyone past second year apprenticeship should be able to lend a bit of magic. In practice, I made the commitment as Yew Primus that I, or someone else directly involved in the Inheritance Court, will check and see to it on a scheduled basis. While the room is open to all seven Courts, and we'd be glad of additional volunteers, this is my project and my responsibility. Anyone interested in helping should leave their name, and Charlus will be setting up a rota."

Christopher nodded. Nestor opened his mouth, then thought better of it, apparently. When there were no other questions, Griffin pushed himself upright, murmuring, "Places, please." Annice went to the right and Helios went to the left, each of them standing at the centre of one of the long walls. That had been one of the tricks with the space. For this kind of magic, a long rectangle was harder than a square. A ritualist could pretend a square was a circle, but once things got into ovals, what might be best translated as odd orbits of energy turned up, and it took longer to pass some distances than others. That was something they'd had to solve with the stones.

He was proud of the solution. The actual talisman pieces were amber, washed up on the Norfolk coast a few years ago. They were near perfect matches in colour and clarity, a warm honey gold that glowed when lit by magic. The stones were held at about chest height, set into the top of the panelling. Part of what made this work was the amber and jet, both formed from ancient trees, the light and dark echoing and anchoring each other in a particularly potent cycle.

Unbroken copper wire ran in a channel set along the top of the wainscoting, then up over each door, with smaller pieces of jet set at the corners. More copper wire ran up the corners overhead to an additional talisman set in the centre of the ceiling. The last set ran down to the floor, all of it dotted with alternating jet and amber.

Once Helios and Annice were in place, Griffin smiled and took his steps to under that centre point. Normally, there'd be a charmlight there, but they'd taken the fixture down for this work. He began the incantation with six pure tones, pitching them perfectly and holding them as they echoed, building one on the other. Then he chanted the whole thing into being.

It wasn't the words that mattered here. All the detail of the work had been done in the talismans. What he was doing now was waking the magic, bringing it into a living, breathing clarity of purpose. Of course, having some words worked better. He'd given some thought to whether one of St Hildegard of Bingen's chants might suit. But this was a space for people of all beliefs and practices, and even the less overt choices like "O Virtus Sapientie" had seemed a bit too much.

Instead, he'd chosen a chant from about the same time, written by one of the Schola professors - though interestingly not the Ritual Mistress of that era. It was really properly designed for a formal work room and to echo off the walls without furniture softening it, but it had beautiful arcs to the melody, and the words called out the four elements as well as the mystery of what came before and what came after.

The fact that it suited his voice well didn't hurt one bit. He was in good voice, and once the first line or two was sung, he picked up the magical work. Not everyone could do both simultaneously. He knew several of the people in the room preferred not, for one thing. For him, it was about trusting his magic, trusting the music to bring movement and enforce the need to breathe. He was trained in Incantation, and while he wasn't the most competent singer in Trellech, he knew this deep into his bones and the depth of his lungs.

At their cue, perfectly on beat, both Annice and Helios pressed their hands against the amber, sending their own smaller pulse of magic into the system. Griffin felt it catch, a bit like a fish biting, delicate but absolutely there. Then they moved to circle to the short walls of the room, and the other talismans. Again, on the proper beat, they repeated it, and then Griffin could let the whole thing flow.

He knew he'd done it, even before there was a wordless gasp. His eyes were closed, but he could see the glow through his lids. The amber had flared into light, and he could smell the faint scent of it added to the vanilla and cedar as the magic warmed it. It would not be like this again, at least not until they had to do refurbishment, but he basked in the glow. Another line or two of song, and then he felt everything click into place with a sensation that was felt and heard, both. The last few lines of the chant brought him to the end, finishing the thing properly and ensuring that the magic would continue to flow.

When Griffin opened his eyes, everyone was looking around - and more importantly, everyone had shifted how they were standing to something a little more relaxed and open. Even Nestor had uncrossed his arms. The glow was still visible, like standing in a sunny meadow on a summer day, but it was beginning to slowly fade.

Lamont smiled at him. It was a thing of warmth and deliberate information, letting everyone see it. "There is no doubt of your success, Griffin. Thank you for your work on this, and for being willing to make the demonstration of your skill and workmanship public. We'll discuss further at our meeting tomorrow afternoon, three hours, we've a fair bit of business to cover. I believe that's all, unless there are any questions?" It was the tone he used when dismissing a meeting, one they all knew well.

For a moment no one moved. Then there were murmurs from everyone else, congratulations, mentions of having an idea for the use, or a desire to talk about an aspect. Niobe exchanged glances with Lamont, and then said cheerfully, "Annice, my dear, and Charlus. How about we go along to Griffin's office and give him a minute?" Griffin could hear Charlus complimenting Helios's work, and encouraging him along as well, mentioning some biscuits.

Griffin very much wanted one of those, and he was leaning on the cane hard enough to aggravate his wrist now. He managed to hold everything together long enough for the door to close, leaving him alone with Lamont.

"Here. A chair." Lamont went and fetched one of the wooden chairs from the table himself, setting it so Griffin could sit. "Do you need a moment?"

"I know what your diary is like this afternoon." Griffin tried to make it a joke, and it came out flat. The sitting wasn't a moment too soon. He'd unbalanced himself a bit, and not falling over was seizing a lot more attention.

Lamont pulled another chair over, settling down on it. "They were all out the door before it was obvious how much exertion that involved. Would it have been easier with Charlus helping?"

Griffin twitched a shoulder. "If I hadn't had to make a show of it, I'd have done more of the setup over multiple days. Or sat down for this part. But the show was part of it, so." He shrugged. "A bit of food and drink in a few minutes when I can manage them." Right now there was the undeniable thread of nausea that made that a bad idea. "And a little care tonight, but I planned for that."

Lamont nodded. "And right now? Up for a little more conversation?" His tone had turned amused, and Griffin blinked at him once or twice, focusing on his face. "Pleasant for you, at least."

It made Griffin a little more sure of what the topic must be. "Of course, sir."

"I assume you are still both willing and interested, or you wouldn't have gone through this with the conditions you agreed to," Lamont said. "My plan is to have a quiet word with Nestor and Harriet this afternoon. They're both booked for meetings with me at the end of the day. And tomorrow, I will let everyone know I have chosen you as Heir."

Griffin couldn't breathe for a second, and then he made himself, playing lines of the chant through his memory to remind him. When he met Lamont's eyes again, he managed not to stammer. "Thank you, sir. For the advance warning on all counts."

"I do not expect Nestor to be happy about it. If he gives you any trouble at all, tell me. I know you can deal with it, but managing it is my duty." Then he broke into a smile. "And perhaps a dinner out somewhere in public, later in the week, once the formal announcement goes out. Thursday or Friday? Discuss it with Mistress Matthewman. Any of the places that allow one to see and be seen are fine. Let me know what's to your taste and ease." He made a slight gesture at Griffin's knees. "How about we meet on Wednesday morning, to sort out an ongoing schedule. You can get a good look at your new office and decide what you want to move and what you don't. There's a budget for redecorating, of course."

"Of course." Griffin managed a breathy response, then took a moment to gather himself. "I'm sure it'll be hitting me every few minutes for the rest of the day. Thank you for your trust in me, sir."

"You've more than earned it. Not just in what you did today, either, but how you've gone about it. Generative, collaborative, not combative." Now he waved a hand. "I'd suggest getting out of the building promptly. Go tell the people in your office and make whatever celebration you like. I'll see you tomorrow."

Griffin felt he could just about manage the walk back to his office now. He stood, and let Lamont go out first. The older man disappeared off toward his own office at the front of the building. Griffin did his best to keep from calling out from joy as he went back to the office that would soon be someone else's.

CHAPTER 44
MAY 17TH

Annice was outright antsy. Griffin hadn't turned up at four, which was the earliest likely time. Nor at half four or five. He'd warned her he might be late, and he hadn't sent a note with a messenger, so she assumed he'd be back by six, but that didn't help. She was on the list for one of the magical journals, but they were backlogged, so it'd be another week or two before she had one of her own.

She'd been worried about him yesterday. The magical work had been exhilarating on one level - and Lamont's decision, even more so. But he'd put off people who'd wanted to go celebrate. Not yet, he'd said. When they'd got in, he'd immediately washed up, and she put together a tray of things he could eat in bed. When she'd asked how he was, he'd shrugged and said, "It was worth it. I didn't - well. I couldn't have gone out. We can go out some other time. And besides, I shouldn't make it obvious yet. Not until tomorrow."

Annice didn't know how to play the politics of the thing,

and besides, it was Griffin's life. He got to make the choices. She'd settled in, bringing some mending in, and working on it quietly while he ate and then read. He'd fallen asleep early, of course, though that was at least partly because of one of his potions. Griffin had seemed much better in the morning. He'd got up early, and while she was sleepily putting breakfast together, he said, "I made arrangements for an hour in the baths at the Temple this morning, yesterday. You can come if you like, or walk me over. I'm due there in half an hour."

It gave her something to tease him about. How he could have let her know last night. It brushed the cobwebs off. She'd walked over with him before picking up some pastries to bring to Niobe's. She was apparently already a person who had preferences about bakeries in two different areas of Trellech, and she suspected it'd be more before too long.

Finally, about twenty past five, she heard the warding and lock shift, and the door opened. Annice had been reading - well, not reading but pretending to - on the sofa, and she immediately got up. Griffin wheeled himself in, looking pleased. It wasn't a smug sort of pleased, exactly, it wasn't a 'better than'. It was Griffin, joyful at the world. He immediately pulled up short. "Sorry for being late. There was a fair bit of talking after the meeting, several ways round."

Annice took a breath. "I was worried, and I knew you'd let me know if you'd be much longer, and I'm glad you're back, and tell me about it?" It came out all in a burst, and Griffin just grinned at her.

"Give me a minute, and is there something for supper, or do you want to figure out takeout? I can journal the local." The pub around the corner, down to the west and south, would put things together for them quickly enough. Annice shook her head.

"There are potatoes and some chicken cutlets in the warmer when you're ready." Not that she'd had to do much with them. The housekeeper was a wonder. "And asparagus, you liked it so much on Sunday."

"Tis the season." Griffin beamed at her and then went off to wash up. She heard the shift from the chair to the crutches and the opening and closing of the bathroom door. Five minutes later, he came out looking refreshed, joining her in the kitchen. She set a mug of tea down in front of him and took the other chair.

"Tell me about it? The main meeting, I mean. Were either of them horrid? What was everyone else like?" She had so many questions.

"It's..." Griffin let out a breath. "Nestor's a prick. But we knew that. He was all rigid and formal and exquisitely polite, so Lamont made his options exceedingly clear yesterday. I hope he gets over it. Lamont and I are going to talk about that more tomorrow." Griffin considered. "I wish he'd be more honest about things. With himself, first. It'd do him some good."

"Honest?" There were a number of things that might apply to.

"He comes from one of the newer families with aspirations. Him being Heir would be a coup, and also I think they're a little uncertain how things are going right now. One of the nephews and, hm, I think one of Nestor's in-laws found themselves in a bit of trouble a few years ago. Nothing that involved Nestor, and he made all the proper oaths on that. It was a web of related cases. But he feels he needs to prove himself, I think. Being Heir would be tidy. Steady work in an area of the Courts that's rather abstruse to anyone who doesn't do contract law, that's not so visible." He shrugged. "If he settles down, good. If he doesn't, I am currently assuming Lamont has a plan."

"And Harriet?" Annice considered. Supper would take another twenty minutes, so she went and brought out two savoury scones from the keep-fresh box, and two plates and the butter. She nudged that and the butter knife over to Griffin, who cheerfully buttered a scone, not entirely at her, but certainly in punctuation.

"Harriet's most of why I'm late. She came round to my office - well, still my office, for a few days more - to congratulate me. She's sorry it's not her, and she said so - see, that's useful honesty. But she's also glad it's not Nestor, and we talked about what she'd really like to accomplish with the Court of Equity. My support would make it more likely, so we're planning to have a number more conversations."

Annice wrinkled her nose up. "Lots of figuring out how to get things going the direction you want, then. Give me stones, please. I understand stones. Or at least, I'm learning to. Each one's a bit different."

"It'd be terribly boring if we all did the same thing. Though that brings us to your part in this. For supper Friday, how about Percival's? Traditional food, a good portion rather than one of those places where every dish is about three bites. It's the right sort of fancy for the people we want to be seen by, but it doesn't require an excessive number of forks."

"I appreciate that. What's my, um. Obligation? That's not the right word." Annice fumbled for it. It wasn't as if he hadn't talked this part through with her before, but now it was real. Now people were going to be looking at her.

"Mostly, you smile and nod and you let me introduce you and mention you're apprenticing with Niobe, and that will carry about nine parts in ten of the necessary conversation. For supper, other events will vary. We are very much both expected to make an appearance at the Council rites at Solstice. Though after this one, you don't need to come every time. I mean, I hope you won't hate it and you're willing to come, but making the right show to start off is a thing."

"And what does that involve?" Annice had run out of scone, and it left her hands to fidget.

"There are formal dances - the Council and chosen partners, not us. Don't worry about that. There's a time when everyone goes and presents a token from their lands, the Lord and Heir, or Lady and Heir or whatever, and we go down the line. You'd sit that part out, but I have some ideas about who to introduce you to."

"Oh?" Annice considered. "More people you know. That I haven't met yet, or it wouldn't be an introduction."

Griffin grinned. "Quite. As to who, several people who came up via their own skills. And one who didn't. The odd one out is Healer Rhoe Belisama. Her brother's on the Council, Cyrus Smythe-Clive, and she oversees the baths at the Temple. That's why I could get a slot on no notice. She'll take a message from me outside of her usual hours."

"Hah," Annice said, amused. "And you don't abuse it."

"No. She helped me demonstrate I was fit to come back to the Courts when I did. Her brother helped too, he's a ritualist. Anyway, she'll be there. There's Rathna Edgarton, she's just had a baby, two months ago, but she should be there in June. She's a Portal Keeper - she can talk about stones day and night. And her husband's a Penelope. Mason had some of the training of Gabe, though not officially. He's his father's Heir. You've heard me mention Captain Edgarton. That's his father. And then there's Thesan Wain - well, socially, Fortier - but I heard from Seth she's expecting, so she might not be there. They've not announced it formally yet. She's the astronomy professor at Schola."

"Right. Explains why you know her."

"Also, she enjoys knowing interesting people?" Griffin shrugged. "And I do try to be interesting. And interested. Anyway, her husband Isembard is his brother's Heir, and Garin - that's the brother - is also on the Council, and his wife as well. Dour fellow, barely smiles. But Isembard's always got good stories. He's also a teacher at Schola. Protective magics. He might be interested in your big jet stones, sometime, if you wanted to talk more about them."

"Huh." Annice leaned back. "So a range of people. But they don't sound too terrifying."

"There are plenty of other people, but Thesan's from good farming folk a generation or two back. You met her brother, she's a lot like him in manner. Easy to be with if you're a decent person. And Rathna's parents worked in East London." Annice knew how to translate that well enough, as decidedly not posh. There was a story there, somehow. "And Lamont's wife, too. Her name's Magdalena, she's a little younger than he is. She does a bit of consulting as a theoretical magical researcher, but mostly she works on her own projects. There's some family money on her side. She knows a lot of interesting people, though, too."

"You think they'd be willing?" Annice asked, finally. "That's the part I don't know about. I mean, that and the clothes, though you have plans for the clothes. Oh, I got the confirmation - final fitting for that frock you thought I'd want tomorrow, so I can wear it Friday."

"That, now, is excellent timing on my part, and Mistress Castalia's. And I'll check with her about settling up the account."

It wasn't just one frock - Annice had been promised several dresses, suitable for a range of events, and then some ordinary day clothes as well. But they'd aimed at having one ready sooner, for whatever came up, or a nice evening out like that summer. Annice hadn't been able to resist a sea-blue, with little tiny round jet beads, proper jet, just enough to be subtle and decorative. There was a much fancier frock coming in a paler blue, suited for something more like the Council rites. She'd put herself entirely in Mistress Castalia's hands, and Griffin's, in terms of what she might need.

Shoes, at least, were simpler. Magical shoes were so much more comfortable and easy to walk in. She already had a comfortable pair from Griffin's friend Owen, and a dress pair in the works. And, well, she and Niobe had some plans for jewellery. With any luck, she'd have not only Griffin's piece done, but something to match it. And there were apparently such things as hairdressers and people to help with cosmetics. "So what do I need to know before Friday, then?"

Griffin grinned at her. "Well, we can talk through the menu. Charlus got me one. And the space. We can decide what topics you'd feel comfortable talking about, and which you'd rather avoid. A united front."

Annice nodded. "Facets," she said. "Oh! I should tell you about that. I learned something new today."

"Bring out the food, then, if it's ready, and tell me. Though I suppose pótatoes are not the ideal medium for demonstrating gem cutting, they might give a gesture at the shape, with a little deftness." The idea of it made her laugh, and now she'd have to try that. She stood to go get the food out of the warmer and pour more tea, while Griffin leaned back and watched her, entirely appreciative.

EPILOGUE
JUNE 22ND AT THE COUNCIL KEEP, WALES

Griffin was, on the whole, rather pleased with how the day was going. There was more than a bit of a crush, of course, with the several hundred people here. Even if some of them had drifted to the side rooms - or outdoors in the courtyard - during the formal presentations.

He was, of course, impeccably dressed, down to the talisman at his throat. Annice had presented it to him on his birthday, four days ago, a beautiful tie pin with his namesake griffin inscribed. The blue chalcedony glistened just below the knot of his deeper blue tie. Two smaller pieces, set as cufflinks, made up the matched set, and she was working on a fob for his pocket watch. All of them were gorgeous, but the thought and care - and the fact it was all Annice's work - made them a treasure. Best of all, they were things he could wear every day, if he wished. They'd suit the rhythms of daily life, not just special occasions.

This was definitely one of the latter. Everyone was dressed well, the women in all shades of summer frocks, the men in sharply fitted suits. There had been some back and forth about whether to bring the chair or manage with the forearm crutches.

Lamont had been clear - quietly, but firmly - that he would push the staff at the Council Keep into some suitable ramp if required. But most of the gathering would involve people standing around talking, and the chair wouldn't help with that. Everyone's arses, right at face height, even before the part where people would back up without looking where they were going. Lamont had left the decision to him.

In the end, Griffin had decided on the crutches. But he'd also let Lamont know that if there was more strain than he hoped, he might take the next day off or work at home. The court was in Solstice recess. It wasn't as if Lamont minded terribly. Whichever way it went, he should be sufficiently recovered for a day at the Midsummer Faire on the Saturday. He'd made arrangements for space in the Court tent, which meant he and Annice would have seating when they needed it without fighting with the crowds. If he weren't up for much walking, she could go and take in the faire and come back to him.

And she would come back to him. That was the thing he was still getting used to, though every time it hit him, it made him happier. They both had busy lives, full of unique skills. And yet, morning and evening, whatever else had happened, they had the quiet time together. Sometimes entirely without words, for long stretches, sometimes chatting about the day or who they'd talked to or what they'd done. Nothing confidential, of course, all either cases Griffin was assisting in or clients Niobe saw, but all the rest of it.

Seth had turned around a suitable table exceedingly promptly - he'd refused to tell Griffin how many places in line he'd jumped, though Golshan had reassured Griffin privately that it wasn't many hours of actual work. Most of the time had been spent waiting for stains and the wood polish to dry between applications. The last fortnight, he and Annice had begun having people over for supper once a week or so, and that was a tradition Griffin wanted to deepen.

Now, Griffin glanced over to make sure Annice was still in good company. Magdalena, Lamont's wife, had taken to her - especially when they got onto theories of stones and magic. They were talking with Rathna Edgarton, who was gesturing vigorously about something.

Lamont leaned over. "They're getting on splendidly, I think. Magdalena reminded me to arrange regular suppers out together. Good for the image, but it's rare she's the one encouraging me to get her out of her study."

Griffin grinned as they inched forward. "You've both been very generous with your time, but we've enjoyed the suppers so far tremendously, all three of them. And it's been a help, making the show of it." The gossip of the choice had mostly settled, thankfully, though Nestor was pointedly civil and only that.

Finally, they made it up to the head of the line. Griffin felt the shift in Lamont before anything else, as Lamont let the magic of their oaths and the Courts settle on him. It wasn't the same way as it was done when calling the truth magic, but it was a cousin. A recognition of their role and the land and people they tended. Griffin inhaled, doing the same. Lamont had talked him through it a fortnight ago, in one of the ritual rooms, until Griffin could do it smoothly, between two breaths.

Normally it would have been Griffin's role to carry their token - a bound book, recording notable events in Trellech of the year, the usual offering. But because of his need for the crutches, Lamont was carrying it. He handed it over with a slight bow to Hesperidon Warren, the current Head of the Council. Then Lamont was speaking, his Court voice, all velvet and bass. "May I present my Heir, Magister Griffin Pelson, Esquire, Senior Solicitor and Keeper of the Courts, Yew Chair Primus. He has a long history in the Courts. I am confident in his magic, his skills, and most of all, his love of Trellech and all she is."

Griffin had expected the first sentence, with the full title. He'd even expected the second. The third was a surprise. It was true, of course, Lamont wouldn't say something untrue, not here and now. That was what the Lord of Trellech's Justice brought with him, when acting with that robe of office so clearly in place.

Council Head Warren inclined his head. "It took you some time to decide." That had a barb to it, but then he went on smoothly. "Be welcome, Magister Pelson, as Heir to Trellech's Justice. We look forward to what you make of Lamont's choice." That was a suitably enigmatic approach. It covered waiting for Griffin to fall on his face - metaphorically or literally - or bring something interesting to the table.

Griffin extracted his right hand from the crutch, offering it for a handshake. "Most fruitful of solstices to you, Council Head. I look forward to getting to know many of the people here better." Then it was time for them to move on down the line. The next few weren't terribly difficult - Philomena Gordon, Frederica Hastings, and Owain Powell were all entirely cordial, with no hidden implications.

After that came Cyrus Smythe-Clive, who beamed. "Glad to see you made the choice I, for one, was hoping,

Lamont. A pleasure to welcome you formally, Griffin. Rhoe is looking forward to some time to chat with you and Annice as soon as your duties allow."

Beside him, Mabyn Teague also smiled. She and Cyrus had taken up with each other as partners within the last six months, at least in any public form. They'd been all the gossip after winter solstice. She leaned a little closer to Griffin. "We'd be glad to have you both to supper, when we can find a time. And Lamont, you and Magdalena, as well."

"I would be pleased, and I suspect we can get Magda out of her library for that." Again, they couldn't hold up the line further, but it left Griffin more relaxed. Next down, Alexander Landry made a formal greeting and then had a question about something Griffin had written up the previous year, hoping for a further discussion.

Not everyone was so welcoming. Both Livia and Garin Fortier were cordial, but only that. Not that they had a reputation for warmth, but Griffin couldn't decide if it was him, the crutches, or something else. Working down the line, most of the reactions were not worth fussing about. Two glanced at the crutches, considered saying something, and then chose not to. It wasn't until Silvia Warren - Hesperidon's wife, and only a year and change on the Council herself - that there was anything more definite.

"I gather you often use a chair?" She'd made a cursory nod at the formality.

"For ease, yes. It lets me do more in my day. But it's not so pleasant for a gathering like this." Griffin did rather want to get to the part where he could sit down. They'd been in line for a good while before their own presentation. But he also knew better than to be rude. "I think of it rather like magic, picking the tool for the moment. There's a skill in knowing which will serve best, task to task." Then he paused, the exact right amount, from all his Incantation training, to indicate that he was unflustered and that he found other topics more interesting. "I'm delighted to get to know many here a little better."

At that point, Lamont nodded. "We won't keep you, Council Member. There are many more waiting their turn. Later, perhaps?" With that, he gestured Griffin away, and they could retreat to the women and the waiting chair that Annice had been guarding for Griffin's use. He sank down in it, suppressing a grunt of relief.

"Drink, love?" Annice bent down, a hand on his shoulder. "A bit of quiet?"

"Yes, to the drink, if you can get someone's attention. Wine or the punch cup, either is fine. And no, I'd love to know what you were talking about." He took a breath or two, steadying himself, while Lamont kissed his wife's cheek, whispering a couple of things in her ear. Rathna didn't look offended by any of it, just patient.

"Oh, working stones, and the implications for some of what I'm doing with Niobe. Rathna keeps saying it's not her speciality, but she knows a great deal. I've got a list of references to read. Can we go haunt the bookshops at some point?" Annice straightened up cheerfully.

Rathna chuckled. "I know the most about the stones I need for my work - mostly alignment and flow, of course." She was a Portal Keeper, tending Albion's portals. "But my husband has never met a bit of knowledge he didn't want to pick up. If you put him and Annice together, they'll be going for days, I'm sure." She then weighed something. "I gather you got a bit more grief for the crutches than he gets for his cane."

"Your husband also has a reputation as a duellist. I suspect it makes people cautious about giving too much offence." Griffin said, amiably. "It was—" He caught Lamont paying attention. "Full report once we're done and back in the office, sir, but it was on average about a third better than I was afraid of. A good measure to work with."

"Ah, well. We'll see about directing the interesting people this way." He lifted a hand, and one of the serving staff appeared promptly, allowing Lamont to put in an order for several drinks. "And I expect a proper accounting of anyone who gives trouble."

Griffin spread his hands once he'd rearranged the crutches to stay put. "You've made your expectations clear, sir." His tone made it obvious he was teasing a little. "Now, though, we can begin with the drinks and - oh, there's Rhoe." He could see her coming across. Her arm was through her husband's, the two of them gliding through the crowd like the great ocean liners of his line of work. It reminded him to add to Annice, "Cyrus and Mabyn would like to have us for supper, so we should compare diaries after this week."

Annice perched on the arm of the chair, apparently deciding that was more pleasant than the other options. Certainly more pleasant for him. He could get his arm around her waist comfortably. "As you like." Then Rhoe and Hugh were arriving, and there were introductions all round, before Rhoe asked about a particular case related to medical care that had been decided a fortnight ago. Lamont and Griffin hadn't been part of the formal handling, that had been Harriet's duty. But they'd both sat in on the Court. It was the sort of thing likely to set precedent about old injuries - from the War, in this case - aggravated by unsafe environments in a workshop. Not the most pleasant of topics, but important.

And that was, in fact, what Griffin was here for, as much as any offerings for the land and the people.

IF YOU ENJOYED *Facets of the Bench* and would like to read more of this series, please sign up for my mailing list to get all the latest news and fun extras.

Your reviews (on whatever review site you use) are much appreciated, too!

Read on for more historical details about this book (including a lot about Whitby, jet, and the origins of Trellech).

AUTHOR'S NOTES

Thank you so much for joining me - and Griffin and Annice - for this story. I hope you've enjoyed both Whitby and Trellech! As always, tremendous thanks to Kiya Nicoll, my editor. Thanks too for this book go to my friend Elise Matthesen, who not only said "You should do something with Whitby jet." but who shared many stories of her own visit there and samples of jet and coal. My early readers as always helped improve things as well, with special thanks to a reader who gave some great advice about Griffin's mobility needs and approaches. Any remaining typos are my own fault.

If you'd like to see a bit more of Griffin earlier in his life, you can find him in *Shoemaker's Wife*, when he's newly back in the Courts and working with Captain Donovan and others to help deal with a legal problem. Griffin also appears in *Point by Point*, in 1926, where he's the one overseeing the legal aspects of a situation along with Antimony Orland.

And if you like Niobe here, she's a significant secondary character in the Mysterious Fields trilogy, out in late 2024.

That takes place in 1889 and 1890, when Niobe's in her mid-30s.

On to some general notes, and then a few chapter notes.

Griffin's disability is similar to a number of autoimmune disorders. Sometimes triggered by an injury or shock of some kind, they can cause a wide range of symptoms and things to deal with. Griffin describes his pretty accurately: balance, some muscle weakness that affects his lower body more than his upper half. And if he exhausts himself or does too much, there are consequences to that. By the time we get to *Facets of the Bench*, he's a lot better at managing that most of the time.

~

I've been asked where **Trellech** is, and my answer is that it's on the map. There are a couple of alternate spellings in various sources: Trelech, Treleck, or Trelleck. Whichever spelling you're using, it's currently a tiny village in Monmouthshire in south-east Wales. Find the mouth of the Severn - or Tintern Abbey - and go just a bit north, and you should see it.

It's a tiny village these days. That wasn't always true. For several centuries, it was one of the major towns of mediaeval Wales. The most likely history, from what I've read, is that it was deliberately established by the de Clare family. It was conveniently placed to use iron ore from the Forest of Dean and charcoal from the woods in order to make munitions for their ongoing skirmishes and military activity. Some numbers suggest there were about 20,000 people living there at various points, at a time when London was about 80,000 people.

However, a lot of the city was destroyed in 1291, with

further destruction due to the Black Death, and then further fighting and military campaigns in the area. By the middle of the 1400s - a few decades before Albion's Pact - it was down to being basically a tiny village with a long history.

In Albion, the city picked up population after the Pact. It was still well-positioned for resources and trade, with a river and the coastline not too far away. There is in fact a healing spring in the area. (All right, this is Wales and England we're talking about, if you look at maps of such things, there's a healing spring of some sort every mile or three.) There are limestone caves not far away, used by the Trellech banks for their vaults and storage. (More about that is in *Fool's Gold*.)

Trellech has grown up, been built and rebuilt, into its own city with its own customs. There are walls around the city, as much to contain the area that's magically protected as for physical fortification. Outside the walls, a series of illusions and enchantments help keep people without magic away from the city, and the vast majority of traffic in and out comes by portal rather than road or river (so it's not visible outside the city).

In my mind, the city is a vast and gloriously varied range of architectural styles. There are sections of the city built out at particular times, with particular architecture. The Temple of Healing is very much like a Gothic cathedral in design, although for at least four centuries it's been explicitly open to people of all beliefs (or none) who seek healing and respite. I imagine other buildings in a range of styles - a row of Georgian townhomes here, a few Tudor buildings still in good order, others of varying styles and periods.

You can find a map of the different areas of the city on

my authorial wiki at bit.ly/celia-lake-wiki . (Search on "Trellech" and you'll find the map.)

I'm delighted we actually got to spend substantial time in Trellech in this book, and focused on the particular traditions, celebrations, and customs of the people who've made Trellech their home. I have some more in mind about that. Sign up for my newsletter for a treat in December 2024 that will include more, including a bit more of Griffin and Annice (and a few other people mentioned in this book).

Annice gives an excellent explanation of **jet and jet simulants** when she's talking to various prospective customers. The more I read about jet and the simulants, the more fascinated I was.

Jet was a huge industry in Whitby, but for a surprisingly short period of time. Jet was worn as a mourning stone before Queen Victoria. It turns up in graves that are thousands of years old, and then it becomes used for jewellery in various forms. It's easier to cut, somewhat more forgiving, and it allows for carving and decorative designs and patterns in a way that harder gemstones refuse. But it exploded in popularity and demand when Prince Albert died in 1861. Queen Victoria wore mourning for the rest of her life, and jet was one of the few types of jewellery permitted for women wearing mourning throughout the Victorian and into the Edwardian periods.

Workshops opened up all through Whitby, training up generations of carvers, and needing all sorts of related services and skills. If you explore the history, you'll find workshops like Annice's tucked into rooms all over the city.

At the height of the trade, there were over two hundred in the town.

Jet is also tricky to find. Whitby jet comes from a stretch of shoreline that's seven and a half miles in length, starting more or less at Whitby and running south along the coast. As Annice explains, a lot of what washes up is coal or tar-like substances from the ocean. Sometimes larger pieces erode out of the coastline. And at the height of the jet industry, there were also mines in the hills near Whitby.

However, in the wake of the Great War, demand for jet fell off. The explanation I've seen in multiple sources is that people didn't want to be faced with the visible signs of grief at that point. Jet made mourning visible, and when the entire country was mourning so much loss, it became overwhelming. Almost overnight - certainly over a few years - the workshops shut down, with just a few hanging on.

The jet industry in Whitby has kept going, and these days, there are several jewellers working in jet. In one case, they've even discovered and opened up a Victorian workshop that had been walled off for decades. It's possible again to buy beautiful pieces of Whitby jet (and ammonites, if you like ammonites).

The modern era has also made identifying jet simulants easier to do. Those are materials that look rather like jet but aren't. There's currently research to better understand what jet actually is, but also how those simulants can be identified without destructive testing. Sometimes it's fairly obvious - how a piece is mounted, if aged horn is flaking along the edges. Sometimes it's a lot harder. Or sometimes as Annice discovers in this book, a material is jet, but not from Whitby.

We'll cover some of the details about Whitby as I talk about specific chapters, for tidiness. But the city is as described - a long coastline, a lot of fishing trade, and homes and shops and other spaces built into the cliffs on either side of the river. It has some quite interesting history, ranging from the Abbey to Dracula's arrival point in England, to Captain James Cook's home for some years. (He was an apprentice in Whitby, learning the sailing trade.)

Chapter 4: The local pub and inn - there for centuries - on the east side of the river is in fact called the **White Horse & Griffin**. In that spelling. I couldn't make this up if I tried.

Chapter 12: The history of **mining** in Yorkshire is unfortunately full of awful mine disasters. The explosion at Swaith in 1875 was particularly bad, and the worst mining disaster since the Oaks Colliery disaster in 1866. 143 men lost their lives. It's the sort of event that people use as a marker, especially anyone who had family members working in the mines.

Chapter 15: I want to give all the thanks to the self-named "church nerds" on my authorial Discord, who were a tremendous help with figuring out what Anglican worship might look like in Albion in the 1920s.

They also all have very strong opinions about **Saint Hild**. And with good reason! She's a fascinating figure who doesn't get nearly as much attention as she ought. While working on this book in stages, I was reading (for other reasons) a lot of Anglo-Saxon and Northumbrian history, prior to the Norman Conquest.

St Hild gets more paragraphs here than she gets in most non-fiction works about the period, and I've done my best to do her history justice. The abbey is, as described, not the one she founded, but it is a beautiful architectural marvel. As Griffin notes, it was damaged by bombing from the coastline in the Great War, but mended by the time he sees it. **Caedmon**, the poet, is also a real person (or as probably as we can be, given the time), and a few fragments of his poetry survive, including the part Griffin quotes.

The 199 steps are a particular landmark of Whitby, rising from the east side of the river up the cliff to the abbey and cemetery. There are regular benches along the way, but the lore, at least, has it that they were designed not for people to sit on, but for pallbearers to rest coffins on, when carrying them up for burial. The stairs do have a road that runs alongside, but it's very steep, so most wheeled traffic goes a little north, then comes at a shallower climb toward the abbey.

Chapter 33 : The local building stone around Trellech is a red sandstone known as the **Old Red Sandstone**. It would lend a warm reddish glow, especially at particular times of day or in certain kinds of light to the city. Certainly not everything is made of it, but enough buildings and civic structures are to give a consistency to the city. If you'd like to look at pictures, it was heavily used in the construction of Raglan Castle, Tintern Abbey, and Brecon Cathedral, also in Wales.

Chapter 36 : To begin, for various reasons, **Christianity** is no longer the most dominant religion in Albion. That's due to a combination of factors following the Pact in 1484 that accelerated first with the formation of the Church of England, and then expanded even more with Cromwell's Protectorate.

Long story short, some families and individuals continued as Christians, other families reconstructed family traditions, created some new ones, brought in a focus on local spirits of place, or embraced Roman or Celtic or other relevant traditions. There's a lot of variation, and of course as new strands of Christianity emerged, those are present as well. (Kate, in *Wards of the Roses* and *Country Manners* is Welsh Chapel, for example.)

Both Annice and Griffin are **Anglican**, but their experiences are a bit different. We ended up doing quite a bit of discussion on the Discord as I was working on this section. At this time, the *Book of Common Prayer* (the liturgy and other worship materials for the Anglican church) were still in Latin, though readings might be given in the local language.

This brings up an interesting note. Trellech is a Welsh city, and has held onto Welsh language and customs more than some places in this period (in large part because there was less pressure to give up those things from the surrounding overculture). But many people who live in Trellech as adults grew up elsewhere - crafters and Ministry staff, for example - or people live elsewhere part of the year. As a result, Trellech mostly runs in English, but people who grew up there often would know Welsh. We don't see Griffin use much of it here, because he's with Annice or other people who don't speak it, but he absolutely is fluent in it.

Thinking about what magic would change in a given service was also fascinating. The **vigil service** as described was done in the Anglican Church of the period, but not very often. It is, however, one of my favourite liturgies. It runs as described, with the kindling of a fire outside, a procession and then lit candles providing light in a dark church with nothing on the altar. The readings cover many of the most evocative Biblical texts, starting with the very opening of Genesis. And then, at a particular point, there's a triumphant roar of music and sound, and the altar is filled again with all of the items for ritual and celebration.

It's a long service, but it can absolutely be so moving you forget you've been there for an hour or three. Magic, of course, makes part of it far more showy, like being able to bring up all the lights, or using magic to bring all the altar items to the proper places. (Or make them visible.) I loved having the chance to see this through Annice's eyes, and the mix of the known and unknown she experiences.

Working out the details also involved figuring out how many parishes are in Trellech. Three parishes, each with a different focus and core community, felt about right for a city of about 20,000. Many other people find their celebrations in other ways, or at the Temple of Healing, or through specific networks of community and family. Or they have private beliefs, and participate in the larger communal festivals like May Day processions or the solstices, just as many people do now.

One thing was clear, though. **Saint Hildegard von Bingen** would absolutely have been of interest to Albion. Getting her named as a saint took a long and complicated process, but she appears on lists of saints in the Roman Catholic church from the 16th century on. She pioneered a great deal of medical advice, as well as having detailed mystic visions, and many of her comments about materia (stones, herbs, and other items) made it into texts about those topics for centuries to come.

For the other two parishes, it also makes a great deal of sense to me to have one parish focusing on **Saint Matthew**, patron saints of civil servants and accountants (among other things) in the Ministry-focused city of Trellech. And **Saint David**, of course, as the patron saint of Wales, for the third. The balance is very much the way modern parishes often fall out, with parishes near each other developing something of a niche in the larger ecosystem.

Thank you again for joining me for this journey and a glimpse into Albion's courts and the wonders of Trellech. The best way to get all my news is by signing up for my mailing list. Check out the contact page for other places to find me and more about my Patreon and Discord.

The next book in the *Mysterious Arts* series is *Weaving Hope*. Set later in 1927, it's all about weaving, restoring some ancient tapestries, and tending a venerable old estate so it has a future. It'll be out in February 2025.

Before that, we'll be taking a step back into 1889 and 1890 with the Mysterious Fields trilogy where a series of bad choices change lives forever. Vitus (one of the protagonists) is a talisman maker finishing his apprenticeship with Niobe Hall. *Enchanted Net* (book 1) will be out in September 2024. *Silent Circuit* (book 2) will follow in November and *Elemental Truth* (book 3) in December.

ALSO BY CELIA LAKE

The Mysterious Charm Series

Outcrossing

Goblin Fruit

Magician's Hoard

Wards of the Roses

In The Cards

On The Bias

Seven Sisters

The Mysterious Powers Series

Carry On

The Fossil Door

Eclipse

Fool's Gold

The Hare and the Oak

Point By Point

Mistress of Birds

The Mysterious Arts Series

Bound for Perdition

Shoemaker's Wife

Perfect Accord

Facets of the Bench

Charms of Albion

Pastiche

Sailor's Jewel

Four Walls and a Heart

Land Mysteries

Best Foot Forward

Nocturnal Quarry

Old As The Hills

Upon A Summer's Day

Illusion of a Boar

Three Graces

The Magic of Four

Other stories

Complementary

Winter's Charms

Forged in Combat

Learn more about the world of Albion and future books at my website, celialake.com. Additional information linking characters, places, and timelines is available at my authorial wiki at bit.ly/celia-lake-wiki (or get there from my website under the menu that says "more information").

Sign up for my newsletter to be the first to hear about future books and learn about fascinating bits of research. Happy reading!